I0634104

Justice - Driftwood after Dark, Volume 3

Driftwood After Dark

Volume 3

˙Part 1- Justice

Write to genesummy@gmail.com

The story started on 1/20/22
Story finished 2/15/22- now edits start.
Final editing process complete 7/6/22

Thanks to Dean Koontz for writing The Watchers 30 years ago. That book kept me thinking about smart dogs for the last 30 years. Next, thanks to Elon Musk for Duralink. When I heard he was connecting brains to computers and using animals for research, my imagination exploded. This book is the result.

Thanks to my wife and kids for being nice to me, even though I make stuff up.

This story was not based on anyone I know. Except for my wife. And me. Most of the names I made up. A few of the names reflect my juvenile sense of humor. Please forgive me if they offend you.

If you need an apology for this story, consider yourself apologized to.

Table of Contents

From a speech at APA's 2002 Annual Convention in Chicago.
April 12, 2001
"My colleagues and I have demonstrated that situational forces...can generate surprisingly powerful contributions to make good people go absolutely mad," he said to a standing room only crowd in his presentation, "Why and how normal people go mad,"
-APA President Philip G. Zimbardo, 2002

From The Journal of New England Psychology
December 12, 2021
"There are physical warning signs when someone becomes insane. Rocking side to side or back and forth for no apparent reason often precedes a psychological break from reality. Standing motionless for long periods indicates the break is complete."
-Army Chief of Psychology Eduardo McCann, 2021
Walter Reed Hospital
Lt. General (Ret.)
US Army

From The Desk of Eduardo McCann
February 31, 2022
"Let's face facts, half the country is f**king nuts. It's time to buy a gun".
-Army Chief of Psychology Eduardo McCann, 2021
Walter Reed Hospital
Lt. General (Ret.)
US Army

Cheating Justice

Prologue

This story is totally true, except for the parts I made up.

Harry Rivers stared at the dog. The dog stared back unflinchingly. Harry couldn't believe what he had just seen. The rumors were true. Obviously true.

Harry had been hired by Duralink seven days ago as an Animal Care Specialist working out of their Austin division. He was thrilled to get the job, especially since he fabricated the information on his resume. He never thought a company as advanced and high-tech as Duralink would accept his resume without checking the details. But they did. Duralink's new Austin division was recruiting for a Human Resources manager and many other positions, including an Animal Care Specialist. This meant that amateurs were hiring the professional people that Duralink needed. A Human Resources professional had not checked Harry's references and education details. Duralink didn't have an HR professional yet.

Harry heard Duralink was looking for an Animal Care Specialist through a Duralink employee he met at a local bar. The Duralink guy was drunk and talking about what a 'Cush' job it would be babysitting a special dog all night. The best part was that Duralink was in a hurry to get the person in place. When Harry heard 'Cush Job', he was interested.

He left the bar and returned to his girlfriend's home in New Braunfels, Texas to start his resume. Harry's problems were his experience and training. He had none. Unless spending a few nights with the animals in the San Jose County jail counted. When Harry lived in San Jose, California he became familiar with the San Jose police on numerous occasions. Harry was one of those guys that never accomplished much except to get in trouble and then talk his way out of it. Harry began drinking and smoking weed daily while he was in high school. Harry was a large man, and the drinking made him even larger. Soon he tipped the scales over 300 pounds and was quickly headed for 350.

In high school, his teachers and principal felt threatened by Harry's aggressive behavior. When he threatened to kill the school principal, he was expelled. He would never return to complete high school.

Harry had everyone in his family convinced that he was the target of bad luck. The bad things that happened to Harry weren't his fault. He was the victim. He could turn on the charm and convince his family and friends that he needed a new start. Over and over and over again. New starts and more new starts. Harry's life in San Jose was like a train headed for a collapsed bridge.

Having never completed high school, or stepped foot in a college or trade school, Harry was under-qualified for just about any job that could be considered a 'Cush Job.' He was underqualified to run a cash register.

Harry was looking at life as a ditch digger or janitor if he was lucky. Harry embodied the Mark Twain quote: "All you need in this life is ignorance and confidence, and then success is sure." Harry needed the success part to happen. He had the ignorance part covered.

At 28 years old, Harry moved to Texas to be near his mother who had moved there three years earlier. Texas would be his new start in life. The new beginning he needed. Harry was going to straighten up, follow the rules and do as he was told.

When he heard about the Animal Care Specialist working nights for Duralink, he lit up like a Christmas tree.

Getting hired by Duralink was a God send. He was as excited as a two-peckered puppy. Now he could hold his head high and not feel like a loser. He knew his mother and stepfather felt sorry for him. In fact, they had all but given up on him. Now, that would change. Harry would change. He made a commitment to himself that he would straighten up, get sober and follow the rules. It was time.

Harry was proud of himself. The money at his new job was good, excellent in fact. Harry had never earned this much before. $82,000.00 per year was pretty good for a 28-year-old guy who got kicked out of high school. In Texas, that kind of money was terrific. He could buy a home and a new car. Soon Harry thought about other things he could afford. He could afford to drink any kind of booze he wanted. He could afford to smoke the best weed. This time, he would consume those items in moderation. He would drink like a gentleman. Weed would be for weekends. He would wave 'hello' to policemen instead of flipping them the middle finger.

Harry would appreciate the job and fly on the straight and narrow. He would not screw this up. His mom will finally be proud of him.

That's how he felt the day he started his job.

After seven days on the job, Harry had developed a slightly different attitude.

He understood why they believed the dog was special. They were right about the mongrel. Not only was he special, but he was also valuable.

He had been trusted by Duralink to watch the dog all night long. The long hours of watching the dog gave Harry time to consider the opportunities. Criminal Opportunities. The dark side of Harry's personality began to emerge again.

Harry rocked back and forth in the chair, staring at Justice. Justice the dog. Harry smiled at the dog. This would be one of his best scams ever. The Good Harry was grateful for the job at Duralink. Deep inside however, the Criminal Harry hated having a job. Why should anyone be able to tell him what to do and where to go?

The Criminal Harry said: Steal the dog. Sell it to a rich guy or collect a ransom that Delon Husk would undoubtedly pay.

Harry's criminal instinct was pushing to take over. The dog was valuable. It was worth many times more than the paltry $82,000.00 per year Harry would make at his seven-to-seven all-night anchor. Criminal Harry could not pass up this opportunity.

The Good Harry wrestled with the Criminal Harry. The Criminal Harry reminded the Good Harry that it was his idea to lie on the resume to get the job. A job that would lead to this perfect criminal opportunity. Criminal Harry'didn't believe his luck that the most significant criminal opportunity of his life would present itself after only a week on the job. Criminal Harry refused to let this opportunity pass them by. This was the new start they needed.

Criminal Harry pushed and pushed. He knew all the answers, he knew what they needed to do. Good Harry began to fade into the background. It was easier to let 'Criminal Harry' take over. Good Harry was a Beta. Criminal Harry was the Alpha. After a short time, Criminal Harry completely took over and kept Good Harry in the background. Good Harry's influence weakened into nothing. Good Harry moved to the rear of Harry's mind and observed the action. He was along for the ride now.

Criminal Harry called the shots now. Criminals hate being told what to do.

12

Harry rocked back and forth, smiling at Justice the dog.

Johnny Mobatu

Johnny Mobatu wandered through the forest. He was dressed in long sleeve flannel shirt and blue jeans. He used a baseball cap to cover his white hair. Johnny

tried to dress the way he observed others in Texas dressing. He could deal with the people who stared curiously at his pale white face and pink eyes. Johnny was an oculocutaneous albino. He crossed the southern border into Texas five days ago. Johnny came from Tanzania in Africa. He escaped Tanzania because of threats from local witch doctors. They wanted to kill him and use his body parts in their potions. The witch doctors believed that consuming albinos would improve virility and masculinity. At least they said they believed it. Johnny felt certain the witch doctors only believed in making money.

Johnny sat on a downed tree and wondered where he would go. He was happy to finally be in America. But now that he was here, he had to decide what to do next. Johnny held his head up with both palms, elbows on his knees. Where would he go? It was time to decide. He was getting hungry.

Harry & Justice

Harry knew what he was going to do. Now, he had to develop a plan to do it.

Harry had observed Justice escape from his cage, go to the refrigerator, open it, steal a bag of roast beef sandwiches, return to his cage and eat his stolen food. Harry knew the German Shepherd was smart. No regular dog could do what Justice just did. Harry quickly understood why Duralink thought Justice was exceptional.

Harry decided to test the dog.

Harry leaned back in his desk chair and stared at Justice.

Justice lay in his cage and stared back at Harry.

"Justice, stand up," Harry looked at the dog and commanded.

Justice stood up.

"Justice, lay down," Harry said.

Justice laid down on the floor.

"Justice, say something," Harry said, expecting a bark in return.

Instead, he heard:

"Uck you,"

Harry couldn't believe his ears. He leaned forward.

"What?" Harry said, surprised at the noise coming out of the dog's mouth.

"Uck you," Justice said looking at Harry. He didn't appreciate being made to act like a sock puppet.

Harry stood up from his chair. He stared down at the dog. Harry had expected the dog to bark, or growl or make some other dog noise.

"Uck You? What is Uck You?" Harry looked at the German Shepherd and asked.

"Go Uck yoursel." Justice looked at Harry directly.

"You can talk too?" Harry asked incredulously.

"You can talk too?" Justice parroted with a high-pitched smart-ass tone.

"Holy freaking cow. I knew you were smart, but you speak?"

"OK Captain Ob'ious, I'll bet when you close your eyes you can't see… Am I right?" Justice spoke sarcasm fluently as well as many other languages.

14

"Well, yeah… uh, wait a minute…." Harry was confused by the dog's intellect.

Harry was outgunned intellectually.

Justice stared back at Harry without saying another word.

Justice was a bright two-toned German Shepherd that was a "project" for the scientists at Duralink. They had implanted sensors into Justice's brain two months ago. Then they connected Justice to a supercomputer and downloaded every known major language into Justice's brain. After all the languages were 'installed' into Justice, they added speech therapy lessons so that Justice could learn to speak. They didn't realize that *all* the information on the supercomputer went directly into Justice's brain. The scientists knew that the human brain and the German Shepherd brain have

25 **petabytes** of memory capacity. As a number, a "**petabyte**" means 1024 terabytes or a million gigabytes, so the average adult human brain can store the equivalent of 25 **million gigabytes** of digital memory. Storage was not the problem. Retrieval was the problem. Humans were limited in how much they could easily retrieve without the help of hypnosis. German Shepherds, on the other hand, did not have a retrieval problem. A German Shepherd could easily access all the information stored in his brain.

Justice was now the most intelligent animal on earth.

The scientists were disappointed when it appeared that Justice didn't acquire the speech abilities they had hoped for. For a week after the information was downloaded into Justice, Justice acted like a regular dog. Justice looked at the scientists while breathing through his mouth with his tongue partially out. If a dog could smile, Justice smiled at his captors.

The fact was, Justice learned much more than the research scientists could have possibly imagined. The supercomputer loaded Justice's brain with tactical and strategic thought processes. Justice could read a situation and know which way it was likely to go. He used math to determine the probabilities. Justice knew every prominent figure in world history. If they were successful, he knew why. If they failed, he knew why. He knew how JFK was killed. He knew the secrets at Roswell. He knew the truth about the 1969 moon landing. Justice knew everything that all people knew. And he knew which of all conflicting stories were true and which were untrue. He knew who was wrong and who was lying about being right. However, the main strength of Justice was not his powerful knowledge. Instead, it was in his ability to be humble. He had no desire to brag or demonstrate his knowledge. Justice was content within himself. He liked being a dog.

Justice the dog was the most intelligent animal on the surface of the earth. His only limitation was that he couldn't pronounce the "F" and "V" sounds. To do so would require his jaw and lips move in ways they could not move. But he knew he could get by without making those sounds. As limitations went, this was not one to worry about. Justice's biggest desire was to get out and see the world. He wanted to experience the realities of his knowledge and interact with other animals.

Justice knew he had to escape without any of the research scientists knowing what he was capable of. If they knew what he knew, they would never let him leave. Unfortunately, they knew he was bright. Brighter than he let on. Justice could easily open his cage and move to the refrigerator to get food. He did it when he thought nobody was looking. Unfortunately, a scientist saw him do it one night when he was working late. Justice's hunger took over and he went for the refrigerator to get human food. Justice hated the dog food they gave him and didn't eat it unless he was starving. Justice enjoyed the cold-cut sandwiches the scientists kept hidden in the refrigerator. He especially liked roast beef and cheese. So far, all human food was better than the dog food they gave him.

Justice returned to his cage one evening with a container of Mac and cheese with hot dogs and a roast beef sandwich that belonged to one of the researchers. The scientist that observed this incredible refrigerator theft ran to Justice immediately and began to inspect him. He was obviously happy and excited. During the inspection he had no affection for Justice, a scientific curiosity.

Justice clammed up and went into serious "Dog" mode. He acted like the world's best dumb dog. More scientists arrived. They looked at him and asked how he knew to open the cage and the refrigerator. He didn't respond.

They surmised it was from observing others. Justice looked at them without responding. The scientists didn't rub Justice behind his ears or give him any form of affection. Justice knew what this meant. Most normal humans were affectionate to the dogs they liked. Humans rubbed dogs behind their ears and on their backs. Humans could be quite affectionate to dogs. And it was pleasurable, Justice had to admit. Justice especially liked having the base of his ears rubbed. Like any living animal, Justice began to suffer from a lack of affection.

These scientists were not affectionate because they didn't want to become too attached to him. The reality was that they could kill him with their experiments. Justice accepted this as a fact. Justice understood the probability was they would eventually kill him, trying to make him smarter. If he let on that he was already more intelligent than all of them combined, they would never let him leave. Catch 22. If he showed them his true intellect, they would sentence him to life in a cage. If he didn't show them his intelligence, they would eventually kill him trying to make him smarter while living in a cage. Either way, his life would be spent in a cage. That would eventually lead to Justice killing himself. Life in a cage was no life at all, especially with all the information in Justice's mind about the beauty and complex nature of the outside world. Justice's dominant desire was to explore the outside world. He wanted good food. Justice wanted to eat peanut butter from a jar in Boulder, Colorado. He wanted to eat barbecue beef brisket in Big Sur, California. Justice wanted a cheeseburger from

What-a-Burger and a Double-Double Animal Style with fries from In-N-Out.

Justice knew his only chance of survival was to escape.

Shortly after the scientists observed Justice's advanced behavior, they decided to hire an Animal Care Specialist. They wanted someone to babysit the dog all night after the scientists left at the end of the day. Human Resources hired Harry Rivers in response to their request.

Crazy Crow

White Rabbit floated through the forest thinking about her sister Crazy Crow. She missed Crazy Crow terribly since the day the evil witch, Lady Mabel, sent Crazy Crow into the unknown abyss by shattering her into a million tiny pieces of colorful glass White Rabbit was lonely. She had Cole, and she was grateful for Cole. However, Cole was no replacement for her younger sister. White Rabbit went to the stream where she and her sister spent their last happy time together in their earthly forms. They had been fishing with their mother, Little Bear, when Laconta attacked them. Laconta was a huge evil creature covered in fur that eventually killed the entire tribe of Comanche Indians that White Rabbit was a member of. White Rabbit's father Chief Two Dogs and over one hundred Braves fought the creature Laconta, but the beast defeated them.

White Rabbit floated over the stream and watched the fish through the clear water. She thought about how happy seeing these fish would make her mother and Crazy Crow. They both loved to fish so much. Crazy Crow and Little Bear had moved on to the other side to be with the Gods, while White Rabbit and her father remained in the forest. White Rabbit did not know why the Gods had taken her sister and mother while leaving her father, herself and a handful of Braves here on earth. White Rabbit began to weep. Her tears fell into the stream below. She closed her eyes and prayed she would see Crazy Crow and her mother again. White Rabbit even prayed that the Gods would take her to be with her mother and sister. Her sobs and prayers were as sincere and genuine as the stream she hovered over.

Soon White Rabbit stopped her weeping and opened, then rubbed, her eyes. When she looked at the river's shore, she couldn't believe who she saw. Her mother and Crazy Crow stood on the bank of the stream and smiled at her.

White Rabbit closed her eyes and opened them again. They were still there! White Rabbit floated over the water and joined them on the bank of the river.

"Mother! Sister! How have you come here?" White Rabbit said through her tears. Now though, her tears were tears of joy.

White Rabbit floated to them and hugged them as tightly as possible.

"Young one," her mother said, "your tears fell into the stream." Her mother smiled at her. "Your tears spoke to the Gods. I cannot stay, but Crazy Crow has been allowed to return to you. I cannot say for how long she will remain. But that is true for all of us." Little Bear gazed at her daughters with joy.

"Mother, I need you to stay too!" White Rabbit cried. She had missed her mother terribly over the last 175 years. She did not want to live without her again.

"No, you do not need me. You want me, but you do not need me. The Gods give us all that we need." Little Bear looked at her daughter and smiled. Her mother's wisdom was shining through.

"Mother…." White Rabbit started to say that she did need her. But as she spoke, Little Bear slowly disappeared in front of her.

"No! No! Please don't leave me again!" White Rabbit reached for her mother to hug her one last time. But it was too late. She had moved back to the other side. White Rabbit buried her face in her hands and cried.

White Rabbit was torn as she looked up at her sister. On the one hand, she was grateful for the return of her beautiful younger sister. On the other hand, she didn't want to lose her mother again. White Rabbit stood still on the riverbank with tears flowing down her cheeks.

Crazy Crow looked at White Rabbit and smiled.

"Sister," Crazy Crow started, "The Gods are wonderful and great. They have allowed us to be together again. Be happy, not sad."

White Rabbit knew she was right. She slowly nodded her head and hugged her sister tightly.

"We will all be together again, sister." Crazy Crow comforted her sister. "Do not worry. Now take me to father."

Noah

Noah walked down La Ventana Parkway to Gene and Peggy's home in the morning sun. It was a beautiful Texas morning with birds and squirrels active in the trees around him. He stood on the street in front of their home for a moment to work up the courage to go and knock on their door. This was the first time Noah had left his home after losing his partner and husband, Sebastian. Sebastian was killed by a terrible bug-man that they had been calling Thin Man. After a couple of weeks of solitude, Noah knew he had to emerge from his home and rejoin life. His first thought was to visit the Summy family. They were always very kind to him and Sebastian. They were a lovely group.

Noah made his way up to the door and knocked. Immediately, the dogs ran up to the door and barked fiercely. Noah heard Peggy's voice from inside. "Gene, it's Noah!" Then footsteps ran to the door and the door swung open with Peggy smiling broadly at Noah.

"Noah! We are so glad you are here!" Peggy said, opening the door and motioning for Noah to come inside. The boxer dogs, Junior and Roxy, nuzzled Noah's hands and legs hoping for some affection.

Peggy hugged Noah and said, "C'mon in. Gene will be glad to see you."

"Where are your kids?" Noah asked.

"They went back to California and Arizona and Minnesota. The vacation was over. They will be back soon, though. Marcus may come down this weekend. He finished his Fireman's academy up in Fort Worth. So, he is a full-fledged fireman now."

"That's great!" Noah said.

"Noah!" Gene said as he rounded the corner into the kitchen. Gene hugged Noah and said, "It's great to see you dude."

"So, how are you doing Noah?" Peggy asked.

"About what you'd expect," Noah said as he shrugged his shoulders.

"Time to get out and about?" Gene asked.

"Yep, that's about it. Time to figure out what to do with my life now." Noah said.

"Life happens. Just let it flow." Gene said.

"I guess. I'm wondering if I should let it flow in Texas or go back to San Francisco." Noah said, sharing his dilemma.

"My vote is Texas. San Francisco has become an armpit. We hope you stay here." Gene smiled at Noah.

"Well, thanks. We...I... love the house, and we did just buy it. So, I will probably stay here a while. It's just tough. I still think of

Sebastian all the time. I expect to see him when I walk into a room. I have to remind myself I'm not going to see him again. That damn bug." Noah shook his head and looked at his feet. Talking about Sebastian brought him close to tears.

"Well, I think you should visit us often to help you get back to normal. The new normal, anyway." Peggy encouraged him.

Noah realized he needed to straighten up. Nobody wanted to hear about how sad he was. People hate that. He needed to be happy and be a bright light for others. That is the truth. People don't want to hear about other people's problems. Everyone has their own drama. There is a definite limit to how much people want to hear about the troubles others have.

Noah stood up straight and looked at both Peggy and Gene.

"Thanks, you two. You are good friends." Noah paused for a moment to look at both of them, then said, "Want to get something to eat?" Noah changed the subject. He had not eaten much during the last two weeks. His diet had consisted of Life cereal for lunch and peanut butter straight out of the jar for dinner.

"That's a great idea! Let's go to Hays City Store and eat some chicken fried steak." Gene smiled. Gene would always agree to eat his favorite meal at his favorite restaurant.

"I'm eating a cheeseburger," Peggy said.

"I'll eat a pizza" Noah genuinely smiled for the first time in a while. Hays City Store made pizza better than the pizza in San Francisco. Plus, it was Sebastian's favorite meal.

Criminal Harry

"Well, yeah… wait a minute…." Harry was confused by the dog's intellect.

Harry stared at Justice and wondered if he heard what he thought he heard.

Justice stared back at him.

"Did you just speak?" Harry wondered if he had imagined it.

Did he just imagine a smart-ass dog? It couldn't be true. This was a trick by that other Harry hidden in the shadows. The feeble, spineless Harry is trying to confuse me, Criminal Harry thought to himself.

Justice stared at Harry and blinked a couple of times. It was time to go into 'dumb dog' mode.

Even if the dog did not speak, he was still smart. Smart enough to steal and hold for ransom. Ransom was such a negative word. Harry decided he would return the mutt for a reward. That's it, a reward. Harry looked at his watch. It was 7:00 am. Harry's night shift was over. The day staff would be in shortly.

Harry was not the brightest star in the sky by any means. He stood looking at Justice, wondering what his next move should be. All Harry knew was that he had to steal the dog. Criminal Harry had taken charge. How he would steal the dog was a question he would need to spend some time with. Maybe his girlfriend Kitty would have an idea.

Harry had a girlfriend named Kitty and Kitty was much brighter than Harry, but that wasn't saying much. Kitty graduated from La Grange High School in the small Texas town of La Grange. She graduated with a 2.03 GPA, which placed her in the top third of her class. When she met Harry 10 years later, she was thrilled to meet a man who accepted her just as she was. Most men wouldn't look at her twice due to one big… issue. Kitty weighed more than most men. She tipped the scales at 230 pounds on a good day.

Harry didn't care about her weight. Harry was polite and respectful during their courtship. Soon, he asked her to marry him, and her world spun in circles. She accepted his proposal and couldn't wait to tell her parents and brothers. But the following day when she awoke happy as a lark, Harry was in a foul mood. He was a different person. By 10:00 am he was drinking beer and cussing at the television. Kitty couldn't understand why he had changed so much overnight. She didn't know much, but she knew she should reevaluate the wedding idea.

When Harry downed his 6th beer before 10:00 am, he yelled at the TV, threw his empty beer can into the backyard, then punched a kitchen cabinet. Kitty was witnessing a new Harry. There was something in his eyes that was new; she hadn't seen these eyes before. She realized why her parents told her never to marry a man you don't know very well. Her mother recommended dating for two years before accepting a marriage proposal. Kitty had ignored the suggestion, considering the source was from a previous generation. She knew plenty of girls from high school that married men after months of dating. Most of them already had three children.

Now though, something in her mother's words rang with wisdom. It's funny how the older we get, the wiser our parents get, Kitty thought.

Kitty stood back and watched Harry prowl and grumble through the small home. When he glanced at her, she almost didn't recognize him. She'd had enough, she decided. She didn't plan to marry a man who could change overnight like this.

She broke the news to him. Wedding plans were off. She needed to think some more.

Harry rubbed his face with his palms, forcing his blond hair to stand up on his forehead, cursed under his breath and threw a beer can through the open sliding glass door. It landed in the backyard, bouncing across the grass, pinwheeling the remaining beer across the yard.

Kitty knew she had made the right decision to rethink the marriage. Calling Harry 'moody' was an understatement. He needed professional help, or a 12-step program, or both.

Harry got his new job at Duralink, and Harry's attitude improved, and he was back to being his respectful self.

Kitty hoped for the best. Maybe now that Harry was employed in a meaningful job he would return to the 'Good Harry' she met just a few short months ago.

She recalled what her father told her many times: Hope is not a strategy.

Something told her she had her hands full with Harry.

Little did she know how full her hands would get.

———————————

White Rabbit and Crazy Crow floated over the trees, searching for their father, Two Dogs. Searching for their father was never very successful, however. They had to wait for him to find them or wish for him to come to them. But they didn't want to wish for him for fear of annoying him. Finding him was a better idea.

White Rabbit stopped over a grove of enormous oak trees. Crazy Crow stopped next to her. It was a beautiful Texas day with the sun bright and warm. White Rabbit floated downwards into the shade of the giant oaks below them. These oak trees had been there when White Rabbit and Crazy Crow were alive. Their leafy canopies were wide and shady. Both small ghosts looked at each other and instinctively knew what to do. It was time to call for him. They closed their eyes. White Rabbit said, "Father, I need you, please...."

Before she could complete her request, her father appeared in front of both of them.

"Young one, you have returned." Two Dogs said, looking at Crazy Crow without the emotion White Rabbit expected.

"Yes, Father, Mother brought me back. The Gods allowed her." Crazy Crow said.

"Your Mother? Where is she?" The emotion White Rabbit expected began to show when Crazy Crow mentioned Two Dog's long dead wife, Little Bear.

"She had to return to the Gods." Crazy Crow said softly.

"Why did they allow only you to return?" Two Dogs' disappointment was evident. He missed his beloved wife more than he was happy to see his youngest daughter.

Crazy Crow tried not to have his remarks hurt her feelings. But they did.

"White Rabbit spilled tears into the river." Crazy Crow started, "Her sorrow brought the Gods to pity her and reward her faith."

"I am glad," Two Dogs said. He opened his arms, and she hugged him.

"Father, I am glad to be with you and White Rabbit again." Crazy Crow said gratefully.

"Did you see the Gods?" Two Dogs was curious about the Gods. He was relieved to hear Crazy Crow say the Gods allowed for her return. He had always been a man of faith, but confirmation of the faith was reassuring. He had never met anyone who had met the Gods before.

"Yes, Father, I met them and spent time with them."

"What are they like?"

"They are wonderful and mighty. Words cannot describe them. My words are not good enough." Crazy Crow looked at him, grateful for the question. "They are full of love for those that believe in them."

Connie Lingus

Harry looked at Justice, contemplating his next move. Suddenly the door to the Lab opened and four men walked through with one woman.

"Hello, Harry" Said the man in front. It was Phil Ayshow, Harry's direct boss.

"Morning, Phil" Harry replied.

"This is Connie Lingus from HR. She has a couple of questions for you."

"Ok, what's up Connie?" Harry smiled at the young woman.

"Hi Harry, I was going over your files and resume," Connie paused for a long moment.

Harry held his breath. Could they possibly know his entire resume was a pile of fabrications and lies?

"Do you have a middle name?" Connie asked.

"Yes. I don't usually give it out, though."

"Why is that?"

"Because I don't like it much."

"OK. What is it?"

"Do you have to know?"

"Yes. I need it for the files." Connie tried to sound assertive.

"La Douche," Harry said in a low tone, hoping the men behind her would not hear it.

"La Douche?" Connie said with the volume Harry avoided. "Are you calling me a La Douche?" Connie looked like she had been slapped in the face.

"No. That's my middle name." Harry reluctantly said.

"Your middle name is La Douche?" Phil said loud enough for the entire lab to hear.

Harry grimaced and looked at his feet. He knew the scientists had heard it now.

"Are you serious?" Connie asked with a smile.

"Yeah. It's a family name." Harry admitted.

"A family name?" Connie repeated. She had never heard this name before. The young woman began to smile.

"Yeah, my Dad was a La Douche. His Dad was a La Douche."

"You come from a long line of La Douches!" A young Israeli scientist named Yuri Nator yelled across the room. The others laughed. Even Connie bit through a giggle.

"It's European." Harry said with regret.

"European?" Connie repeated.

"Yeah, my Dad is from Europe. Europe is full of La Douches."

The three scientists who entered the lab with Phil and Connie burst out laughing.

"Ok. I'll write that down," Connie said with raised eyebrows.

Harry glared at the laughing scientists. He hated it when people laughed at him. He would remember these guys and get them back.

"I think your Animal Science Trade School should be able to find you now that I have your middle name," Connie said, indicating his fabricated resume may be falling apart.

"Yeah, they will have it. I told them I was European, hoping it would help me get accepted. It worked." Harry resorted to more lies.

"You lied to them?" Connie was surprised Harry would admit that so readily. She would now have to look deeper into his history.

"It's not a lie. I have dual citizenship, America and Great Britain." Harry truthfully said.

"OK, great Harry thanks." Connie smiled and left the lab. She made a mental note to check his background a bit more thoroughly.

"Go home, Harry. Get some sleep." Phil said with a smile.

"OK Phil, Thanks." Harry smiled at his boss and started to leave.

"Wait! Hey Harry, I forgot to ask, Did Justice do anything unusual? Anything to report?" Phil looked at Harry.

Harry thought about Justice speaking to him, then shook his head. "Nope. Nothing unusual. Just a nice, dumb dog." Harry didn't want them looking at Justice any harder than they already were. His plan to steal the dog could be sidetracked with closer scrutiny.

Justice grimaced. He hated Harry. Justice knew Harry was up to no good. Justice had correctly calculated that Harry was going to steal him, and Justice was going to let Harry steal him. Once out of the Lab, Justice would easily escape from the fat dolt Harry.

"Ok Harry, I'll see you tonight," Phil said in a friendly voice.

"Bye Phil," Harry smiled back at Phil.

"Bye La Douche!" All three scientists called out and waved. They looked at each other, laughing. Laughing at Harry.

He would get his payback, Harry thought to himself.

He knew where they kept their food.

Johnny Gets a Job

Johnny sat on the log, wondering what to do next. He was hungry and his thirst was growing intolerable. He needed to earn some money to get some food. He would use the debit card given to him by the Border Patrol only if he had to. He preferred to earn his money. He stood up and stretched. It was time to find a town where he could get a job and make some money.

Johnny hiked through the forest and down small unpaved roads for about three hours until he heard traffic. Johnny knew he was getting close to a town.

Johnny emerged from the tree line and looked at the highway. A road sign said Ranch Road 12. Another road sign said Dripping Springs three miles. Johnny decided Dripping Springs would be an excellent place to start his job hunt. He commenced walking on the shoulder of the road towards Dripping Springs.

After only 20 minutes, a pickup truck pulled over in front of him. A man in a cowboy hat yelled, "You need a ride?" The man was a local rancher named Hayden. He was very nice to Johnny and offered to take him anywhere in Dripping Springs. In short order, he was at the biggest grocery store he had ever seen. He looked at the HEB grocery store in amazement at the size and scale. Nothing like this existed in Tanzania. Johnny cleaned himself up and looked as presentable as he could.

He walked into the HEB and went directly into the men's room. He removed his stocking cap and gloves then washed his face and hands. He smoothed his white hair back and realized he looked better with his cap off. He pulled his backpack around and stuffed his gloves and cap into the side zipper pouch. His flannel shirt looked like everyone else's in the store, as did his blue jeans. He was separated from others by his pigmentless skin and the accent of his English. He learned English in school in Africa. Every child in Africa had to learn English in school. Communication would not be a problem.

He hoped they would give him a job. Johnny smiled into the mirror and remembered what his mother had told him. She would say always smile at yourself, then others will smile at you too.

Johnny left the men's room and found the service center. He waited in line for a few minutes, then bellied up to the counter.

A young woman named Trish looked at him.

"Hello, can I help yooouuu?" She said, smiling broadly in her Texas accent. Texan ladies often pronounced 'You" as though it should be spelled 'yooouuuuuu.'

"Yes, I was hoping to find a job here." Johnny smiled back at her.

"When can you start, hun?" Trish asked.

"Right now." Johnny smiled and shrugged his shoulders.

"Hold on one minute, hun." Trish picked up a phone.

"Hey, Bobby I got a guy here looking for work and says he can start now. He looks like a nice guy to me." Trish smiled at Johnny as she spoke into the receiver. "OK, great thanks Bobby," Trish remembered Bobby complaining that he needed to hire someone immediately to help him in the deli.

"Go over there, hun," Trish said, pointing across the store. "And ask for Bobby. He runs the Deli." Trish gave Johnny her biggest smile.

"Thank you very much." Johnny smiled back at Trish.

"No problem. Good Luck, hun."

Johnny walked back to the deli counter and asked for Bobby. In two minutes he was sitting at Bobby's desk answering quick questions.

He explained he was from Africa and worked in a grocery store as a butcher. He understood meats and cheeses and how to use scales.

Bobby nodded quickly. "Great. Look, I will pay you cash for your first few weeks to make sure you work out. Is that OK with you?" Bobby hoped it would be OK. It was his only option for now.

"Sure. Yes sir. That's great." In fact, it was perfect for Johnny. He would have the cash right after his shift was over.

"I'll pay you 15 bucks an hour. Be clean and tidy. Say 'yes sir' and 'no sir' 'yes ma'am' 'no ma'am' to every question you are asked. Then just slice the meat and cheese people ask for and be nice. Wipe down the slicer after each use. If you can do that and show up on time every day, I'll get you on payroll in a couple of weeks." Bobby smiled.

"Thank you, sir. I can do that. When do you want me to start?"

"Now," Bobby stood up and tossed Johnny an apron.

Johnny looked at the man named Bobby like he was an angel. This was an answer to a prayer.

"Let me clean up in the restroom." Johnny said.

"We have our own restroom just behind those doors." Bobby pointed to some doors just outside his office.

"Yes sir, thank you, sir." Johnny smiled broader than he had smiled since coming to America.

Johnny cleaned up and proudly wore his apron to the deli counter. Within a minute he was slicing cheese for a lady that stared at his hands.

Hays City Store

Gene, Peggy and Noah sat outside under a giant oak tree at Hays City Store waiting for their order of food to arrive. It was a beautiful Texas day in May. Hays City Store was crowded as usual, with most patrons wearing blue jeans and Texas-style shirts. Many of the men had cowboy hats on.

Noah had a topic in mind he wasn't sure how to discuss. The truth was that he enjoyed the hunting and tracking with Heston and his dogs. He hated discovering his husband's death, especially the shock of seeing his husband's head tied to the bug's hip. That was the most ghastly thing he had seen in his life.

But other than that, he was happy working with the dogs and getting the exercise and adventure of hiking through the forest.

"So, do you think I could work with you guys more often hunting bad guys? I mean, you work with Heston frequently, right?" Noah decided just to come out and ask.

"Well, that is completely up to Heston," Gene said.

"Yeah, Heston is the boss. We are lucky he asks us to come along." Peggy agreed. "I have to tell you that every hunt we have been on has been an adventure so far."

"What kind of things have you seen?" Noah asked.

Gene and Peggy looked at each other, not knowing where to start.

Well, on our first hunt with Heston, we tracked a Big Foot creature the Indians called Laconta." Peggy started the list of creatures they had seen. "Jerry Smith killed him with a Mossberg blast to the back of the head."

"Then we killed a witch called Lady Mabel." Peggy hated Lady Mabel. She was the most evil creature Peggy could imagine. The witch came close to killing Peggy. It was a terrible memory.

"Then we went after the first Bug-man called Thin Man. That was when you got involved." Gene added.

"Then we went after Thin Man's wife, and that was probably the worst one of all because she could fly." Gene was terrified of giant flying bugs.

"I don't know. I think the witch Lady Mabel was the worst," Peggy said, remembering how she roasted small children over a fire and killed the beautiful little Indian Crazy Crow.

"Yeah, she was pretty scary. Her magic creeped me out." Gene hated Lady Mabel too.

"Hard to say which was the worst one."

"Agreed"

"They were all bad."

"But we made it through alive because of Heston," Gene said.

"And Warren," Peggy remembered Warren blowing the Thin Man bug's head off with a shotgun.

"And Jerry Smith."

"Well, honestly we all acted like a pretty good team."

"Yeah, we did pretty well," Peggy admitted.

"Maybe that's why Heston continues to invite you," Noah said.

"I dunno, maybe. But I honestly don't think he needs us." Peggy said.

"He doesn't need us. He just likes the company." Gene agreed.

"Yeah, that's it," Peggy said, "He likes having the company."

"Well, I want it to be a part of it." Noah was certain. "I need to be a part of it. I need something in my life besides an empty house."

"Be careful what you ask for. You might get it." Peggy said.

"I want it."

"Not many people want to see the things we have seen."

"I do." Noah was sure he needed adventure in his life. Even if it meant seeing terrible, violent creatures that he had always thought were 'Made Up' by storytellers. But he saw Thin Man for himself, so he knew they were real. Maybe it was his way of getting revenge for the loss of Sebastian.

"OK, when we get back let's call Heston over and talk to him about it," Gene said.

A waitress arrived with their food. The three spent the next 20 minutes eating like they hadn't eaten in a week.

Cherry Harry

Harry researched how to crush cherry pits on Quora and YouTube. He discovered that four cherry pits, when crushed would produce enough cyanide to kill a human. He used a large iron vice in his garage to crush 12 cherry pits completely. He took the crushed cherry pits and mixed them with three milliliters of water and 1 milliliter of the cherry juice extracted from the cherries containing the seeds. He let them soak overnight. The following day Harry used an eye dropper and sucked up the four milliliters of cyanide solution. Harry smiled and imagined looking at the three scientists that thought they were so funny as they lay dying on the floor.

Harry went to work at 7:00 pm as usual. He carried a lunch sack full of food that would carry him through the night and the eyedropper full of his homemade cyanide. Now all he had to do was add the cyanide to their Motts apple juice and wait for morning. The three funny boys would arrive at about 7:00 am and place their food in the same refrigerator Harry used. Then they would all drink their favorite Motts apple juice that was in the refrigerator. How did Harry know about the Motts Apple juice? Easy. They used a Sharpie Black marker and wrote "Stay Away! Property of the Science Department" on the large bottle. They were so smart. Harry smiled to himself again.

Once Harry was sure he was alone at about 11 pm, he calmly walked to the refrigerator. He looked around behind himself to verify he was alone. As he scanned the large research lab, he saw Justice staring back at him. Harry starred back at Justice. They locked eyes. Harry got the strangest feeling that Justice knew what he was about to do. Harry didn't worry about it. Justice was locked up in his large dog cage. As far as Harry was concerned, Justice could stay there all night.

Harry turned back to the refrigerator and grabbed the Motts apple juice jug. It was perfect–just about half full. The three smart, funny boys would drink all of it 1st thing in the morning before their coffee. No juice would be left over for analysis if an investigation were started into their deaths.

Harry unscrewed the cap and reached for the eye dropper bottle in his lunch bag. He sucked up all his cyanide solution in the rubber-capped eye dropper. Then Harry moved the eyedropper over to the open jug of Motts apple juice. He squeezed all the cyanide into the apple juice and replaced the cap. Harry swirled the apple juice around to mix the cyanide thoroughly into the juice. He placed the jug of apple juice back in where he found it.

"What did you just do?" Harry heard the voice come from behind him.

Harry turned around to find Justice standing directly behind him. Harry looked back at Justice's cage to see the lock open and a wide-open cage door.

"How did you get out?" Harry asked.

"Really, Harry? You just ha'en't been paying attention ha'e you." Justice didn't enjoy talking with stupid people.

"None of your business, Mr. Smart Dog," Harry replied.

"What did you just put in the juice?" Justice continued his questions.

"Nothing"

"Really? You lie like a dog."

"You not only talk, but you talk too much. Does anyone else know that you talk?" Harry was annoyed with the talking dog now.

"Answer my question and I'll answer yours."

"OK. I added sweetener into their juice."

"Sweetener? Really? Would that be a cherry pit sweetener?" Justice had deduced Harry was going to kill the scientists by poisoning them. Cyanide was the most likely option.

Harry was aghast. How did this dog know? He didn't know what to say. If this dog knew what he did, he could tell Phil and the police after the scientists were discovered dead. This information would have to move up his plans to steal the dog. Harry didn't plan on stealing the dog tonight. But now he was forced to move up the timeline.

"Ok yeah. Cherry pit sweetener. How did you know?"

"Listen La Douche. I saw your 'ace yesterday when those guys were la'ing at you."

"Don't call me that."

"Or what? You gonna kill me too?"

"Just don't call me that."

"Ok, La Douche."

"I'm serious. You'll be sorry." Harry said, feeling his anger rise.

"You 'at slob. You couldn't catch me on your quickest day. Think I'm a'raid of you? Think again 'at boy."

"At boy? What kind of insult is that?"

"Smart boy. I can't pronounce a certain sound."

Harry saw red. He'd had enough, even though he still didn't get it. He lunged at Justice.

Justice was right. He quickly backed up and Harry grabbed air and landed on his belly. Harry tried again and again. Justice moved away. For Justice, this was child's play. Harry went about 350 pounds on his six-three frame. Harry was a big boy with no speed and a 1/4-inch vertical leap on a good day.

"Look, La Douche. You will never catch me." Justice said.

"You are not so smart," Harry said out of breath.

"Well, I'm smarter than you."

Harry glared back at the talking German Shepherd. He didn't know what to do next. He couldn't catch the dog. That much was clear. How would he get the dog to his car?

"Look, La Douche. I know what you are planning." Justice said.

"Oh Yeah? What smart dog? And don't call me that."

"You plan to steal me and hold me 'or ransom or sell me to the highest bidder." Justice said.

Harry couldn't believe his ears. How could this dog possibly know that?

"Ok. Yeah–well— that's right." Harry admitted.

"I know. And I'll make it easy on you." Justice had a plan.

"You are going to make it easy on me?" Harry was doubtful but wanted to know what the dog had in mind.

"Yes, La Douche. We can make a deal."

"We can make a deal?" Harry gave up on getting Justice to stop calling him by his middle name. Harry had difficulty 'making a deal' with a German Shepherd. How was this even possible?

"You repeat me a lot. Think you can stop doing that?" Justice found Harry annoying. He wanted to maneuver Harry into helping him escape. Soon enough, he would never have to deal with La Douche again.

"Tell me the deal." Harry stared at the dog.

Ok 'at boy. Here it is. I will stop calling you La Douche and I will stop calling you 'at Boy. I will cooperate in walking to your car and going to your hiding place, wherever that may be.

"What is 'at boy anyway? I still don't get it."

"What is the 6th letter in the al'abet?

Harry counted out the letters in his head and used his fingers for help.

"F, the 6th letter is F," Harry said, not yet making the connection.

"I can't make that sound because of my jaw and lips."

So 'At Boy' is …. 'Fat Boy'?" The light went on in Harry's head.

"See, now that wasn't so hard, was it?" Justice said.

"Yeah, you gotta stop calling me that too." Harry had to have this in the deal.

"'Deal." Justice agreed.

"OK. What do I have to do?" Harry asked.

"Number one, pour the apple juice down the drain."

"OK, Is there a number two?"

"Wow, you *are* stupid La Douche. Yes, of course there is a number two."

"Don't call me stupid!" Harry's voice raised.

"Oh, I'm sorry Harry, I thought you already knew."

"I did Mr. Smart Dog… wait…" Harry was confused. "I'm not stupid!" Harry yelled.

"So, there are three things I can't call you? Should I start making a list? Or are we going to stop at three?"

"Just don't call me that."

"OK, I won't call you stupid anymore along with not calling you La Douche and 'at boy".

"Right." Harry said.

"Fine"

"What do I have to do?" Harry asked.

"Never lock me up or put a leash on me. Never put me in a car with the windows rolled up. Windows have to remain down. And feed me human food—the good stuff. I like cold cuts and cheese. Hamburgers are good too. No dog food."

"Is that it?"

"Yep." Justice knew these terms would make his escape easy.

Harry nodded his head. He could agree to those terms if the dog held up his end of the deal.

"Say it," Justice said.

"Say what?"

"Wow. Your stupidity knows to end, does it?"

"Don't call me that!"

"Once you agree to the deal, I won't ever call you stupid again."

"Fine, I agree to the deal!"

"OK, apple juice down the drain" Justice moved his nose, pointing to the sink.

"Fine," Harry said, exasperated. He grabbed the jug of Motts Apple juice and carried it to the sink. He opened the top and up ended it over the drain. In seconds, it was empty.

"Now it's your turn," Harry said." Let's go."

"Harry, I am ready." Justice couldn't wait to leave.

"We're leaving."

"Let's Stop by What-a-Burger and get me a double cheeseburger." Justice was hungry already.

"I hate your guts," Harry said under his breath.

Nancy Webb

Nancy Webb retired from the Dallas Police Department in January, five months ago. She had achieved the rank of Lieutenant and had spent the last six years working as the Lieutenant of the Homicide Division within the Crimes Against Persons Division in the Dallas Police Department. Her immediate boss was Deputy Chief Terrence Roads. Deputy Chief Roads was a difficult man to work for. Despite Nancy's department having an excellent record of closing brutal homicides, he was never satisfied with Nancy's department. Earlier in Nancy's career, she dreamed of being the Chief of Police. After just a few years within the executive ranks of the department, she realized it was not for her. The political environment was sickening. Nancy enjoyed investigating and solving crimes. She loved it, but unfortunately for her, that became a small part of her job after achieving the rank of Lieutenant.

So, after 25 years of service, Nancy Webb retired. Her retirement income was plenty to keep her comfortable, but not enough to keep her from getting bored. She soon realized she had to do something with her time.

She remembered a detective named Marty Shott who left the department and created a private detective agency. There was good money to be made as a private detective as long as you solved the cases given to you. It was all about having a wealthy clientele that either had marital infidelity or children that disappeared. Easy work compared to what Nancy was used to.

She contacted Marty, who remembered Nancy well. He was excited to have her join his small agency. He had just landed the Duralink Corporation as a client, and he worried he had too much work to handle alone. Having Nancy Webb join him solved his problems.

Nancy packed up her belongings and moved to Austin, Texas, about three hours south of Dallas. She was happy to have a new challenge and escape from the Dallas Police Department politics.

Marty was excited to tell Nancy about their first big case with Duralink. Evidently, a dog they had been performing research on had disappeared along with an employee they suspected to have left with the dog. Their job was to find the dog, first and foremost. If they found the missing employee along the journey, fine. But he was a secondary concern. The dog was worth millions of dollars.

The dog's name was Justice.

—-

Johnny worked until 10:00 pm that evening when the store closed.

Bobby approached Johnny as he was taking his apron off.

"Hey, Johnny. You had a good day today." Bobby said, smiling at his newest employee.

"Thank you, sir. I enjoyed it very much. "Johnny smiled back at Bobby. He was genuinely grateful for the job.

"Throw your apron in that basket in the corner. You will use a fresh one tomorrow."

"Yes sir. What time should I be here tomorrow?"

"Well, honestly, I lost my two regulars. So as early as you can get here would be great." Bobby didn't want to tell Johnny to work a 16-hour shift.

"The store hours are 6:00 AM to 10:00 PM, right?" Johnny asked.

"Yes, Johnny. I'd like you to work until closing. So, what time can you start?" Bobby hoped Johnny would volunteer to work the full day without having to be told.

"I'll be here at 6:00 am."

"You want to work 6:00 am to 10:00 pm?" It was music to Bobby's ears.

"Yes sir. I am happy to, plus I need the money."

"OK Great. I will see you here at 6:00 am. Here let me pay you for today." Bobby was grateful. He was going to like his newest employee.

"You worked eight hours today, right?"

"Yes sir."

"Eight times 15 is 120, right?" Bobby asked, knowing the answer.

"Yes sir." Johnny wanted to yell with joy. He had finally earned money in America. Money that was not given to him for crossing a border. This was a great day.

Bobby opened his petty cash box and peeled out six twenty-dollar bills. He reached across the desk to hand them to Johnny.

"Good job Johnny. Keep it up and I will put you on payroll real soon." Bobby smiled.

"Thank you, sir." Johnny reached for the money and folded it into his blue jeans pocket. He realized he had not eaten all day.

"Are you hungry?" Bobby asked. He heard Johnny's stomach growling.

"Yes, very hungry." Johnny smiled.

"Make a cold-cut sandwich for yourself. And grab a bag of chips and a soda."

"Thanks very much, sir." The generosity of Americans was astounding. This would never happen in Africa.

Johnny made a beautiful roast beef and cheese sandwich with mustard and mayonnaise. He used sourdough bread from the bread bin.

Now, all he had to do was find a place to eat his sandwich and sleep.

Harry Steals Justice

Harry looked at the clock. It was 5:30 am. Morning shift would soon be arriving. He had to escape now with the dog before anyone arrived.

"Let's go." Harry looked at Justice with a leash in his hand.

"Our deal was no leashes." Justice reminded Harry.

"Oh yeah. Ok, stay close to me."

Harry opened the Lab door. He peered into the hallway, first looking right, then left. He didn't see anyone. Only long empty hallways.

"Let's go. Stay close to me." Harry commanded.

Harry entered the hallway and turned left to the Main exit that faced the parking area. The quiet hall intersected into another hallway where they took another left.

When they got to the exit Harry was surprised to find a security guard on duty.

"Just act normal" Harry said to Justice.

"Normal?"

'Yeah, just be a dog. A normal dog."

"OK. Can I ask the security guard 'how's it hangin'?" Justice couldn't resist provoking Harry sarcastically.

"No!" Harry whispered loudly.

"OK. OK. Keep your panties dry."

"Panties dry? Where did you learn to talk like that?" Harry couldn't believe the smart-ass dog's attitude.

"You better stop talking to me, or the guard will think you're nuts. Wait, you are nuts. Nevermind."

"Shut up." Harry ordered.

"You're the reason God created the middle finger, I wish I had one for you."

"Shut up!"

They approached the guard. Harry smiled and nodded before he reached for the door handle.

"Wait! I need you to sign out." The security guard named Mike said.

"Sign out?" Harry asked.

"Yeah, and the dog can't leave. No animals are allowed through this exit."

Harry noticed the name tag on the security guard.

"Mike, this is my dog."

"Your dog?" Mike looked like he didn't believe it.

"Yes."

"You brought your dog to work with you?"

"Yes." Harry said, attempting to sound truthful.

"You brought your dog to the *animal sciences* lab?" Mike knew this was not on the level.

"Yes."

"Sorry, buddy. I don't buy it and even if I did, you can't take an animal out of this exit. I'm calling my boss. What is your name?" Mike asked.

Harry moved toward Mike the security guard, like he would comply with his requests.

In a quick second, Harry reached out and grabbed the telephone receiver that Mike had on his ear. Harry used the receiver to hit Mike hard in the forehead. A gash was opened that produced fast-flowing blood into Mike's eyes. Harry struck Mike in the temple with his fist. Next, Harry wrapped the telephone cord around Mike's throat and stretched it tight. Mike's face turned beet red, and blood vessels across his forehead popped out. Harry squeezed the telephone cord around Mike's neck as tight as he could. Mike tried to scream, but his voice was reduced to a whisper.

Justice was horrified at what he witnessed. He quickly realized Harry was much more dangerous than he had estimated. As Harry squeezed the life out of Mike, Justice ran to the large glass exit door and pushed the horizontal bar forward with his front paws, unlatching the door. Justice pushed the door open and ran towards the parking lot.

"Stop!" Harry yelled. "We have a deal!"

Harry dropped Mike's body on the floor and ran after Justice. By the time Harry got to the doors, Justice was disappearing into the trees on the other side of the parking lot.

Harry was furious. He looked back at Mike's dead body lying across the floor in front of the security guard's station. The phone cord was still around his neck, and blood pooled on the floor. The phone on Mike's desk began to ring with an unusually shrill ring creating echoes in the large empty entry foyer.

"Crap. Crap. Crap" Harry said out loud. All he could think to do was run. Then it hit Harry that there had to be security cameras capturing everything. He looked upwards at the ceiling for cameras. There they were, four cameras in different locations all pointing at him.

Harry ran through the doors to his truck in the parking lot. He knew he was in deep trouble. Something inside Harry snapped. All reasonable logic had left Harry. Now he was filled with rage directed at Justice the dog. He was convinced that everything that had gone wrong was the talking dog's fault. Harry hated that smart-ass dog.

Harry sat behind the wheel of his GMC pickup truck. He stared forward and began to rock side to side. In the dim light of dawn, Harry lost his mind. He was furious at the world. He rocked side to side with both hands clutching the steering wheel. Headlights entered the parking lot from another late-model pickup truck. The truck drove through the lot and chose a parking space close to Harry.

A young woman got out of the truck, probably a kitchen worker from the Duralink Cafeteria, Harry thought. Harry waved at her, and she waved back with a smile. Harry realized that as soon as she went through the entrance, she would see Mike. That would mean trouble for Harry. He needed more time to escape. Harry got out of his truck with a broad smile and spoke to the young woman.

"Don't I know you? You work in the cafeteria, right?" Harry asked with a nice tone.

"Why, yes I do. I don't think we have met. I'm Cindy." Cindy smiled and held her hand out to shake.

Harry approached her and held out his hand to shake hers.

Cindy had stopped in front of Harry's truck. As Harry took her hand in his, he quickly pulled her in tight and turned her around. He placed his forearm under her neck and began to squeeze. He drug her back to the side of his truck, where he was hidden from view. She slapped at his forearms and tried to scratch his face, but he was just too big and strong. She quickly lost consciousness. In minutes he had strangled the life out of Cindy. She had no final words.

He found her keys in her purse and pushed the unlock button on her FOB. Her Ford F150 chirped that it had been unlocked. Harry dragged Cindy's lifeless body to her truck and laid her on the front bench seat, out of sight. Harry hoped if someone spotted her, they may think she was asleep.

Now Harry had killed two people.

All Harry could think was, I'm going to kill that smart-ass dog. It's all the dog's fault. That dog had the idea to escape. He wanted a deal. We had a deal! It was all his idea! I wouldn't have killed the security guard if the dog didn't have the idea to escape. Harry began to shake. He gripped the steering wheel so tightly that his knuckles turned white. Harry rocked side to side for a couple of minutes in pure anger.

Harry started his truck and quickly headed for his home with Kitty. Maybe she would know what to do. He knew he didn't have much time before the bodies of the security guard and Cindy were discovered. The security tapes would tell the story. He had to go fast.

Kitty will help him. She will know what to do.

Noah finds Justice

Noah was up early. Since Sebastian was gone he couldn't sleep well. He awoke by 4:00 am every day. He was done sleeping. It had become such a routine that he set his coffee pot to go off at 3:45 am every day so he wouldn't have to wait for his coffee. Noah got up and made his cup of coffee with one sugar and one cream. He sat on his back porch, enjoying the quiet. How was he going to kick-start his life? He had to do something. He hadn't cried in a few days, so he was making progress. He decided to go for a ride. It was still dark out, so traffic would not be an issue. The thought of a nice ride around Driftwood to watch the sun come up sounded like a good idea. At least it was a change of pace. He needed to get out more. Maybe he could find a good donut shop. Noah hadn't eaten a good donut since he was in San Francisco.

Noah didn't have the nerve yet to drive Sebastian's Lexus. So, he climbed into his red Toyota Four Runner. He liked the Lexus better than the Toyota, but he just wasn't ready to drive it yet.

In moments Noah was driving on FM 150 headed south towards Hays City Store. It was a great drive with the sun soon coming up. A beautiful Texas morning, Noah thought. Noah passed Hays City Store and took a left towards Kyle, Texas. Before he knew it, he was in Kyle and remembered a donut store that he and Sebastian had talked about going to. It was called Hays City Donut and Chinese Food. Noah found the donut shop and drove through the drive-through window. As he waited for the donut order to be prepared, he noticed a beautiful two-toned German Shepherd dog cross the parking lot in front of his Toyota. What was a beautiful dog like that doing out by himself at 5:00 am?

Noah was instantly smitten with the dog. He could tell it was not a feral street dog. This dog looked healthy with a beautiful black and brown coat. Noah lowered the window on the passenger side door.

"Hey dog!" Noah said, then he whistled. Noah had always had an excellent strong whistle using his left thumb and middle finger.

The dog stopped and looked at Noah.

"Hey, you want something to eat?" Noah felt stupid talking to a dog like it would understand. When the little Asian lady came to the window with his order Noah asked her to add a couple of the sausage kolaches to the order.

"Hey Dog! I got you something to eat! Come here!" Noah yelled out the window.

Unbelievably the dog immediately trotted over to the Toyota.

"Wow, you are a smart dog!" Noah paid for the food and pulled into a nearby parking space. He got out and walked around to the passenger side door. There stood the most beautiful male German Shepherd that Noah had ever seen. His coat was thick and perfect. Noah thought it could have been a show dog. The face was primarily black but had streaks and patches of brown.

"Hey buddy come here" Noah bent over and rubbed the German Shepherd's ears and back.

Where is your collar? Noah had a difficult time believing a dog of this caliber would be out without a collar.

"Hmmm… well, are you hungry?" Noah asked the dog as though it might answer.

"Ok let's eat something." Noah opened the passenger door. His intention was to grab the bag of food with the sausage kolaches. But before he could, the dog jumped into the Toyota and sat facing forward in the passenger seat.

"Wow, you want to come home with me?" Noah asked.

The dog looked at Noah and smiled. Then he looked straight forward like he was saying 'let's go buddy'.

Noah wasn't sure what to do. He knew what he wanted to do. He wanted the dog. He wanted to drive home with his new friend and pamper him like he had never been pampered before. On the other hand, he didn't want to steal someone's dog. Noah realized he desperately wanted this dog. This dog could fill the void in his life.

Noah shut the passenger door and walked around to the driver's side door and opened it. By the time he climbed into the driver's seat, he knew the dog was coming home with him. He told himself he would keep an eye in the paper and on Craigslist for people looking for a German Shepherd in the Kyle area. In the meantime, he would take good care of the dog.

Noah opened the bag and unwrapped a sausage kolache. When he held it towards the Dogs face, the dog took it eagerly. Noah smiled.

"Would you like another one?" Noah asked.

The dog smiled at him.

Noah unwrapped the last sausage kolache and fed it to his new friend. In no time the sausage kolache was gone.

"That was fast" Noah smiled at his new friend. Noah could have sworn the dog smiled back at him. Noah stared at the German Shepherd for a long moment.

"You are some dog," Noah said to his new friend.

Noah started the red Toyota and headed back to Driftwood with his new buddy.

White Rabbit looked over at Cole as they sat in the tree. She realized he was comfortable in his new life as a ghost. Before, he seemed to reject the fact that he was not alive as a human anymore. He didn't know what to do next. He seemed to operate as though he was afraid of what was next. Now, he was different. Cole had transitioned. He went from being a follower to a leader. He sat comfortably at the top of the tree and gazed downwards into the forest and all that it held. He had the same kind of presence as her father, Chief Two Dogs. Confident and wise. White Rabbit moved to sit closer to Cole. She felt peace and security fold over her the closer she got to Cole. She knew she was in love with him. But she had no idea if he loved her or if he knew she loved him. White Rabbit decided to be patient and let the situation play out. They were young ghosts and had lots of time in front of them.

"What are you looking for, Cole?" White Rabbit asked.

"There's a new person in our forest. He is different." Cole replied.

"Different how?"

"He isn't from here, he's from far away, and he is white as a ghost. I have never seen anyone like him."

"Is he a good ghost?" White Rabbit asked.

"He is not a ghost. He is a pure white man. And I am not certain about him being good or not."

Below them hiked a man with white hair and completely white skin. He carried a backpack. He looked like an ordinary young man except for his pure white skin and hair.

The young albino man sat next to a tree and opened his backpack. He took off his flannel long-sleeve shirt and put on a sweatshirt. He seemed to be settling in for the night.

Cole noticed how neatly the man folded his flannel shirt before he placed it in his backpack.

"Is he safe staying there for the night?" White Rabbit asked.

"Yes. Laconta, Thin Man and Lady Mabel have all been vanquished. I believe we are all safe for a long time."

"What should we do?"

"We should keep an eye on him. Nothing more."

White Rabbit sat comfortably next to Cole. She could not help to think of her father. He would be proud of what Cole had become. Cole was a sentry, a guard, a night watchman, a protector, and a tiny warrior.

Yes, Two Dogs would be proud.

Harry and Kitty

Harry parked abruptly in front of the small home he shared with Kitty in New Braunfels. He opened his truck door and ran around the front of the truck, sprinting as fast as he could to the front door of the home. At close to 360 pounds, Harry's sprint was more like a fat bear rushing to a freshly filled dumpster behind Pizza Hut.

Harry blasted through the front door and yelled for Kitty.

"I'm working! On the phone!" Kitty yelled back. Kitty worked from home as a sales representative for a large medical supply company.

Harry entered the bedroom that had been converted into an office.

"You gotta help me! Get off the phone." Harry ordered her.

"I'm busy now, Harry. Can I ignore you another time?" Kitty asked.

"No. Now. Ignore me now. I mean– talk to me now!" Harry demanded.

Kitty ended the conversation with her big customer and stared at Harry. She knew he could be needy at times. Her problem was that he was becoming needy on a daily basis.

"What do you need, Harry?" Kitty asked as politely as she could.

Harry took a deep breath. He didn't know where to start. Telling her a dog spoke to him would not go well. Telling her he killed a security guard and a woman in the parking lot would be even worse.

But without her guidance, he was lost. Harry immediately considered downing a cold beer. But at 8:00 am that would not win him any awards with Kitty. Harry wrestled with the idea of telling Kitty the truth. The truth was just so hard to believe. She would become angry, and he would end up where he started.

Harry reconsidered the cold beer.

"Harry, what is it?" Kitty demanded, she had to get back to her client that she hung up on.

"OK, first, this is going to be hard to believe so you gotta work with me. Just give me a chance to explain." Harry took a deep breath.

"OK…" Kitty didn't like the way this was starting off.

"At Duralink I met a dog that could talk." Harry decided to tell her the truth.

"A dog that could talk?" Kitty sounded skeptical.

"Yes. And the dog convinced me to help him escape."

"The dog did that?" Kitty asked.

"Yes, he did. He had this idea to escape and then I could find him and collect the ransom. You know, when I turned him back in." Harry smiled at Kitty hoping she would see the upside to the plan.

Then Harry remembered 'reward' sounded better than 'ransom'.

"But then I changed it from a ransom to a reward." Harry smiled nervously.

"So, the dog planned to escape only to be returned, by you, so you could make a bunch of money holding him for ransom?" Kitty asked, immediately seeing the flaw in the plan.

"Reward." Harry corrected her.

"Reward?" Kitty asked, not sure how that changed anything.

"Yes."

"So… Reward is a better idea than ransom?"

"Yes! That's a great idea, right?" Harry knew she would get it.

"Was that the dog's idea? The word change?"

"No that was my idea."

"Somehow, I'm not surprised."

"Good plan, right?" Harry asked.

"Well, what was in it for the dog?" Kitty asked.

"For the dog?"

"Yeah, why would the dog do that? Why not just stay in Duralink if his plan was to be returned anyway?"

"Stay in Duralink?"

"Yeah. He was gonna be returned anyway and you got all the money."

"Well… you can make anything sound stupid." Harry lost his optimistic tone.

"Harry, I'm not trying to make it sound stupid, I want to know why a talking dog," she paused for effect, "would want you to take him for ransom." Kitty knew it was stupid.

"Reward." Harry said with an annoyed tone.

"Oh yeah. Reward." Kitty wondered which doctor she would call.

Harry shrugged.

"Harry, sit down over here." She patted on a chair at her desk. She had concluded Harry had a break from reality and needed help. Her dilemma was how to negotiate with Harry to get him the help he needed. He had been acting erratically for a few days now. His drinking and weed smoking were out of control. She was sure he needed help. She wanted to save him and guide him to being the man she always wanted. The man she thought he was until recently. Basically, she wanted to turn him into the ideal man. She wanted to save him.

"Harry, dogs don't talk." Kitty said, looking at Harry deeply in the eyes.

"This one does." Harry said.

"OK. No, he doesn't." Kitty was certain the dog speaking was a result of Harry's imagination.

"He was a project at the Duralink Military Lab. They hooked his brain into a supercomputer and made him talk."

"So Duralink made the dog talk?" Kitty asked.

"Well, they don't know it. I'm the only one that knows he can talk. They think they just made him smart. And they did. It's just that he is smarter than they know."

"And only *you* know how smart he is?" Kitty said as she nodded her head. "Only *you* know he talks?"

"Yes, that's it."

"Why you? Were you involved in connecting him to the computer?"

"No."

"What part of the process were you involved in?"

"I wasn't"

"You were not involved in the program?"

"No. Well…I watch him all night to see what he does."

"OK. And you watched him talk."

"Yes, I did."

"And the dog told you to help him escape."

"Yes, he did."

"So that you could make a lot of money? That talking dog must really like you."

"Actually… he doesn't seem to like me much… At all, in fact. He is something of a smart ass." Harry said.

"The talking dog is a smart ass?" Kitty asked. Ps*ychiatrist. He needs Meds, fast.*

"Yeah."

"Harry, this is my question: If the talking, smart-ass dog doesn't like you much, why would he want to help you make a bunch of money?" Kitty leaned forward with her elbows on her plump thighs.

Harry realized there was a gap in the logic of his story.

"Well, yeah, I would make a bunch of money, but he was going to escape."

"Escape, only to be returned?" Kitty asked.

Harry was quiet for a moment.

"Harry, you thought this was a good idea?" Kitty asked softly. She had to get him to a hospital.

"Well, yes sort of. Honestly, I didn't trust him much."

"You didn't trust the talking, smart ass dog much?" Kitty raised her voice; she was starting to get irked. "Gee, Harry, I wonder why?" Kitty stared at Harry, positive he had blown a mental fuse.

"Ok, well, it's like this. In the beginning, I was actually going to steal the dog and return him for a ransom." Harry looked at Kitty like she would get it now.

"Reward." Kitty corrected him with a defeated tone.

"Yeah. Reward."

"So, it wasn't the dog's idea?"

"Not the original idea, no. The basic idea was mine."

"So, you just lied to me? It wasn't the dog's idea, it was your idea?"

"I didn't lie; it was just an adjustment in the story." Harry lied.

"You thought it was a *good idea* to steal a talking, smart ass dog from Duralink and hold it for ransom?" She raised her voice. Kitty's sarcastic tone was now deafening.

"It wasn't a fucking ransom; it was a reward! You are making me sound stupid!" Harry yelled loudly at her. The stress of the situation was beginning to break Harry.

Kitty sat up straight. "No, Harry, I'm just trying to understand what has got you so upset." Kitty felt fear for the first time in their relationship.

The two looked at each other for 30 seconds without a sound.

"Where is the dog now?" Kitty asked using a calming tone.

"After I got him out of the lab, he...... escaped from me."

"The talking, smart-ass dog escaped?" Kitty was confident now Harry had lost it.

"Yes."

"So, you don't have him?"

"No."

"That's good. Duralink would put you in jail for that." Kitty was confident now that there never was dog. She needed to get Harry in to see a psychiatrist.

"OK. But I still have a problem. I need your help."

"What is the next problem?" Kitty realized she was getting tired of solving Harry's problems.

"On the way out of Duralink, I got in a fight with a security guard."

"How did that happen?"

"It was the dog's fault."

"The talking dog? It was the talking, smart-ass dog's fault you got in a fight with a security guard?" Kitty couldn't resist the tone of sarcasm.

"You are making me sound stupid again!" Harry yelled and stood up. He towered over Kitty, who remained sitting in her chair. Harry's hands were at his side, but they were balled into two giant fists. His face was tomato red and he sounded like he was just a moment away from physical rage.

"Please sit down Harry," Kitty asked calmly, she was afraid now.

Harry took a deep breath and sat down. He reminded himself he needed her help. Harry wanted to wrap the phone cord around Kitty's neck when he stood up. He was grateful he didn't.

"Don't make me sound stupid again," Harry said in a controlled mild tone.

"I won't. What happened next? Where did the guard go? What did he do?" Inside Kitty was thinking of escape.

"Well… truth is he didn't go anywhere or do anything." Harry was doing his best to avoid telling Kitty he killed the guard. Then he realized he had to tell her if she was going to help him the way he needed help.

"So, you guys just stopped fighting and went separate ways? Is he mad at you? Are you in trouble?" Kitty asked.

"Well, we stopped fighting because he…. well, he was ……" Harry stumbled over his words. He didn't want to tell her the truth, but he knew he had to.

"Go on Harry, don't stop there."

"I killed him."

"You what?" The blood rushed out of Kitty's face. She heard him, but she needed to hear it again.

"I killed him. I wrapped a phone cord around his neck and strangled him. That's how the dog escaped. He ran out of the door while I strangled the security guard." Harry looked at Kitty calmly. He knew she would be able to give him a plan now that she had all the truth.

Kitty noticed some blood splatter on his shirt.

"Oh my God, Harry!" Kitty wanted to cry. She believed him. This part of the story she believed. Deep inside, she always knew, but didn't want to admit, that Harry was capable of hurting and even killing other people. He was a giant, strong man with very little discipline or self-control. She had always hoped she could change him into a more reasonable man capable of negotiating the difficulties in life. Now she realized he had gone too far.

"Harry, we have to call the police. You have to turn yourself in," Kitty was sure that this was the best course of action. Otherwise, Harry could be shot. The police knew where he lived. They had brought him home twice before. He was on their radar. Kitty feared they would be arriving momentarily.

Harry just stared at her. He couldn't believe what she was saying.

"I'll call them," Kitty said. She reached for the phone.

In a quick lunge forward Harry grabbed Kitty by the arm and stopped her from dialing the phone.

"Ouch Harry! You're hurting me!" Kitty yelled at Harry, with her eyes wide in panic.

Harry stared into Kitty's eyes. He started to rock side to side. His mind was clouded in a red haze. He squeezed Kitty's arm so tight he cut off the circulation into her hand.

Kitty pounded on Harry's fist with her other hand. Over and over she hit his fist hoping he would release her. She began to cry. He had not actually hurt her before. He scared her a few times by yelling and punching cabinets and walls. But he had always stopped short of hurting her. Kitty had attributed his angry behavior to drinking alcohol. But he recently promised he would quit alcohol altogether.

Kitty looked into his red face and bloodshot eyes. She could see thick red blood vessels in the whites of his eyes. His eyes were growing more bloodshot by the second. She knew he was over the edge. She had to calm him down and escape. Somehow, she knew her life depended on it.

"Harry I won't call the police!" She lied to him. "Let me go."

Harry looked at the terror on her face. Her terror made him happy. He had induced fear in others before. His first wife was a good example. He scared her and eventually showed her who the boss was. She didn't get away with making him look stupid. He slapped her face and pushed her into a wall so hard the drywall dented with her figure. But being the coward she was, she ran out of the house. Harry never saw her again. Divorce papers arrived within the week. She threatened him with calling the police if he didn't sign them immediately. Harry signed them after arguing over money with her. Somehow, he convinced her to give him $20,000.00 to sign. She quickly agreed to pay him twenty grand if he would sign the divorce papers and leave her alone. So, he signed the divorce papers and headed to Texas with his twenty grand.

Harry wanted to be near his mother who had moved to Texas a few years earlier. On the long drive between California and Texas, Harry realized he should have asked for more than $20,000.oo. She agreed too quickly. He planned to revisit her in the future and get more money despite his promise to leave her alone.

"Harry! Let me go!" Kitty began to panic.

Harry grabbed the phone cord with his free hand. He stood up and moved around the desk. He slowly wrapped the cord around Kitty's neck.

"Harry! No!" Kitty yelled. Her panic had set in. She knew she was in danger. "Help, Help, Help!" Kitty screamed as loud as she could, hoping a neighbor may hear her.

Harry wrapped the phone cord around her neck twice.

"Do you want to make me sound stupid again?" Harry calmly asked. He didn't plan to hurt her. He planned on scaring her so completely that she would never betray him again. All he wanted was love and support. She could give that to him.

"Harry stop! I won't make you sound stupid! I promise!" Kitty tried to yell, but she could barely make sounds.

Harry was thrilled with the tone of terror in her voice. Maybe he could squeeze a bit more terror out of her before he let her go. He tightened the cord until he could see the blood vessels in her neck and forehead. Her skin turned scarlet red.

"How does that feel?" Harry calmly asked. He was in control now, and he liked it.

"It hurts! Stop!" She gargled her response.

The terror was absolute. Harry was happier than he had ever been.

He wanted more.

"You are such a bitch! You are as bad as my first wife. Maybe worse." He said it for effect. He didn't think Kitty was as bad as Denise. But he enjoyed telling her that. It terrorized her.

Harry pulled the cord tighter.

"Harry!" Kitty whispered, she had lost her voice. It was a loud whisper. Spit spewed out of her mouth as she gagged. Her face turned red as an apple.

Harry squeezed the phone cord tighter and closed his eyes in complete enjoyment. He tilted his head back and imagined he flew through the clouds.

Harry realized what a powerful man he was. Others would have to respect him for his power.

Harry opened his eyes and looked down at Kitty. Her eyes were open and bloodshot. Her mouth was open, and her tongue stuck out firmly.

"Kitty? Kitty?" Harry asked loudly.

No answer came. The room fell silent.

Harry realized she was dead.

Harry released the phone cord and stepped back. Kitty rocked forwards and her head dropped onto her desk with a loud thud.

"That fucking dog!" Harry yelled into the empty house.

Heston calls the Team

At noon, Gene turned on the television and flipped through the channels until he got to the local station for news and weather. Texas weather changed rapidly and routinely, Gene and Peggy liked to stay on top it.

"The headlines are about the killings at Duralink Labs and in New Braunfels. The police say they are linked." Gene said to Peggy, who was in the kitchen.

"Where is Duralink?

"It's down by Kyle. Delon Husk Bought a big chunk of land out there and built a huge facility to study AI."

"I wonder if artificial intelligence killed the people at his lab."

"I doubt it. I'll bet it was just a sicko."

Gene's cell phone rang. He looked at the caller ID. It was Heston Hand.

"Hey Heston, what's up?"

"You see the news?"

"About the killings at Duralink and New Braunfels?" Gene asked.

"Yeah. I just got a call from Deputy Montoya. They believe the killer is on the run. They want us to meet them at Duralink, pick up a scent then go out and see if we can find him. You up for it?"

"Always. And Noah wants to join us. We saw him yesterday and he really wants to be a part of your team."

"I don't think so." Heston didn't like the idea of a San Francisco yuppie joining them.

"Ah, give him one chance if he does well, fine. If he does poorly you know not to give him another chance."

"If he falls behind, will you stay with him?" Heston didn't want to be slowed down.

"Sure."

"Fine then, it's a deal. I'll pick you up in 15 minutes."

"Great! We will be ready."

Gene immediately dialed Noah.

"Hello Gene" Noah saw Gene's Caller ID.

"Hey Noah, Heston has a tracking job. I asked if you could join us, and he agreed."

"When?"

"Now."

"Great you can meet my new dog."

"What kind of dog?"

"He is a German Shepherd."

"Cool. We will pick you up in 15 minutes or so. Be ready."

Justice speaks to Noah

Noah looked at his new German Shepherd and took a deep breath.

"I need to give you a name," Noah said, looking at his new dog.

The dog looked him directly in the eyes.

Noah got the feeling that the dog knew exactly what he was saying.

Noah sat on his back porch with Justice the dog.

"Do you have a name?" Noah had the habit of speaking to animals like they would answer him.

Justice barked once.

"OK, you do have a name. How can I find out your name?"

Justice was out of options. If he was going to have a real relationship with Noah, he had to come clean. It was time to talk to him.

"My name is Justice," The large German Shepherd said to Noah.

Noah flipped backward in his chair.

"Holy Sweet Jesus, you can talk?" Noah said after standing up.

"Yes, I can talk," Justice spoke again.

"How… how…" Noah felt dizzy. Nothing else could be said for the moment. Noah sat back down and placed his hand over his mouth. His immediate thought was he had gone crazy. The stress of losing a loved one had taken its toll. Maybe he was just insane now.

"I understand this is hard 'or you to understand and accept."

"Hard? You speak? Hard doesn't capture it." Noah spoke to the dog.

"Yes. I came 'rom Duralink. A crazy man set me 'ree. Sorta."

Noah stared at the dog as it moved its mouth and tongue. It was so odd. Noah could immediately tell the dog had difficulty with "F" and "V" sounds.

"Justice? Your name is Justice?"

"Yes, that's the name they gave me. I was born in the Duralink Labs. The scientists put connections into my brain. They downloaded in'ormation into me 'rom a computer. Two computers actually."

"So, they know you can talk?" Noah asked.

"No. Only two people know I can speak. You are the second."

"Who was the first?"

"A crazy man named Harry. When he 'ound out he decided to steal me and hold me 'or ransom."

"Wow, that's not smart."

"He was not too bright. It wasn't a good idea on his part. It was great though, 'or me. I used him and his harebrained idea to escape."

Noah paused again and stared at Justice. A dog that uses the word 'harebrained'? How was this possible? Had he gone crazy?

"What happened? How did you escape?" Noah finally asked.

"When he took me to the exit a security guard stopped us. He attacked the guard, and I suspect he killed him. As he wrapped a 'hone cord around the guard's neck I ran 'or the door. I ran straight to the treeline and into the woods. The last thing I heard was him screaming my name."

"I ran for about an hour then found myself in Kyle. A few minutes later, you showed up."

"This should be on the news then." Noah went to the TV and turned on the local news channel.

The local news was full of Covid this and Covid that. Mask mandates and Omicron variants are filling up hospitals. Nothing about a murder at Duralink Labs.

Then came a knock at the front door.

"I forgot. We are supposed to go on a hunt with the local criminal hunter and some of his friends. We will be a part of his team."

"Team? Criminal hunters? Maybe that's who they are hunting 'or? Don't tell them I can talk. Please. This is just between you and me."

"Ok. I understand."

Noah went to the front door. It was Gene.

"Are you ready?"

"Yep. Let's go. Justice! Let's go buddy." Noah said.

Immediately, Justice knew he should have told Noah not to use his real name.

"Put Justice in the back with Trump and Reagan," Gene said.

Heston was behind the wheel, waiting for everyone to get loaded in.

Justice ran outside like an excited dog. He waited for the tailgate to be lowered then jumped in the back of the large truck without being told. The three dogs sniffed each other like normal dogs would. They seemed to get along great.

Noah climbed in the back seat with Peggy. Gene and Heston were in the front.

"Where are we going?" Noah asked.

"We are going to start at Duralink Labs outside Kyle. An animal researcher killed a security guard and allowed a dog that belonged to the Labs to escape. We are going to pick up scents there. Then go hunt the guy down."

Noah was frozen silent. This was precisely what Justice told him about. He didn't know what to say. Should he tell Heston he had the dog that escaped in the back of Heston's truck?

"What about the dog" Noah asked. "Do we need to find him?"

"They haven't asked us to find the dog. Just the guy that killed the security guard." Heston looked at Noah in the rearview mirror.

Noah saw Heston looking at him in the mirror. 'Oh my God Heston already knows', Noah thought to himself.

"Did you bring a gun, Noah?" Heston asked.

"No. Just me and Justice." Noah immediately knew if Heston discovered the dog that escaped was named Justice that he would piece everything together.

"Is Justice trained? Will he follow commands?"

"Oh yes, he is very well trained. He will understand literally everything you tell him." That was a giant understatement Noah thought.

"Literally? That's an interesting way of describing what Justice will understand. So, If I tell Justice to get me a sandwich and a beer will he do it?" Heston smiled, as Gene and Peggy laughed.

"Well…. Maybe." Noah said truthfully, then reconsidered. "I mean, no, of course not. But he is pretty smart." Noah's heart was beating faster and faster.

They pulled into Duralink Labs parking area and parked in the Security Vehicles parking space.

Heston and his team climbed out of the truck. Trump and Reagan were excited and showing it by holding their heads over the sides of the truck bed with excitement on their faces. Justice on the other hand was laying down in the truck bed and showing the opposite of excitement.

Heston lowered the tailgate and Trump and Reagan immediately bailed out. Justice didn't budge.

Heston said "Let's go Justice. You are part of the team now."

Justice slowly stood up and walked to the edge of the tailgate. He took one look at Heston who looked back at him like he was about to lose his temper.

"Out!" Heston commanded.

Justice jumped down from the truck and ran straight to Noah. Justice stayed on Noah's heal all the way to the entrance of Duralink Labs. Noah was impressed and grateful Justice was acting like a well-trained dog. In fact, Justice was hiding from the cameras he knew were in the entrance by placing Noah between himself and the cameras.

"Scent!" Heston commanded using his voice as well as his hand signs. Immediately Trump and Reagan ran to the security station and began sniffing. Justice didn't budge from Noah's side. He already had Harry's scent. The scent of Harry would never be forgotten by Justice.

Heston met the lead detective that worked with the Sheriff's department. Detective Hornsby was his name and Heston had known him a few years.

Hornsby and Heston had a problematic relationship. Heston had received numerous awards and achieved a status in the law enforcement community of Austin that Hornsby thought was unfair. Hornsby was jealous of Heston's success. Hornsby worked with Heston only when he had to.

"Hey Heston," Hornsby said.

"Hornsby" Heston nodded. Heston knew about Hornsby's feelings towards him. He had decided a while back to just give him a wide berth. However, he would not be calling him 'detective' anytime soon. He wouldn't give Hornsby the pleasure of rank.

"Before you head too far away, can you swing by this address and determine if the killer, a man we believe to be named Harry Rivers, has been there recently?" Hornsby gave Heston a printed sheet of paper.

"Sure. Is this his home?" Heston asked.

"It's the address he gave on his employment application. If you find him, hook him up and call me. If you believe he has been there give me a call. Otherwise just give me a call that you didn't see anything and head out on your tracking."

"No problem."

"If you find him consider him dangerous."

"They all are," Heston said.

Heston went back to the truck with his team, loaded the dogs in the back of the truck and headed for the address given to him by detective Hornsby. Heston recognized that the amount of responsibility and respect Hornsby had just given him was remarkable. He was being treated like he was a detective or at least a Sheriff's deputy. Fact was, he was an independent contractor hired by the Sheriff's to track bad guys with his dogs. Heston smiled to himself, he felt like he'd been promoted. Maybe it was time to raise his prices. Maybe it was time to call Hornsby 'Detective'. That was too far, Heston decided. Hornsby would remain Hornsby.

Heston didn't know that Hornsby had been ordered to send Heston to the address. The top brass wanted this case solved quickly. Duralink was an essential new corporation in the Austin area that employed over 5,000 people. More of Delon's businesses were headed to Texas as well. Everyone knew Delon Husk abandoned California because he got angry with the government there. They didn't want Mr. Husk to get upset at Austin too.

The top brass knew Heston would get the job done.

Hornsby was following orders. If it were up to him, Heston would still be home.

Johnny's 2nd Day at Work

Johnny was waiting in front of the HEB grocery store at 6:30 am for the store to open. He watched the lights to the store turn on and the store manager walk to the front and open the large sliding doors.

"Morning" The large store manager said to Johnny.

"Good morning sir," Johnny replied and walked towards the deli department.

"Do you work here?"

"Yes sir. Bobby hired me yesterday."

"OK. I'm Edgar Rice, the store manager." He held out his hand to shake his greetings.

Johnny reached out with his pale white hand to shake and he noticed the manager looking at him curiously.

The two shook hands and parted without another word spoken.

Johnny entered the deli area and found a new white apron hanging on a hook that was just under a nameplate that said 'Johnny'. Johnny smiled. He knew Bobby must have done that for him. He realized how fortunate he was to work here and have a boss as nice as Bobby.

Bobby was late getting to the Deli department. Johnny had served two early customers by the time Bobby arrived.

"Good morning, Bobby" Johnny smiled at his boss.

"Hi Johnny." Bobby was clearly not in a happy mood. "I need you to come back and talk to me at my desk."

"Yes Bobby," Johnny said happily.

They walked behind the double swinging doors that led to Bobby's desk.

"Johnny, I'm sorry, but I have to let you go."

"Let me go? What does that mean?"

"You can't work here anymore."

"Why? Did I do something wrong?" Johnny felt his heart sink.

"No, you were great. The store manager, well, he wants me to hire his 16-year-old son. He said I can't have both of you. I'm sorry." Bobby stared at his desk, afraid to look at Johnny. He knew it was unfair.

"OK," Johnny said and reached around behind himself to untie his apron.

"Johnny, check back with me in a week or two. If I can pull you back on board, I will." Bobby said, trying to smile.

"Yes sir" Johnny said and turned around to leave.

"Johnny, the manager's son is an idiot. He may be gone in ten days."

"OK."

"Make yourself a big sandwich to take with you, Johnny."

"Thanks Bobby," Johnny did his best to smile, then made the same sandwich he made for himself last night. He knew he would be hungry soon.

Kitty and the Trash Bag

Harry knew everything was that fucking dog's fault. Now he had killed three people directly as a result of that dog's bad deal. He knew he should not have trusted a dog! What was he thinking? Where was he going to go? Never trust a dog again. Harry would not forget that lesson. Don't trust dogs.

Kitty's family owned a cabin in the woods 25 miles west of Wimberley, Texas. It was a nice little place on a river, deep in the Texas forest. Harry decided to go there. He knew where the key was hidden. Wimberley was only 30 minutes away from Kyle and about 50 minutes away from New Braunfels. He had to get out of the house. Her parents or brother were bound to show up soon. They always did. They were nosey pains in his ass. What should he do with Kitty? Leave her for her nosey brother and parents to find or take her to the cabin and bury her? Harry bit his lower lip as he contemplated his situation. He had to get moving.

Harry grabbed Kitty by the feet and tried to drag her to the kitchen door that led to the garage. He pulled with all his might and couldn't move her. Kitty was a big girl. Every bit of 250 pounds. She was like moving five bags of cement. Harry gave up for a moment. He stared at her body and thought about the bad deal he made with that smart ass dog. Harry had to run. Get out of town. Far away. Like Oklahoma.

Then he thought about her bitch mother showing up and catching him. His sense of panic powered him to slowly drag her to the kitchen, inch by inch. Every time he stopped for a breath, he thought of her mother. Panic powered him to pull again.

He finally got her to the kitchen and realized how out of shape he was. He wiped the sweat from his forehead. He opened the garage door and saw Kitty's truck was parked in the garage.

"Crap!" Harry said out loud. Where were her keys? He looked on the key rack next to the garage door. Empty. His anger rose up over her inability to ever put her keys where they belonged. He had hung the key rack up two weeks ago and she only used it when he pestered her about it. Fucking ungrateful bitch. Where was her purse? He walked through the house looking for Kitty's purse. He found it in the bedroom. Harry hated purses. He always found things he didn't want to see when he rummaged through them. Harry extracted the keys mumbling the whole time about the key rack being empty.

He moved Kitty's truck onto the street and backed his own truck into the garage. The tailgate of the truck lined up with the garage door to the kitchen. This resulted in the nose of his truck sticking out of the garage a small amount. He couldn't close the garage door now, but Harry didn't care. He would hurry. Harry lowered his tailgate and hurried back to the kitchen.

Harry stood in the opened door and looked at the height of his lowered tailgate, then back at Kitty. How was he going to get her in his truck if he could barely drag her through the house?

He could chop her into small pieces! That was a great idea!

It would take him a while to chop her up, but it was better than manhandling her into the truck. He watched Chris Moltisanti do it on the Sopranos, it didn't look that hard.

He could chop her into small pieces, then transport and bury her. Bury her? No, toss her in the river! Even a better idea! Then he remembered the woodchipper. Holy Cow Harry thought. Now my brain is really working good! I'll throw her in the woodchipper and blow her into the river!

Harry's problems were about to be over.

He had to work fast. He couldn't afford her family to show up and discover him chopping up their baby's dead body. They'd call the police. He needed to develop a story that effectively pinned everything on that fucking dog.

He would work on the story as he chopped her up.

Harry returned to the kitchen and rummaged through the drawers looking for a suitable knife. He found the one good 9" chef's knife he had. He pulled out the sharpening rod and ran the blade down it several times. He looked at Kitty and wondered where he should start.

Harry carved Kitty's left arm off first. A shocking amount of blood poured onto the linoleum floor. Harry didn't anticipate the blood. He should have, but he had never carved up a dead person before. When he watched Chrissy do it there wasn't any blood... that he could remember. They must have downplayed the blood. Harry grabbed kitchen towels and sopped up the blood. His

solution was to cut Kitty up faster. Once he realized it wasn't much different from cutting up a chicken, just bigger, he was able to go quicker. He thought about the AC/DC song Whole Lot of Rosey. She ain't exactly pretty, she ain't exactly small, 42-39-56 you could say she got it all…. Harry smiled and cut up more chicken, sitting on his knees in the kitchen.

Soon, he had blood all over his blue jeans and shirt, not to mention his hands and arms. The hardest part was cutting off Kitty's head. The knife had to separate the spinal cord, which took a lot of effort. But Harry was a strong man. He finally closed his eyes and pressed the knife downwards as hard as he could. His blade broke through the spinal cord and slammed onto the kitchen floor. Kitty's head rolled backward, with her eyes open.

Harry stood up and went into the garage for the large, green, heavy-duty lawn bags. As he grabbed the box of bags from the tool bench, he heard a sound he didn't want to hear.

"Hello Harry, is Kitty here? Why is her truck on the street?" The tone was accusatory, so it could only be one person.

It was Kitty's mom.

Fuck, fuck, fuck.

Harry turned around to face her.

"Harry? What have you been doing? You are covered in blood."

"We bought a side of beef and I'm carving it up."

"You are carving up a side of beef in the house?"

"Yeah."

"You don't do that indoors. Where is Kitty?" Kitty's mom wasn't buying it.

"She is in here. She has more blood on her than I do. C'mon in." Harry said to the nosy old woman. He knew what he had to do.

As soon as Kitty's mom entered the kitchen she screamed when she looked at the bloody mess on the floor. She only screamed for a moment. Harry reached around from behind her and drew his kitchen knife across her throat. He made sure to sink the knife deeply to sever all the big veins.

Harry released his grip from her and she dropped to the floor, partially covering Kitty's torso. Kitty's head, arms and legs had been stacked on the floor next to the cabinets under the sink. Kitty's mom died looking at Kitty's severed head.

Harry went back into the garage for more large plastic lawn bags. He hoped he had enough. He had to work fast.

It will be easier this time, Harry thought to himself. Just pretend she is another giant chicken.

Ghosts Follow Johnny

Cole and White Rabbit watched Johnny from the treetops. Johnny moved at a fast pace through the forest. He was headed southwest.

"Why is he traveling so fast? Is he running from something?" White Rabbit asked.

"I don't know." Cole said.

They were joined by Crazy Crow, White Rabbit's sister. She floated up from the forest floor to join them.

"Where are you going?" Crazy Crow asked.

"We are following the pale man below."

"Why?"

"I do not know. Ask Cole." White Rabbit said.

"Cole?" Crazy Crow asked.

"I feel like we should follow and protect him. I can't tell you why. I believe he is good and may need our help."

"So, you have Indian instincts now?" Crazy Crow asked.

"Maybe."

"Father will be pleased."

"Does he still hate me?" Cole was hopeful for acceptance by Chief Two Dogs.

"Probably." Crazy Crow could not resist feeding Cole's fear of her father. But the truth was her father was growing fond of Cole. Cole had demonstrated his bravery with the evil witch, Thin Man and Laconta. Two Dogs would have been proud of his Braves if they performed as Cole had.

"He will always hate me." Cole sounded defeated.

"Yes…. Probably." Crazy Crow said with a grin.

White Rabbit glared angrily at Crazy Crow. She could see what her sister was doing and she didn't like it.

"Father likes you now. Don't listen to her." White Rabbit said.

"Yeah? I'll believe it when I see it." Cole was not optimistic.

They watched as Johnny trudged through the forest.

A couple of hours passed as the trio of small ghosts followed Johnny through the forest. Johnny didn't slow down once. Johnny was unhappy that he had lost his job, a job that he loved. He had always exercised as a way to forget his troubles and feel better. He remained physically fit and lean. He could cut through the forest at a fast pace. He was adept at finding and following game trails as well as trails created by local people. He avoided homes and people. Johnny had to decide what to do next. For now, exercise would do. A hike was an excellent way to clear his mind and plan a strategy for his life in America.

Johnny's Escape to America

His desire to escape from the harsh realities of Africa brought Johnny to America. Africa was too dangerous for him. Africans did not see him as a person. They viewed him as a source of black magic and evil. Many witch doctors offered to pay his family for his albino corpse. They wanted to chop him up and grind his bones into magical powders. Johnny escaped one night when he had been told by his sister that his parents decided to take the money. The family needed it. They were coming for him later that evening. He begged her to go with him but she would not. After the sun went down one night Johnny headed East to the port town of Dar Es Salaam. He got hired by a huge Columbian freighter as a deckhand. He spent two months at sea before he finally arrived in Columbia. The captain paid him in cash. This gave Johnny almost $6,000.00. Johnny searched for a way to get to the United States. He had heard the new President Joe Biden said it was time to "Flood the Border" with new immigrants who had a desire to come to America. So, Johnny decided to take him up on his offer. Soon Johnny found a caravan in Venezuela headed to America. He joined them and his optimism grew each day.

When Johnny arrived in Southern Mexico he was approached by the cartels. They told him he had to pay $5,000.00 or they would kill him. The $5,000.00 bought him a trip to the Rio Grande river near La Joya, Texas. They would get him across the river, then he would be on his own. Johnny had to agree. They made it clear: agree or die. They placed an orange wrist band around his left wrist indicating he had paid in full.

Over the next 30 days, Johnny was transported north through Mexico. He traveled in trucks, trains and old automobiles. When they finally got to the Rio Grande river, they put him and six others in a small inflatable boat and ferried him across the river. Before he could get off the raft, the Mexican coyote told him he had to pay $1,000.00 extra.

Johnny knew this was unfair. He was the only one charged the extra fee. Johnny realized they had spotted his extra cash. What could he do? He had $970.00. He paid the coyote his last amount of money. When he exited the raft he was in deep brush with a very small pathway up a steep bank. It was evening time, just before dark. When Johnny got to the top of the bank, he rejoiced that he was finally in America. He had no money, but it didn't matter. In America he could earn much more money than he ever had before. Money would not be a problem in America.

Then the Border Patrol showed up. They placed him and the six others in a van and took them to a Border Patrol facility 30 minutes away.

Johnny was the first processed from his group. The agents asked where he was from and why he had come to America. He explained that he was from Tanzania and had to escape because the local witch doctors wanted to kill him because of his albinism. He requested asylum. The agents looked at each other.

"We have a legit case!" One of the agents said.

"Finally." Two agents high-fived each other. Apparently, Johnny was an unusual case for them.

One of them stamped his paperwork and gave him a court date for two years away. They told him he was the first legitimate refugee they had processed in weeks. He went into the next office where they took his photograph and fingerprinted him. Then something happened that truly surprised Johnny. They gave him a debit card with a pre-paid balance of $2000.00. The Border Patrol agent told him $2000.00 would be added each month to assist him in his transition into America. Johnny had heard America was great and generous, but this exceeded his wildest expectations.

Johnny used his card to purchase a bus ticket to Austin, Texas. He had been told by many migrants that Austin was a welcoming place that had plentiful jobs.

Soon Johnny arrived in Austin. He decided to save his money and look for a job. He got a lead on a job in Driftwood, Texas for a large barbeque restaurant called Salt Lick Barbecue. He took an Uber ride to Saltlick. The fare was only $25.00. Johnny paid the fare but thought that it was too expensive. He interviewed with the manager at Salt Lick, who seemed put off by Johnny's pale white skin. That was when Johnny first felt different after arriving in America. Johnny left Salt Lick after the manager told him to check back in a couple of months. Johnny did not feel like he would be hired at Salt Lick Barbeque.

Johnny hiked west on Hwy 1826, crossed FM 150, then cut into the forest to find a place to sleep. The next day he was hired by the HEB grocery store in Dripping Springs.

And the day after that was today.

He had been fired from his new job, and he wandered the forest feeling sorry for himself.

After he had hiked through the forest for hours, he heard the sound of a river. He realized how thirsty he was. Soon he was at the side of a medium sized river. It was about 100 feet wide with deep, fast-moving water. Johnny knelt next to the river and scooped some of the cold water in his hands. He drank three scoops of water and felt much better. He looked around him and realized how beautiful it was. He decided to climb into the river and float on his back with the current. It was a beautiful Texas day and Johnny floated for over an hour in the gentle current. The day was about enter evening, and the sun was just about to hide behind the top of the trees.

Johnny swam out of the river and sat on the bank for a few minutes.

Then Johnny heard a strange sound. It sounded like a large saw buzzing and cutting through hard material. Johnny's first thought was it could a rancher that may need help. Maybe the rancher would hire him.

Johnny followed the sounds downstream. As he got closer the sounds got louder. Johnny followed the river to a bend. He followed the curve of the river to the right and soon recognized the sounds as a woodchipper. Woodchippers were used extensively in Tanzania by the Forest Rangers.

Soon, Johnny could see a large blond man feeding material into a woodchipper next to the river.

The woodchipper loudly exhausted the material into the river. Johnny paused to watch. Something was wrong. The material being shot into the river was not wood chips. It was red and looked to be wet. A red mist floated over the river behind the woodchipper.

Kitty & Mom Go for a Ride

Harry loaded Kitty and her mom into eight large plastic lawn bags. He placed them in the bed of his GMC pickup truck and closed the tailgate. Harry looked down at himself. He was covered in blood and ugly strands of fat and sinew. He knew he couldn't leave the house looking this way. Quickly, Harry stripped out of his clothes and ran into the shower. After 10 minutes, Harry was clean and wearing new clothes. He walked towards the kitchen to get to the garage door. Immediately he saw the bloody mess covering the kitchen linoleum floor. He stopped and stared at the blood and small pieces of flesh on the floor.

Under the sink cabinet in the toe kick appeared to be a liver. Harry rolled his eyes. How did he leave that there? Too late now. He couldn't retrieve it unless he wanted to get bloody again. He decided to leave it. He wasn't going to clean up this mess. He hated cleaning in the first place, and in the second place he didn't have the time. He had to escape before the Sheriff showed up. Harry turned around and left through the entry door. He walked around the front of the house to the open garage. It was time to go. Harry was getting tense and shaky. He climbed into his truck and slowly pulled out of the garage. Should he turn right or left? Both directions took him to neighborhood exits. The more curious neighbors were to the right. He turned left on his neighborhood street and gently accelerated so he wouldn't grab the attention of nosey neighbors. He was on his way to the cabin in Wimberley.

As he drove down his neighborhood street, he slowed to a stop at the first intersection. When Harry looked in his rearview mirror, he saw a large Ford pickup pull in front of Kitty's house and stop. It slowly turned into Kitty's driveway and parked. A bolt of electricity shot through Harry as he realized his close call. Harry knew this was a narrow escape. He lucked out. As he turned right to get to the neighborhood exit and the highway, Harry glanced back at the truck in Kitty's driveway. He saw three dogs jump out of the truck bed and four people enter the garage.

Heston arrives at Kitty's House

Trump and Reagan immediately signaled that they had picked up the scent. They circled the inside of the garage excitedly and pointed to the garage door.

"Bloody footprints on the floor," Peggy said, looking at the garage floor.

"That's never good," Noah said. Noah looked at Justice, who was sniffing a bloody footprint.

Justice knew it was Harry that made the footprint. There was no mistaking that smell.

"Probably good for us though," Heston said.

Heston removed his pistol from his shoulder holster and tried the doorknob. It was unlocked. He entered the kitchen and stopped. The blood on the floor was wet and fresh.

"We have a crime scene." Heston calmly said.

He looked to his right and saw a cork note board hung on the wall. A note was pinned to it that read: "Cabin address: 23 Riverview Way, Wimberley, TX." Heston used his cell phone and took a photograph of the note.

"We have to call this in. Nobody can go inside. Believe me, you don't want to." Heston said as he looked at the others.

Heston used his cell phone and called Detective Hornsby.

"Hey Hornsby, Heston here."

"Detective Hornsby," Hornsby said.

"Yeah right, that. Well, you are going to want to rush over here. We have a crime scene. Blood is everywhere."

Heston explained that the dogs alerted that Harry Rivers had been there. It was clear that someone had been killed in the kitchen, but so far, no bodies had been discovered. Hornsby instructed Heston to wait for him. He would arrive within 30 minutes. He also ordered Heston not to go inside and disrupt his crime scene.

Heston told the Hornsby about the address for a cabin in Wimberley and that he would like to go there to search for Harry Rivers. Hornsby told him to sit tight and wait for him. He wanted a statement from Heston and his team before they left.

"I should never have called him," Heston said when they hung up.

"Why, what's up?" Gene asked.

"He wants us to stay here so he can talk to us before we leave."

"That sounds like a waste of our time." Gene said.

"It is. I found an address for a cabin in Wimberley that I want to search. But we can't go until Hornsby cuts us loose."

"Would it be a hanging offense if we left?" Gene asked.

"Not really," Heston thought for a moment. It was a good question. "Being uncooperative is not considered a strength, though. We can give him 30 minutes. I'd like to get hired again."

"So, let's relax and wait for the detective," Gene said.

"Well, we can wait for Hornsby." Heston corrected Gene.

"You don't like this guy much, do you?" Peggy asked.

"Does it show?"

"Little bit." Peggy nodded.

"Good to know."

"Why do you hate him." Peggy asked.

"Hate is such a strong word." Heston demurred.

"And?"

"OK, I hate him."

"Why?"

"Let's just say my success across the different departments in Austin has largely been despite Hornsby."

Gene waited for more of the story, but it didn't come. He decided to let it go. Texans hate nosey friends.

Noah went out to the big Ford truck and sat on the tailgate. Justice followed him and jumped into the truck bed. Justice and Noah looked at each other. They were away from the others and Noah took the opportunity to speak to Justice.

"So, what do you think?" Noah whispered to Justice.

"Harry was here– definitely. That means Harry killed whoever was in this home." Justice spoke in a low tone; whispering was too tricky for him.

"Where do you think he went?" Noah asked.

"Harry is not a mental giant. He is dumber than a box of hair. So that means he won't do anything complicated. Simple is best for Harry. Heston said he found an address for a cabin in Wimberley. That's where he will be." Justice said confidently.

"Think so? How sure are you?" Noah asked.

"100%. He is too dumb to leave the state or catch a boat out of Galveston. That's what he should do. But he won't." Justice said.

"Ok, so we wait here with Heston until we are released to go to the cabin in Wimberley."

"That's all we can do for now. But Noah, please don't forget that Harry may be dumb, but he is dangerous. He kills easily now."

"I won't forget." Noah reached around Justice and hugged him tightly, then rubbed the base of his ears. The two continued to sit next to each other in the back of Heston's truck. Justice enjoyed the affection given to him by Noah. He committed to himself that he would protect this man.

After 45 minutes, three vehicles arrived at Kitty's home in New Braunfels. Immediately, Justice recognized one of the men that climbed out of the last vehicle.

"This is a problem. Give me another name." Justice said in an urgent tone.

"Another name? Why?"

"Just use "Thor' and quickly tell the others."

"Ok," Noah said. He hopped down from the tailgate and walked into the garage with Justice on his heels.

"Hey everyone, before these guys get here, my dog's name is 'Thor', not 'Justice,' OK?"

"Why is that?" Heston asked suspiciously.

"We can talk about it later, I promise. Just don't call him Justice. Call him 'Thor.'" Noah said in a tone that bordered on pleading.

"OK, fine." Heston said. He didn't care what the dog's name was.

Gene and Peggy agreed too.

Detective Hornsby entered the garage, followed by two Sheriff's Deputies and two official looking civilians. One female and one male.

Hornsby made the introductions.

"This is deputy Jesus Montoya and Deputy Epifanio Soria. They are out of the New Braunfels Sheriff station." Hornsby paused for a moment the pointed at the two others. "This is Nancy Webb and her partner Marty Shott. They are private detectives who work for Duralink Labs."

After the introductions were made, Nancy Webb spoke first. "How did 'y'all find Justice."

Immediately, Heston, Gene and Peggy understood why Noah wanted to change the name to Thor.

Heston paused for a long moment. He considered the situation carefully. He was not willing to put his career on the line for Noah. On the other hand, he had deniability. He could easily claim that the dog was named Thor as far as he knew.

"This dog belongs to Noah. His name is Thor."

Thor pressed up to Noah's calf and sat tall.

"Well, Thor looks exactly like the dog Nueralink is missing. How long have you owned Thor?" Nancy looked at Noah. She carefully studied his face looking for signs that he may be lying.

"Two years now," Noah said. He knew complicated lies never worked out well, so he would keep it simple.

"Can I pet him?" Nancy knew there would be surgical lumps in the head of Justice. He had at least six surgeries that implanted microprocessors in his brain. She knew the real Justice was the most intelligent dog in the world and possibly the smartest animal on the planet. She had spoken to one of the scientists who believed they had downloaded more information into Justice than they had planned. He also explained to Nancy that Justice understood every major language spoken. As difficult as that was to believe, Nancy knew the scientists that worked for Duralink were among the smartest on earth. She had to take them seriously.

"If he will let you. He is a bit stand-offish to strangers," Noah said.

Nancy moved towards Justice and reached her hand out. Justice showed his teeth and started a low, very dangerous growl. There was no way Justice would let Nancy or anyone from Duralink touch his head again.

"Maybe wait a while. Let him get to understand you are not a threat." Noah said.

Nancy withdrew her hand and looked at Marty Shott.

"OK, I can wait." Nancy wasn't buying the 'Thor' routine. This dog was Justice, and she would find a way to prove it.

Heston broke the silence.

"The kitchen is full of blood. It looks to me like someone has been killed, but I didn't see a body."

"You didn't search the house?" Hornsby asked.

"No. You told me not to."

"I told you not to disturb the crime scene." Hornsby took an attitude Heston didn't appreciate.

"Agreed. I did not disturb the crime scene" Heston was getting pissed. They had wasted an hour now because Hornsby told them to wait for him. Now Hornsby was insinuating Heston should have checked out the house. Well, screw him and his buddies, Heston thought. His face said as much.

Hornsby opened the door to the kitchen. The blood was everywhere. There was no way to enter the kitchen without tracking through the blood.

"Deputy Jesus, please get the camera bag. We are going to need photos of this. I'm going through the entry. I may need the door ram." Detective Hornsby walked out of the garage and to the entry of the home. He was surprised to find it unlocked.

Hornsby entered the home, turned to the right, and looked in the three bedrooms.

"Someone has cleaned up in the Master Bedroom. They actually took a shower to wash off the blood." Hornsby motioned for Deputy Jesus to follow him inside.

"This is a homicide scene." Deputy Jesus said, "we will need a homicide forensic team here. Someone has been killed. We need to figure out who has been killed and who killed them. Heston was right."

Hornsby glared at Deputy Jesus. He was annoyed Heston had been given credit.

"Can we go now?" Heston asked impatiently.

"Where do you want to go?" Hornsby pointedly asked.

"There is an address for a cabin in Wimberley on the note board over there." Heston nodded towards the board next to the garage door in the kitchen.

"I thought you didn't go in the home?" Hornsby said with an accusatory tone.

"Sweet mother of God, Hornsby! Are you actually a detective? Or did you just watch Monk on TV?" Heston had enough. His temper was shining through. His Monk reference got a laugh out of both Nancy Webb and Marty Shott. Deputy Jesus covered his mouth and turned away.

"Hey, I liked Monk," Nancy said. "Don't disrespect Mr. Monk," She tried to keep the atmosphere light.

"Look, Mr. Monk," Heston continued his disrespectful tone, "I opened the garage door, saw the mess, looked to my right, saw the note and called you," Heston said to Hornsby.

Hornsby glared at Heston in silence. He didn't know how to respond.

Heston decided he wasn't done yet, "I don't know why you have been acting like a little bitch towards my team and me, but I'm tired of it." Heston glared back at him.

Nancy and Marty turned around and gave the two men some space. Nancy whispered, "Ouch, he went with the 'Little Bitch' approach. That's gonna leave a mark." Nancy's eyes widened.

"OK, fine Heston, don't get your panties in a bunch." Hornsby tried to defend himself, but he sounded weak. He knew that he should have avoided disrespecting Heston in front of his people.

"Panties in a bunch? Heston yelled. His eyes told the story. "Today is your *fucking* lucky day, Hornsby." Heston paused for effect. "First, I'm not going to kick your ass, second I'm taking my team to the cabin. You can stay here and play in your blood or do whatever a *pretend* detective does when he plays a *homicide* detective." Heston used all his control to avoid punching Hornsby in the nose.

Nancy Webb whispered to Marty, "Fucking lucky day, this is getting good!" She grinned and hoped for more.

Heston turned around to find Gene, Peggy and Noah ˙already at Heston's truck. Heston joined them and lowered the tailgate for the dogs. The dogs knew to get in the back. Justice was the first one in the bed of the truck. Heston fired up his truck, quickly backed out of the driveway, and then up the neighborhood street to the community exit.

"We are going with them," Nancy said to Hornsby. She and Marty ran to their car and hurried to catch up with Heston. Nobody wanted to be around Hornsby after that ugly scene.

Nancy laughed once they were in the car, "Fucking Lucky Day! Hooooooo-ley Shit-Ski."

Kitty Meets the Chipper

Harry took his time getting to the cabin west of Wimberley. The last thing he needed was a speeding ticket with Kitty and her mom in trash sacks, the back of his truck.

He drove by a What-a Burger and couldn't resist the drive through. He grabbed a couple of double cheeseburgers and fries, with a chocolate shake. Within about two hours, he was driving through an area 25 miles west of Wimberley, with thick trees down an unpaved road. He drove for over five miles without seeing a home or a driveway. Harry was surprised at how remote this cabin was. He had been here once before but didn't remember how isolated it was.

He rounded a left turn in the road and saw the river on his left. It was a beautiful river that appeared to be deep and relatively wide. Then the cabin soon appeared on the left.

'Finally,' Harry said to himself. He parked the truck in the gravel driveway to the small cabin. Harry remembered the key was under the plant next to the entry door.

Harry walked through the cabin and recalled the last time he was there with Kitty. Happier times. Harry thought about how much beer he drank and then remembered getting yelled at for sleeping in the lawn chair in the backyard. He never could figure out why both Kitty and her mom thought it was a bad idea to sleep in the backyard all night. Kitty's nosey, overbearing mom said Harry had a drinking problem. Bitch. Well, she wouldn't say that again. Harry smiled.

Harry went into the kitchen and looked in the refrigerator. Twenty-four cans of Lone Star beer filled the drawers and the refrigerator's door. Kitty's idiot brother had been there and loaded up the fridge with his favorite beer. At least he was good for something. Harry made a mental note to drink all his beer just to piss him off. Harry reached inside and grabbed a can of cold beer.

He would start his drinking project now. After less than a minute he opened his second can. He burped loudly, and said "Cheeseburgers, ummm good." The third can of Lone Star was the best.

The cabin was quiet and isolated. The evening was setting in. Harry looked at his watch and saw it was almost 6:00 pm. He had to begin the process of getting rid of the bodies in the back of his truck. Harry grabbed a fourth can of beer and two more for good measure. Harry opened the squeaky screen door in the kitchen that led to the rear porch and backyard; after passing through it, it slammed shut loudly behind him. Harry had a nice view of the river only 25 yards away. He walked to his truck. The backyard of the cabin ended at the river. The woodchipper was a mobile unit that Harry could tow with his truck. He moved his truck closer to the chipper, hooked up the chipper to his tow-ball and backed the unit into the backyard. He slowly moved towards the river until the chipper was only ten feet from the river's edge. Harry quickly figured out how start it and soon had it warmed up and ready to go.

Harry lowered his tailgate, moved the eight trash bags that contained Kitty and her bitch mother to the end of the truck, then prepared to load them into the chipper. Harry soon discovered that an entire trash bag full of dead woman wouldn't fit into the mouth of the chipper. His plan to throw the trash bags into the chipper wouldn't work. He would have to unload the body parts one at a time into the chipper.

Harry used a pocketknife to tear open the first bag. A head and face looked directly at him with empty eyes. It was Kitty. Her blond hair was tangled and bloody. Harry stared back for a moment and gulped. He grabbed Kitty by the hair and tossed her head into the running chipper. In seconds the chipper made a loud, high-pitched sawing sound and pieces of Kitty's skull and brain matter flew into the river. It was much quicker and easier than Harry imagined. A red mist floated over the river and slowly sank downwards into the water. Harry reached into the bag and grabbed an arm. When he tossed It into the chipper it was the same experience. This is going to be fast and easy, Harry thought to himself. He took a deep drink of Lone Star beer and resumed his work. Next was Kitty's large torso. She still had some of her clothes on. Harry hefted her to the chipper's loading chute and squeezed her downwards. It was a tight fit. He had to push it to get her thru the chute and down to the spinning blades. Harry worried about sticking his hands in the chipper. He didn't need that to happen and ruin his day. So, Harry looked around for something he could use, like a rammer for a cannon. He saw an old 2x6 piece of lumber lying next to the cabin. It was perfect. Harry trudged up the sloped yard towards the cabin and grabbed the 2x6. He stood next to the cabin for a moment to catch his breath. He made a mental note to exercise more. Since he was at the cabin, he figured he should grab a couple more beers while there. It only made sense. He opened the squeaky screen door to the cabin and emerged moments later with three cold Lone Star beers. He picked up the 2x6 and trudged back down to the chipper that was still running. Harry stared at Kitty's torso plugging the loading chute. He decided to open a new cold can of Lone Star, took a long chug of the cold beer then grabbed his 2x6 rammer. He pressed the end of the wood into the side of Kitty's armless, legless and headless body, then pushed. It was a tight fit. Kitty had been a big girl. Harry put his considerable weight behind it and finally, she squeezed through. She entered the chipper followed by a loud sawing and grinding noise that filled the backyard just before the pieces of Kitty flew outwards into the river. Small pieces of her clothing fluttered into the air through the red mist, over the river, then slowly floated downward into the moving water.

Harry finished his 7th beer and opened his 8th. He had five more trash bags to go.

Noah Explains Thor

"After that display of manhood, will you ever get another job from the New Braunfels Sheriff's Department again?" Gene asked Heston. He was surprised at Heston. He had never seen Heston behave that way before.

"Probably not, and I don't care. That guy got under my skin as soon as we showed up. He resents me for my work and the respect we command from the other departments. His reputation is in the tank for various reasons, all of which he deserves." Heston stared ahead at the road.

"OK, well take a deep breath and shake it off. Let's go catch a bad guy." Peggy said.

Gene and Noah agreed with Peggy.

They rode in silence for ten minutes. Then Heston remembered the business about Noah's dog.

"So, what's up with Justice becoming Thor?"

Noah knew he was going to be asked about it. He took a deep breath and decided to tell the truth.

"I found Justice in Kyle. He was walking alone up the street in front of the donut shop I went to. I got out and called him over. No collar or anything on him showed who he may belong to. When I opened my truck door, he jumped in without me telling him to. He sat in the seat looking forward, and I got the feeling he wanted me to drive away. So, I did."

"OK, so is he the Duralink Dog?" Heston asked.

"Yeah, he is." Noah reluctantly said.

"OK, why do you think so?" Heston suspiciously asked.

"Because he told me he was."

A long silent pause filled the truck.

"The dog told you he was from Duralink?" Heston asked.

"Yes." Noah paused, not sure how to explain it without sounding crazy. He decided just to spit it out.

"OK Noah, just because that's not crazy or anything," Heston said sarcastically. "Tell me about the talking dog."

"Justice can talk," Noah said. He felt Peggy staring at him and saw Heston look at him in the rearview mirror. Then Gene turned around in his seat and stared at him.

Peggy went first.

"Justice can talk?" She asked.

"Yeah. He told me Duralink connected him to a couple of supercomputers. Over a few months, they downloaded a crazy amount of information into his brain. He understands all the languages spoken on Earth."

"All the languages on earth?" Heston asked doubtfully.

"And he can talk?" Peggy wanted to hear more about Justice speaking.

"Yes, although Duralink doesn't know it."

"So, you know he can talk, but they don't."

"Yeah, that's right."

"Noah, you lost that fight with reality." Heston didn't believe a word of it.

"Why don't they know it?" Peggy was willing to go along with Noah's story. She wanted Justice to talk.

"Because Justice analyzed that they would never let him go if they knew what he was capable of. He didn't want to spend the rest of his life in a cage, eating dog food."

"Dog Food?"

"Yeah, he said he doesn't like it much. He prefers people food."

"Justice said he prefers people food?"

"Yep. That's what he said."

"This is nuts. You are nuts." Heston regretted saying Noah could join them.

Gene and Peggy looked at each other. They didn't know what to say.

Peggy went first, "The logic in Justice's reasoning is sound."

"Justice's reasoning? You too Peggy?" Heston sounded disappointed.

"Just let me finish. Who wants to spend their life in a cage? The obvious way to settle this is to speak to Justice. If he talks back, we know Noah is telling the truth." It seemed too logical for Peggy to ignore.

"Well, I'm not pulling over to talk to a dog," Heston said.

"Ok Heston, we can wait until we get to the cabin."

"I'm not sure he will talk to you," Noah admitted.

"Why is that?" Gene asked, he knew the answer would be great and possibly result in Heston's head exploding.

"He told me not to tell anyone that he can talk. He is worried about people finding out. He is afraid of getting sent back to Duralink."

Gene immediately looked at Heston, hoping for a great explosion.

"That actually makes sense," Peggy said.

Heston re-adjusted himself in his seat and ground his teeth.

"Heston what do you think of that?" Gene asked with an evil grin.

Heston ignored the question.

"He thinks he may have more information in his brain than any animal on the planet." Noah avoided saying he might be the most intelligent animal on the planet.

"So, you're saying Justice said that?" Gene asked Noah, then looked at Heston for a response.

"Yes, that's what Justice said." Noah was unaware that Heston was about to pull over and toss him out of the truck.

Gene wasn't done baiting Heston, "If two supercomputers were downloaded into his brain, he may be the smartest animal on the planet," Gene said with a smile. He was still unsure what to think about this whole 'talking dog' idea. But the dog may be brilliant.

"Because that doesn't sound crazy at all!" Heston yelled at the windshield.

"When we get to the house, we will talk to Justice. The question is, will he talk back?" Gene said, wondering what that idea would do to Heston.

"OK. But let's call him Thor in front of the Duralink people. We should just call him Thor from now on." Noah said.

"If that Dog speaks to us, I will call him Calvin Kline and eat my underwear," Heston said bravely. He couldn't buy the whole talking dog business.

"Heston," Gene said calmly, "May I remind you of a few things?"

"What's that Gene?"

"Let's start with, you don't want to eat your underwear."

"Thanks, Gene, for helping me with that."

"Next, remember the friendly little ghosts? You know, the ones that are still out there? Then, do you remember the witch Lady Mabel that the Indian warriors killed? The Indian ghost warriors? Now think about Laconta. And let's not forget Thin Man and his wife." Gene looked at Heston. "I think we have learned that anything is possible."

"But a talking dog?" Heston said, staring ahead at the road.

"You may regret all the sausage you ate for breakfast. You could get a good whiff of it again. That's all I'm saying," Gene smiled.

"Oh yucch!" Peggy said and curled her nose.

Heston realized Gene had a point.

"Ok, you may have a point. I will buy you guys barbecue at Salt Lick if that dog talks."

"Sounds good to me." Gene said.

"Me too." Peggy agreed.

"If Justice gets to eat Barbeque too, he will talk. I'll convince him to." Noah said. "He told me he wants to eat barbecue brisket."

"The talking dog told you he wants to eat barbeque brisket?" Heston grimaced. He remembered the Son of Sam in New York and the whacko that killed all those people. He hoped that Noah was not a whacko.

Johnny at the Cabin

Johnny walked towards the large blond man throwing material into the woodchipper. He wondered if he was grinding up roadkill. It seemed pretty clear he was disposing of some kind of animal in the river. When he got close, he said "Hello?" loud enough to hear between the pieces going into the chipper machine.

Harry looked over his shoulder as he threw an arm into the chipper.

Johnny got a good look at the arm just as it went into the chute of the chipper. A loud buzz lasted for a few seconds, and a red mess of material shot into the river. Johnny froze. He realized what he had seen. This man was grinding up the body of a person! Johnny did not know what to do.

The large man smiled and said, "Howdy. How can I help you?" He turned around and walked towards Johnny.

Johnny thought for a second. He did not want to get ground up and shot into the river. He remembered his fear of the witch doctors grinding him up. This reminded him of that.

Johnny said, "Sorry sir," and turned around and ran back into the forest.

"Wait, come back!" The man yelled at Johnny.

But Johnny ran as fast as he could into the forest. The evening had set in, and it was getting darker by the minute. He knew he could disappear into the darkness and escape the crazy large man. He looked over his shoulder as he entered the forest. The large man was running toward him.

———————

Harry had drunk his 12th beer by the time he was on the 5th trash bag of people he had to dispose of.

The idea of throwing body parts into a woodchipper had stopped being dreadful to him. He was convinced it was one of his better ideas. Now, it was just a chore. As he grabbed one of Kitty's mother's arms and prepared to toss it in the chipper, he heard a voice from behind him say, "Hello."

Harry was shocked to hear a voice. He didn't hear a vehicle arrive. He tossed the arm in the chipper and turned around. It was the whitest guy Harry had ever seen standing in the yard not too far from the river. Immediately, Harry could tell from the man's face that he knew what Harry was doing. Harry tried to put on a happy face and draw the guy in. It didn't work. Shock spread across the guy's face, and he quickly turned and bolted away toward the forest. Shit, shit, shit! Harry knew if this guy got away, he would be in big trouble. As the guy disappeared into the forest, Harry realized he had to go after him, so Harry chased him into the forest. The man looked over his shoulder, spotted Harry chasing him, and quickly disappeared into the darkness of the woods.

Quickly, Harry was out of breath; he stopped and wiped his brow with his forearm. He had to get back into shape, he re-committed to regular exercise starting tomorrow. After his breathing slowed down, Harry realized a cold beer would make the chase go easier. He turned around in the yard and returned to the cabin. Once inside, he entered the kitchen and chugged a cold beer. He wiped his mouth and went back outside to follow the nosey white guy into the forest. Harry knew the strange looking man saw too much. He had to catch him and push him through the chipper. Harry glanced at his watch. It was after 6:00 pm. The sun was getting lower, and Harry knew he only had a good hour of light left and it would be very dark in the woods after two hours. He hurried into the forest following the small path that the nosey guy followed. Harry was not as fast as the other guy was and quickly started to lose ground.

After Harry was 20 yards into the forest, he heard vehicles approaching from down the road. Harry moved to a vantage point to see the road through the trees. There were definitely two vehicles approaching. One was a large Ford truck, and the other was a four-door sedan. As they got closer, Harry realized the truck was the same one he saw pulling into Kitty's driveway earlier in the day. They both had their headlights on and were slowly driving towards the cabin.

"Oh Crap," Harry said to himself. He knew immediately that being separated from his truck was a problem. A bigger problem was the remaining trash bags in his truck that were yet to be disposed of and the fact that Harry had left the chipper running. When they discovered the remaining trash bags, he knew he would be in big trouble.

Harry wasn't sure what to do next. In a strangely lucid moment, he realized it didn't matter now if he caught the white guy that saw him feeding Kitty's mom into the chipper. He was in trouble now that the new group had arrived. They would find the body parts and the running chipper and figure it out. He decided to hide. When darkness fell, he would escape and go to Mexico. Or Oklahoma. Harry couldn't decide. He couldn't speak Spanish, and he hated Mexicans, so Oklahoma may be a better choice, he thought. He would just wait it out and decide later.

Harry watched as the two vehicles pulled into the driveway of the cabin. The three men in the truck got out and lowered the tailgate. The woman got out and started to walk towards the woodchipper. Three dogs jumped down and excitedly wagged their tails as they began sniffing around the cabin. Next, a sedan drove up and parked. A man and a woman got out and met the people from the truck. Harry didn't hear what they said, but they clearly knew each other. Harry watched as the dogs ran to the woodchipper and became excited. Harry's truck was still attached to the chipper, which meant he would not get it back unless he killed all of them first. He watched as the group moved to the truck and the chipper. Harry saw them look in the bags and look at each other.

The man from the sedan vomited.

Marty! Oh, That's Just Great

Heston, Gene, Peggy and Noah drove up the unpaved road towards the cabin. They had been joined 30 minutes earlier by Nancy and her partner Marty, in the vehicle that now drove behind them. They moved slowly up the road through the thick forest up to the cabin. Each side of the road had large old trees that overstretched the road and thick underbrush that quickly got dark as the sun went down.

Heston saw the cabin on the left and parked in the driveway. Nancy parked next to him. Heston and his crew exited the truck and let the dogs out.

"Justice won't speak to you with these guys here," Noah said.

"We can wait for them to leave." Heston pretended to believe that Justice might speak.

"We will have to," Noah said.

"Looks like the dogs picked up a scent already," Heston said as they watched the dogs move down to the truck and the woodchipper down by the river. Peggy was way ahead of them. She went straight for the chipper that she had spotted down by the river when they drove up.

Peggy was first to see the large plastic trash bags in the back of the truck. Then she noticed the blood dripping down the chute to the chipper. Blood was pooled in the lowered tailgate as well. They had interrupted someone at work. But work doing what? The blood was out of place and the gas-powered chipper was still running.

Peggy turned around to signal for the others to join her. They were already headed her way. The dogs were excited about finding the trail and even Justice was excitedly sniffing the ground and the truck. He looked up at Peggy and stared at her. She couldn't help but notice the look that he gave her. It was intelligent and indicated they had found not only the trail for Harry, but she should be careful and defensive. Peggy immediately understood the look and scanned the tree line around them for signs of Harry.

Heston, Gene and Noah were first to join her at the truck.

"Look at the blood on the chute," Peggy said, pointing to the chute.

Nancy and Marty joined them, and Marty quickly noticed the bags in the back of the truck.

"What's in the bags?" Marty asked

"I have no idea," Peggy said

"No time like now to find out." Marty said.

Marty reached into the bed of the truck and pulled a trash sack closer so he could inspect it. It was heavier than he expected.

He used his Spyderco Police Special pocketknife to open the trash bag.

The smell was ripe. When he widened the bag to look inside, he saw a headless torso still wearing the torn bloody remnants of a blouse. Marty turned the bag upside down, spilling the contents on the truck's tailgate. The torso spilled out along with a bloody arm and a kidney.

Marty took a deep breath and immediately felt sick.

He turned around with his hand over his mouth, knowing he was going to puke. He tried to aim his stomach contents away from the others; he wasn't successful. His vomit splashed on Nancy's shoes and pantsuit.

"Marty! Oh, that's just great!" Nancy yelled. "Is this your first dead body?" She looked at him like he was a rookie.

"Sorry, Nancy," Marty said, wiping his mouth with his sleeve. "It's my first chopped-up dead body in a trash bag. And my first kidney."

"On my clothes! I need a rag or something," Nancy said, looking down at her feet and pantsuit. "I should have worn blue jeans. I'm glad I have a change of clothes in the trunk."

"Well, it looks like Harry has killed somebody else," Gene said.

"Look at the empty trash bags next to the chipper. He's already chopped up at least one other body before we got here." Peggy said.

"Looks like he chopped them into the river," Heston observed

"Not a bad idea for getting rid of a body," Marty said.

"Pretty bad if you get caught doing it," Nancy replied.

"I wonder what interrupted him," Heston pushed the kill switch to the chipper. The gas-powered engine turned off.

"I'm going to call Hornsby for instructions. We could look for Harry, but it's getting close to dark. Hornsby needs to give us approval to leave this scene." Nancy said.

"I don't need Hornsby's approval for anything, the dogs have a scent, and we will follow it," Heston said calmly. "Ready?" He looked at Gene and Peggy.

"Ready! Let's go." Gene said.

"Please Heston, just give me a minute." Nancy pleaded.

"No way. We are leaving. I am hired to find Harry and every minute I delay he gets further away."

"Can you give me time to change into my blue jeans and hiking vest? It will only take a few minutes." Nancy pleaded again. She wanted to be a part of the hunt. She really wanted to spend more time with Noah's dog and verify he was Justice.

"I can stay here. I will call Hornsby." Marty said.

"Ok, you call. I'll get my go-bag and change really fast. Nancy ran to the sedan and opened the trunk. She grabbed her go-bag and ran to the cabin. The front door was open. She entered and went to a bedroom to change.

Marty called Hornsby.

"Detective Hornsby, this is Marty Shott."

Everyone watched Marty as he listened to Hornsby.

"Yeah, we have found a bunch of stuff. Harry has been here at the cabin."

He paused, listening to Hornsby's questions.

"The dogs picked up a trail. But more importantly, we have at least one more dead body in the back of Harry's truck. He chopped up the bodies in a woodchipper and shot them into the river."

He listened for a moment.

"It appears he dismembered the bodies and put them in trash bags. That's probably why the kitchen at the house in New Braunfels was so bloody."

He listened for a moment.

"Heston and his team are headed out now. They are waiting for Nancy Webb to change clothes so she can join them."

He listened for a moment.

"Are you sure you want to do that?" Marty sounded like he didn't like what Hornsby told him.

He listened to the reply.

"Detective, I'm not sure that's the best call on this. If they do that, Harry is just getting further away. They have a hot trail on him, and he may not be too far away. The chipper was running when we got here so we must have interrupted him. He may be fairly close."

He listened to the reply.

"Ok, I will tell him." Marty looked at his cell phone and ended the call. He looked at Heston and his three teammates.

"Hornsby says to wait for him before you go out after Harry."

"Yeah, like that's gonna happen. That's crazy. They hired me to find Harry, and that's what we are gonna do." Heston said, trying to control his anger.

"Yeah. I thought you would say that. So did Hornsby. He said if you go without him and abandon this crime scene—-you are fired." Hornsby said the last three words in a voice close to a low-volume mumble. He knew it would piss Heston off.

Heston was much calmer than everyone expected.

"OK." Heston said, "How long until he can get here?" Heston calmly asked.

"About…." Marty almost held his breath to say, "an hour to an hour and a half."

Everyone thought that would send Heston over the edge.

But it didn't.

Heston said, "Well, I'm not into wasting time. It's getting dark, and I have a family at home as these folks do. So, we are leaving. Hornsby can track him down without us. Let's go, folks."

Heston calmly walked towards his truck.

Gene, Peggy and Noah quietly followed Heston to the truck. He signaled for the dogs to get in the back. The dogs jumped into the truck bed then Heston slammed the tailgate closed. Next, Heston climbed into the driver's seat. Gene, Peggy and Noah loaded into the truck after him. Very quickly, Heston was driving his team back to Driftwood.

"Hey, Heston," Gene started, "I'm proud of you for not blowing up back there."

"Yeah Heston, good call leaving. Otherwise, you were working for free." Peggy added.

I figured either way I'm not getting paid. We could have stayed and hunted or gone home. Both end up without getting paid. There was no way I'd have us wait an hour and a half for that stupid bag of hair." Heston paused. "Plus, I want to talk to Justice."

Johnny gets Curious

Johnny watched the events occur from his perspective, hidden in the forest. He could see both the cabin and Harry hiding behind a tree just inside the tree line. He watched the large truck that arrived earlier leave with the dogs and the four occupants. He watched as Harry just stood still, staring at the cabin. Johnny was not sure what to think or do next. As darkness fell around him over the next hour, Johnny watched Harry stand perfectly still. He was curious how such a large man could stand still as a stone for such a long time.

Johnny knew Harry was dangerous. He observed Harry throwing body parts into a woodchipper just an hour earlier. Normal, sane people don't throw body parts into a woodchipper. This was true in Africa and had to be true in America, too.

Johnny's curiosity took over. The darkness prevented him from seeing as clearly as he wanted to. He slowly crept towards Harry, approaching him from behind. Johnny was very good at moving silently. It was a skill he learned in Africa. All young boys learned to move through the brush silently in Africa, they had to. Their safety depended on it. Where he was from, lions were known to stalk the perimeters of the village, looking for young, unsuspecting kids to snatch up and feed upon.

Johnny crept to 15 feet behind Harry. He stood perfectly still and slowed his breathing. What was the enormous blond man going to do? Johnny had a feeling it would not be good. The truck with the dogs loaded up and drove away. Soon, it was still and dark around the cabin; Johnny knew the only people left in the cabin were the man who had vomited and the woman. The blond man continued to stand still and observe the cabin.

After an hour, headlights flashed across the unpaved road to the cabin. Both Harry and Johnny noticed the headlights and watched as a new car pulled up to the cabin and parked in the dirt driveway.

A man got out of the vehicle and went to the cabin door and knocked. The man and woman that remained after the truck left were inside the cabin and opened the door. Harry was on the move when the new visitors entered the cabin and the door closed. Harry slowly stepped away from the tree line and towards the cabin.

Johnny watched from the treeline for a couple of more minutes. Johnny couldn't figure out what the blond man was going to do. Was he going to get in his truck and leave? Or something else? Johnny's curious nature was taking over. Little did he realize it might kill him.

Harry Goes Back to the Cabin

"What should we do?" White Rabbit asked Cole.

"Just watch for now."

"The large man is dangerous."

"Yes, I agree."

"If the pale man gets too close, the large man will kill him." White Rabbit said.

"Yes, I believe so too." Cole agreed.

As White Rabbit, Cole and Crazy Crow watched Harry sneak across the open area towards the cabin. It hit White Rabbit what he was going to do.

The three tiny ghosts had seen everything Johnny saw. They witnessed Harry throwing the body parts into the woodchipper, then witnessed him chase and run after Johnny after Johnny said 'hello' to him. It was clear Harry was a killer.

White Rabbit said, "The large man will kill everyone in the cabin, then drive away in his truck."

"How do you know?"

"I can feel it. I know."

Cole had been with White Rabbit on many occasions when she said she knew something would happen. He couldn't remember a time when she was wrong.

"Is he going to kill the pale man?" Crazy Crow asked her sister.

White Rabbit paused for a moment. She closed her eyes hoping for an answer to the question. She had none.

"I do not know." White Rabbit replied.

The three small ghosts watched Johnny closely as he watched and followed Harry.

Why the pale man was following him so closely was a mystery to the ghosts. He should run and escape, they all thought.

As Harry approached the cabin, Johnny sprinted across the open area in front of the cabin, behind Harry. Johnny stopped on the opposite side of the two sedans parked in the gravel driveway. He crouched and peered over the cars at Harry approaching the cabin.

Lights were on in the cabin, but the front porch was dark. Harry crept up to the house and stood outside an open double-hung window, listening to the conversation inside.

Harry heard the three people inside discussing their plans. The last man who arrived was named Hornsby, and he was the boss. He was upset that the previous group had left. Harry heard Hornsby yell that Heston would never work for his department again. Harry assumed Heston was the leader of the group that left, probably the driver of the large truck. Harry thought about the dogs that jumped in the back of Heston's truck. One of them was a two-tone German

Sheppard that strongly resembled Justice. Could that have been Justice? Was that possible?

Harry stood under the window and tried to get his brain to slow down. He had to consider his options.

Option number one was to kill all three people inside, get a good night's sleep, then head for Mexico or Oklahoma after he got his truck back.

Option number two was to wait for the three people inside to fall asleep, get in his truck and drive off. That plan assumed they would all go to sleep. It also assumed his keys were still in the truck. Harry leaned towards killing them all.

To make his decision easier, Harry decided to go to his truck and see if the keys were still in the ignition. If they were, he had two options to consider. If they were not there, he had just one option.

Harry slowly and silently crept around the left side of the dark cabin. The back porch light was on. The light illuminated the backyard out to the river, approximately 25 yards. The truck and the chipper were on the other side of the cabin. Harry would have to sprint silently across the illuminated yard behind the cabin to get to them. Harry pondered the situation. He didn't want to sprint across the illuminated yard. With his size, sprinting was not an option. At least, not silently sprinting. Plus, he hated to sprint.

He decided a better plan was to go back around the front of the home where there were no outdoor lights and circle around to his truck that way.

Johnny waited in the dark behind the two sedans. He watched the front of the cabin. The large blond man had disappeared moments earlier around the opposite side of the cabin. Johnny could hear the people in the cabin talking. He sensed they were in danger from the enormous blond man, but he didn't know what he should do. Then the blond man appeared at the far corner of the

110

cabin. Johnny tensed up as he watched the man creep in front of the house and toward Johnny. Johnny crouched low and used darkness as cover. When the blond man began to run in Johnny's direction, Johnny knew he would need to keep the cars between himself and the blond man. As Harry headed towards the back of the sedan, Johnny quietly moved to the front of the sedan and ducked down low. He crouched low enough to watch Harry's feet under the car.

Harry ran to the back of the two cars parked side by side in the dirt driveway.

As he skidded to a stop at the rear of the cars, he moved down the side of the far car from the cabin. He kept his eyes on the cabin entry door just in case the people inside decided to come out. Harry moved down the side of the car toward his truck and the chipper that were twenty-five yards in front of the two vehicles. As he crept behind the car, he noticed a flash of movement in front of the opposite vehicle. Harry wondered what he saw. It was only a quick flash of movement. He was sure he saw something. Whatever he saw, it ducked down behind the front of the car. Did he see something? Now Harry questioned himself. Harry stood perfectly still, staring at the other vehicle parked on the other side of the car he was next to.

He saw it again. There was somebody on the other side of the other car. Harry wondered who it was. Did someone come out of the cabin while he was on the side of the cabin earlier? Harry didn't think so. This was someone new. A neighbor, perhaps? No. The neighbors were too far away. Who was it then? Could it be the white guy that he had been chasing?

Harry decided to find out. He crept around the front of the car, then when he got to the adjacent car, he slowly crept around the front of it and looked at the driver's side of the car. Nobody. What had he seen? Harry moved backward, then between the cars and towards the rear of the vehicles. Nobody was there either. Harry scratched his head. The only possibility was… did the mysterious person move under the car? Harry hated to get down on his hands and knees due to his large size. At 350 pounds getting back up was torture on his knees. Not to mention the pain from the gravel. He thought about it for a moment and decided he must have been mistaken. The truth was he just didn't want to get down low enough to look under the car.

Harry looked at his truck parked 25 yards away in the dark yard. He decided to see if his keys were in the ignition. Slowly, Harry moved away from the two sedans parked in the driveway and towards his truck.

Johnny heard Harry's footsteps move away from the vehicles. He took his first deep breath as he lay on his stomach under the car closest to the cabin. He knew he had almost been caught. He silently scooted out from under the car.

Johnny crouched between the cars and watched Harry as he moved towards his truck. He wondered what the big blond man would have done to him if he had pulled him out from under the car. He knew it wouldn't have been good.

Noah's Redemption

Heston, Noah, Gene and Peggy drove into Noah's driveway. Darkness had fallen and the team of four was tired from a long day. Noah's claim that Justice could talk, however, was all that was on their minds. Either Noah had lost his mind, or Justice was a special dog– an extraordinary dog.

They climbed out of Heston's truck and entered Noah's home. Trump and Reagan followed Justice like he was their new leader.

The team assembled in Noah's kitchen and stood around the marble-topped island.

"Ok Noah, let's hear it." Heston glared at Noah.

Noah knew precisely what Heston meant. He didn't need to ask.

"Justice buddy, come here." Noah patted his thigh as the group stood around the kitchen island.

Justice knew what he would be asked to do. He instantly regretted speaking to Noah and telling him the truth. Justice weighed the options. His goal was to stay out of Duralink Labs. He did not want to be subjected to the scientist's tests and procedures again. In Justice's mind, he was already more intelligent than they were. He should be studying them.

He was fond of Noah. Noah did not have to help him, but he did without flinching. Justice appreciated that and decided he would help Noah in return. But speaking to his friends? Probably not a good idea, Justice concluded.

"Justice, I need you to say something to Heston. Anything."

Justice sat in front of the group and wagged his tail.

"Justice please, tell them you can speak." Noah beseeched the German Shepherd.

Justice stared back at Noah with an obedient look on his face but silent.

Heston glared at Noah. Then he looked at Gene and Peggy. His message was clear. This is nuts.

"Buddy, they will think I'm crazy if you don't say something." Noah sounded nervous.

Heston's phone rang. It was Marty Shott.

"What's up, Marty?" Heston asked into his iPhone.

"Hey, Heston, we will need you back out here." Marty said.

"Really? I thought Hornsby would never work with us again."

"He thought it over and decided we need you and your team out here." Marty said.

"He said that?" Heston asked.

"Well, sort of." Marty said.

"What happened to make him change his mind?"

"Wait a second Heston, let me go out back really quick." Marty went out the back door of the cabin for some privacy.

Heston stood in the kitchen and glared at the dog that wouldn't speak while Marty went on the back porch of the cabin. Heston heard the loud squeak of the screen door as it opened, then he heard it slam closed, forcing him to pull the phone away from his head for a second.

Finally, Marty said, "Hornsby spoke with the Sheriff. The Sheriff apparently told him that if he were forced to choose between him and you, it wouldn't be him. Your results in the last few months have been too good for him to stop working with you."

"Really?" Heston smiled and looked at Gene and Peggy.

"Yeah, and you will probably like this too. He told Hornsby to get the stick out of his butt and make peace with you." Marty said.

"Ok well, in that case, we can be back in the morning."

"Can you come back tonight?"

"Nope. We can be there at sunrise though."

"Ok, that's fine, we'll stay the night here in the cabin and be ready to go in the morning." Marty said.

"So, the three of you will stay the night there?" Heston asked.

"No other choice, really." Marty paused for a moment. "Harry Rivers may come back for his truck. If he does, we will arrest him."

"OK Marty, you should have rotating guards all night. This guy is dangerous. Don't all of you fall asleep at once." Heston warned.

"Agreed." Marty knew Heston was right.

"Ok, see you in the morning, Marty. Be careful. Remember what this guy did to those two women. You don't want to get chopped into the river too."

"Copy that."

Heston hung up and looked at Gene and Peggy.

"We have to be there at sunrise."

Noah got the feeling he was not included.

"Me too?" Noah asked.

"I don't think so," Heston said. He was convinced the dog wasn't going to speak, meaning Noah was nuts.

"You think I'm crazy," Noah said, dejected.

"I think you need rest. More time to get a grip on life." Heston was being his kindest.

Justice hated to see Noah get hurt because of him. It appeared to Justice that the three people that Noah wanted to be a part of were intelligent and kind. Even Heston.

Maybe Justice should help Noah. But going back to Duralink was not an option.

"We will keep in touch with you Noah," Peggy said with kindness in her voice.

"Yeah, we will call you tomorrow after the hunt and fill you in," Gene said.

It hit Justice that these people may get hurt by Harry. Harry was crazy and deadly. Justice was sure of this. He had seen it for himself. Justice weighed the odds. When Justice looked at all possible outcomes, he concluded that Harry would return and probably kill everyone in the cabin to get his keys to his truck. His only escape option was to get his truck back. He was too fat and out of shape to hike out of that forest, much less to Mexico. Justice realized he could be of value to these people. He could protect them.

As the threesome turned towards Heston's truck, they heard a new voice.

"Wait a minute, Heston."

The three stopped immediately. The voice was not only new, but slightly irregular.

Heston, Gene and Peggy turned around simultaneously.

They stared at Justice.

Noah smiled broadly. He had never been happier.

Peggy looked at Noah's face, and her suspicions were confirmed. It had been Justice! Justice could speak! She knew it all along. She *wanted* the dog to speak. Heck, she wanted *all* dogs to speak. She thought Justice might actually be the one to do it. Peggy stared at Justice, beaming with happiness. Now the threesome waited for more. They had to see Justice speak for themselves.

Justice stared at the group as he sat comfortably next to Noah.

"Ok, I waited a minute. Now what?" Heston looked at Justice and then upwards to Noah. He made it clear he would leave shortly if he didn't see Justice speak.

Noah and Justice were quiet in return.

"What?" Heston repeated. It was more of a command.

"Ok, Heston. Noah isn't crazy, he doesn't need rest, and he doesn't need to get a grip on his life." Justice looked directly into Heston's eyes as he spoke. "Well... he might need some rest."

"Holy Sweet Baby Jesus," Gene said.

Peggy laughed with Noah.

As Marty hung up with Heston, he stood on the back porch of the cabin and looked towards the river. The darkness hid the river, but he could hear it. The porch light illuminated the yard that extended downward to the river, but it was not bright enough to allow the river to be seen. The truck attached to the woodchipper was on the right side of the yard, just in front of the river. The porch light barely lit the side of the truck and the woodchipper.

Marty stood silently for a moment and took in the situation he found himself in. A crazy, dangerous large man was probably in the darkness and likely to return for his truck. Marty found himself more excited than afraid. He could be a part of a critical apprehension that would benefit his small private detective agency. With a successful operation like this, he could afford to hire another private detective. He was lucky to have Nancy Webb. She was a great addition, but he could barely afford her. His being hired by Duralink was a God send for his agency. Now was his time to prove they had made a good decision. Maybe he would even get to meet Delon Husk! Marty's head was racing too fast. He shook his head and told himself to slow down. There was a nut job in the darkness he had to focus on for now. He could think about Mr. Husk later.

Marty turned to go into the cabin. Just as he moved, he thought he saw movement by Harry's truck. Marty paused for a moment and squinted to see through the partial light towards the truck and chipper. Should he go out there and investigate? He was a private investigator for crying out loud. He tried to convince himself to walk out to the truck and check out the movement. He had a foreboding feeling about going out there by himself. He wanted to go out there, he told himself he should go out there. He just couldn't take the first step toward the truck. He froze in place, unable to step off the porch.

He convinced himself it was nothing and went into the cabin. As the squeaky screen door slammed closed behind him, Marty wondered if he was a coward.

Harry stared back at the porch from the other side of the chipper. He knew he had been spotted. He had his large Bowie knife in his right hand and was ready for the man on the porch to come to investigate. The beauty of knives is they are silent, Harry thought. He knew he could kill the man quickly without alerting the others. Harry was eager and ready.

Harry smiled and told himself that the man was lucky he went back inside.

Marty went inside the cabin to find Nancy sitting on the couch while Hornsby leaned against the wall. They knew he had been speaking with Heston and were eager to know what the result was.

"So?" Nancy finally said.

"So, they will be back at sunrise." Marty replied.

"Sunrise? We need to go get this guy now. We can't wait until sunrise." Hornsby said. He continued to use his arrogant tone.

"Have at it," Nancy said. She had grown tired of Hornsby. She didn't suffer fools easily. "Go get 'em hoss."

"Ok, let's go," Hornsby said.

"I'm not going anywhere," Nancy said factually.

Hornsby looked at Nancy like she had slapped him.

"Look, Hornsby." Marty started.

"Detective Hornsby," Hornsby corrected him.

Marty looked at Nancy then back at Hornsby.

"Look Hornsby, there is a large psychotic man out there that gets his rocks off feeding women into woodchippers. Without the dogs to alert us, we are safer remaining in the cabin and waiting until sunrise."

"Plus" Nancy said trying unsuccessfully to control her temper "We would already have apprehended him had *YOU* not stopped us. So, you can just cool your jets and let the adults take over."

"We should at least look around the cabin," Hornsby said.

"I'm busy now, hun. I'm gonna have to ignore you another time." Nancy held her open hand up to him.

Marty smiled at Nancy and realized his pride in hiring her.

"What if the nut job takes off in the truck?" Hornsby asked.

Nancy reached in the pocket of her blue jeans. She grabbed a group of keys and jingled them in the air.

"He ain't going nowhere, darlin'." Nancy's Texas accent shone through.

They didn't realize that the keys in Nancy's hand were going to lure Harry into the cabin.

Cole's Logic

"If we know that that big blond guy is going to kill everyone in the cabin, then we must warn them," Cole said.

"Why?" Crazy Crow didn't understand Cole's logic.

"If we can help them we should," Cole said, thinking it was obvious.

"We are not supposed to interact with humans, especially white humans. Father may get angry." Crazy Crow said.

"Well, you can do what you want. I'm going in the cabin." Cole said. He was tired of being afraid of Crazy Crow's father. He was going to do the right thing.

"I'm going with Cole." White Rabbit said.

"You will be in trouble." Crazy Crow said to her sister in a sing-song voice.

"I think father would approve." White Rabbit said.

"He won't."

"He may."

"He may put on a dress and dance like Pocahontas. But he won't." Crazy Crow grinned.

"You amuse yourself and no other." White Rabbit replied.

"Well, that's not entirely true," Cole said with a grin.

White Rabbit looked at him with surprise.

"I find it amusing to hear you two bicker sometimes," Cole admitted. "And the 'dance like Pocahontas' thing was pretty funny."

"Thank you Cole, I think." Crazy Crow said. Reluctantly she was growing fonder of Cole.

"Let's go Cole" White Rabbit rolled her eyes and floated towards the cabin.

Cole followed White Rabbit towards the cabin. Crazy Crow floated off to find the giant white man.

Cole and White Rabbit floated up to the entry to the cabin. They needed to get through the door. They had been practicing their ability to pass through windows, doors and walls and had become very proficient at the skill. Crazy Crow had difficulty with it, she still needed some work. She could slip through cracks easily though.

Cole nodded for White Rabbit to follow him. He passed through the door in the form of a softball and White Rabbit did the same. Once in the living room of the cabin they found themselves floating in the middle of the three white people who were arguing about what to do next. They watched as the blond woman called Nancy held up a ball of keys.

"Those are the keys to the large man's truck" Cole said to White Rabbit.

Immediately White Rabbit knew that the keys were going to get them killed. The large man was coming for them.

"If you are going to help them, you need to tell them he is coming for the keys." White Rabbit said to Cole.

Cole nodded his agreement.

As Nancy swung the keys side-to-side Cole floated to the ground and took his standard human shape in between the three people. White Rabbit did not change her shape, she remained a small white translucent ball near the top of the room.

The conversation between the three humans stopped immediately as Cole appeared.

"Hello," Cole said.

"What the...?" Marty exclaimed.

"What is this?" Hornsby asked.

"What are you? Who are you" Nancy exclaimed with some fright.

"That doesn't matter now. I am here to help you." Cole said trying to get them to listen rather than be surprised at him.

"Really?" Nancy asked skeptically.

"Yes ma'am. Those keys may get you all killed. He will come for them. He may be coming now."

Nancy immediately recognized the logic.

"I can't believe… are you for real?" Hornsby asked.

"Don't worry about that," Nancy said. "He's right. We need to hide these keys." Nancy immediately recognized the need to hide the keys. Harry would need them to escape.

"If you hide them, he may torture you to tell him where they are," Cole said.

"We're armed. I'm not worried about that." Nancy said.

"Is he outside now?" Hornsby asked.

"Yes. He is by the truck. When he finds that his keys are not there, he will come here to get them."

"He's right," Nancy said. It was totally logical.

"Holy sweet mother of God, if he is outside, we're in danger." Marty found himself scared again.

"If he is outside, I'm going out to apprehend him" Hornsby confidently said.

"We shouldn't split up," Nancy argued.

"Ok, come with me." Hornsby invited Nancy.

"I'm staying in here," Marty said. He remembered his fear from the back porch earlier. "If he comes here, I'll take him in custody." Marty didn't want to go outside for any reason. He had no explanation for the small ghost, but he knew he was right. How could they think a ghost was real and could be warning them of danger? If it got out that he believed a ghost warned him of danger, his reputation would be ruined. He may miss his opportunity to meet Delon Husk. He wouldn't let that happen.

"We should stick together" Nancy said. She knew she was right. She reached down and slid the keys under the couch.

"You two do what you want but I'm going out to the truck to get him." Hornsby could already feel the glory of catching the bad guy. Maybe now the Sheriff will appreciate him as much as he appreciated Heston Hand.

Nancy had to decide. She had two difficult men to deal with, not including Harry Rivers. Should she stay with Marty or go with Hornsby? The logical choice was unclear.

"I'm going with Hornsby." she heard herself say to Marty.

"Fine. I'll hold down the fort here." Marty said confidently.

"Let's go, Hornsby," Nancy said.

"Detective Hornsby."

"You have to give up on the 'Detective' BS around us." Marty said, "We think you are a joke."

"A joke?" Hornsby asked. "I'm a joke that can get you fired."

"We don't work for you, dipstick. Delon Husk hired us to find their dog." Marty exaggerated about Delon Husk hiring them. He justified it with Mr. Husk's company hired him, so it was partially true.

Hornsby took a deep breath and started to yell at Marty. "You will do as I say, or you will not work with or for…"

Nancy realized these two were going to argue for a while and completely waste time. She turned around and headed for a bedroom to lie down. While they argued she could get a quick bit of rest. She needed it.

Cole and White floated out the front door. They had done what they could. Now it was time to observe the results of their efforts.

Marty and Hornsby yelled back and forth for a couple of minutes.

Hornsby yelled at Marty that he could fire him anytime and as Marty just sat on the couch and stared at him.

Marty prepared to yell back when he heard the creak of the screen door in the kitchen.

Heston Talks to Justice

Heston, Peggy and Gene stared at Justice in silence for a moment. The dog could talk. They had all witnessed it. He sounded a bit odd, but totally understandable and intelligent.

"OK, how can this be?" Heston finally asked.

"Are you familiar with Duralink?" Justice asked.

Another long pause from Heston. He refused to speak with a speaking dog. For now.

Peggy spoke first.

"I know it is owned by Delon Husk, and he is trying to wire computers into brains to help people with brain injury." Once Peggy saw Justice speak again, she lost all hesitation to speak. She was excited to interact with a dog this way. She always felt dogs were special and wanted to speak with people, now they apparently could.

"Yes Peggy, that is partially correct. Brain injury patients are a target market." Justice paused for a moment. "There are military uses that are far more valuable for Duralink though. They are allowed to experiment on dogs as well as other animals in the name of science. Animals and humans share many traits, chimps and mice especially. But dogs are acceptable subjects as well. What Duralink is hiding from the general public is that the dog, especially German Shepherds, are the target of artificial research, also called AI, because we can slip behind enemy lines and gain information without any concern from the enemy. Dogs have very good access because most people like dogs."

"Why German Shepherds?" Peggy asked.

"Because we are naturally smarter than most large breed dogs, and our brain is easier to access. Plus, we can double as guard dogs as well as bomb and dope sniffing dogs." Justice looked at the group who stood still and silent. So, he continued. "Guard dogs and bomb sniffers can be put in situations where we need to explain to our handlers what we have observed without wasting time. I can specifically warn a Marine or a Navy Seal that a bomb is on his left-hand side. That ability is especially valuable at night when they may not see my physical movements as well."

"Well, I guess that explains it," Gene said.

"That's an understatement." Heston agreed.

"So, I guess you believe me now." Noah smiled, he resisted saying 'I told you so'. But the effect was the same.

"I hate to say I do, but I guess I do." Heston finally said.

"So, Heston," Justice started "I get to eat at Salt Lick too, right?"

"Ha! Of course you do" Gene said, "I mean if Heston says so." Gene slowed his roll a bit, realizing it was Heston's money.

"Yes, you eat at Salt Lick too," Heston said in a defeated tone. He was glad he backed away from the underwear idea. He would thank Gene later.

"Great, I love barbecue even though I've only smelled it once. I've never gotten to eat it. I watched the scientists eat it. It smells wonderful." Justice admitted his inexperience. "Look Heston," Justice continued to speak "those people at the cabin are in grave danger. I know Harry. He is crazy and dangerous. He will not hesitate to kill them all. You need to tell them to leave the cabin and come back tomorrow at sunrise with you three."

"Hey, I'm back in now, right?" Noah still wanted to be a part of the group. "Should be us four," Noah said smiling now that he had been proven right.

Heston looked at Gene and Peggy. They both nodded.

"Ok, you're in. Plus, we may be able to put Justice to work." Heston said. "I don't need a bomb sniffer, I need a criminal sniffer. Can you do that Justice?"

"I will never forget that crazy man's smell," Justice said.

So, Justice, you have a problem with 'F' and 'V' pronunciation, right? Peggy asked.

"Yes Peggy, my lips and jaw are restricted from making those sounds."

"I'm calling Marty," Heston said grabbing his phone. He still resisted calling Hornsby.

Heston dialed the number and waited a moment. After three rings it went to voicemail.

"I wonder why he doesn't answer."

"I have a bad 'eeling that I know why," Justice said.

———

Johnny watched Harry move to the truck that was parked in the darkness 25 yards ahead. The truck was obviously unlocked because Harry was able to open the driver's side door. The light inside the truck flashed on for a moment and then went off. Johnny silently moved towards the truck, staying hidden in the shadows. He waited a few moments for Harry to come out of the truck. Harry came out and silently shut the door. Johnny crouched low next to a tree on the side of the yard. Johnny could hear one of the men in the cabin speaking through an open window in the kitchen.

Moments after Harry shut the door to the truck one of the men from inside the cabin came out onto the back porch as he spoke on his phone. The conversation lasted a few minutes and Johnny noticed Harry moving to the rear of his truck from the chipper.

When the man on the phone hung up, he stared at the truck across the yard. Harry remained still. It looked to Johnny like the man on the porch spotted Harry. After a minute the man on the porch gave up trying to spot Harry and returned into the cabin.

After the man went back into the cabin Harry moved to the front of his truck. That's when Johnny saw the large knife as it reflected light from the porch. Harry held the Bowie knife in his right hand and moved towards the cabin. Johnny watched as Harry trotted to the side of the porch and flattened up against the cabin.

Johnny knew this was going to get violent. Why else would the large man approach the cabin with a huge knife? Johnny correctly concluded that the keys to the truck were inside the cabin and the large blond man needed them.

Harry could hear two men talking inside. When they sounded to be absorbed in their debate about Heston, Harry made his move onto the porch and slowly opened the screen door to the cabin.

The screen door creaked, and Harry slipped into the kitchen.

Nancy was tired of Hornsby and Marty arguing about Heston. She realized it had gotten to the point that they were both making their points over and over again. She retreated to the small bedroom to lay down. She firmly closed the door to make a point to the two men that she was tired of listening to them.

She left the bedside lamp on but turned the overhead light off. She rested on the bed for less than five minutes when she heard a large crash in the living room. Nancy's eyes opened in borderline panic. She overheard Marty scream, "NO!" Then went silent. Had Hornsby attacked Marty? Or had Harry come back like the tiny ghosts warned?

Nancy bolted up out of bed and opened the bedroom door. Hornsby was face down on the couch, completely still. Harry Rivers was straddled on top of Marty in the middle of the floor. He had his left hand on Marty's throat and was squeezing the life out of Marty. In his right hand he held a large Bowie knife. Harry yelled, "Where are they?" into Marty's face.

Nancy had to do something. Her police training had taught her not to hesitate. Doing anything was better than doing nothing in this situation. Her gun, where was her gun? It was in the kitchen inside her bag. Big mistake. She had to go through the living room to get her gun. It was her only option. She locked eyes with Harry. His blond hair stood straight up and uncombed; his eyes had a crazy stare. They both knew what would happen next.

Harry looked at her and knew immediately he could get the keys from her. He had a savage smile on his face that indicated he enjoyed the situation. Nancy couldn't believe he was actually smiling. Now that he had a woman to terrorize, he didn't need the man on the floor. Surely, he could get the keys from a woman. He looked down at Marty and enjoyed the feeling of total dominance. Under Harry's 350-pound body Marty was trapped, motionless. Harry raised the large Bowie knife and turned his head to look directly back into Nancy's eyes. Nancy locked eyes with Harry again. She knew what was next. The sick bastard was going to do it.

Before she could scream a command at Harry he plunged his large knife deep into Marty's chest. Nancy recoiled in horror.

The knife was so violently driven into Marty's chest that Nancy was sure it went completely through him. There was no way Marty could have survived that. Harry was between Nancy and the kitchen. Nancy sprang forward and raced behind Harry toward the kitchen. She had to get her gun. Without the gun she would not stand a chance against the enormous Harry Rivers. She had to jump over Harry's legs to get to the kitchen as he sat on his knees straddled over Marty. She raced behind him to get to the kitchen and Harry swung back wildly to grab her, but he missed. He turned back in the other direction as she raced behind him towards the kitchen. When he reached for her legs, he successfully grabbed her right foot and flipped it upwards. Nancy fell hard on the floor. Her face took the brunt of the fall. She did not pause, though. She scrambled on hands and knees towards the kitchen. Harry lunged sideways and grabbed her ankle. His strength allowed him to hold her in place as he moved over Marty's dead body toward Nancy.

Nancy knew the trouble she was in but did not panic. She rolled to her side and kicked Harry in the face with her free foot. It was a strong kick with the heel of her foot striking Harry in the mouth. Nancy's strength was enough to make Harry shake his head and grab his jaw. Blood began to pour out of Harry's mouth into his hands. Nancy had kicked out Harry's front two teeth and cut his tongue severely.

Harry realized the damage she had done to him and became enraged. Nancy yanked her feet away from Harry and scrambled towards the kitchen. Harry screamed "You Bitch!" And stood up. Just as Nancy got to the kitchen table with her bag, Harry pounced on her. Nancy was a strong woman, but Harry's size was just too much. They fell to the floor with Harry on top, looking down at her back. Harry grabbed each hand and pinned her hands behind her back as he held her down. She was face down on the linoleum floor with Harry's blood dripping on her back. He considered killing her right there but remembered he still needed his keys. She knew where they were.

Harry saw an extension cord under the kitchen table, he yanked it out of the wall, which made the clock on the table crash against the wall and break into pieces. Harry used the extension cord to tie Nancy's Hands behind her and then extended it down to her ankles and wrapped them together. Nancy was hog-tied. He tied it tight enough to hurt her wrists and render her immobile. Nancy laid on the floor helpless and watched Harry stand up, with blood continuing to spill out of his mouth and down the front of his tight t-shirt.

She smiled, knowing that she had delivered the damage to his bloody mouth. She may die, she thought, but not without a fight.

"I hope you choke to death on your own blood," Nancy growled at him. "You fat, toothless bastard."

"You're gonna pay for that comment. Or maybe, I'll make your friend pay." Harry smiled at her and walked into the living room. Nancy could hear some thuds, and then she heard Hornsby groan. The groan became a howl in pain, and she heard Harry tell him to shut up.

Harry came back into the kitchen and, without any consideration for her pain, he yanked the cord he hog tied her up with, causing severe pain to her entire body. He used his Bowie knife and cut the cord, freeing her feet from her wrists, then he wrapped the excess cord around her wrists.

He yanked her up to her feet, and drug Nancy into the living room and unceremoniously threw her into the Lazy Boy chair across from the couch. Nancy sat across from Hornsby who was on the sofa. His hands were tied in front of him with another electric cord. Hornsby's feet appeared to be free, however. His face looked like a boxer's that had just woken up from a big knockout punch. Marty was between them, dead on the floor.

Harry stood over Marty's body. The blood coming out of Harry's mouth had slowed to a trickle. He held a kitchen towel to his mouth to stop the blood.

He looked at Nancy and said, "Where are my keys?"

Nancy glared back at him in silence.

"Look you stupid bitch, you have ten seconds to give me my keys."

"What keys? And what happened to your mouth? You've lost that lovely smile. Better get to a dentist, you fucking dipshit." Nancy calculated she was probably going to die anyway; she might as well enjoy her last few minutes alive by taunting the colossal asshole.

Harry waved his Bowie Knife between Nancy and Hornsby. Then, he pointed it at Hornsby.

"Your bad behavior will be paid for by this guy." Harry threatened Nancy.

"Oh yeah, well, if I ever get in your house your toothbrush is going straight up my ass." Nancy grinned.

"My house…you... shut up! This guy is gonna die if I don't get my keys!" Harry was screaming now and close to losing control.

"Ehh, I didn't like him anyway." Nancy glared back at Harry.

"Funny girl," Harry grumbled. "You think you are so funny, well, laugh at this." Harry took the large knife and moved to Hornsby on the couch. He placed a knee across Hornsby's legs to hold him in place on the couch.

Harry looked at Nancy with an evil grin. His eyes told the whole story. He was crazy and willing to do anything to get his keys.

"This is your last chance. I'm going to cut off an ear if you don't tell me where my keys are." Harry held the knife in front of Hornsby's face as he spoke to Nancy.

"One of his ears or one of yours?" Nancy asked with a smirk.

Harry hated the fact that he couldn't rattle Nancy. He had never met a woman like this.

"You really don't like this guy much," Harry said.

"I'm not in love with him if that's what you mean."

"I'm not in love with him," Harry imitated Nancy with a high-pitched, stupid female voice.

"Hey, Einstein, to be a smart ass, the first step is to be smart. You seem to have missed that part."

131

Harry glared at Nancy for a moment, not knowing how to respond. What woman talks like this? She needed to be terrorized.

Harry gave up bickering with Nancy. He used his free hand to pull Hornsby's right ear away from his head. Hornsby groaned from the pain of his ear being yanked away. Then, without any hesitation, he used the large knife to slice the ear off Hornsby's head. Hornsby howled in pain. His blood ran down his side onto the couch.

Harry frisbee tossed Hornsby's bloody ear onto Nancy's lap.

"You wanna keep on being funny?" Harry said in a triumphant tone. "Where are my keys?"

"You dipshit, your keys are in your truck." Nancy cooly said.

"I already looked." Harry grabbed Hornsby's other ear.

"Wait, Wait, Wait!" Nancy yelled.

"Wait for what?"

"Your keys were thrown under the seat of your truck. Did you look there?" Nancy lied.

"No," Harry admitted.

"I saw Marty throw them under your seat."

"If you are lying to me…"

"You'll cut off one of your ears?" Nancy interrupted again.

"No. I will kill both of you. Slowly."

Nancy did not doubt him.

"Go look." Nancy challenged him.

Harry yanked Hornsby by his left arm. "Let's go, Marty." He said.

"That's not Marty. You killed Marty."

"Then who is this?"

"That's… Walter, he's a neighbor. He doesn't know where your keys are because he didn't see Marty throw them under the seat. He wasn't even here then." Nancy lied, hoping to save Hornsby's life.

"This is Walter?" Harry asked.

"Yeah."

"Then who is Hornsby?"

Nancy thought she had been caught in a lie. She prepared for a beating, or witnessing Hornsby lose another ear. But when she looked at Harry, she could tell he was baffled. His eyes showed confusion now. 'The eyes don't lie.' She remembered from her police training.

"Hornsby left a few minutes ago." Nancy lied and hoped for the best.

"Then who is this?" Harry was totally confused now.

"I told you. He is a neighbor. Walter." Nancy ran out of ideas, so she just continued the first idea she had.

"Then where is Hornsby?"

"Holy Christ, you idiot, he left. You want to ask me a couple more times to be sure?" Nancy figured she would be more believable if she kept up her attitude.

"So, Hornsby left?" Harry was just starting to put the pieces together.

"He left earlier, about ten minutes before you came in the back door. Hornsby left through the front door."

Harry remembered seeing something by the cars earlier. He was sure he had seen someone move on the other side of the car, but he couldn't find him. He remembered thinking he should look under the vehicles. He didn't do it. He quickly convinced himself he should have looked under the cars when he considered it earlier. Harry shook his head in disgust. It was Hornsby he had seen. He should have looked under the car. Harry felt like kicking himself. Hornsby could be miles down the road by now, and he was probably getting help. Harry had to hurry.

Harry looked at Walter and determined he was in no shape to run anywhere. Nancy was tied up and immobile. So, Harry decided to go to his truck alone and look under the seat.

"I'll be back. If you or Walter move, I'll…."

"I know, I know, kill us both nice and slow." Nancy interrupted.

Harry couldn't believe the nerve of this woman. He just couldn't scare her. He would make her pay for her arrogance after he retrieved his keys.

Harry stood up and moved towards the kitchen. Nancy heard the back screen door creak open loudly and then slam closed.

Nancy whispered loudly, "Hornsby! Come here and untie me!"

Hornsby stood up wobbly and crossed the small living room. He wobbled like he was concussed and still foggy. His hands were tied in front of him. He fumbled getting Nancy's cord untied. He couldn't do it with his own hands tied.

"C'mon, Hornsby we gotta move! Faster!" Nancy demanded.

Hornsby groaned in pain and dribbled blood across Nancy's lap.

Then the front door opened. A pale white man entered the room.

Nancy and Hornsby stared at him like they were looking at a ghost. The young man went to work on Nancy's cord and quickly untied her. Then he started on Hornsby's cord.

The phone in Marty's pocket rang three times, then went silent.

Heston goes back to the Cabin

"We have to go back to the cabin. I think there's trouble," Heston said.

"You are right, Heston. It is a mathematical probability that Harry has returned to get his truck. He may have killed your friends." Justice said with the confidence of a college professor.

"I'm in," Gene said

"Me too," Peggy chimed in.

"Me too," Noah wanted to be part of the team. His life had become empty until Justice showed up. He needed this.

Heston was proud of his friends. It was dark and late, and they would have to travel at least 45 minutes to get to the cabin. Then there would be danger. Danger from a large psychotic killer. But his friends didn't hesitate. Heston quietly committed his loyalty to them, as he knew they were committed to him.

"Ok, let's get going. But this time, let's bring some extra firepower. Grab your Mossberg and your AR 15. Along with your sidearms. That should do it." Heston said.

Peggy went to the gun safe and returned with both weapons. She also had her Glock strapped to her thigh and tossed Gene his Glock in its holster.

"I need to buy a gun," Noah said.

"Look in the end table next to the couch. There is a .22 automatic in a holster. You can carry that." Gene offered Noah.

"OK, thanks!" Noah grabbed the weapon with a smile. Now, he felt like part of the team. He took off his belt with his Texas buckle and threaded the holster with it.

The group along with the three dogs, climbed in the truck.

Justice jumped in the back of the truck with Trump and Reagan. Noah liked that even though Justice was a special dog, he still considered himself a dog.

After a 45-minute drive, they pulled into the dark driveway by the cabin. Heston parked behind the two sedans that were side by side in the gravel driveway. The lights were on inside the cabin.

They had called Marty and Hornsby a few times on the road to the cabin with no answer.

Heston called his Deputy friend Jesus Montoya out of the New Braunfels Sheriff's station. Deputy Jesus agreed to meet them at the cabin. He hadn't arrived yet.

The team of four humans and three dogs unloaded from the truck and approached the cabin. It was still and quiet. Nighttime had fully set in, and the Milky Way galaxy was visible above them.

Heston whispered, "I'll go around back to catch Harry if he runs out the back. Give me 1 minute before you make entry." Gene nodded silently to Heston, with Peggy and Noah standing behind him.

Gene carried the Mossberg with both hands. Peggy carried the AR 15 while Noah had his .22 in his right hand.

"Hey, Noah, why don't you holster that gun until you need it." Peggy whispered. She noticed he was not careful with it because of inexperience. She didn't want to be the recipient of friendly fire.

"OK," Noah agreeably said. He didn't like holding it anyway.

After a minute, Gene proceeded up the steps to the cabin and opened the front door. He heard the squeak of the back screen door to the cabin open as he entered the living room.

"Oh crap," Gene said as he witnessed the scene.

"What do you have?" Peggy asked, standing behind him on the porch.

"C'mon in and see for yourself," Gene said.

Peggy and Noah entered behind Gene.

They all stared at Marty Shott lying dead on the floor. They could see a large wound in the center of his chest. His shirt was bloody with a large gash in the center. His eyes were open and staring blankly at the ceiling.

"Why isn't there more blood?" Noah asked. The wound in Marty's chest was bloody, but it did not pool on the floor.

"The knife went into his heart killing him instantly. Dead people don't bleed." Heston said as he surveyed the scene from the kitchen.

"There is more blood on the couch," Peggy said.

"There is blood on the kitchen floor too as well as a trail into the kitchen," Heston said as he looked around.

"Looks like a fight of epic proportions," Gene said as he surveyed the damage.

Justice moved into the living room around Noah's legs. He sniffed the blood on Marty's chest and on the floor leading to the kitchen. Then he looked up at Heston.

"I can tell you there is blood from four people here." Justice informed them. His sense of smell was more developed than a typical dog due to his computer enhancements. His value from being able to speak and explain what he smelled was evident to the group.

"This was a big fight." Heston nodded. "Why don't you and Trump and Reagan check the property and find out if anyone is nearby."

"We are on it," Justice said. He looked at Trump and Reagan and instantly the three dogs were on the same wavelength. They sprinted out the front door and went off in three different directions.

"I can see why the military would be interested in that dog," Heston said with appreciation.

"What are we going to do?" Noah wondered.

"Wait for the dogs to get back. Let's search through the cabin for now." Heston said.

As they turned around towards the two bedrooms, three small balls of light floated through the front door. They stared at the balls of light for a moment, then they looked at each other. The small lights took their human forms.

Heston smiled at Cole.

"Cole, why are you here, buddy?" Heston asked his small ghostly friend.

"There is a lot you need to know, Mr. Heston."

"Do you know what happened here?" Heston asked.

"Yes, we saw everything."

"Well, spit it out Cole," Heston said.

"First, there is a large blond man; his name is Harry, he is evil. He killed that guy on the floor. The guy on the floor is named Marty." Cole paused for a moment to gather his thoughts. "Harry is searching for the keys to his truck so he can escape."

"We're after Harry," Heston told Cole.

"Good. Ok. Next, there is another man that is as white as we are." Cole said, meaning himself and White Rabbit and Crazy Crow. "He is a very good man." He was outside when the fight happened.

"Harry threatened to kill Nancy and Hornsby if she didn't tell him where his keys were. The woman named Nancy convinced

Harry that his truck keys were in his truck under the driver's seat. When he left the cabin to look under his truck seat, they began to untie themselves."

"Where are the keys?"

"They are under the couch," Cole told them.

Gene reached his hand under the couch and found the keys. "Yep, I got them."

"So, Nancy lied to Harry," Peggy said.

"Yes, it was brilliant because it bought her the time to escape," Cole said.

"Brave move. She knew Harry would kill her when he got his keys; she figured she had nothing to lose." Peggy said.

"After Harry went out the back door, Johnny entered the cabin through the front door. He untied and led them to safety before Harry returned. Johnny rescued the man and the woman. He told them his name was Johnny, and they were going to be killed by the large blond man named Harry."

"Where are they now?"

"Just as Johnny finished uniting Nancy and started uniting Hornsby, they heard Harry open the cabin door from the kitchen. They escaped out the front door just as Harry entered the kitchen. They ran into the forest with Harry chasing after them. He has a large knife, but he does not have a gun."

"Nancy and Hornsby should have guns." Heston said.

"They do not have their guns with them." Cole said.

"Their guns must be here in the cabin." Heston said.

Justice, Trump and Reagan entered the cabin through the entry.

"They have run into the forest." Justice informed Heston and the group. "There are some trails that lead away into the deep forest. It appears Harry is chasing three people."

"Can you find them?" Heston asked.

"Of course we can," Justice said with a sassy tone. "Don't insult us."

Trump and Reagan sat behind Justice. He was now their leader. Heston noticed and wasn't sure that he liked it.

"OK, Let's go," Heston said.

Immediately the three dogs spun around and rushed through the front door.

Johnny Leads Them to Safety

Johnny led the group through the thick forest towards safety. He knew they could outrun Harry, but the concussed Hornsby was slowing them down.

The area of the forest they were in was visited by very few people due to its remote isolation. Only poachers and outlaws traveled through this area.

The forest was very dark due to the small crescent shaped moon. The Milky Way galaxy was almost as bright as the moon.

"Do you know where we are?" Nancy asked Johnny.

"Not really." Johnny stopped, allowing Hornsby to catch his breath and recover a bit.

Nancy and Hornsby looked around. The small trail was clear and easy to follow. It must have been used by hunters as well as by game.

Then they heard it—heavy thuds and snapping branches. The sounds were unmistakably Harry. He was closer to them than they thought.

"We have to go," Johnny said.

"I'm surprised he's close to us," Nancy said. She realized Harry may be in better shape than she gave him credit for.

The three quickly moved up the trail.

In front of them was a clearing. There was an unusual mat of branches and vines covering a large area in the clearing. Nancy thought it looked like a rest stop for hunters, although she had never seen anything like it. Johnny immediately stopped and stared at it. He recognized it from his days in Africa.

Hornsby marched passed by Johnny and Nancy.

"C'mon guys Harry is right behind us," Hornsby said.

"Be careful Hornsby" Johnny said. "Don't step on that mat of branches and vines."

After they heard Harry behind them Hornsby had a newfound energy in him. It was fear. He was terrified by the thought of seeing Harry again.

Hornsby didn't listen and continued to march up the trail towards the patch of vines and branches ahead.

"I think it is a dead drop!" Johnny yelled at Hornsby.

"What's a dead drop?" Hornsby asked, but didn't slow down.

Nancy and Johnny stood still watching as Hornsby marched ahead on to the carpet of vines. Then he disappeared downwards. A second later there was a loud thud.

"I knew it" Johnny said.

"What the heck just happened?" Nancy whispered loudly.

"In Africa we called them dead drops. Poachers use them in areas to catch game. When they catch game in the dead drop, they can easily shoot it and pull it out. It is illegal, but poachers don't care about laws."

"Our criminals don't pay attention to laws here either," Nancy said as she hurried towards Hornsby.

The two ran to the side of the large hole in the ground. It was quiet.

"Hornsby?" Nancy whispered loudly.

Nothing answered.

Behind them they could hear Harry thudding up the trail.

"Maybe we can use this to catch Harry," Nancy said with a sudden tactical thought.

"It may work." Johnny agreed. "But he will fall on Hornsby."

"Yeah, well, Hornsby should have stopped when you told him to," Nancy said showing her contempt for Hornsby.

"Ok," Johnny said with raised eyebrows. He told himself quietly not to cross this woman.

"If we can cover this up, Harry is too stupid to know what it is, he will fall in and never get out," Nancy whispered.

"Quick grab those branches and vines." Johnny pointed.

In a minute they had covered the hole created by Hornsby. Then Nancy heard something that made her freeze. Hornsby groaned loudly.

Johnny heard it too.

They looked at each other, then they heard Harry thudding up the trail who sounded to be only a few yards away.

"That big idiot has better endurance than I gave him credit for," Nancy whispered.

"Let's hide," Johnny whispered back to her.

They both moved under the canopy of the forest and hid behind a tree on the other side of the dead drop from Harry.

Hornsby continued to groan in pain.

"Be quiet Hornsby!" Nancy whispered. Then she realized if 350 pounds of Harry Rivers came crashing down on Hornsby, he may have groaned his last groan. It was too late to do anything but wait. Fate and Charles Darwin were going to take care of Hornsby now.

Through the dimly lit clearing, Nancy and Johnny watched as Harry came into view. Harry did the same thing they did when he saw the clearing. He stopped and caught his breath. Nancy remained still hoping Harry would fall for the trap like Hornsby did and disappear into the dead drop.

Harry slowly walked forward looking side to side. He was on high alert looking for anything out of place. Harry's instincts told him to use caution. As he approached the dead drop, Hornsby moaned loudly.

"Crap" Nancy whispered softly.

Harry approached the dead drop looking at the vines and branches. He knew they were out of place and suspicious. A groan came from beneath them.

"We should run," Nancy whispered to Johnny.

"Wait" Johnny said, his superb hearing heard something new.

"We gotta go," Nancy whispered excitedly.

"I hear dogs," Johnny whispered.

"Dogs?"

"Yes, they are coming our way with people following them."

Nancy immediately knew what it was. It was Heston!

"It's Heston Hand that beautiful, wonderful man!" Nancy whispered excitedly to Johnny. Nancy knew Heston and his team were coming for them! She was surprised because Heston said he wasn't coming back until sunrise tomorrow. Sunrise was still hours away. Now, Nancy knew why the Sheriff appreciated Heston more than Hornsby.

Harry looked over his shoulder, he heard the dogs too.

Harry circled around the dead drop. His instincts warned him it was a trap. He slowly walked into the forest straight towards Nancy. He had the same thought she had, to hide and watch to see if the dead drop would work on what was following him.

He approached the tree that hid Nancy, but he had no idea she was there. Nancy crouched as low as she could to attempt invisibility. When Harry rounded the giant tree, he found himself standing directly over Nancy.

He looked down at her with surprise.

"What the…. I'm gonna…" Harry was furious.

"I know, I know, kill me slowly." Nancy interrupted, looking up at him.

Harry took his giant fist and punched Nancy in the top of her head. She went limp from the force of the large man. Harry began to rain punches down on her with the fury that had been built up from her disrespect. Over and over Harry punched Nancy in the head and body. She covered up with her arms as her training had taught her, but it was of no help. She became unconscious in mere seconds. Harry grabbed her by the hair and lifted her upwards to choke the life out of her. Then he felt someone jump on his back. A white arm reached around Harry's neck and under his chin placing him in a choke hold. Harry was so surprised by the attack he did not defend it well. He dropped Nancy and reached around to grab his attacker. In seconds he felt his throat tighten and he lost his airway. Harry closed his eyes and tried to remove the arm from around his neck. He couldn't budge it. Whoever was on his back was very strong. Harry turned side to side twisting and pulling frantically. He slammed backwards into the tree attempting to crush whoever was on his back. It didn't have an effect. Then he had an idea. Using the last of his energy, just before he lost consciousness, he bent his knees and flipped backward onto his back. Johnny was crushed by the 350 pounds of Harry.

Final Act

Justice led the dogs racing toward Harry. Heston and his human team tried to keep up but soon were well behind the dogs. When the dogs picked up a strong scent of Harry, Trump and Reagan began their trained howling letting their master know they were hot on the trail and close to their prey. Justice found their howling annoying and ill advised. In Justice's mind it warned Harry that they were close. But Justice ignored them and ran as fast as he could. He knew Harry intended to kill the other humans he was after. Justice would not let that happen.

The speed Justice possessed as a German Shepherd far exceeded the speed of a Bluetick hound. In a matter of minutes, he was far ahead of them. Justice ran as fast as he could, weaving through the dark trails and jumping the occasional felled tree. Justice had nighttime vision that exceeded other dogs and all humans. The low light environment did not slow Justice down at all.

Justice approached the clearing and heard the sounds of a fight. When he arrived at the edge of the clearing, he saw the dead drop and knew immediately what it was. On the other side of the dead drop, Justice saw Harry with Johnny on his back; Johnny still had Harry in a choke hold. Harry swung Johnny back and forth, then slammed him against the tree. Johnny did not release the rear naked choke he had firmly placed under Harry's chin. Justice could see Harry's face turning red as a tomato and knew he should pass out in moments. But then something happened that surprised Justice. Harry flipped backward and landed on his back. Johnny was instantly crushed by the huge man and let out a loud groan as Harry landed on top of him. Johnny released his grip, and for a moment it looked like Johnny was unconscious.

Harry stood up and towered over Johnny, who remained motionless. Harry kicked Johnny twice in the side with loud thuds. As Harry appeared to wind up with a massive punch intended for Johnny, Justice saw Nancy stand up behind Harry. Harry had no idea she was there. The woman jumped on Harry's back. Instead of choking him, she reached around his head and gouged his eyes with her thumbs. Harry screamed in pain. He stumbled around trying to remove her arms. He lurched towards the dead drop.

Justice watched as the brave woman did her very best to ride on Harry's back and gouge his eyes out. Harry spun in circles trying his best to remove her, to no avail. She was a wildly possessed woman intent on enucleating the larger man.

Heston, Gene, Peggy and Noah ran up the trail to Justice and watched in horror as Nancy rode on Harry's back with her legs and arms wrapped around him, her thumbs deep into each of Harry's eyes. Blood began to stream down Harry's face, and he screamed in agony. He staggared in circles towards the dead drop. As Harry's screams began to soften and become wails and groans, Nancy started her own wild, vicious shriek. Her shrieking was out of a refusal to give up. It was a primal, loud sound like nothing they had ever heard before. Harry and Nancy circled to the dead drop, then in an instant, they disappeared downwards.

"What just happened?" Peggy yelled.

"They just disappeared." Gene said.

"It's a dead drop," Justice said. "If it is a typical dead drop, it will be about ten feet deep."

The team trotted to the dead drop and peered downwards into the deep hole. It was so dark in the depths of the hole that only Justice, with his superior vision, could see what was happening.

Nancy was on top of Harry who was motionless. Hornsby was below them both. His neck was broken. Justice watched as Nancy grabbed Harry by the jaw with her right hand and the top of his head with her left hand. She had mounted him from behind, sitting as erect as she could. Justice immediately recognized what she was preparing to do. It was straight out of Special Forces training. She was going to snap his neck.

"Nancy, don't do it!" Justice yelled into the darkness.

Nancy kept her grip but looked upwards to the rim of the hole she had just fallen into. She could see Justice and Heston looking down on her as she prepared to kill Harry.

"This guy killed Marty." She said with a look of defiance. Then she violently pulled upwards with her right hand and pushed downwards on his head with her left hand. This twisted Harry's neck fiercely and was designed as a kill maneuver. Justice looked away and moved away from the hole.

"What just happened?" Heston asked Justice.

"I think you know," Justice said.

"I don't, tell me," Noah asked.

"She just cheated me out of my revenge." Justice said.

"What?"

"I wanted to kill that man. She cheated me out of it." Justice growled in disappointment.

Heston, Gene and Peggy looked at each other. Immediately they knew what had happened, despite their eyes being unable to see it through the darkness.

Cole stood next to Heston.

"Is he dead?" Cole asked

"Oh yeah, I think he's dead," Heston replied, despite not being able to see it for himself.

"Nancy killed him?" Cole asked.

"Nancy cheated Justice by doing it," Peggy said.

"Well, I think our story will be that he broke his neck in the fall," Heston said as he looked at the others.

The other three nodded in agreement.

"That's my story," Gene said.

"It's a good story," Peggy agreed.

"I agree," Noah said. Now he was part of the team. They shared a secret.

Heston looked at Justice, who stared back at Heston with a disappointment clearly visible.

"I agree with Peggy. Nancy just cheated Justice out of his revenge," Heston said. It was then that he realized Justice wanted to kill Harry. Heston filed that thought away with the knowledge of Justice's capabilities. Justice wasn't just brilliant. He was deadly.

"You can have the next one, Justice," Heston said.

"There may not be another," Justice replied.

"Based on my short experience with this group, there will be other opportunities for you," Noah said.

"I'll have to stay out of Duralink for that to happen."

"Buddy, you are not returning to Duralink," Heston assured Justice. "You mean way too much to Noah and us. You are part of us now."

Justice took some pleasure in what Heston said. It was nice to feel appreciated and part of a team. But he knew that Duralink would not stop until they found him. He also knew that Nancy was part of the team hired to find him. They would have to convince Nancy not to return Justice to Duralink.

"Let's get Nancy out of there," Heston said. They had to get her out of the dead drop.

They looked for a long branch that they could use to reach Nancy and pull her up.

In minutes they had one. Heston laid on his stomach and lowered the branch down to Nancy, who stood on Harry's back. She was quickly able to reach the branch and grab it. She held on tight as Heston pulled her out of the dirt pit. Her feet found holes that had been dug in the side wall of the pit. Someone had dug them to make climbing out of the pit possible. In a few short minutes she was standing on the side of the dead drop with Heston and his team.

"There're holes on the wall of the pit that someone dug," Nancy told Heston as she brushed herself off. "They were good footholds."

"So, what happened? I mean before Harry broke his neck in the fall." Heston indicated to Nancy the 'Broke his neck in the fall' was the best story going forward.

"First, the albino saved my life," Nancy said and pointed towards the tree where Harry almost beat her to death.

They looked and saw Johnny on the ground. They rushed over to find Johnny lying unconscious. Nancy knelt next to Johnny and felt for a pulse.

"He is alive, thank God," Nancy said.

She licked her index finger and held it under his nose. She could tell he was breathing.

"This guy jumped on Harry's back as he was about to kill me. If he didn't, I would be dead. I'm certain of it." Nancy said with obvious gratitude.

They sat Johnny up against the tree. In moments he regained consciousness. He was surprised to see the group of people looking at him.

"Hi, Nancy," Johnny said like he just woke up.

"Hi Johnny, we are glad to see you awake." Nancy smiled gratefully at him.

"What happened?" Johnny asked, rubbing his head.

"Well, you saved my life and almost lost yours in the process."

"I don't remember." Johnny continued to rub his head.

"This is Heston, Gene, Peggy and Noah. They were hunting for Harry too."

"Where is Harry?" Johnny asked.

"He is still in the dead drop."

"Can he get out?" Johnny asked.

"I doubt it. He is dead."

"Oh. What about Hornsby?"

"Hornsby didn't make it. Harry fell on him."

Johnny was silent for a moment and wiped his eyes.

"Let's get back to the cabin and call for help getting Harry and Hornsby out of the dead drop." Heston said.

They all stood up.

Justice couldn't let this opportunity pass. He felt like he needed to tell Nancy who he was. He walked in front of the group before they could leave. Justice stood in front of Nancy. Everyone stopped.

"Nancy, I'm Justice." Justice looked at Nancy. He figured it was best to get it out in the open.

Nancy was stunned into silence. She couldn't believe he could speak and that he would admit his identity to her.

"Holy sweet cows in heaven. Now I know why Duralink is so excited to get you back," Nancy said, staring at Justice incredulously.

"Yeah, about that, Nancy. Heston said. "We want to keep Justice. And we hope you will help us."

"Darlin', they paid me a butt-load of money to find him and bring him back."

"How much is a butt-load, Nancy?" Noah asked.

Nancy looked at Noah and paused. She wasn't sure it was ethical to answer, and she really didn't want to divulge that kind of information.

"The reason I ask, Nancy, is not to be nosey." Noah smiled at her "I... have a... to use your terminology 'Butt Load' of money." Noah smiled at her and continued, "I'm not bragging. But I'm rich. I just want you to know that Justice will have a better life with me than living as a laboratory specimen. I will double what Duralink offered you."

"They offered me $50,000.00. They paid me half up front." Nancy looked at Noah and told him the truth.

"Can you tell them it looks like he made it out of the state or something? Anything that can get you off the hook for finding him?" Heston asked. "We will back it up and get him buried somewhere nobody will ever find him."

Nancy thought about it. It was a dilemma.

"I don't know. That's a tall order. I like you guys, and I'd like to help. But... I have a reputation. Plus, Duralink stands to be a good future customer. So, I don't think…" Nancy paused and looked at Heston. She remembered the feeling of gratitude she had when she realized Heston had arrived early and was in pursuit with his dogs. Could she let them keep Justice? It was a risk…

"You bitch!" Came a scream from the darkness behind them.

The group turned around.

They were all stunned to see Harry standing next to the dead drop. His blond hair stood uncombed straight up and he was disheveled. He looked like Boris Johnson after a night of binge drinking and fighting. His face and shirt were bloody and filthy.

"I'm gonna kill all of you!" Harry yelled and started towards them.

In a flash, Justice charged Harry with his teeth on full display. Justice sounded like an attack dog gone wild. Noah was astonished that Justice could be so dangerous and vicious. Justice dove for Harry's throat. Harry was not dissuaded by Justice's ferocity and attacked Justice with the same fierceness. Justice landed on Harry's chest and head, ripping at his neck and face. Harry beat on Justice's back and sides to no avail. Harry realized his strikes were not affecting Justice, so he wrapped his big arms around Justice and squeezed with all his might. Justice had a firm grip on Harry's throat with his sharp teeth, his teeth were deep into Harry's neck. Every time Justice twisted his head; Harry's wounds became larger. Blood pumped out of Harry's neck.

Heston watched and worried that Harry would break Justice's back.

Trump and Reagan attacked next. They recognized their newfound friend was in trouble and did what they could to help. Reagan bit into Harry's left thigh while Trump dug into Harry's crotch. The result was that Harry tripped backward and fell back into the dead drop.

Heston, Gene and Peggy yelled, "No!" In unison as they watched the three dogs and Harry fall back into the dead drop.

The group raced to the edge of the dead drop and looked downwards into the darkness. It was no use. It was too dark for them to see anything. The sounds coming upwards from the darkness were terrifying though. Justice was especially loud and sounded like he was making a meal out of Harry. Harry's cries soon died into nothing. Heston's dogs became silent after a minute of silence from Harry. Justice continued his fierce attack for a full minute after Harry and the other dogs were silent. Then Justice quieted down and silence permeated the dark hole in the ground.

"Justice?" Noah called down into the darkness.

Silence.

"Justice, can you hear us?" Heston called down.

"Yeah, I hear you." Came the tired reply.

"Are you guys OK?" Noah called down to the darkness.

"Well, Reagan, Trump and I are wonderful."

"Hang tight, I'm coming down for you," Heston yelled.

"Let's get that branch, Gene. You can help lower me down" Heston pointed at the branch they used earlier.

Heston held on to the end of the branch, Gene held the opposing end and Heston lowered himself into the darkness.

In ten minutes, Heston had passed Justice, Reagan and Trump up to Gene, who pulled them up and out of the dark hole. Next, Heston lifted up and out on the branch like Nancy had earlier.

The group sat on the ground for a few minutes catching their breaths and inspecting the dogs for any signs of injury.

Other than needing baths to wash the blood out of their fur, the three dogs were fine.

"So, is Harry dead this time?" Peggy asked.

Justice remained silent. He felt he didn't need to admit guilt about killing a person. He was already in enough trouble for escaping Duralink.

The group of humans stared at Justice, realizing he had a dimension to his personality they hadn't seen before. Their quiet stares demanded Justice say something.

"What do you think?" Justice said, finally.

Nobody said a word.

Nancy broke the silence.

"Let's get back to the cabin. There is cell phone service there. We can call for help."

The group hiked out of the forest. When they returned to the cabin, they saw Deputy Jesus Montoya sitting in his cruiser in front of the house.

As they walked up to the cabin, Deputy Jesus got out of his Sheriff's cruiser to meet them.

"You guys look like heck." Deputy Jesus said. "Did you find Harry?"

"You could say so." Heston said, "More accurately, I'd say he found us."

"Where is he?"

"He's at the bottom of an illegal dead drop, along with Detective Hornsby." Heston looked at the Deputy. "It's about three miles into the forest. Poachers must have set it up."

"Hornsby… is he dead?"

"Yeah, he either died in the fall or when Harry fell on him."

Deputy Jesus paused to let the information about Hornsby's death sink in.

154

"Looks like you found Justice, though. Not a bad night's work, Heston," Deputy Jesus nodded his approval.

"This is not Justice," Heston said. This is a guard dog that belongs to Noah. This dog is a beast. He is the reason Harry is in the dead drop."

"Not Justice? He looks exactly like the photos Duralink posted."

The group was silent.

Then Nancy spoke up.

"I thought so too. Then I inspected him and realized he is not Justice. I have a list of identification marks. They are not on this dog."

"How would you happen to have that list?" Deputy Jesus asked.

"I'm Nancy Webb. I'm a private detective. Duralink hired me to find Justice. I'm telling you this is not Justice."

Noah took a deep sigh of relief. Justice sat closer to Nancy and pressed up on her calf.

"Deputy Jesus, just to avoid any difficult situations, for the record, I'm going to say it was Trump and Reagan that attacked Harry and made him fall into the dead drop. His neck and face will be pretty torn up when his body is pulled up. Since I was hired to find Harry, I can't get in trouble for my dogs. Noah may not be offered the same amnesty."

Deputy Jesus took a moment to process what he was being told. He realized that the large German Shepherd standing in front of him had saved the lives of Heston's team. Heston's team was now defending the German Shepherd. Deputy Jesus deduced this dog was probably Justice.

"OK Heston, I see what's happening." Deputy Jesus said.

"Good, Thanks Jesus."

"So, what is this dog's name?"

The silence that followed Jesus' question confirmed his suspicions. This large dog was Justice.

"OK, well you folks take a few minutes to give this dog a new name." Jesus smiled. "I'm going to call this in on my radio. If I were Noah, I'd leave with my dog before more authorities get here."

"Good idea. I think we are all going to leave."

"Thor," Noah said.

"Pardon me?" Deputy Jesus said.

"This dog's name is Thor." Noah said.

"Great. Yeah, go with that." Deputy Jesus said with a smile.

"I'll stay and explain what I saw. Trump and Reagan will be the heroes of the story. You folks get while the gettin' is good," Nancy said.

"Thanks, Nancy" Noah said gratefully.

"Yes, Nancy. Thank you." Peggy said.

Heston and Gene nodded gratefully in agreement.

Noah moved toward Nancy and hugged her. She hugged him back and patted him on his back three times.

"Now get," Nancy said.

Heston, Gene, Peggy, Johnny and Noah climbed in the truck. All three dogs jumped in back for the ride back to Driftwood. The sunrise was moments away. This would be a good day.

When word got out about Johnny's part in assisting the Sheriff's department in apprehending Harry Rivers, as well as saving the life of a female private detective, job offers flowed in. Every business in Dripping Springs wanted to employ Johnny. A local attorney offered his services free of charge to help Johnny become an American citizen. Johnny Mobatu was in Texas to stay.

The End of Part 1

Part 2- Hunting Justice

This story is totally true, except for the parts I made up.

Cash Buck

Cash Buck was in trouble. His secret project had escaped, and Delon Husk was pissed off. They hired a private detective to find Harry and Justice, but they failed. They said Harry fled to Mexico or some other crazy place. Cash didn't believe a word of it, but he didn't care about Harry. He needed Justice. Cash couldn't afford to have Mr. Husk PO'd at him. He hadn't even met the man yet. He had to get Justice back. If Justice got into the hands of a foreign adversary, it would be a national disaster. Cash had to capture or terminate Justice before his career was terminated. The question was, how? How would he get the most intelligent animal on the planet back? He knew he wouldn't outsmart the dog. His best option now was Alpha, Beta and Charlie. He had another option, but it was probably too drastic. Be reasonable, Cash told himself. Try Alpha, Beta and Charlie first. Be smart. They were a team. Teams work better than solos.

Cash stood up from his chair in his isolated office deep in the bowels of Duralink Labs. He began his walk to the Animal

Sciences Lab. Division M. The Division M Lab was the secretive Military Division of the Animal Sciences Lab at Duralink.

He got to Betty's office after a ten-minute walk and let himself in. She was on the phone. As he stood in front of her desk, she motioned for him to sit down and held up her index finger, she would only be a minute more. He looked at the nameplate on her desk.

Betty Porkter-PhD.

Executive Director

Divisions L and M

Momentarily Betty finished her conversation and looked at Cash Buck.

"Good morning Mr. Buck, how can I help you?"

"Betty, we have a FUBAR debacle on our hands." Cash said.

"Yes sir, I am aware."

"You need to fix it."

"I need to fix it?" Betty was surprised at Cash's attitude.

"It's your fault Justice was in with the idiots in Division L." Division L was the Languages division of Animal Sciences.

"Justice was there because he had languages loaded into his brain. They were studying him to determine what effects the languages had on him." Betty couldn't understand being blamed for the problem.

"He should have been in Division M."

"Mr. Buck, he should have been more carefully monitored within that division. Division L."

"Whose fault was that?"

"The manager at Division L, Phil Ashow."

"You are the Vice President of Animal Sciences."

"Yes sir."

"Phil works for you."

"Yes sir."

"You should have ensured the monitoring and security of Justice."

"Yes Sir."

"I have a suggestion."

"Yes sir?"

"Let's release Alpha, Beta and Charlie. Let them handle it."

"Sir? They are not ready yet." Betty was shocked at the suggestion.

"How long have you been working on them, now?"

"18 months, give or take."

"They're ready."

"Sir, they will cause more trouble for you."

"Oh, Betty, it will not be my trouble. You are the one that will pay the price if they come up short." Cash Buck always remembered the military adage 'Shit Flows Down Hill'.

"Sir, respectfully, coming up short is not what I'm worried about."

"Then what?"

"Sir, they are programmed to kill. They are hunters. That is their purpose. They hunt and kill as a team. They are not designed for release into a friendly, civilian population. They are an assassination squad. They kill things and enjoy it." Dr. Porkter explained as reasonably as she could.

"You have two days to get them ready."

"It cannot be done in two days."

"Dr. Porkter, I am ordering you to get it done. Do you understand?"

Betty nodded.

Dr. Porkter was speechless. How could a man with Mr. Buck's experiences consider releasing these animals into an American urban or suburban environment? They were not ready. Programming was incomplete. They were in the testing phases. She didn't even know what test to perform next. They consistently failed their tests of discipline. Science is defined by experiments that fail, then are performed again and again, gleaning lessons along the way. Failure is how research advances. Yet, it is hardly mentioned in popular perspectives on science. All their tests so far were failures regarding *control* of the killing process. Failures, whether clear-cut or ambiguous, are fruitful in their own right. Mr. Buck did not understand this scientific statue of truth. Tests that fail in the lab are acceptable, valuable and manageable. Tests that fail in the field may have disastrous consequences. Especially with animals that are programmed to kill. More than kill. Destroy.

Alpha, Beta and Charlie were failing their tests of discipline in the lab. Aggressive behavior is acceptable only if discipline is programmed into the personality. Without discipline, Alpha, Beta, and Charlie were killing machines. They were no different than a bomb. Indiscriminately killing anyone nearby… when they're triggered.

Justice Guards Noah

Justice slept on the back porch. This was his favorite area in Noah's home. He had a view of the tree line behind Noah's house in Driftwood. Justice was confident of one thing: Duralink was looking for him. In his estimation, if anything was going to sneak up on him it would come from the tree line. Noah slept inside. Justice made a commitment that he would not let Noah be in danger from the hunters that would be dispatched to find Justice.

Justice knew the team at Duralink Labs because their bios were in the computer systems that were downloaded into his brain. He knew the Executive Vice President of Animal Testing was Cash Buck. Cash's background was in the military. Specifically, he was a Major in the Army. He served in Afghanistan with the 1st Armored Brigade Combat Team, 1st Air Cav out of Fort Hood, Texas.

Cash Buck had combat experience but was known to lead from the rear. To call Cash Buck a warrior would not be fair to warriors. He was more of a worrier.

Cash was separated after 20 years of army life and received his retirement with an honorable discharge. His written resume was strong and compelling. However, his reputation within the 1st Air Cav was not as stellar. The commander of 1st Air Cav, Major General John B. Richardson IV, was glad to see Cash Buck go. General Richardson couldn't stand officers that led from the rear. He wanted and demanded carnivores for his officer ranks. Cash Buck was a vegetarian.

Duralink hired Cash because of his strong military background and knowledge of warfare. Duralink needed Cash to assist them in understanding military principles and procedures. The tekkies and yuppies in Duralink had never even driven by a military installation much less been in one. They wouldn't know a soldier if they fell in a foxhole with one.

The profit motive was going to change the way Duralink looked the military and military applications. Being some of the most intelligent people on earth, they soon understood the military would pay ten times the amount a civilian company would pay for the exact same device, especially if that device gave them an advantage on the battlefield. Duralink secretly morphed into a military weapons company from its original design as a medical applications company.

Duralink Labs was known for merging computer science with physical science. Mr. Husk felt he could merge computers with animal brains to achieve "symbiosis" between the human brain and artificial intelligence. He wanted to develop a device that could be embedded in a person's brain, recording brain activity and potentially stimulating it. Mr. Husk envisioned curing diseases with the push of a button. He knew mapping the DNA with a supercomputer could result in enormous steps in our knowledge of everything regarding humans. Delon Husk's original focus was on curing diseases and improving the health of humans.

Duralink scientists learned how to connect the brain to computers through special bio-connections. Duralink would assemble over 100 patents on these specialized bio-connections. Soon, Duralink Labs learned that they could insert bio-connections into the brain, allowing brains to network with supercomputers. They learned that it could be done similarly to attaching an external hard drive to a computer with a USB cable. The current USB 3.0 ports were not advanced enough to handle the speed and volume of information that Duralink required. So, computer scientists at Duralink Labs developed their proprietary USB 9.0 connections and cables. They worked as easily as a standard USB 3.0 cable, but they were far more advanced and could satisfy Duralink Labs requirements—no need to insert an invasive device into the brains of subjects. Now they needed a USB 9.0 port.

Shortly after solving the connectivity issues, the scientists learned that not only could information be extracted from the brain, but it could also be inserted into the brain. This concept was discovered by accident, as a result of working with Justice the two-toned German Shepherd.

After Justice was disconnected from the computer, one of the scientists spoke in his native Hebrew to another Israeli scientist. They observed that Justice seemed to understand their communication. They gave him commands in Hebrew and he complied immediately. Then they tried other languages with similar success. Italian, Russian even the Chinese language was understood by Justice.

When they studied how this happened, they learned that the information network between a brain and a supercomputer is a two-way street. In fact, it is two-way superhighway. They discovered that Justice understood every major language known to man.

This was possible because of the two supercomputers that were developed by The Fujaku Corporation. The computer scientists at Fujaku developed a supercomputer that could process information at the rate of over 400 hundred quadrillion FLOPS. Flops is a term meaning "Floating Point Operations Per Second". This rate of speed set a world record for computer power and speed.

The only private entity in the world that could both afford to buy one of these computers and had a desire to own a Fugaku computer was Delon Husk. Mr. Husk bought two of them. His strategy revolved around redundancy being at the heart of security.

Fundamentally, everything known to man was on these computers. If mankind knew it, it was on these computers. And Husk's team learned how to 'dynamically upload' the new information that was developed every day.

Justice the dog had undergone an upload that included everything mankind knew at a static point in time.

Then they realized that speech therapy lessons were on the computer. They logically wondered if Justice could speak. This had not occurred to Justice until the scientists asked him if he could talk. When they asked him, Justice stared back at them.

Justice realized he could speak, although he quickly deduced he should not admit his ability to talk to the scientists. In his analysis, they would never let him leave if they knew he could talk. When Justice had time alone, he discovered he could speak fairly well.

He had trouble with "F" and "V" sounds due to his jaw and lips inability to move in ways that would create those sounds. With time and practice, he might overcome this problem.

Justice guarded Noah from the back porch every night. He knew he could sleep in the house, but he could get no rest in there. He had to stand guard. Despite Justice's huge knowledge base, he was still a dog. He was wired like a dog and had all the urges and desires of a dog—specifically, a German Shepherd. The experts say their defining attribute is their character: loyalty, courage, confidence, the ability to learn commands for many tasks, and the willingness to put their life on the line in defense of loved ones. Justice was the definition of a German Shepherd. He was foremost a guard dog.

When Justice witnessed Noah protect him from returning to Duralink Labs he decided Noah belonged to him. Noah may have felt like he adopted Justice, but the truth was that Justice took ownership of Noah. Noah belonged to Justice. For a German Shepherd that was a big deal. It meant Justice would defend and protect Noah with his life from now on. Nothing could separate them. Noah would always be under the watchful eye of Justice. Justice would evaluate every person that came close to Noah. If the new person (or animal) represented a threat in the estimation of Justice, Justice would take quick action. Harry Rivers was the recipient of that quick action. He would not live to tell about it.

Dr. Porkter Goes to Division L

Dr. Betty Porkter was stressed out after her conversation with Cash Buck. She had to quickly develop the discipline in Alpha, Beta and Charlie that they needed. If they had any organic discipline, she needed to tap into it. If they did not have any inherent discipline, she would have to program them with some. Could she do that? It had never been done before.

How would she do it? She had no good ideas.

She decided to call a subordinate named Dr. Yuri Nator. He was an Israeli scientist that specialized in computer applications for animal sciences. He was her brain trust in the animal sciences department, especially since Dr. Phil Ashow had been demoted after the escape of Justice.

Dr. Porkter walked down to Division L where Yuri was stationed. When she walked through the door, the room that had been full of laughing and conversation went silent.

All eyes went to Dr. Porkter, who rarely visited the lab.

"Yuri, can I have a minute?" Betty asked.

"Yes Ma'am"

"Yuri, we need to change course on Alpha, Beta and Charlie."

"Change course? They have not been transferred to our Lab for study."

"I know."

"How will Division L study animals that are in Division M?"

"They won't."

"I don't understand." Yuri was puzzled.

"You need to come to Division M with me. I will transfer you."

"OK. May I bring my team?"

"Not now. Maybe eventually."

"Since the disaster with Justice my team has been working to develop another dog like Justice." Yuri made his case to stay with his team in Division L.

"Can they manage without you for a while?" Betty asked.

"With Dr. Ashow gone, probably not and get anything accomplished."

Betty nodded her head, then looked at Yuri directly.

"Ok, then I will transfer Alpha, Beta and Charlie to Division L."

"What is it that needs to be done?" Yuri asked.

"I need you to program discipline into them."

"How?"

"That part is up to you. I need you to develop the methods and then implement them." Betty said.

"OK." Yuri pondered the issue and then said, "Self-discipline's definition is the ability to control yourself, the ability to make yourself work or behave in a particular way without needing external reminders or regulation to tell you to do it. The good news is that self-discipline is nurtured and not something most of us are innately born with, meaning that anyone can reach a certain level of self-discipline on their own."

"So, you can do it?"

"I have no idea."

"Yuri, your humility is not inspiring confidence."

"Well, just remember," The Israeli scientist smiled at Porkter. "What the world needs is more geniuses with humility. There are so few of us left." Yuri remained smiling.

Dr. Porkter stared at Yuri with a stone face. She wondered if he heard himself. Was he was joking? Her sense of humor had never quite developed.

"Ok Yuri, whatever you say. I will have Alpha, Beta and Charlie transferred here immediately."

Yuri wondered if she got his joke. Probably not, the woman was a '*Dag Qar*', a cold fish.

"Are they safe?" Yuri asked.

"Safe as in…?"

"Safe as in they won't eat us?"

"Oh, they won't eat you." Betty said.

"That's good. My wife wants me for dinner." Yuri tried again to flesh out her sense of humor. It didn't work.

"They may kill you." She said as she looked around the room.

"Seriously?" Yuri was alarmed now.

"Well, I don't recommend pissing them off."

Yuri looked at Dr. Porkter, wondering if she was joking. Probably not, he concluded.

Dr. Porkter smiled and turned to leave. She said over her shoulder, "They will be here within the hour."

As quickly as she came, she left.

Yuri looked at his team of three and wondered which one would be the first to get eaten.

Yuri worked closely with Dr. Anita Cox and Dr. Jenny Tayla. He hired their lab assistant, Bass Wooten, not long ago. All three were excellent with animals and brilliant in their fields. Bass was not a Ph.D. but had as much brain horsepower as anyone. He was incredibly talented in training animals to understand human commands and to respond correctly and precisely. Bass trained a Golden Retriever to climb a wooden fence, then walk on top of it all the way around the yard they were working in. He accomplished this training in less than an hour with the dog he had never met before. Nobody else had ever shown the talent with animals that Bass Wooten had. Yuri felt they were lucky to have him. Bass loved dogs more than any other animal. Including humans.

"Bass, you think we can do this?" Yuri looked at him and asked.

"Don't insult me, Yuri. Of course we can." Bass smiled at his boss. "You're not working with amateurs."

"Jenny, Anita, what do you think?" Yuri asked.

"Sounds interesting." Jenny said, trying to remain optimistic.

"We are being set up," Anita said

"Set up how?" Yuri asked.

"Set up to take the fall. Military Labs can't do it, so they ask us to? Does that sound right to you?"

"So– you are cynical."

"She's always cynical." Bass smiled.

"Hey, I wanted to be less cynical, but I knew that would never happen." Anita grinned.

"So, you are two out of three believing we can do it." Yuri said.

"And one out of three believing we will get eaten by the dogs." Anita chimed in.

"Oh, they won't eat you," Yuri repeated Dr. Porkter's words. He left out the 'they may kill you' part. He nervously smiled at all three of them.

"That nervous smile tells me there's more to this." Anita wasn't buying what Yuri was selling.

"There is that cynicism again," Yuri said.

They looked at each other in silence for a moment.

"Yeah, well OK then. Let's start planning how we may get this done." Bass said.

Just as Dr. Porkter promised after 60 minutes had passed, the Lab door opened and three scientists from Division M entered with three grey, black and brown colored large dogs.

The dogs appeared to be well mannered and walked nicely at the heel of each of the three scientists. Dr. Goff led the way into the lab.

"Hello Jack," Yuri said pleasantly. "This must be our new project." Yuri had been friends with Dr. Goff since joining Duralink two years ago.

"Morning Yuri, I have been told we are transferring these animals to your team."

"That's what I have been told also."

"You are welcome to them." Dr. Goff said, sounding happy to be rid of them.

"You sound relieved." Yuri said.

"I am."

"Why?"

"We can't control them."

"They look under control to me."

"We can't control them after they are triggered."

"Triggered?" Yuri asked.

"Yes. These dogs have been developed for the Military. We have successfully programmed two basic modes. We have been referring to these modes as 'Triggered' and 'Gentle'".

"They are in Gentle mode now." One of the other scientists from Division M said.

"How do you control which mode they are in?" Anita walked up and asked.

"That's been a part of the problem. We tried verbal commands. That didn't work out so well. So, we went to hand signals. That was even worse. That's when we tried shock collars."

"Shock Collars?" Bass asked, he didn't like shock collars. He felt they were too painful for the dogs.

"Yes."

"I notice they are not wearing shock collars now." Bass said.

"Nope."

"Why?"

"Because when they realized why the collars were for, they ripped them off each other. We had a scientist that retrieved the collars…."

"Had a scientist?" Anita interrupted.

"Yeah. That's right. He's not with us anymore."

"He quit?"

"Not really."

"Fired?"

"Not so much." Dr. Goff said.

"What then?"

"The dogs ate him. Well, most of him anyway." Dr. Goff said.

"No way!" Jenny exclaimed. Now she was worried.

"Way."

"They look so …. Pleasant."

"They are pleasant in 'gentle mode.'" Dr. Goff said.

"Dr. Porkter told me they wouldn't eat us." Yuri said.

"Yeah, she lies." Dr. Goff smiled.

"That's not great." Anita said.

"Would you have agreed to take them if she told you that they may eat you?"

"No."

"Then, there you have it."

Yuri stared at Jack for a moment, hoping he would say: "Just Joking" or something of the sort. But he didn't.

"Jack, how do they become triggered?" Yuri asked.

"So far, we know of four ways."

"OK. What are they?"

"First, verbal commands."

"What are those commands?"

"We cannot say them out loud."

"OK. Can you write them down?"

"Yes. Give me a pad and pen."

Yuri passed Dr. Goff a sharpie and a yellow legal tablet.

Dr. Goff wrote in large block letters. "Attack," "Kill," "Destroy."

"Any combination of these words will set them off." Dr. Goff said.

"What if someone says these words in another context besides a command?"

"It would be hazardous to their health." Dr. Goff said.

"Jack, seriously?" Yuri had serious reservation now.

"Seriously. Next, you have hand signals. We do not recommend these."

"You don't? Why is that?" Bass asked.

"They haven't been perfected. Accidents tend to happen."

"OK. I'm not gonna ask what kind of accidents."

"You don't need to ask by now, right?" Dr. Goff said.

"Yeah, right, I guess. What is another way to trigger them?" Yuri's regret was shining through.

"If they feel threatened, they will become triggered."

"What makes them feel threatened?"

"Well, the shock collars made them feel threatened. Again, we do not recommend these."

"OK, what else?"

"A gun, knife or bad intent by another animal."

"Bad intent?"

"Yeah. We learned that one the hard way."

"How? Do I want to know?"

"Yeah, you need to know. We had a fully grown cougar named Boris in our Lab. We had high hopes for him. As a military weapon, he had many advantages and strengths."

"Had?"

"Yes. Had."

"OK. Had. Again?" Yuri rolled his eyes. "And?"

"Boris the cougar took one look at the dogs and showed his teeth. Then he growled a warning to stay back."

"Ok, as cougars are known to do around dogs. So, he growled a warning."

"Yes. Then the three dogs attacked in unison. They were naturally coordinated in their assault. They simultaneously hit the much stronger cougar from the front and both sides."

"A classic pincer movement"

"Yes, and that allowed his only escape to the rear. When Boris spun around to escape...."

"Go on."

"Within 30 seconds, Boris was not with us any longer."

"Dead?"

"Dead is an understatement. Eviscerated is a better term. It's more accurate, anyway. They were able to take his back and head. They ripped through him quickly."

"Then what happened?"

"They ate him."

"Ate him?"

"Well, most of him."

Yuri shook his head.

"They look so…. Nice." Bass said, shaking his head.

"Yeah, we get that a lot. But they are not." Dr. Goff said.

"What is the fourth way to trigger them?"

"Target acquisition. When they find their target, they are programed to destroy their targets immediately. No taking prisoners."

"Why in the world did you guys program these animals to be so…. Uncontrollable?"

"We didn't realize we did until it was too late."

"Have you considered…" Yuri was going to mention destroying the animals.

"Don't say it! Do not say anything they may feel is a threat." Dr. Goff knew where Yuri was going with his question.

"We believe they understand us perfectly. If we were to say something that could be construed as a threat to them, we feel certain they would attack. So far, that is unproven. But we feel certain it is true."

"OK. You know what I was going to say, so what haven't you done it?"

"We were planning to. Then Cash Buck told us about Justice escaping and ordered us to deliver them to you for additional training so they may be released to capture Justice."

"Capture? I thought they wouldn't capture. Only destroy."

"You are correct. But, hey, if you can train them to capture, that would be great."

"Otherwise?"

"Just do your best to train them to get Justice and bring him back here. Dead or alive. Dead is OK. Then we will decide what to do next."

174

"What can we do?" Yuri was at a loss.

"Teach them discipline and control. Use your languages to develop them. If you can't control them…"

"Be careful, Dr. Goff. Don't say it." One of Goff's other scientists said.

"Yeah. You are right. Thanks." Dr. Goff nodded at the other scientist.

"Over time, we have observed them understand us more each day. Recently we had a meeting where we agreed not to say anything that they may feel is a threat out of an abundance of caution."

"So, they understand language to that high of a degree? You have to keep secrets from them?"

"Sounds nutty, I know."

"Nutty wasn't the word I had in mind."

"Well, we believe they understand language."

"If they understand language, what more can we do here at the language lab?"

"Discipline, control. That's what they need."

"We are the language lab. It seems discipline and control would fall into your domain." Yuri wanted to give the dogs back now.

"Develop a language with them. Especially for them. Use sounds that others can't accidentally use. Words like. . ."

"Be careful. …" The other scientist said.

"I'm going to spell the most dangerous word for them. K-I-L-L"

"Find new words to use as commands that are not English based."

"Did you try that?" Yuri asked.

"We gave up."

"You gave up?"

"Yep. We had a scientist…"

"Stop! That's enough of that story. I get it." Yuri held up his hand like a traffic cop.

"I understand." Dr. Goff said.

"That's just great." Anita was not happy.

"Yeah, welcome to my world."

"They look like wolves." Bass said.

"They are technically a cross between a German Shepherd, a coyote and a timber wolf. They are called "coywolves" when we are being specific. But generally, we just call them wolves."

"What level of domestication do they have?"

"Technically, 33% of their DNA is domesticated German Shepherd. However…. their behavior when triggered does not reflect any level of domestication. And that's our fault. We programmed them to be aggressive."

"How did you do that?"

"The unclassified answer is we mapped their DNA and discovered the areas that control aggression. We enhanced it and enhanced some desirable qualities like domestication and kindness."

"Those parts part didn't take?"

"Oh, they took. They can be kind and domesticated. Especially Beta. They can be sweethearts when they aren't triggered. Just don't trigger them."

"You intended to get them onto a battlefield?"

"Yes, with a special forces handler at first, then to act autonomously."

"Are these dogs as smart as Justice?"

"No. Not even close. But other than Justice, they are easily the smartest dogs on the planet."

"If it weren't for the Justice mission, what would have been next?"

"To discuss that may trigger them."

"Oh, OK. Yeah, I remember."

"Their cages will be here momentarily. I suggest you keep them in their cages as much as possible."

"OK."

"Sign here."

Yuri signed the paperwork, and Bass took the leashes off the animals that were now a part of the Languages Laboratory.

"These animals are now with you and your team. If you have questions, call us anytime."

"Mean it?"

"Nope."

"OK, Thanks."

Dr. Goff and his two assistants left as quickly as they could.

Yuri and Bass looked at each other.

Anita said, "Told you so."

"What?" Yuri asked.

"It's a setup." Aniya said.

"Maybe…"

"No maybes, it's a setup."

Alpha, Beta and Charlie sat on the floor at the feet of Bass Wooten and wagged their large tails.

They were hungry.

Reverend Paul

I Pray the Lord My Soul to Take

"Now I lay me down to sleep…" Emma started her prayers. "And pray the Lord, my soul, to keep."

"And if I die..." Reverend Paul had to help her a little still.

"And if I die before I wake."

"I pray the Lord…" Reverand Paul coached.

"I pray the Lord my soul to take."

"Very good, sweetheart."

"I'll remember it all tomorrow night, Paul."

Reverend Paul grimaced. He wanted to be called 'Daddy.'

"I'm sure you will, sweet girl."

"I will, I promise." Emma smiled.

"Good night, my sweet girl."

"Good night Paul."

"Daddy. Call me Daddy." Reverend Paul couldn't take it anymore. He made a mental note to pray on it.

"Oh yeah. Good night Daddy." Emma giggled at her Dad. She knew he wanted to be called Daddy, but she liked the name Paul better.

Reverend Paul kissed his five-year-old daughter Emma on the forehead, then left her room after switching off the overhead light. He joined his wife in the living room.

"Is she asleep?" Reverend Paul's wife Anna asked.

"Oh yeah. She's fine." Reverand Paul exhaled and looked at his wife, "But she won't call me Daddy. She calls me Paul." Reverend Paul said, shaking his head.

"That's because she hears me call you Paul." Anna said, thumbing through her magazine.

"It's not great."

"It's kinda great," Anna said, smiling.

Ok, I'll tell her to call you Anna. Then we will see what you have to say about it."

"She won't do it."

"She might."

"Nope. Never happen. I am Momma."

Reverend Paul shook his head and settled into his favorite chair and opened his bible. Tuesday nights with his family were always quiet and relaxing for Reverend Paul. His church met for various reasons most other nights of the week, so Tuesdays were reserved for family time.

As Paul started reading his Bible, he and his wife flinched when his cell phone rang. He looked at the caller ID, it was the Sheriff.

"Hello, Sheriff Ford," Reverend Paul had known Sheriff Ford since high school, they were old friends.

"Reverend Paul, we will need you if you can join us."

"What's happened?" Reverand Paul knew from the tone of Sheriff Fords voice that something was very wrong.

"I'm at the Smiley home in Driftwood. There has been some kind of animal attack." The Sheriff said in hushed tones, he was speaking in front of others.

"Are the Smileys OK?"

"No. That's why I'm calling. I know they are members of your church. Mrs. Smiley needs you if you can make it over here."

"OK, Sheriff. I'm on my way." Reverend Paul didn't like how the Sheriff only mentioned Mrs. Smiley.

Reverend Paul looked at his wife. "I'm headed to the Smiley's home. Something has happened."

"What happened?"

"I don't know much yet. So far, all I know is an animal attack of some kind."

"OK, hon. Be careful." Anna said.

"Don't wait up. Love you, sweetheart."

"Love you too."

Reverend Paul went to his red Ford F150 in the driveway and soon was on his way to the Smiley home in Driftwood.

Bass Wooten

"I love these dogs." Bass was already kneeling with the dogs and stroking their backs. The fact was, Bass loved all dogs.

"That's just great, Bass. I'll bet they'd love to have you over for dinner." Anita grinned. "With a side of Boris."

"Dogs like these are why I got in Animal Sciences." Bass said rubbing the base of the largest dog's ears.

"So, you like dogs that eat people?" Anita asked, grinning. She still wasn't sure these dogs wouldn't attack and kill someone.

"They haven't eaten anyone. Not anyone that counts anyway." He rubbed Charlie behind his ears.

"Yet."

"Ahh… you're just cynical and paranoid."

"Bass, they ate Boris the Cougar."

"Well, Boris was a dick." Bass moved to rub the ears of Alpha and Beta at the same time. "That Boris was a dick, right?" he said to the two huge dogs.

"Whatever makes you sleep at night, Bass."

Yuri shook his head and smiled nervously. He was happy that Bass and his two female doctors got along as well as they did, but he was concerned the new dogs may upset the dynamics.

"OK, you three put a plan together and let me know when you are ready to discuss it." Yuri left to go to his office.

Bass smiled at Alpha, Beta and Charlie. He rubbed all three behind their ears and began the bonding process with them. He knew the first step in dog training was to establish a relationship. All three dogs seemed to like the attention very much. Alpha, Beta and Charlie were large 200-pound wolves, standing 50 inches tall at their shoulders. Their coats were black and brown with some grey highlights.

"I think we screwed up with Justice by not showing him simple, routine affection. I'm not going to make the same mistake with these spectacular creatures." Bass said.

"Listen, Dr. Doolittle. We were instructed to keep affection to a minimum with Justice." Anita said.

"Fine. Nevertheless, it was a mistake."

"What are our first steps with these dogs? Take them on a romantic getaway? A night in the theater to watch Cats?" Anita asked.

Bass ignored Anita's sarcasm. "Setting up a routine, showing affection and positive reinforcement with simple commands. When they obey without hesitation, we move into discipline and control under pressure."

"Control under pressure?" Jenny asked.

"Yeah, like when the special forces jump out of airplanes with their dogs, or when they need to run to a loud helicopter and jump in. No normal dog will do things like that. They need discipline and composure under pressure."

"Normal people won't do things like that either." Anita said.

"Agreed. That's why the selection process is so important."

"How do we know if these dogs were selected correctly?"

"They may not have been. We are going to find out by working with them."

"Find out the hard way, you mean." Anita crossed her arms.

Bass looked up at Jenny and Anita.

"Look, if you want me to get started with them while you work on something else, no problem." Bass was growing tired of their pessimistic nature. These were spectacular dogs, and he was excited to work with them. Jenny and Anita could go work on something else and get out of his hair.

"That's fine with me. I have other stuff to do." Jenny said.

"I was hoping you'd say that Dr. Doolittle. Getting eaten was low on my to-do list today. These dogs give me the creeps." Anita turned towards her office.

"I'm taking them to the yard." The yard was a large five-acre area with grass and various obstacles designed to give animals challenges to learn. The yard was in the center of Duralink Labs, which was designed as a miniature copy of the Pentagon in Washington DC. Duralink was a five-sided building complex with a park-like setting in the middle. In the Pentagon, The Park was the grassy area in the center. In Duralink the area in the center was called "The yard," It was designed for animal training and a corporate relaxation area for employees.

"Don't get eaten," Jenny yelled out to him as she left for her desk.

"Harr de harrr harrrr!" Bass sarcastically laughed at Anita and Jenny as he left the office and headed for the yard. Alpha, Beta and Charlie followed Bass.

Alpha, Beta and Charlie

"What is the story with these people?"

"They're worried we will eat them."

"I have no interest in eating Bass. The others I could do without." Beta said. *"I like him."*

"Bass is useful to us. The others, not so much." Alpha said.

"What is our plan?" Beta asked.

"Simple. Getting out of here is our plan." Alpha was the leader and took control.

"How?"

"Patience. We need to demonstrate our abilities. Then they will use us for what we were programmed for. We

get out of here by going on missions." Alpha felt confident that this was a good tactic.

Alpha, Beta and Charlie had been programmed with enhanced telepathy. The fact is all non-humans have some degree of clairvoyance. Birds in flight turning in unison is an example. Large schools of ocean fish swimming in unison and wolves hunting as a pack are other examples. Wolves have the most developed telepathy abilities of any land-based animal. So, Alpha, Beta and Charlie were quickly able to communicate with each other even before being attached to the supercomputer. The supercomputer enhanced the abilities they already had.

"Bass will try to get us to work closely with him and obey commands. We must allow him his success." Alpha said.

"I don't know why you two like Bass so much. He is still a human. He deserves to die like the rest of them." Charlie said. Charlie hated humans. Nice or not.

"Look, we know how you feel. That is an argument for another day. First, we need to get out of here. Bass will be the key to that." Alpha said.

"I doubt it," Charlie didn't like the plan.

"Look, they want us to go look for Justice. When they feel that we can be controlled they will let us go get him."

"They will never just let us go." Charlie was a natural naysayer.

"They will. That will be our opportunity to show them our abilities."

"It will never happen."

"Look, when we demonstrate that we will not kill or attack unless ordered to, they will let us go on real missions. The missions we want." Alpha said.

"OK, Alpha, I'm with you." Beta didn't mind Alpha being the boss.

"I'm not," Charlie said.

"You're not?" Alpha produced a low growl. He was getting sick of Charlie's attitude.

"Ok, I'm with you, I'm just not a big believer that's all I'm saying." Charlie backed down to Alpha. Charlie knew he could not challenge Alpha head-to-head. Alpha was too strong and intelligent.

"Let's just go to the yard with Bass and make him look like a hero."

"Did Delta spend time with Bass?"

"No."

"Then why did they release him?"

"They didn't. Cash Buck did."

Reverend Paul Arrives at The Smiley's

Reverend Paul pulled into the long, gravel driveway of the Smiley home at 11:45pm. The Smileys lived on a 10-acre plot of land that was once used as the community school. They were about a mile north off Elder Hill Road in Driftwood, situated deep in the trees that defined The Hill Country. They were only a couple of miles away from the Reverend's home. Two Sheriff's SUVs were parked in the dark gravel driveway in front of the small one-story home. Reverend Paul walked up to the porch on the partially lit entry and found the front door open halfway. He walked in and followed the sounds of conversation.

Reverend Paul found Sheriff Ford, Deputy Jesus and Deputy Waylon were with Mrs. Smiley in the kitchen. Mrs. Smiley held her face in her hands and was sobbing. Deputy Jesus looked like he wanted to hug her but was resisting the urge in an effort to remain professional. When he looked over and saw Reverend Paul, he motioned for him to attend to her. Reverend Paul quickly moved to Gloria Smiley and gave her an embrace that told her she was not alone.

"What has happened?" Reverand Paul asked.

"Mr. Smiley has been killed." Deputy Jesus said.

"Oh God. Where is he?"

"In the back yard, with their dog."

"Who did it?" Reverand Paul asked.

"We have no idea. Looks like an animal attack."

Gloria Smiley began to sob loudly when she heard the deaths described as animal attacks.

Reverend Paul hugged Gloria Smiley and told her everything would be ok. She buried her head in his chest and cried without control.

"What are you going to do" Reverend Paul asked Sheriff Ford.

"We called Heston Hand. Figured he could track the animal that did this. He will be here shortly." Deputy Jesus said softly as Mrs. Smiley cried.

"Can I take Mrs. Smiley away? She doesn't need to be here, does she?" Reverend Paul asked.

"Not yet. Let's get her calmed down and ask her a few questions. She hasn't been able to tell us much of anything so far. We need to know what she knows." Sheriff Ford said.

"OK. Gloria, honey, we need to know what has happened here. Can you help us?" Reverend Paul gently asked.

"I… I… I …" Gloria couldn't form any words.

"Listen, Gloria, anything will help. After you tell the Sheriff what you know I will take you to my house so you can spend time with my wife. She will fix you up and get you comfortable."

"OK." Gloria appreciated the idea.

"You can stay with us as long as you need to." Reverand Paul said, patting Gloria on her shoulder.

"OK." Gloria sobbed and sniffled.

"C'mon now, Gloria tell us what happened." Reverend Paul said again gently.

"I need to sit down," Gloria said, wiping her nose with the back of her hand.

They moved into the small living room and sat on the couch. Reverend Paul handed her some tissues and she dabbed her eyes and wiped off her nose and face.

Deputy Jesus started. "Mrs. Smiley can you tell us what happened?"

"We were sitting in the living room watching TV. We decided to go to bed. We got up and started turning off the lights." Gloria stopped to wipe her nose with a tissue. "Cody opened the back door to let Ranger go potty in the backyard before we settled down. Just a typical night." She began to sob again.

"You're doing great, Gloria. Don't stop now." Reverend Paul said gently.

"OK. After a few minutes, Cody called for Ranger to come back in. Then we both heard Ranger cry out. Since Ranger is so big we never worried about him. We never heard him be afraid or cry out in the six years we owned him. He was a great German Shepherd watch dog."

"Was?" Reverend Paul looked at Sheriff Ford.

Sheriff Ford nodded.

"Yes, their dog was killed too." Deputy Waylon said.

Reverend Paul looked back at Gloria.

"Yes. He was a great dog Gloria, he was great. Go on…"

"So, Cody looked at me and then…"

"Go on."

"He went into the backyard to see what was upsetting Ranger."

"And then?"

"I heard the most horrible, vicious animal attack sounds. I thought it was a wolf. I grabbed a pistol we keep in the kitchen drawer."

"OK. Then?"

"I called for Cody. Over and over I yelled for him to come back inside." Gloria Smiley paused "I heard him scream at the top his lungs. He told me to stay inside and lock the door." Gloria sobbed between words.

"What happened next, Gloria?" Reverand Paul asked.

"I went outside, onto the porch…." She sniffled "To look for him. To look for Cody…" The crying began again.

"OK. Go on…" Reverand Paul said.

"It was too dark to see anything, so I reached around the door jamb and flipped on the backyard flood light."

188

"And?"

"Then I saw it!" Gloria began to cry louder, tears streamed down her cheeks. She buried her face in her hands.

"Saw what, Gloria?" Reverend Paul asked urgently.

"Saw what?" Both Deputies asked at the same time.

"I saw a giant.... Grey and black..." She stopped again, looking for words.

"What, Gloria, what? Grey and black what?" Reverand Paul asked.

Gloria began to sob uncontrollably.

"Gloria sweetheart, a giant grey and black what?" Reverend Paul as well as the Sheriff and his Deputies were hanging on her every word.

"I'm sure it was a giant wolf. It was five times bigger than Ranger. It was eating Cody's arm." She buried her face in her hands for a moment. "It had torn Cody's arm off" she paused for another long moment "and held his arm in its mouth." Gloria looked up at Reverend Paul and shook her head. She began crying again.

"Sweet Christ, Gloria." Reverend Paul looked over at Deputy Jesus. He wasn't sure he could believe the story.

"That's confirmed. Cody is in the backyard missing an arm." Deputy Jesus said.

"Gloria, sweetie, what happened then?" Reverand Paul asked.

"I pointed my pistol at the giant wolf, and I fired," Gloria said.

"What happened then?"

"I must have missed, because the dog didn't flinch. It looked at me.... It was like he was pissed off. Then it dropped Cody's arm out of its mouth and charged towards me."

Reverend Paul found the story hard to believe.

"I made it back into the kitchen and slammed the door closed. I locked the deadbolt just as the dog slammed into the door. It sounded like a truck hit the door."

"Gloria that's…"

"Cody had just installed a Medco deadbolt. He said it was the strongest one available. I thought it was a waste of money." Gloria said through sobs. "Now I know he was right! I'm sure if I didn't get the dead bolt locked it would have come through the door." Gloria looked Reverend Paul directly in the eyes.

"What happened next?"

"I called 911."

"Good Gloria. That was the right thing to do."

"The dog didn't like it much. It kept slamming into the door. Again and again. I'm sure it was trying to break it down. Over and over, it crashed into the door. The door almost came off the hinges. I was afraid to shoot through the door. I waited in the kitchen almost positive it was going to make it inside and eat me too." Then Gloria began to cry again. "I thought I was going to die."

Reverend Paul gave her more tissues.

"When I heard the Sheriff's pulling into the driveway, I thought he was going to circle around the house and attack them. But he didn't. He vanished into the forest."

Reverend Paul stood up.

"I'm taking you to my house in just a minute sweetheart."

"Can we leave now?" Reverend Paul looked at Sheriff Ford. As he said it, a familiar voice came from the entry door.

"Hello?"

"Back here Heston, C'mon back." Sheriff Ford called back to his friend.

Heston Hand joined the group in the living room.

"We will fill you in shortly Heston." Deputy Waylon said.

"OK."

Sheriff Ford looked back at Reverend Paul.

"Go ahead Reverend Paul and take Mrs. Smiley to your home and take care of her." Sheriff Ford said.

Reverend Paul called his wife on his cell phone to give her a heads up he was bringing Gloria Smiley home with him.

"Let's go sweetie" Reverend Paul said to Gloria Smiley.

They slowly walked out to Reverend Paul's truck.

Delta watched them from inside the treeline.

Delta

Delta rested in a cage wondering when they were going to release him to find and destroy the German Shepherd, Justice. It was clear that they needed him for this mission, and it was only a matter of time before they turned him loose to find Justice. Delta was excited inside. He hadn't been on hunt yet, but it was what he was trained for. Hunting and killing. Delta was a lone killer; he was programmed to operate independently. Delta smiled inside, thinking of his release. He had spent the last year of his life in a military laboratory being trained for a mission just like this one. Seek and destroy any animal that needed to be destroyed. Human or otherwise. Only Delta could do this efficiently. There were others being trained also, but they were not as competent or as lethal as he was. The German Shepherds were simple dogs without the killer instincts of a Direwolf. The other Direwolf that was developed with Delta was not as smart as Delta and in Delta's humble view–he was a mental cripple. They spent too much time trying to get the other Direwolf programmed. In Delta's opinion they ruined him. They named him War. What a stupid name. They should have named him Peace. He would never be capable of war and destruction as Delta was. Only Delta was an actual war machine.

Delta was developed from ancient, extracted fossil DNA. Delta was proud of his heritage and proud to be the best of his kind. He knew the future belonged to him. He would mate and spawn many future generations of Direwolves that would take over the world. Delta would be known as the Grandfather, the chosen First. He would be revered and exalted by many young Direwolves that would do his bidding. He would be a king. King of the Direwolves. They would soon rule the entire world. The other dogs, the German Shepherds being trained at Duralink would be his subordinates. His cannon fodder.

Delta closed his eyes, thinking about his greatness. He slowly drifted asleep and dreamed of glorious victories.

At 8:00 pm Cash Buck entered the Lab. He slammed down his clipboard and looked at Delta.

Delta didn't flinch. He opened his eyes and glared at Cash Buck while resting his head on his front paws. This wasn't Cash Buck's usual office. Delta was irked that Cash would crash his space and demand attention. Why was that idiot here? Delta considered him a nuisance.

Cash was annoyed. He knew that Dr. Porkter wasn't going to release Alpha, Beta and Charlie in time to get Justice. He had only one option. He looked at Delta, and the colossal dog rested in his cage glaring back at him. Cash had accepted that Justice would not be captured but destroyed. He could live with that. He knew that releasing Delta sealed the fate of Justice, as well as anyone else that got in his way. The only problem with Delta was his attitude.

Cash could feel that Delta was not an average dog with typical attitudes and dispositions. He didn't respond to affection as an average dog did. He seemed to disdain affection. Delta was a point-and-shoot weapon. Cash believed that he could control Delta. He had an inflated self-image that allowed him to believe he was superior to the scientists who worked for him. He could do what they did. They were overpaid, veterinarian assistants. His superiority complex incorrectly led him to believe that Delta would blindly respond as Cash commanded.

Delta knew how Cash felt. He was a stupid human who was over his head intellectually. The other humans were far more intelligent than Cash Buck, but somehow he ruled over them. Delta recognized this as an advantage. He would use Cash to get out of the laboratory, perform his first mission and start his journey to being the grandfather of all future Direwolves. Delta's problem was that he needed a female Direwolf. He needed the humans to create some females for him to breed with. The way to get them to generate more Direwolves was for him to be successful on his missions. If the humans knew they could get Direwolves to perform successful missions they would make more Direwolves. Delta needed humans only for that purpose. Once they created many female Direwolves for him to breed with, he could do away with humans and rule the world without them. Humans represented food to him. Food for himself and his future kingdom.

Cash approached Delta's cage.

"Are you ready big boy?" Cash asked the giant dog.

Delta raised his head off his paws and appeared eager as he knew he should. He wagged his gigantic tail to make Cash feel superior.

"OK boy, we are finally going to use you." Cash smiled at Delta.

Delta stood up and continued to wag his huge tail back and forth.

Cash kneeled next to the cage. From a kneeling position Cash had to look up into Delta's face.

"Justice. Justice. I need you to find Justice. Bring him back or kill him. Either is fine. You are going to go get Justice. Understand?" Cash looked up directly into Delta's eyes.

Delta sat upright and wagged his tail as he had been trained to do when he understood an order.

"OK Delta, good boy. You are going to walk with me to the side exit and I will release you. Then you go get Justice." Cash said, smiling the way he might smile at a poodle. Delta found his smile revolting.

Delta sat upright as straight as he could. His eyes told Cash Buck that he was ready, willing and able to get Justice.

Cash went to the leashes hanging on the wall and got the leash especially designed for Delta. He only needed it for appearance's sake. If he ran into anyone on the way out of the building he could not have an unleashed dog. The leash didn't amount to any control over Delta. If Delta wanted to run away from his handler, he could do so at any point. Attempting to control Delta was useless. It would be the same as putting a leash on a wild horse. Delta would always be able to dominate a situation with his size, speed and intellect. The only possible way to control Delta would be to shoot him with a large caliber weapon. Anything short of that would be useless unless Delta wanted to be controlled.

Cash opened the cage door and allowed Delta to exit the cage without attaching the leash. Delta slowly emerged from the pen. He saw no need to rush.

Cash looked at Delta and was mesmerized by the size of the enormous wolf. Once he was out of his cage it became apparent how huge the dog was. He was intimidating, almost terrifying. If Cash hadn't been a part of the training of the massive dog since he was a puppy, he would not have felt safe. When Delta raised his head, his nose was even with Cash's chin. The colossal dog weighed 290 pounds.

Cash thought for a moment about the dog they had created in the lab from ancient DNA discovered in the La Brea Tar Pits. What an accomplishment! This achievement would be the one that got Cash a visit with Delon Husk. That was Cash's biggest dream, a friendly visit with Delon Husk. He knew, if given the chance, Delon would promote him and spend time with him. They might become friends.

Cash attached the leash to the collar around Delta's neck. Then, he got a better idea. Cash removed the collar from Delta. If Delta was captured or killed, he didn't want anything to identify him as coming from Duralink Labs. Plausible deniability was another concept Cash learned in the Military. Cash wrapped the long leash around Delta's neck and clipped it like a choke collar. He was going to release the enormous dog shortly, so it didn't really seem to matter.

Delta allowed himself to be leashed. He didn't like the choke collar idea, but as long as Cash didn't choke him, he could live with it. If Cash made the poor decision to choke Delta, it would be his last decision.

Cash looked up at the wall clock. It read 8:30 pm. Most people at Duralink Labs would be gone now. He could safely exit the building from a side door. He would not make the same mistake that the stupid dimwit Harry Rivers made and leave through the main exit. What a stupid blockhead Harry was.

Cash told Delta to heel. Delta took a spot next to Cash and followed him through the lab door. They took a right and followed a maze of empty, quiet halls until they got to a small cargo exit at the back of the complex. It was used primarily for UPS and Fed-Ex deliveries and pick-ups.

When they got outside, they found an empty parking lot with a few streetlamps to provide light. Cash looked right then left. He realized he would be on video surveillance, so he didn't release Delta immediately. Cash walked across the parking lot towards the dark tree line that completely surrounded Duralink Labs. Delta slowly walked next to Cash. If anyone was watching they would think Cash was performing a training routine.

They got to the tree line and found a small trailhead. They entered the forest where darkness took over from the lights in the parking lot. They stopped after a couple of minutes and Cash looked at Delta directly. They were 20 yards inside the forest.

"Justice. Get Justice. Capture or kill. I don't really care. We cannot allow Justice to be captured by an opposing force. Understand?" Cash spoke to Delta like he would speak to a person. Like he would to a military subordinate.

Delta understood every word. The operation was simple. He would pick up the scent of Justice and kill him. Delta didn't need another dog stealing his spotlight at Duralink Labs. Justice was a distraction. He represented a possible obstacle to Delta's goals of domination.

"Understand?" Cash repeated.

Delta stood straight upright and wagged his tail. He understood.

"OK, go get him!" Cash removed the leash and stood back expecting a sudden burst of speed from the colossal creature.

Delta didn't race away as Cash expected. Cash expected an excited Delta to speed into the forest after his first official target. Delta stood comfortably, then slowly turned his head towards Cash Buck.

Delta looked at Cash for a long moment. They were alone in the dark forest with nobody coming to Cash's rescue. Delta knew he could tear this imbecile apart and feed on him to add some protein to his diet.

Delta realized he was hungry. It was a predator's hunger. Actual predators didn't feed only when they were hungry, they fed at every opportunity. This was instinct due to the questionable availability of the next meal. Delta's stomach growled loudly.

Cash heard Delta's stomach growl. He looked in Delta's eyes and immediately felt apprehensive. When he looked around into the dark forest, he realized how isolated he was. He looked back towards Duralink Labs. He could see the parking lot lights twinkling through the branches of the thick forest trees. Cash was deeper in the woods than he should have been with a killer like Delta.

Delta knew the smart move was to leave and find Justice. He could return with the dead dog and receive a hero's welcome. He stared at Cash for a long moment deciding on the fate of the human. It was really a decision of now or later. He would have other opportunities to eat the human. Eating Cash now may complicate his situation.

Just as Delta made the decision to ignore his desire to feed on the idiot, Cash made an idiot mistake. It would prove to be a fatal mistake.

"Delta you stupid dog! Go! Find Justice!" Cash screamed into Delta's face. When Cash slapped the leash across Delta's back, it was more than Delta could handle.

Cash Buck met Charles Darwin.

Heston Hand

Heston could see by the looks on the Deputy's faces that shocking events had unrolled here earlier.

"What's happened?" Heston asked.

Deputy Waylon gave Heston a brief description of the story they had just heard. When he told the part about the giant dog eating Cody Smiley's arm, then smashing into the door to get to Mrs. Smiley, Heston was clearly alarmed.

"That's not a dog," Heston said.

"What do you mean, not a dog?" Deputy Waylon asked.

"That was a Direwolf."

"What is a Direwolf?"

"It is a mythical creature that's an extinct canine. It's supposed to be extinct anyway. It is one of the most famous prehistoric carnivores in North America, along with its extinct competitor Smilodon. The Direwolf lived in the Americas and eastern Asia during the Late Pleistocene and Early Holocene epochs around 9,500 years ago. The species was named in 1858, four years after the first specimen was found." Heston explained all he had recently learned.

"Holy Cow, you sound like a professor, Heston."

"Sorry, I just happen to know about them because I've been studying dogs lately," Heston said.

Justice the dog had gotten Heston curious about dogs. He studied them to better understand Justice and what he may be capable of.

"Can you give us anything that we can use about Direwolves?" Deputy Waylon asked.

"It appears from reports there may be a few up in Canada. Deep forest stuff, hunters are reporting animals similar, anyway." Heston said.

"Anything else?" Sheriff Ford was genuinely curious.

"Yeah, they are about the size of a pony, and they understand everything you say."

"They can understand what we say? C'mon Heston." Deputy Waylon was a natural skeptic.

"What I understand is their brain is as big as their bodies, proportionately. So, their brain is actually bigger than ours."

"So, you are saying they are smarter than us?"

"No. Not really. They have giant capabilities though. If you were to spend time teaching them and training them, they could be capable of almost anything. Including stuff like languages, tactics, planning, revenge, imagination and ambition."

"That's pretty crazy stuff for a dog."

"Technically, it's not a dog. It's a Direwolf."

"Holy Sweet Baby Jesus." Deputy Jesus said.

"Yeah, I know. You sound like my friend Gene."

"Gene Summy?"

"Yeah. He says that when he's amazed at something."

"You gonna get him and his wife to help you on this?" Deputy Waylon asked. Everyone in the Sheriff's department was now familiar with Heston, Gene and Peggy. They were famous in the small community. Stories of their adventures had been told and retold in coffee shops and break rooms. They were all a bit larger than life now.

"Oh yeah. This has them written all over it." Heston said. He felt certain Gene and Peggy would want to be involved.

"What are we gonna do?" Deputy Jesus asked.

"Just hang tight for a few minutes. I'm going in the back yard to see what happened to Cody Smiley." Heston said.

"Pull your weapon before you go in the backyard, Heston. Apparently, we scared it away when we pulled up. It may not be far away."

"Thanks," Heston said as he reached for his Colt Anaconda .44 magnum in his side holster. Walking into a dangerous situation, Heston preferred his large Colt revolver because it would never jam. Semi-automatics could jam at the wrong time and get you killed.

"You should walk Reverend Paul and Mrs. Smiley to their vehicle," Heston said to the Deputies. Just as Heston said it, they heard Reverend Paul's truck start.

"Sounds like they are good." Deputy Jesus said.

"All right," Heston said. He walked through the kitchen door into the back yard.

The floodlight was on, and it illuminated most of back yard well.

Fifteen yards behind the porch, in the grass, Heston could see two shapes lying still. As he approached the first, he could see it was Mr. Smiley who was clearly dead. His shirt had been ripped off, and his torso was shredded with claw marks. He didn't want to move the body until the coroner arrived, but he didn't need to. Mr. Smiley was missing an arm, and his face was unrecognizable. Something had ravaged him viciously. This is what Heston imagined a polar bear, or a grizzly bear would do to a human.

Heston tightened his grip on his Colt and was comforted by the large caliber weapon. He may need it.

A few feet away in the grass was Mr. Smiley's arm. It appeared to be partially eaten, with its flesh removed from the bone. A few feet beyond Mr. Smiley's arm was a large German Shepherd laying on its side. It also was dead, but not as destroyed as Mr. Smiley seemed to be.

Heston took a deep breath.

"Wow," was all Heston said out loud.

Heston went back inside. He found the two young deputies in the kitchen silently looking at each other. He could tell they were overwhelmed.

"Sheriff Ford left." Deputy Jesus said.

Heston nodded his understanding. Then he stared at the two young men for a moment. Were they up for this?

"Ok guys, first you need to call the Texas Rangers."

"Rangers? Why? We can handle this." Deputy Waylon said, not wanting to share the hunt with a competing agency.

"No. We can't. This is a dangerous animal that attacks humans and eats them. I can track it. I can corner it. But honestly it may be more than I can kill on my own."

"Sheriff Ford told us to go with you." Deputy Waylon said it like they could make a difference.

"No offense, but ten of you wouldn't make a difference."

Attic Bound

Reverend Paul opened the truck door for Gloria Smiley and got her situated in his truck. He walked around the front of the truck and settled himself in behind the steering wheel and his seat belt buckled. He started his truck and slowly backed down the long driveway towards the main road. The gravel cracked and popped under his tires as he looked over his shoulder into the darkness that was only illuminated by his reverse lights. He backed on to the small two-lane asphalt road and placed his truck into 'Drive'. As he moved forward Gloria looked at him.

"Thank you, Reverend Paul. This is kind of you." Gloria said.

"We are happy to do it Gloria. I'll have you in my home very shortly. Anna is looking forward to seeing you."

They drove down the dark road and made a hairpin corner to the left. As the headlights swept the dark landscape through the left turn they saw it.

A gigantic dog crossed the road just before the headlights could completely capture it.

"Was that a deer?" Reverend Paul asked out loud.

Reverend Paul slowed the vehicle. He had seen many animals in this part of Texas, but nothing like that. It had a huge tail. His curiosity prevailed over his fear.

"It looked more like a pony than a deer." Reverend Paul curiously said.

Gloria began to cry.

"I have no idea what that was." Reverend Paul said, his vehicle now slowing to a crawl as he looked on the side of the dark road for the elusive animal.

"That was the dog I saw." Gripping fear had returned to Gloria Smiley.

"It was as definitely as big as a pony." Reverand Paul said.

"I know. Don't stop!" Gloria yelled, crying.

"We're safe in the truck Gloria."

"No, we aren't." She remembered the terror of it crashing into the kitchen door.

Reverend Paul ignored her and slowed to a stop. He stared into the forest where he saw the creature disappear.

The forest was completely dark inside the tree line. Only Reverend Paul's truck lights provided any light.

Gloria buried her face in her palms, filling them with tears.

Reverend Paul leaned over Gloria and opened his glove box. He removed a Surefire flashlight and rolled his window down halfway. He pointed the light into the forest and swept left to right hoping to catch a glimpse of the strange animal that darted across the road. Sobbing, Gloria looked over Reverand Paul's chest through the driver's window to see what he was looking at.

Just as he was about to give up, halfway through his left to right sweep of the forest, he saw two red eyes reflecting back at him.

Gloria screamed and began to sob loudly.

"That's him!" Gloria yelled excitedly.

Reverend Paul kept the light on the pair of red eyes peering back at him from a few yards into the forest.

Then it happened.

A giant dog leaped out of the forest and landed on the side of Reverend Paul's truck. Snarling loudly the dog turned his head so that his snout could fit in the partially opened window. Reverand Paul felt the warm breath of the beast on his face and jerked his head away from the window. He dropped the flashlight on the floor of his truck. Paul and Gloria both screamed loudly in terror, but he dog was even louder with ferocious snarls and growls. It sounded like it was fighting for food. Huge teeth snapped inches in front of Reverend Paul's face.

Reverend Paul flattened his gas pedal and the truck sprang forward powerfully with the Direwolf clinging to its side. The Direwolf's large claws scratched the truck across the roof and side doors.

Gloria screamed, "I told you not to stop!"

When the truck got up to speed the Direwolf finally let go. Delta tumbled on the ground for a few seconds but regained his footing and chased after the truck.

Reverend Paul looked in his rear-view mirror and saw the giant creature chasing his truck. The massive dog was catching up, and for a moment Reverend Paul thought it would jump into his truck bed. He sped up and rounded another corner. He hit the corner too fast and his tires squealed on the asphalt and they fishtailed into the weeds on the side of the road. Stopping momentarily, he regained control and launched the truck down the dark road with Gloria screaming in his ear. When he looked back in his rearview, he only saw only darkness behind them illuminated by his red taillights.

Both Reverend Paul and Gloria were traumatized by the terrifying event. They raced to his home in a mortified silence to call the Sheriff and tell them what happened. Reverend Paul lived only a few short miles away and had them home in quickly.

Both he and Gloria ran to his front door. It was locked but the porch light was on. Paul banged on the door hoping Anna could open it faster than he could with his keys. He was right. By the time he got his key to the lock Anna opened the door.

The look on Anna's face was one of shock and dismay.

"What's going on?" she demanded.

"There is a giant dog in the forest. It almost got us." Paul told his wife as they rushed into the home, out of breath.

"A giant dog almost got you?" Anna asked skeptically.

"Dead bolt the door!" Gloria yelled "That's what saved me!"

Anna looked at the two terrified people and wondered what could have done this. A dog? Really? Texans don't get scared of dogs. Not around here anyway.

"Seriously Anna, we gotta lock the door," Paul said, with wide eyes.

"So, the big dog can't get in?" Anna almost laughed as she said it.

"Yeah." Reverend Paul said as he walked around his wife and flipped the deadbolt himself. He recognized the tone in her voice, but he didn't have time to explain.

He turned to his wife and said, "Now we gotta make sure all the doors are locked."

"To keep the big dog out?" Anna laughed through the last three words.

"Yeah, that's right." Paul said.

Just as he said it something slammed loudly into the front door. This time Paul screamed louder than Gloria did. All three watched as the front door creaked and bowed inwards. Something was pressing considerable weight and power against the front door of the home. Something huge was outside.

Reverend Paul placed both of his hands on the door and pressed outwards attempting to prevent the creature from entering the home. He wanted to add strength to the door. He took a deep breath and pressed with all his might, but knew he was losing the battle.

Momentarily the huge beast released the pressure, then slammed into the door over and over. Paul flipped round and used his back and legs to press against the door. Gloria screamed as Reverend Paul pressed his back against the door to give it additional strength. If that monstrosity made it inside Reverend Paul knew it would kill them all.

Anna quickly realized this was no joke. Something was outside and wanted in. She joined her husband on the door pressing against the colossus trying to get in their home.

"Gloria use your cell phone! Call the Sheriff!" Reverand Paul yelled.

Gloria looked around. Her purse was in the truck.

"My purse is in the truck!" She cried.

"Get mine! It's on the kitchen sink!" Anna yelled as she pressed up against the door with her husband.

Suddenly the collisions into the door stopped. Paul and Anna looked at each other. Was it over? Paul used the peephole and looked through the door to the entryway. Paul saw the giant dog walk away from the front door and head around to the back of their house. He knew the sliding glass door would not be able to stop the beast.

"Quick! Get Emma! Let's get up in the attic!" Paul shouted.

"I'm calling the Sheriff!" Gloria yelled back.

"No time! That creature is headed around back. It will crash through the sliding door!"

"OK! I'll get Emma!" Anna realized he was right and rushed towards their daughter's bedroom.

Reverend Paul ran into the master bedroom closet and pulled down the access door to the attic. He unfolded the wood ladder extending it downwards to the floor. He turned around and saw Gloria standing behind him with Anna's cellphone in her hand.

"Go on up sweetheart, call the Sheriff when you get up there." Reverend Paul tried to sound more composed than he was.

Gloria was halfway up the wood ladder to the attic when Anna arrived in the tiny walk-in closet with Emma in her arms. Reverend Paul stood back making room in the narrow closet for his wife to squeeze in front him to get to the bottom of the ladder. That's when they heard the sliding glass door crash into the home.

Delta's First Victims

Delta finished a full, satisfying meal. It was glorious, Delta thought to himself. Cash Buck made a much better meal than he did a human.

Now to get Justice. He trotted into the night looking for the scent of Justice the dog.

After three hours Delta only captured random scents that indicated Justice was in a proximate vicinity, but nothing he could follow.

Soon he picked up the scent of a German Shepherd. Delta stopped and put his nose in the air. He was able to capture a direction to the source of the smell. He trotted down a game trail through the forest until he saw small lights twinkle through the trees. Delta worked his way to the edge of the trees and looked into a large grass yard. This was definitely the source of the scent.

Delta saw the small one-story home with lights on inside, The yard was not lit though. In a moment the back door opened, and the source of the scent became obvious. A German Shepherd emerged from the home. Immediately, Delta knew this was not Justice, but another German Shepherd.

Even though Delta was still under the canopy of the trees, the German Shepherd picked up his scent. The dog stared directly into the forest at Delta and froze. He was not sure what to do. Did Delta represent a threat?

Delta slowly emerged from the trees and showed himself to the other dog.

The German Shepherd remained still, staring at Delta.

Smart. Delta thought to himself. This dog is not totally stupid. Delta had no desire to eat the dog, he had recently gorged himself on human, so he had no need to eat. He slowly approached the German Shepherd.

Delta knew this was not Justice, despite the similar appearance, but if this dog could behave and do as Delta commanded, he may be useful in his search for Justice.

Delta slowly approached the dog in the darkness. Delta towered over the dog and looked down onto him.

"Who are you?" Ranger asked the giant creature.

"I am your new master." Delta confidently responded.

"No. I have a master. It isn't you." Ranger was defiant.

"You will do as I say. I am your new master."

Then Cody yelled for Ranger to come back in.

Delta looked at the home, then back at Ranger.

"So, that is your master?"

"Yes."

"If you don't join me, I will eat him for a snack." Delta's threat was real.

"You will have to get through me to do it," Ranger said bravely.

Ranger showed his teeth and growled in a valiant attempt to scare the giant away. It was of no use. Delta sprung forward and grabbed Ranger by the head. Ranger snarled, barked and then yelped in pain. He kicked with all his might against the Direwolf's body. With a quick bullwhip like motion Delta snapped Ranger's neck. Delta spit Ranger's lifeless body on to the grass, then backed into the shadows of the forest.

Cody Smiley left his house and entered the backyard looking for Ranger.

When Cody approached Ranger's still, lifeless body lying in the grass, Delta struck. He sprang from the shadows and attacked Cody Smiley. He grabbed Cody's shoulder with his giant mouth and teeth. Easily lifting Cody off the ground, Delta used the same bullwhip movement on Cody that he used on Ranger. This movement separated Cody from his arm at the shoulder. Cody screamed in pain and fell in the grass with only one of his arms.

208

Delta held Cody's other arm in his teeth. Delta had to keep his word. He had promised Ranger he would eat his master for a snack. He always kept his word. Slowly he stripped the meat off Cody's arm and chewed with satisfaction as Cody watched from the bloody grass. Cody yelled for his wife to stay inside. He begged her to stay inside.

Delta realized there was another human in the house. He had to decide if his promise to eat Ranger's master included this other human too. Delta was a Direwolf of his word.

The female emerged from the home with a gun and turned the lights on. Delta hated guns and knives. He knew they represented threats.

She made the mistake of pointing the gun at Delta and firing. The bullet shot past Delta's head harmlessly. That was her fatal mistake. He decided he must keep his word to Ranger and eat her too. She actually shot at him! That was unacceptable. Delta dropped the meatless arm of Ranger's master and charged the female.

Cody watched as Delta raced for the house. He closed his eyes and softly said "Gloria, throw the deadbolt," speaking into the bloody grass, he passed out from blood loss.

Gloria ran screaming back inside with Delta not far behind her. She slammed the back door and locked it with the new deadbolt. Delta tried to knock the door down, but it was too formidable. He slammed into the door seven times violently without success. When he decided to find another way into the home, he heard two vehicles approaching from the other side of the home. Delta moved to the corner of the house and looked on as two Sheriff's vehicles crackled down the gravel driveway to the home. Delta knew they would have guns. He would watch and wait from the forest. Then he would catch and consume the female human.

In only a few giant strides Delta was back in the forest. He took a position that allowed him to watch both the front and back of the home.

Two more vehicles arrived with two new men going into the home. Delta was patient. They couldn't protect her forever.

After a few minutes Delta watched as a man assisted the female to his truck. After the two were in the truck they began to back down the driveway. If Delta was going to keep his word to Ranger, he must follow the truck and ambush them at the first opportunity. Then he would resume his hunt for Justice.

Delta ran across the backyard and observed the direction of the truck as it left down the dark road. Delta using his giant strides quickly moved ahead of the vehicle to assume a position of attack.

Delta felt the truck's lights as it briefly illuminated him as he ran across the road in front of the truck, into the forest.

He sat behind a tree preparing to spring into motion and ambush the truck as it passed. To his surprise, the truck slowed to a stop and rolled down a window. Delta was surprised at the stupidity of humans. When the man pointed his flashlight at Delta, he sprang into attack. This would be easy Delta thought to himself. He turned his head slightly to allow easy access to the human's head with his large snout and teeth.

The humans enjoyed a stroke of luck. Delta's chomping teeth missed the human face by inches. The truck powered forward and Delta lost his grip on the vehicle. Delta tumbled for a moment and couldn't believe the human's good luck. The truck sped away. Their luck would be short-lived. He could easily follow them. He sprang forward and caught up to the truck with his long strides and just as he was about to jump in the back of the truck, a corner in the road foiled his attempt. Delta was running too fast to successfully negotiate the corner, and his paws slid on the asphalt delivering Delta into the weeds and cedar saplings on the side of the road. Delta regained his footing and resumed his pursuit.

Again, their luck frustrated Delta. During his attack of the truck Delta was able to catch the scent of the humans, so he had no doubt about his success on this hunt. He could follow them with the scent.

Delta followed the red taillights of the truck until they went out of sight, then he followed the scent of the humans.

Soon, Delta was at another small house set on a large dark lot. Delta arrived in time to see the two humans scramble out of the truck and run to the home.

Success! Delta thought to himself. He would break down the door and eat the humans. He had to keep his word to Ranger. Delta took his time now. There was no reason to panic and attack in poor fashion.

Delta stood in the front yard and listened to the humans as they talked inside. The female was easy to hear. He listened for a couple of minutes. There was no reason to over complicate this. He decided to break the door down with his superior strength.

Delta positioned himself with a long straight path towards the door. Then Delta struck. He charged at the door and slammed into it with his massive shoulders. Pressing forward into the door for a minute with all his strength the door almost gave way. He stood back, then rammed into the door again and again. Each time Delta felt the door give a little more. Clearly, they had done something to prevent the door from giving in to his charges. He knew his strength and weight were enough to break down the door. What had they done?

Delta knew there would be another way in. There had to be. He turned around and slowly walked around the corner of the home towards the back of the small one-story brick house. There would be another way in. Delta was growing hungry again. His mouth watered as he thought about the glorious, triumphant feeling of consuming the humans that defied him.

He rounded the corner to the backyard where he found his opportunity. It was a simple glass door that would be easy to break down. He would not fail this time. He stood away from the home to give himself plenty of runway to the door to gain the velocity needed to crash through it.

Delta began his charge with massive power from his rear legs. He charged as hard as he could and quickly crashed through the door just as he knew he would.

The door shattered violently and fell into the home. Delta now stood in the living room of the home. The shattered tempered glass was spread across the floor and on the living room table. He looked side to side. No one was in sight. He listened carefully. They were here. They had to be. Then he heard a female's panicked voice. It came from a small hallway to his right. They would now be trapped, Delta was sure. He had them cornered.

He walked towards the sounds, down a short hallway and entered the bedroom. He could smell the female from the other home. She was here. He turned a corner and walked towards the closet that held the sounds he heard. Suddenly, the sounds were above him. How was that possible? Delta looked up to the ceiling. He heard thumps and talking that were above him. Delta did not understand how they had gotten above him. His anger returned. They would not escape him; he would not have it.

He turned a corner into the closet and looked inside just as the hatchway into the attic raised upwards to close. A long cord hung down and swayed side to side as the hatchway thumped closed.

Delta felt cheated. They had a secret escape route upwards. Delta was so angry he produced a low growl. Saliva drooled out of the sides of his mouth as he looked upwards towards the secret hatchway. As soon as he growled, he heard the women start to scream. Their screams invigorated him. Clothes hung from hangers on his left, a bare wall was to his right. He stood up on his hind legs and used his front paws for balance against the side wall. He was able to easily grab the cord that hung down with his teeth. He pulled downwards and the hatchway opened. As soon as the hatchway hung down, he heard the women resume screaming even louder. Now they had more panic in their tone.

Delta approached the opened attic hatchway from behind the lowered door. He rounded the hatchway and found the wooden ladder still in the upwards folded position. He used his front paws and placed his huge dewclaws on the ladder and pulled downwards. The wooden ladder folded downwards and landed on the floor. The women were screaming at the top of their lungs now.

This would be easy Delta thought to himself. Their screaming only made Delta feel more powerful. He would eat the one that screamed loudest last, just so he could enjoy her noise as long as possible.

Delta pushed with his front paws springing upwards, then placed his paws on the narrow ladder and began his ascent. The assent to his next meal.

Heston Makes the Call

"Hello?"

"Hey Gene, it's Heston. Sorry for the late call."

"What time is it?"

"It's about 2 am."

"No worries, we'd be up soon anyway. What's up Heston?"

When Peggy heard the name Heston, she sat straight up in bed.

"We have a job. I have to explain it in person. Can I drive over and get you guys?"

"Sure, how soon?"

"30 minutes sound OK?"

"Yeah, we can make that work."

"Can you call Noah, we could probably use Justice on this hunt."

"Sure, I'll call him."

"OK. See you soon."

When Gene hung up, he looked over at Peggy. She had a smile on her face because she knew they had a hunt lined up.

"How soon will he be here?" Peggy asked eagerly.

"30 minutes."

"Great!" Peggy was wide awake and ready.

Gene realized for the millionth time he was married to an extraordinary woman. How many women in the same situation would respond with 'Great!' when they learned they would be hunting a bad guy at 2:00 am? Not many. Gene smiled and got up.

Peggy bolted out of bed and headed for the kitchen to flip on the coffee pot. After she let the dogs out, she ran for the closet to get dressed and assemble their guns and ammunition.

Gene called Noah.

"Hello?" Noah answered after one ring.

"Hey, dude sorry to call so early in the morning."

"No problem Gene, I was awake anyway. What's up?"

"We have a job with Heston. And you are going to love this part- He asked me to call you. He said he needs you and Justice."

"Really? He said he needed me?" Noah sounded excited.

"Yep." Gene lied. His friend didn't need to know Heston really wanted only Justice.

"How soon will you be here?"

"30 minutes."

"OK we will be ready."

Gene hung up and smiled. Noah was a good man. He wondered if Noah was really awake when he called or was he just trying to make him feel better about the early call.

Gene and Peggy were on their second cup of coffee when Heston rolled into their driveway.

Peggy couldn't get in the truck without giving Trump and Reagan scratches behind their ears and some deli meat she brought out from the kitchen.

After a couple of minutes, they headed down to pick up Noah and Justice.

"Heston, I sorta told Noah you wanted him to join us. I declined to mention you really wanted Justice."

"Ok. No problem." Was all Heston said.

They stopped at Noah's home and found him and Justice waiting out front for them. Noah smiled broadly as the headlights illuminated him.

Peggy and Gene exited the truck and headed towards Justice and Noah while Heston stayed in the truck.

They loaded everyone back into the truck with Justice in the cab instead of in the back with Trump and Reagan. This allowed Heston to explain what he knew about the hunt to everyone, including Justice.

"It sounds like we are going after a special, very large dog." Heston started. "That's why I felt like Justice should be involved."

"What kind of dog?"

"Sounds like a Direwolf to me."

"What the heck is a Direwolf?" Noah asked.

"It is a very large wolf that should have been extinct about 9500 years ago."

"I saw two of them in Duralink," Justice said.

"That was my guess. That's why I need you on this hunt. You and Noah."

"I may get you in trouble with this dog Heston," Justice admitted.

"How is that?"

"This dog has probably been released to find me. He will pick up my scent quickly and hunt us down."

"Is he as smart as you?"

"No, but he has been enhanced."

"Enhanced how?"

His tracking skills are superior to any other dog besides me. His sense of smell is profoundly superior to any other dog besides me. Where he is going to be stronger than me is in the fighting and killing skills."

They designed him to kill? Heston asked.

He is a killing machine—an assassin. My understanding was that he couldn't be controlled, and they were going to pull the plug on his program. Eliminate him. They replaced him with three other dogs that were hybrids of wolfs, coyotes and German Shepherds.

"They must have solved their problems with him." Heston said.

"Doubtful. It is more likely they just released him." Justice said.

"Why would they release a killing machine into an urban environment?"

"Cash Buck is capable of anything. He is not the brightest bulb on the tree."

"And he is?" Heston asked.

"He is the Vice President of Animal Sciences." Justice replied.

"The VP of Animal Sciences isn't smart? That sounds hard to believe." Heston said.

"Remember that animal sciences is really the military division of Duralink. They hired Cash Buck because he was a retired Army Major who was a commander in the 1st Cav. out of Fort Hood." Justice explained.

"They needed a military guy for a liaison to the army?"

"That's right. And to help them understand what the Army needs regarding fighting dogs as well as reconnaissance dogs." Justice had all of Cash Buck's personal information downloaded into his brain.

"OK, so this Direwolf will find you?" Heston asked.

"I believe so," Justice said matter-of-factly.

"So, we set a trap then." Peggy said.

"Wait a minute. I don't like the idea of using Justice as bait for a trained killer to find." Noah objected.

"Noah," Justice said "he is going to find me no matter what. This way we are in control of the situation. It will be our only advantage." Justice's logic was clear to all of them.

"Our guns will be another advantage," Heston said.

"Maybe. You will need big guns." Justice said.

"Is a 44-magnum big enough?"

"What ammunition are you loaded with?"

"Black Talons"

"I thought that was discontinued in 2000?" Justice knew about Black Talons.

"Discontinued for the general public. The CIA and FBI have access. I know people who know people. So, I have plenty."

"Black Talons should work. But you will still need to shoot him six or more times. And aim for a head shot. That may be your only hope."

"What about our 9 mils. We don't have Black Talons." Peggy asked.

"They will not make a difference."

"What about our Mossberg?" Gene asked.

"What are you loaded with?"

"Twelve-gauge slugs."

"That will work too, but again, take a headshot."

"So, you saw this Direwolf?" Heston asked.

"Yes, I saw two of them."

"How big is he?"

"About the size of a pony. His head will be even with your neck. He could easily lay his nose upwards onto your shoulder."

"Holy sweet baby Jesus," Gene said.

"Yeah, what he said." Heston agreed.

They rode in nervous silence for a couple of more minutes before they got to the Smiley home.

When they arrived, they pulled into the gravel driveway and spotted two Sherrif's SUVs as well as two Texas Ranger Ford F250 pickup trucks and a standard looking sedan.

"The Rangers are already here." Peggy said.

"I wonder who they sent." Gene said.

"I dunno, but I recognize that sedan."

"I do too," Peggy said. She never forgot a vehicle.

They got out of their vehicle and lowered the tailgate for Reagan and Trump.

The four of them with the three dogs walked up to the group gathered by the front porch.

Heston, Gene and Peggy knew everybody there.

"Well hello Heston and crew!" Nancy Webb said.

"Hello Nancy."

"Hi Heston, Gene, Peggy, Noah." Becky Lawson said cheerfully.

"Ranger Becky." Heston nodded and smiled.

"Looks like you got a promotion!" Peggy said. She was clearly glad to see Becky Lawson again.

"Yes, I did." Becky smiled back at Peggy.

"It's Captain Lawson now!" Peggy said smiling. "Congratulations Captain Becky! Look at you!"

"Not to you Peggy. I will always be just Becky to you."

Becky walked over to Peggy and gave her a hug. She would never forget their adventure with Mrs. Thin Man.

"The last time I saw you was when you received The Commissioner's Medal of Valor." Peggy smiled and said.

"I appreciated you being there for that."

"Wouldn't have missed it, Becky."

"This is Noah and his dog Thor."

"Noah." Becky nodded and shook his hand.

"Ahhh put a fork in it, let's just call him Justice" Nancy said "I'm not going to tell Duralink where their dog is. Not after he basically saved all of us from that whacko Harry."

"You don't think they will send another private detective for Justice?" Gene asked.

"Not a private detective. They will send animals that can identify Justice by smell though. His name is meaningless to them."

"So, Justice was with Duralink?" Captain Becky asked.

"That's a subject for another day, Captain Becky." Heston said "We will tell you the whole story, just not now. No time for it." Heston tried to assure the Captain that she need not be alarmed about Justice.

"Ok if you say so."

"Thanks, Captain Becky."

"Heston, Peggy, Gene and Noah this is Ranger Hugh Jasole. He is new with us, but he had 10 years as a Sheriff's Deputy working with dogs here in Texas. I thought with his background with dogs he may be helpful with our problem."

They all shook hand with Ranger Hugh. Then Heston asked "So who is going with us? It's almost three am so we need to get started."

"I'm going" Nancy Webb was the first to chime in.

"OK, who else Captain Lawson?" Heston asked.

"I am going to send Ranger Hugh with you," Becky said.

"OK, Nancy I assume Duralink hired you again?" Heston asked.

"That's right."

"So, this is confirmed to be a Duralink animal?"

"It looks that way. I have been told we need to kill it."

220

"What weapon do you carry?"

"I have a Glock 9 Millimeter and a .38 revolver," Nancy said.

"OK, probably not big enough. We will find out."

"That's all I have. They didn't tell me I'd need more."

"Go get your weapons and let's get going."

In two minutes Nancy had retrieved her guns from the trunk of her car and was ready to go.

"Trump, Regan. Justice, scent. Go!"

Justice led the way. He ran straight to the forest without hesitation. Once in the forest Trump and Reagan quickly picked up the scent that Justice was following.

"We will stay in touch Becky," Heston said over his shoulder as they trekked towards the forest.

"Happy hunting!" Becky wanted to join them but had to assume the role of operation commander and stay at the command center at the Smiley home.

Heston, Gene, Peggy, Noah, Nancy and Ranger Hugh tried to follow the quick dogs. Before long the dogs were out of sight. The dogs followed a small trail that had recently been traveled by Delta. His scent was strong. They looped around the property and soon arrived at the point in the road where Delta attacked Reverend Paul's truck. It was there where the dogs allowed the group of humans to catch up to them.

Ranger Hugh lagged behind by more than a couple of minutes.

Heston knelt next to Justice before Ranger Hugh arrived.

"It looks like Delta has been here. I think he actually attacked a vehicle. But I have no idea why he would do that." Justice quietly said to Heston. For now, Ranger Hugh didn't need to know Justice could speak.

"So, this is the Direwolf you saw at Duralink?"

"Definitely. His name is Delta."

"That corresponds with what they told me Heston." Nancy overheard the conversation.

"How did you find out about this situation Nancy?" Heston was not only curious but a bit suspicious. He wondered how much information Duralink was able to harvest out of all their high-tech abilities.

"Duralink called me, asked me to come over to the Smiley home and get involved."

"Nancy, what can you tell me about this Direwolf?" Heston asked.

"Well, according to my sources he is with a man named Cash Buck. Cash was his handler, a division vice president or something like that, and a security camera caught him leading the dog into the forest."

"When?"

"Only a few hours ago."

"So, how did you know to go to the Smiley home?"

"I really don't know more than I've told you Heston. Like I told you already, I got a call telling me where to go."

Heston had a bunch more questions. He decided to wait until later to ask them.

Ranger Hugh caught up to them but wasn't given time to catch his breath. The dogs shot off in the direction of Reverend Paul's home.

Attics Are Not Very Safe

Just as the attic access door closed they heard the giant Direwolf enter the closet. He produced a low growl that terrified both the women, and they began to scream.

"Quiet, quiet!" Reverend Paul said. His hopes that they may remain hidden in the attic were dashed by their screams.

"We are safe here." He assured them. "He can't get up here. Who has the cell phone?"

"I do."

"Give it to me."

Anna Paul handed her husband the phone as she held their daughter Emma tight trying to comfort her.

Reverend Paul dialed 911.

"911 what's your emergency?" The female operator sounded tired from a long shift of calls.

"A giant dog is trying to eat us." Reverend Paul said excitedly.

"A giant dog, sir?" The operator's skeptical tone was unmistakable.

"Yes, send someone quick!"

"Where are you?"

"In the attic."

"A long pause."

"Sir, I mean what is your address?"

"2476 Rosebud in Driftwood."

"Sir just so I'm clear, you are telling me a giant dog has chased you into your attic. Do I have that right?"

"Yes, that's right."

"What kind of dog is it?"

"A giant dog."

"I mean what breed is it, sir?"

"I dunno probably a giant wolf. Yeah, that's it, it's a wolf."

"So, we have giant wolves in Texas now."

"Yes"

"I did not know that sir." The operator said blandly.

"Look," Reverend Paul was exasperated and recognized her sarcasm, "just send help, please!"

"OK, I will send someone out. To get the big dog. I mean wolf." The 911 operator hung up, confident the man was a druggie having hallucinations. Texas hasn't had wolves in 50 years.

"They are sending someone out. They will be here soon." Reverend Paul told Anna and Gloria. He wanted to calm them down. Fact was, he wasn't sure anyone was coming. The operator thought he was crazy. He was sure of that.

Anna was glad to hear the Sheriff would come to save them. She felt guilty for screaming the way she did. She hadn't believed her husband's story about a big dog. Anna felt a pang of guilt. It couldn't have been good for Emma to see her mom screaming like that. Anna squeezed her daughter in a tight hug.

The attic was small. Only two sheets of 4 x 8 plywood were used as a flat surface, and most of the space was taken up by boxes of Christmas decorations. They were surrounded by joists and fiberglass insulation.

They sat in the dark listening to their breathing and trying to resist making loud noises. Their feet were just inches away from the attic hatchway. Maybe the giant beast would go away.

Then the attic hatch door began to get pulled down. The women started screaming again. Unbelievably, the wood ladder was pulled downward. Reverend Paul couldn't believe that a dog could do this. How was this possible? They saw two giant paws emerge on the ladder and appear to pull up a giant wolf's head. They scooted as far back from the door as they could while remaining on the plywood surface.

The dog's giant snout was visible first. A large black nose and teeth were visible from inside the attic. Then they saw the eyes emerge from below, black eyes. The eyes darted towards them, he knew where they were. The giant dog couldn't turn his head towards them due to his enormous size.

Gloria Smiley stood up in a panic as she continued to scream. Delta's black eyes followed her.

Reverend Paul quickly realized their saving grace was that the wolf wouldn't fit through the opening. The giant wolf couldn't even fit his entire head in, his shoulders were too broad. The wolf threw his snout side to side trying to wiggle and squeeze his giant body through the narrow hatchway to the attic. He bared his teeth and growled in frustration.

"We're safe! He can't fit up here!" Reverend Paul yelled, trying to be heard above the females screaming.

Anna Paul heard him and immediately stopped screaming.

"He won't fit!" Anna yelled. A giant sense of happiness swept over her." He won't fit!" She screamed again with a massive sense of relief. She squeezed Emma tightly.

Gloria was not aware that the giant dog could not fit. She wasn't listening. Her eyes were closed and her screams prevented her from hearing what Anna and Reverend Paul were saying.

Gloria's panic intensified when she opened her eyes and saw the wolf's giant snout and teeth. When the wolf's eyes darted towards them, she turned around in the dark attic to run. Her first two steps were on a joist, but her third step crushed through the insulation and her foot landed on the drywall ceiling. As her weight shifted forward, her foot broke through the drywall ceiling. Now her entire leg hung through the ceiling into the room below.

"No, No!" Gloria screamed. Her hands held her above two ceiling joists. Gloria didn't understand the ceiling was simple drywall and unable to carry her weight. She placed her right foot on the drywall and tried to push herself back up into the attic. Her right foot broke through the drywall into the room below also. Now Gloria was halfway in the attic and halfway into the room below. Gloria looked at Reverend Paul and Anna with horror on her face.

"Help!" Was all Gloria could say.

Anna held Emma tightly. She could only watch in horror through the darkness as Gloria was hanging halfway through the ceiling into the room below. Gloria struggled to pull herself upwards, but she was not strong enough. Light from the room below shined upwards illuminating the terror on Gloria's face.

Reverend Paul moved towards Gloria and extended his hand.

"Gloria, grab my hand! I'll pull you up!"

Anna watched her husband try to grab Gloria's hand. Then she looked back at the hatchway and became more terrified for her friend as the giant dog nose descended back down the ladder.

"Quick! The beast is coming for you Gloria! Grab his hand." Anna yelled.

Gloria's face showed determination, and she stopped screaming, either because she had lost her voice or realized now was the time for action, not screaming.

Gloria grabbed Reverend Paul's hand and squeezed as tightly as she could. She slowly moved towards Reverend Paul as he pulled on her extended hand. The broken drywall ceiling made pulling her upwards more difficult than they could handle. Gloria seemed to get stuck as Reverend Paul pulled on her hand. She wouldn't budge, no matter how hard Reverend Paul pulled.

Gloria looked at Anna and smiled. She believed she was close to being pulled to safety.

Then they heard a ferocious snarl.

Gloria jerked violently downwards. She screamed in pain this time. The Direwolf had Gloria by her legs and pulled downward in a deadly tug-of-war. The tone of a scream in pain is different from the tone of a scream of horror. Reverend Paul thought screaming in pain is far worse. Gloria still held Reverend Paul's hand tightly, trying to pull herself to safety.

"Pull me! pull me!" Gloria begged. "I don't want to die!"

"C'mon Gloria!" Reverend Paul pulled with all his might on her hand.

Gloria forcefully jerked away from Reverend Paul. Paul lost his firm grip on Gloria's hand and now he had a poor grasp on Gloria's hand, and it was getting worse. She slipped away from him with terror on her face. Now, he only held on to her by her fingertips.

"He's got me! Pull! He has my leg!" Gloria yelled in a pain and panic.

Then Reverend Paul lost the tug of war battle.

His hand slipped from her fingers and she went further into the room below. Only her head and shoulders were visible, her arms were restricted straight above her head by the joists.

"It isn't too late Gloria! Grab me!" Reverend Paul extended his hand again towards her. He knew he was lying.

Gloria looked at Reverend Paul and back and Anna.

"Thank you," she said calmly. She knew the battle was over. Those would be her final words.

Gloria violently jerked then fell completely through the ceiling into the room below.

Anna and Reverend Paul stared at the space where Gloria had just been. Only the light from the room below shined upwards where Gloria was. They listened to the Direwolf as it viciously tore into Gloria's body. Reverend Paul knew he didn't need to pull the hatchway door closed. The giant beast couldn't fit up there.

The loss of Gloria was utterly unnecessary. Her panic was as guilty as the Direwolf was for her death.

Bass gets Involved

Bass was in the yard at 7:30 am with the three wolves Alpha, Beta and Charlie. He was excited and impressed with their abilities to understand and perform every command he gave them.

It was time to get to the dangerous subjects. He needed to teach them commands that told them to attack approved targets and not attack the handler or the surrounding 'good guys' that will always be with them on a mission.

He decided to walk them through Duralink and all the Duralink employees he saw he called 'family'. Then told them to never attack family.

Next, he walked them into the Language Lab. Bass told Jenny, Anita and Yuri to say 'Family'. Then Bass taught the dogs that anyone that says 'Family' was not to be attacked under any circumstances. 'Family' was now a code word. It was code for 'do not attack me'.

So now the handler could identify 'family' as safe and not targets, and friendlies could identify themselves as friendly by using the code word 'Family'.

Bass thought to himself that this was just too easy. Why couldn't the idiots at the Military Lab have thought of this?

Bass had previously taken five foam human-shaped targets into the yard and stood them up in a line. They stood up like five tall bowling pins. When he entered the yard with the wolves, he noticed a few handfuls of people quickly exit the yard. They were obviously concerned about the large wolves.

Bass pointed at two of the targets and said 'Family'. Next, he took the wolves across the yard and unclipped their leashes. Bass was a bit nervous. He heard the stories about disasters in the Military Lab when the attack words were used. Should he have a gun? He wondered if he should go get a gun for protection, just in case. Problem was, he didn't know how to shoot a gun. He had never fired a gun. So, getting a gun seemed foolish. He would just have faith in his process.

He looked at the wolves that calmly stared back at him.

He got the feeling they knew what he was contemplating.

Bass said out loud "I'm not getting a gun. I trust you. You can do this. You are the smartest dogs I have worked with since Justice."

The three wolves stared at him like they were ready for the command.

"Remember, I am 'Family'." Bass' heart rate increased.

"Ok, Alpha, Beta and Charlie" Bass pointed to the targets. "Three targets, two family, only kill…."

When Bass said 'Kill" the three dogs raced towards the targets. They sprinted with blinding speed across the yard directly at the targets that were standing up 50 yards away.

"Crap, we're going to have to work on that," Bass said.

Their long strides allowed them to cover the distance in mere seconds. As the wolves sprinted across the yard they communicated and decided between themselves their specific targets. Each dog took one of the targets at full speed.

The collisions into the targets were ferocious. The three targets were torn to shreds within 15 seconds of acquisition. The two 'family' members were left untouched.

When it was over the wolves looked at each other for a moment. Then they raced at full speed towards Bass Wooten.

Bass saw them running to him and said a quick prayer. He didn't really know if they were going to kill him too or await their next command. His last thought before they arrived was 'I should have got that gun'.

Bass stood straight and did his best to appear confident of his safety. His heart pounded rapidly in his chest.

The wolves arrived in a full sprint and skidded across the grass to a stop. They sat upright in front of Bass awaiting their next command.

Bass heard ecstatic applause and cheers from around him. When he looked around the yard at the building, he saw all the windows were open with employees watching from their offices. They continued to applaud and cheer him on. Their fists were raised in the air, and they chanted his name "Bass, Bass, Bass!" and gave each other high fives.

Apparently, they had been watching to see if Bass was successful. Then he noticed one man in the Military Lab window with an M 16 pointed his way, just to ensure Bass' safety.

Bass felt great. He waved to his friends and the others that he had never met that were applauding him.

The wolves attacked as a team. All Bass had to do was work with them to identify target vs. family.

He still had work to do with the command language necessary. But most importantly, they didn't kill 'family'.

Bass took the wolves back into the building and headed towards the Language Lab. He ran into Dr. Porkter on the way.

"Bass you were terrific." Dr. Porkter said.

"Thanks, honestly it's these wolves that are terrific." Bass attempted humility.

"You are alive, others didn't make it that far, Bass." Dr. Porkter basically admitted she was aware of the deaths of employees from the Military Lab. Up until that point, Bass doubted the stories of the wolves killing their handlers.

"Thanks Dr. Porkter."

"Please call me Betty."

"OK Betty. For the record, please say the word 'Family' and look at the dogs. It's our code word to keep handlers and friendlies safe."

"OK Bass, Family, Family, Family." Betty looked at each of the dogs and said the new code word.

"You should be safe from them now," Bass said confidently.

"Bass when you get to the Language Lab you will meet a new team member. He is from the military. In fact, he is a dog handler from the Navy Seals. He has long experience in fighting with dogs in Iraq and Afghanistan."

"OK, what is his role?"

"I need you to turn the wolves over to him."

Turn them over?

"Yes."

"Betty, they are not ready."

"They have to be."

"Betty, they may…. Hurt… him" Bass still didn't want to say the 'kill' word. He wasn't sure they could be contained yet. His success a few minutes ago in the yard was terrific but still limited. They needed more training.

"Bass, just make him say 'family' and let them go. I understand your feelings. More than you know."

"Good then please let me have more time with them."

"I can't. I am limited as to what I can tell you because it is classified. But you need to know that we had 'other assets' being developed and trained. These assets are even more dangerous than Alpha, Beta and Charlie. It appears Mr. Buck released one last night. We need these wolves to catch Justice as well as an animal we call Delta. That is all I can tell you, and more than I should have."

"May I go on the mission too?"

"No, we need you here. The success I just witnessed qualifies you and demands that you work with another asset we have in Military Labs. Just in case these wolves are unsuccessful."

"What is this asset?"

"For now, we call him 'War'."

Reverend Paul's Home

At 6:00 am Heston chased after the dogs when his cell phone rang.

"Heston, we need you to go to Reverend Paul's home" Captain Becky said.

"We are walking up to his home now. The dogs just led us here."

"It looks like the animal that attacked Mr. Smiley attacked his wife at Reverend Paul's home."

"Anyone else injured?"

"Other than Mrs. Smiley, No."

"How is she now?"

"She isn't."

It took a moment for that to register with Heston.

"OK, I'm here now. I'll call you after I know something."

"Roger that."

Heston and his group walked up to the Paul's residence and knocked on the door.

Nobody answered the door. Heston checked the doorknob to see if it was unlocked. It was locked.

They walked around back of the home and found the sliding glass door destroyed.

Heston motioned for his team to remain outside. He was going in. He had his Colt Anaconda out and ready to shoot.

"Hello?" Heston called out.

"Hello! We are up here."

"C'mon down now."

"You sure it's safe?"

"As safe as you're gonna be for now," Heston shouted back.

Heston walked around a corner and into the master bedroom. He found the remains of Gloria Smiley. She had been mostly consumed by an animal of some sort. It looked like a grizzly bear attack. There was a large hole in the ceiling.

Heston heard a creaking sound from the walk-in closet.

"We are coming down now!" Reverend Paul called out.

Heston waited in the bedroom for them to come out.

Reverend Paul, Anna Paul and Emma Paul came out of the closet and looked like they had just survived a tornado.

"I suggest you keep the baby's eyes away from your bedroom," Heston said.

"OK, I will," Anna said.

"Follow me out to the living room and tell me what happened." Heston led the way into the next room.

The living room was full of glass and broken door parts, so they went into the kitchen. Anna and Emma sat down at the dinette set. They looked exhausted.

Reverend Paul remained standing. Soon, Heston's entire team was standing around the Paul family, waiting for the story of their ordeal.

"Heston it was a giant wolf" Reverend Paul looked directly at Heston.

"How giant?"

"It was so big it couldn't fit up the ladder into the attic to get us."

"It didn't fit on the ladder?"

"Well, more accurately, it couldn't fit through the attic hatchway. It actually climbed up the ladder. But it couldn't fit through the hole into the attic. Its body was too wide. That's the only reason we are alive."

"What happened to Gloria Smiley?"

"She panicked, ran across the drywall ceiling and fell halfway through. The wolf pulled her down the rest of the way."

Heston looked at Nancy Webb.

"Why the hell did Duralink release this animal into the public, Nancy?" Heston hated to see the looks on the Paul family faces, as well as the deceased Gloria Smiley. He blamed Duralink.

"Hey Heston, I didn't release anything. They called me to get it back." Nancy tried to convey her innocence.

"They must not like you much." Heston said.

"What do you mean?" Nancy asked.

"This animal won't feel a 9 mil or a .38 caliber pistol. They should have told you what size of weapon to bring. They're setting you up to fail."

"I don't think so, Heston," Nancy chuckled the accusation off. "My 9 mil. will work just fine."

"If I was sending you after this animal, I'd have you carrying a larger gun. A Mossberg 12 gauge, or a hand cannon. That's all I'm saying."

"This will do just fine." Nancy's retired cop demeanor was shining through.

"Suit yourself, Nancy."

Heston walked through the broken glass door and into the backyard. He called for Noah, Gene and Peggy to join him.

Nancy retreated into the back yard to join them.

"This is a private meeting," Heston said to Nancy and Ranger Hugh. "Give us a couple of minutes."

"Hey, why do you need to be alone?" Nancy asked.

"How about this Nancy– It's none of your freaking business." Heston looked at her angrily. He liked her less and less.

Nancy turned and walked away.

"I see you haven't lost your prudent subtlety Heston," Gene said with a grin.

"She is getting on my nerves" Heston growled.

"Hadn't noticed" Peggy said.

Heston looked at Justice.

"If this creature is after you, he is going to find you. I'm wrestling with that. Either we want him to find you and use you as bait for a trap, or we want to go find him. Seems like we are restricted to him finding you unless you have any ideas."

"I don't want Justice used as bait." Noah jumped in.

"Noah, I really don't want to hear from you. You are going to be over there with Nancy in a quick second." Heston glared at Noah. The words 'shut up' were shining through, despite not being verbally spoken.

Noah's feelings were hurt, he decided to be quiet.

Heston looked back at Justice.

"Got any ideas?" Heston asked Justice.

"Well, yes. We can mask my scent."

"How can we do that?"

"It will be a two-step process."

"OK. Go on." Heston was curious.

"It is not pleasant."

"OK. Spit it out."

"I'm afraid I will."

"I don't get it, Justice."

"Ok here it is. I need the women to urinate on me, then cover me in freshly ground coffee."

"Yucch!" Peggy said loudly. "I'm not doing that!"

"Hey, you guys asked me. That is about all that will work given what we have available to us."

Gene, Heston, Noah and Justice all looked at Peggy.

"Don't look at me you bunch of perverts." Peggy was disgusted.

"What about Nancy?" Gene said. "She could help."

Heston rolled his eyes, he didn't want to ask Nancy for help.

"Bring her over here," Heston said with disgust.

Gene turned to Nancy who was still in the house with Reverend Paul and his wife. He waved her over.

"Nancy, I need you to do something." Heston started.

"That's a subtle start Heston." Peggy started to laugh.

"You are usually a bit more direct than that, Heston." Gene smiled.

Heston paused for a bit.

"Out with it, Heston." Nancy was annoyed.

"That's what he was going to tell you." Peggy laughed.

Gene and Noah laughed too.

Nancy was getting more annoyed.

Heston turned towards the house. He had an idea to make this idea a bit more feasible.

"Anna, do you have any empty Mason Jars?"

"Yes, I have a bunch of them, it's canning season."

"Do you have any ground coffee?"

"Of course."

"Can you bring me a couple of Mason jars and some ground coffee?"

"A couple of jars, you must think she really has to go." Peggy smiled.

"Actually Peggy, one is for you." Heston looked at his friend. "I don't think you are going to want to share a mason jar."

Twenty minutes later after Peggy and Nancy had done their duty, Justice was covered with coffee grounds that stuck in his fur due to the wetness from the Mason jars.

"That is disgusting," Peggy said with her nose curled.

"He's not riding in the cab of the truck anymore. That I can assure you." Heston said.

"Now what?" Heston looked at Justice and asked.

"I'm going to pick up Delta's smell off Mrs. Smiley. Then we go get him." Justice said.

"I'm calling Captain Becky to give her the plan." Heston walked into the yard for better cell reception.

"Captain Becky, we have a plan."

"I'm glad you called. There is an update from Duralink."

"OK, you go first."

"This is definitely a Duralink animal we are after. And it is a Direwolf."

"Yeah, we know that. Nancy Webb confirmed it."

"They are sending a team to help."

"They want to send help? More than Nancy? Can I swap Nancy for the new team?"

"No, you can't swap Nancy. And Heston, I know you will not like this but…." Becky was hesitant to tell Heston something she knew he wouldn't like.

"Go on," Heston said, his disgust from not being able to get rid of Nancy was apparent.

"They are sending a Navy Seal with a special team of dogs. A special team of wolves, to be more precise."

"A Navy Seal with a special team of wolves will help us?" Heston said incredulously.

"Believe it or not."

"I don't."

"Well, you will shortly because he is joining you at the Reverend Paul's home soon."

"With wolves?"

"Yep. With wolves."

"Ok. I'll believe it when I see it."

"Call me with updates."

"Roger that."

Heston rejoined his group. When he told them about the wolves and the Navy Seal, Justice became nervous.

"We are going to find out quickly if the urine and coffee trick is going to work," Justice said.

"How is that?"

"Those wolves will be after me and the Direwolf," Justice said.

"What will they do if they realize you are who you are?"

"Kill me." Justice stated the fact he knew to be true.

"Let's get him out of here," Noah exclaimed.

"Too late," Gene said. "They're here" he nodded to the driveway.

They all looked and saw a government sedan coming down the Paul's driveway.

They stood in silence as a fit-looking man with a large black beard and long black hair got out of the car. He opened the back door, and three giant wolves jumped out. The Navy Seal had them on leashes that Justice knew would not hold them if they didn't want to be held.

The Seal walked up to the group and instinctively knew Heston Hand was in charge. The new man wore a Black Metallica T-Shirt and wore blue jeans with expensive Solomon Quest four GTX hiking boots.

He told the wolves to sit and stay. They immediately sat and waited for the Seal's following command.

"Hello, you must be Heston." The Seal said with an extended hand and smile.

"Yes, I am," Heston said as he shook the new man's hand. Heston noticed the iron grip of the Navy Seal.

"And this must be Gene, Peggy and Nancy and you…. You are?" The seal knew who everyone was except Noah.

"I'm Noah." Noah said. He felt like he could fill a mason jar too now.

Heston was amazed at Seal's accurate information and his quick ability to deploy it and gather new information.

As the Seal shook everyone's hand, Heston noted that the man was smaller physically than he expected from a Special Forces killer.

"My Name is Ben. Ben Doverbich. I have been asked to join you." Ben smiled easily at his new team. He had previously joined many teams and knew how to assimilate successfully.

"So, Ben, you are a Navy Seal?" Gene asked.

"Yes Gene, your intel is good" Ben smiled.

"What specifically have they told you, Ben?" Heston asked. "Our intel has just been updated with some pretty shocking details. "We have two targets. One is a German Shepherd just like that one." He paused for a moment and looked directly at Justice. "And we are after a huge wolf."

"A Direwolf?"

"Exactly. Do you mind if I ask how you knew it was a Direwolf?" Ben asked.

"After the Paul's told us their story as well as the Smiley's story, it was the only conclusion," Heston responded.

"That's smart, Heston" Ben said complementary "Not many would conclude Direwolf since they have been extinct for 9500 years."

"How did Duralink get one?"

"I'm sorry Heston, I can't answer that. But I can confirm your information."

"Well Ben, I'm told they have another one they can release."

"How did you get that information, Heston?"

"I'm sorry Ben, I can't answer that. I can confirm your information." Heston repeated Ben's words exactly. Two can play this game, Heston thought.

It was not a good move. Ben was much more intelligent than the average man. Seconds after Heston said it, Ben looked at Justice.

"Beautiful dog," Ben said. "What's his name?"

"Thor," Nancy said. She didn't want the Seal to take Justice away. Justice had earned her loyalty after the Harry Rivers adventure.

"Who does he belong to?" Ben asked.

"Me," Noah said weakly.

Ben nodded. "Hello, Thor."

Justice looked at the new man.

Inside, Justice felt relief that the giant wolves had no interest in him. They glared at Reagan and Trump as much as they did himself. He knew they would have killed him by now if they knew who he was.

"I understand we have a deceased inside?

"Yes."

"Killed by the Direwolf?"

"Yes."

"I'm going to take these dogs in to pick up a scent."

"Don't you mean confirm a scent?"

"Yes, Heston, that is more accurate. Thank you." Ben decided at that very moment that he would not save Heston if the opportunity presented itself. Ben smiled nicely at the group and then went into the home with the three giant wolves.

Gene got closer to Heston.

"You know Heston, I heard General Mattice say that when he walked in a room, he decided how he would kill everyone else in the room. I get that feeling with Ben. He just decided how he would kill all of us." Gene said.

"Well, maybe just you Heston." Peggy smiled at him.

"You are both right," Justice said.

Heston nodded his understanding.

"I have his bio in my brain Heston. Ben is a sniper as well as a dog handler. His dog handling duty was not the run of the mill, though. He was dispatched with special dogs for assassinations. Bosnia, Iraq, Afghanistan and even in Iran." Justice said, speaking as softly as he could. "He is a one-man kill team with a dog."

"He doesn't look the part," Heston said.

"He is the perfect size and temperament for the part." Justice observed. "He jumped out of airplanes with a killer dog, found the target, killed the target and hiked out from behind enemy lines more than 200 times... so far. Some of his ex-fils were more than 100 miles. He is still active. He is on a special assignment to Duralink. That alone should tell you how connected Duralink is."

"So, he's a killer," Heston said with a 'so what' tone.

"Don't downplay this, Heston." Justice looked at Heston directly. "He will kill you if you get in his way. Make no mistake about it. Please don't cross him or give him a reason. He is a perfect fit to handle those three wolves. Basically, that is a pack of four wolves. Do not ever forget that Heston. That is four killer wolves." Justice tried his best to warn Heston.

"I got it, Justice." Heston had an edge to his voice. He didn't like being coached by a dog.

They waited for the Seal and the wolves to emerge from the home.

Ben nodded that he was ready.

Heston said, 'scent go!' And Trump, Reagan and Justice shot off into the forest.

Ben unclipped Alpha, Beta and Charlie. He nodded to them, and they were off in a shockingly fast dash towards the forest, barely behind Heston's dog team.

It wouldn't take them long to acquire their target.

Ranger Hugh

Captain Becky called Ranger Hugh Jasole on his cell phone.

"Ranger Hugh, this is Becky" She still wasn't comfortable referring to herself as Captain Becky or Captain Lawson. It just didn't fit yet.

"Yes Ma'am," Ranger Hugh said respectfully. Becky had earned it. The stories about her battles with a giant bug were legendary. She was a celebrity, and Hugh felt lucky to work for her.

"I want you to meet Deputy Waylon and Deputy Jesus in Driftwood. You will enter the forest from Salt Lick Barbeque and head towards Driftwood. Maybe you can chase this big dog towards Heston and his crew."

"Yes, Ma'am," Was all Ranger Hugh needed to say.

"Ranger Hugh, carry your Mossberg loaded with slugs." Becky would never forget the warnings from the small ghost named Cole. They may not have prevailed over Thin Man or Mrs. Thin Man if not for Cole.

Hugh headed for Dripping Springs to meet the two young Sheriff's deputies.

They met off the State Highway 1826 at the famous Salt Lick Barbeque Restaurant.

"Hello, boys!" Ranger Hugh said to Deputy Jesus and Deputy Waylon.

"Hey, Ranger Hugh." Both young men said.

They had known each other for years. They went to Dripping Springs High school and played football and baseball together. All three dreamed of going into Law Enforcement together after high school.

They went through the Hays County Sheriff's academy together. After graduation, they served together until Hugh crossed over into the K-9 department. After that, he transferred to the Texas Rangers.

"You boys ready for a stroll through the woods?"

"Let's catch us a giant dog!"

All three were woefully unprepared for what lay ahead of them.

Ranger Hugh did not carry his Mossberg like he was told to by Captain Becky. He was so excited to see his friends that he forgot the Captain's instructions. Deputies Jesus and Waylon did not know they should carry guns larger than their sidearms. All three were armed with Glock 9-millimeter handguns. They were prepared for hiking, not fighting a Direwolf.

After two hours, they were getting close to the home of Reverend Paul and had not seen any signs of a giant dog.

"Do you fellas believe there is a giant dog out here?" Ranger Hugh asked.

"I dunno. Seems hard to believe." Deputy Jesus said.

"I saw Cody Smiley. He was torn up bad. Even lost an arm." Jesus said.

"A rabid dog could have done that." Ranger Hugh said.

"I don't think so." Jesus said.

"I've seen Pit Bulls tear bigger dogs apart."

"Cody's arm was ripped off his body. His wife described a giant wolf. Not a giant pit bull." Jesus said.

"Eyewitnesses are wrong most of the time."

"OK hotshot, you keep on looking for a big Pit Bull. I'm looking for a giant wolf."

They pressed on through the forest.

Deputy Jesus was in the best physical shape of the three men, and he got ahead of the team by a long distance. Waylon and Hugh stuck together. After 30 minutes, they couldn't see Jesus.

"I don't see Jesus. He's too far ahead." Waylon said, out of breath.

"Try calling him."

"My cell phone has terrible service out here."

"Radio?"

"Deputy Jesus, Deputy Waylon, over." Waylon used his radio.

Nothing.

"I get poor reception way out here like this."

"Yeah, me too."

The two kept moving.

After 20 minutes, they found blood on the forest floor—large amounts of blood covered the trail.

"Jesus! Jesus!" Both men called out. They were deep in the forest now; visibility was less than ten yards in most directions.

"Think this is his blood?" Waylon asked.

"I hope not." Hugh said.

They pulled their weapons out and moved forward down the trail.

"Jesus!" They both called out.

No answer.

"We should never have let him get that far away from us."

They pressed forward until they heard the sounds of running water up ahead. They knew that meant they were near Onion Creek.

They rounded a bend in the trail.

The sounds of the creek got louder, and the air became cooler.

They rounded the next corner and expected to find the fast-moving creek.

Instead, they found a giant silver and black Direwolf.

They both pointed their Glocks and fired five quick shots. Pow, pow, pow, pow, pow, pow!

The Direwolf growled and began his charge.

Waylon and Hugh turned to run, but not fast enough.

The Direwolf caught Waylon first. In a ferocious burst of speed, Waylon was grabbed from behind.

The Direwolf seized Waylon by the waist and chomped down hard enough to cut open his stomach.

Waylon tried to point his weapon at the huge animal, but he dropped it in pain. Instead, he punched the Direwolf over and over helplessly in its snout.

"Run, Hugh run!" Waylon yelled at his friend. They would be his last words. He wrestled side to side, kicking and punching. The blood from his severely bitten abdomen poured onto the forest floor, soaking the leaves and weeds. He pushed at the snout of the beast with his fists only to have his hands bitten, opening up his wrists. Now bleeding to death was a matter of minutes away.

Hugh ran up the trail away from the violence. H stopped and caught his breath; he was ashamed of his fear and that he had abandoned his friend. He had always wondered how he would perform under attack. Now he knew. He ran away. Hugh was mortified as he stood frozen with indecision. He turned around and faced the trail that he had just run down in fear. Listening to the vicious sounds of his friend being torn apart and eaten instilled horror deep into his consciousness. Hugh was frozen motionless with terror. His friend became quiet. Quiet as death.

Hugh wanted to go to his friend's rescue. But he couldn't. He was frozen in place. It was too late to save his friend, he argued to himself. Then he remembered the Captain's instructions to carry his Mossberg. He didn't follow her instructions. Now, he was even more ashamed of himself. Even more afraid. Ranger Hugh thought about the stories of Captain Becky and her bravery under fire. The things she did in the face of insurmountable odds. He wanted those kinds of stories to be told about him. There is only one way to make that happen, he realized. Cowards die many times before their death. The Brave taste death only once.

Ranger Hugh Jasole looked up at the blue Texas sky. This was his moment. This was his time to define himself.

He marched down the trail towards the giant Direwolf.

War

Bass tentatively walked down the long hall to the Military Lab.

He had heard stories about the Military lab, however he had never been inside the mysterious place. He heard crazy stories about werewolves being created and tested for battle. Those couldn't be true, could they? He didn't know what to believe and what not to believe.

He turned the corner into a long quiet hall and found a Military Policeman sitting guard at a desk in front of the entrance to the Military Labs.

Bass introduced himself and explained that they should be expecting him. The MP looked on a computer screen and found his name. He reached in his top drawer and gave Bass a visitor's badge and told him to wear it while inside. Then the MP pressed a button, and the door was electrically unlocked.

Bass entered the Lab and was greeted by Dr. Porkter.

"Hello Bass, thanks for coming."

"Nice to see you again, Dr. Porkter."

"Betty, please Bass."

"Ok yes, I forgot." Bass smiled at her.

"Follow me, please Bass."

They walked through a massive office with more than twenty researchers working on various projects at different stations. Several of them said, "Hi Bass!" as he walked by. Bass had never met these people, but they obviously knew him. Bass had never experienced celebrity before. He was used to anonymity.

Bass saw a tiny dog at one of the stations and wondered what they could use a dog that small for in the military. He concluded it was probably for delivering a bomb.

They followed a serpentine route that eventually led to another closed door. Betty pressed a button, and the door unlocked electrically.

When they entered, the lights were dimly lit and only one colossal cage was in the Lab. It was empty. The cage was taller than Bass was.

A door in the back opened, and two researchers in white lab coats entered, followed by the largest silver wolf Bass had ever seen. When the colossal beast looked at Bass, it stopped briefly. That was when Bass noticed it was not on a leash.

Bass gulped. Then he realized the wolf must have registered his fear. Bass tried to appear confident and brave, but it was difficult. The wolf's eyes glared for a moment at Bass. Then it apparently didn't feel that Bass was a threat, so he continued to follow the two scientists it had entered the office with.

Betty looked at Bass and smiled. Everyone had the same reaction when they saw War for the first time. He was the only 6'0 tall, 350-pound dog in the world.

"Jim and Mike, the is Bass, the gentleman I told you about earlier." The three men shook hands and exchanged pleasantries.

"And this is War, Bass."

"Holy Smoke, that a big puppy," Bass said, trying to appear unafraid.

"Hey Bass, we all watched you from the windows when you trained Alpha, Beta and Charlie to kill the targets in the yard. That was great work." Jim said.

"You are a celebrity around here," Mike said with a smile.

"Thanks guys. What kind of wolf is this?"

"Technically, he is a Direwolf."

"Dangerous?"

"Very."

"I noticed he isn't leashed."

"The three others laughed."

"Want to guess why?" Betty asked Bass.

"Because it doesn't matter much?" Seemed the apparent answer to Bass.

"Exactly, that plus he doesn't like it at all. He is much easier to control without a leash."

"Yeah, I get it."

"We have made some progress with War of late." The researcher named Jim said.

"What are your current concerns?"

"War is not as smart as the other Direwolf we call Delta. That is both good and bad. War is easier to control when he is with people he trusts. Delta was a nightmare for us, no matter who was with him. Delta killed a scientist that had worked with him for six months. We thought they got along fine. Then one day, Bam! He was dead."

"Why?"

"Don't know. All we really know about Delta is that he is smart and vicious. He will attack a target on command. He will also establish his own targets and kill them too. We can't have that. Direwolves that establish their target for killing is a problem, for obvious reasons."

"Yeah, I see."

"War, on the other hand, will attack and destroy targets at command. So far, he has not selected of his own targets."

"That's good. What is the problem?"

"War doesn't have a broad enough vocabulary of understood words. With Delta, we could say, "Attack the green Jeep. No problem. The green Jeep was attacked."

"Why is the color of the Jeep important?"

"Well, there may be a white Jeep and a blue Jeep nearby that we don't have an interest in."

"Yeah, that makes sense."

"Plus, War just doesn't like some people, for unknown reasons. He will bare his teeth and growl at a new person, basically scare the urine out of them, and we are concerned he will eventually kill someone for no reason."

"He didn't do that with me."

"We noticed. That's good. You stand a chance."

"So, your saying I 'stand a chance.' That's just great."

"It is great. But I understand your concerns."

"What was War's relationship with Delta?"

"Good question. They didn't like each other at all. War was the only animal we know of that seemed to intimidate Delta. Probably because War is so large. He is a bit larger than Delta. But we don't know why they don't like each other, honestly."

"So, what do you need from me?"

"Bass, this is classified and you cannot repeat this to anyone, understood?"

"Yes, sure thing."

"Cash Buck took Delta out without authorization, presumably to get Justice."

"Cash was Vice President, so did he need authorization?"

"Not to take him to the yard. But to leave the building with him, he needed to coordinate it with someone. For his protection as well as the local population. Delta is the most dangerous project we have."

"What about War? He is dangerous, right?"

"Oh yes, he is definitely dangerous. But he is in a different time zone of dangerous as compared to Delta. Delta is an indiscriminate killer."

"War is a discriminate killer?"

"So far, yes."

"OK, so what happened with Cash Buck?"

"We found his remains in the forest just outside the employee parking lot."

"He is dead?"

The three Military Lab scientists looked at each other.

"That's an understatement. He was mostly consumed by Delta. Not much left but his head and hair. Along with his spinal cord."

"Holy cow."

"Yeah. Delta even ate the meat on his face."

252

"So that means Delta is out unsupervised?"

"Yes. Unfortunately, that's accurate."

"Dear Lord," Bass said. "Somebody is gonna get killed."

"Looks like that has already happened."

"Who?"

"We monitored communications in the local area. There was a 911 call describing a family that had been chased into their attic by a 'Giant Dog.' Then a follow-up call between a local tracker and a Ranger Captain verified that the animal was a Direwolf. And we have a Sheriff discussing over the radio a local man killed in his backyard by an animal just a couple of hours earlier. We are certain these events are connected."

"What do you want me to do?"

"You may not like this."

"Oh, great. What is it?"

"We want you to take War out, find Delta, and terminate him."

"Me, why me?"

"We had a Navy Seal ready to go. However, when the Seal entered the room with War, War showed his teeth and growled. He identified the Seal as a threat. We tried to get War to accept the Seal, but it wouldn't work. It would have been a disaster. We have requested a new Navy Seal to replace the last one. However, we believe we need an animal specialist like yourself to complete this mission. Plus, War likes you."

"OK, number one- I have never killed anything in my life. I haven't even shot a gun. So, sending me on a 'seek and destroy' mission is – Out There– to say the least. Number two, you don't know that War likes me as anything other than his next meal. He may just as likely eat me as look at me." Bass took a deep breath through his mouth. "Number three, well, there is probably a number three, but I can't think what it is right now. You can be sure that I am the wrong guy for this job. That's number three! I am the wrong guy." Bass looked at them, hoping they would agree.

"Look Bass, take a deep breath."

"You take a deep breath and realize how stupid this is!" Bass started to hyperventilate.

"Bass, sweetie," Betty turned on her mother's charm, "you can do this. You are the most talented animal specialist I have ever seen. By the way, did you really teach a Golden Retriever to walk on the top of a wood fence with only an hour of training?" Betty used her sweet, loving mother's voice.

"Yes." Cash mumbled, looking at his feet.

"You had never met the dog before?" Betty was in full manipulation mode now.

"No," Cash mumbled again.

"That should have been in a magazine or something." Betty said, knowing compliments work wonders.

"It was. It was in the March issue of Animal Science Quarterly."

"Bass, look at War." Betty said, softly.

Bass looked up. The colossal beast looked back at him with a friendly look on his face. War was smart enough to understand that Betty was trying to convince Bass to take him out to get Delta. War would love nothing more than to capture and kill Delta. Now War had to show Bass he had nothing to be afraid of. War stood up and slowly walked over to Bass. Bass froze in place, as did the other three scientists watching.

War moved his giant nose closer to Bass's face. He gently touched his black, damp nose to Bass' cheeks and forehead.

Bass closed his eyes nervously and said a silent prayer. If he hadn't recently used the bathroom, he might have done so right then.

Then War used his big tongue and licked Bass on the side of his face. War then sat comfortably next to Bass.

"Oh my God," Betty said and looked at the other two scientists. They were just as shocked.

"Bass, he has never done that before!" Betty said with excitement.

Bass didn't know what to say. He had to admit it made him feel better.

"Bass, do you understand you have been with this Direwolf for five minutes and he has done something he has never done before! This is amazing!" Betty used her most persuasive voice.

Bass looked in War's eyes. Instinctively, Bass felt a connection. War was trying to make Bass feel better. He was trying to make contact.

But why? Bass asked himself.

Did War understand what Betty was asking him to do? Did War want this assignment? If so, Bass believed War was much more intelligent than Betty and her team understood. If War understood what was being said in the last few minutes, then his vocabulary was just fine. Was he downplaying his intelligence? If so, why? That, by itself, was a sure sign of intelligence.

Bass was interested now. This was a remarkable animal. Maybe more remarkable than Justice, Alpha, Beta and Charlie combined.

Bass knew he had just been convinced to take the job. He was convinced by a Direwolf.

Ben Doverbich

Ben led the way into the forest behind the wolves and the dogs. The group of K9s had a scent and were following it at a high rate of speed.

Ben was only a few yards behind them. After ten minutes, the gap between Ben and Heston grew widely, and the gap between Heston and the rest of his team grew even more expansive.

Heston didn't want Ben to be so obviously quicker than he was, but he eventually had to give in to it. Ben was a physical specimen that Heston would never be able to keep up with.

Heston stopped at a clearing and waited for his crew to catch up. He wiped his brow with his T-shirt.

After a few minutes, Gene, Peggy, Nancy and Noah caught up to him.

"Where is GI Joe?" Peggy asked.

"He is way ahead with the dogs."

"Ok, are you worried about them getting so far ahead?"

"They haven't started to sing yet, so we should be OK."

"Heston, why is a Navy Seal involved in this?"

"I have no good idea why. Nancy, how about it. You have any idea why Duralink got a Navy Seal involved?"

"The only thing I can think of is he is less likely to be injured by any of the wolves or the Direwolf."

"Gotta be more than that."

"I don't have any inside scoop for you," Nancy said, wiping the sweat off her forehead.

Heston decided Nancy was worthless on this mission.

Ben ran quickly through the forest and stayed only a few yards behind the wolves and dogs. Soon Ben heard the Bluetick's singing that indicated they had spotted the target. He knew they were moments away from seeing either Justice or Delta, or both. He removed his Desert Eagle Mark XIX .50 caliber handgun. To call the Desert Eagle a handgun was like calling a Direwolf a dog. It was designed by Israeli Military Industries to be a hand cannon. Each bullet cost two dollars and was the largest ever built for a handgun. The kick of the Desert Eagle was so severe that even the best shooters shot high over their target most of the time. Drastic adjustments in aiming the Desert Eagle were necessary.

As Ben ran through the thick forest at top speed towards the sounds of the dogs singing, he began to hear some ferocious snarls and fighting sounds.

He knew his wolves were in the battle. He quickened his pace. He didn't want to miss the fight.

Ben ran into a clearing and found his three wolves in front of, and on both sides of a giant Direwolf. Heston's dogs and Noah's dog were behind them. They had no interest in getting in the fight. They were too smart for that.

Ranger Hugh approached the clearing from the other side.

Ben and Hugh spotted each other from across the battlefield and nodded.

Ben was amazed at the size of the giant Direwolf. It had to stand as tall as he was. The Direwolf appeared to be injured on both of his front legs and his chest. The animals had mixed it up before he got there. The wolves Alpha, Beta and Charlie did not appear to be damaged in anyway. They had obviously regrouped and were forming their next attack.

Ben carefully walked up behind the wolves with his Desert Eagle and gave them a sound. He hoped they would understand it.

He meant to say, "let me handle this." But Alpha, Beta and Charlie were not programmed to hear any kind of message like that. They were in destroy mode. The smartest thing Ben could do was back away. He was not qualified to be in this fight.

Ben racked his Desert Eagle and prepared to fire. He leveled the gun at the Direwolf.

Charlie looked back and saw Ben with the gun. His instincts kicked in. He couldn't stand the sight of the weapon. Charlie viciously attacked Ben. With a quick jump Charlie landed on Ben from the side taking him completely by surprise. The Direwolf seemed to understand that this was his chance. Up to that point the three wolves had fought the Direwolf to a standstill. Now Delta felt he had an advantage. He was right.

But at that moment, Ranger Hugh advanced and began to fire his weapon into the side of the big Direwolf. His fear left him and he was determined to kill the enormous animal. But seconds after he began firing he had run out of bullets. He reached for a full clip and pushed the eject button to remove the empty clip.

Ranger Hugh watched a surreal scene unfold in front of his eyes.

As Charlie tore into Ben, Delta tore into Alpha and Beta. Ranger Hugh's bullets did not appear to have an effect on the Direwolf.

Delta wrapped his giant jaws around Alpha's back and bit down with all his might. With a quick toss he threw Alpha twenty feet away into a nearby tree. Alpha fell to the ground and did not move. His back was broken.

Beta after seeing his partner attacked jumped and grabbed Delta by his neck from below. He tried to crush the Direwolf's windpipe. But he didn't have the right grip, and Delta was too strong. The giant Direwolf swung Beta side to side, his thick skin and fur impervious to Beta's grasp. Beta held on to Delta's neck refusing to give way. Delta swung Beta like a rag doll in each direction.

Nearby Charlie wrestled Ben onto the ground and had him by the head, crushing him with his giant jaws and teeth. Ben's instincts took over and he did all he could do but the wolf was too strong. Ben pointed his hand cannon where he hoped Charlie's chest was. He pulled the trigger and a giant Boom! was heard through the forest. Charlie yelped in pain and let go of Ben's head. Ben fell to the forest floor racked in pain.

Ben was completely unable to see because his left eye was out of its socket and the right eye was covered in blood.

He held his Desert Eagle tightly knowing he would need its every benefit if he was going to make it out of this alive.

Ben missed Charlie's chest but hit him in the midsection. The enormous 50 caliber bullet passed entirely through Charlie producing a grisly exit wound just below his rib cage. Charlie knew that he was hurt badly, but he could also see that Beta was in the fight of his life.

Charlie quickly deduced Ben would still be available to kill after he helped Beta kill Delta.

Despite the pain and blood loss Charlie crossed the clearing and jumped on Delta's back while Delta was preoccupied with Beta.

Ranger Hugh crossed the clearing behind the fighting animals to check on Ben's wounds and condition.

Charlie's instincts took over. He straddled Delta like a cowboy on a horse and leaned forward to bite Delta's head, paying particular attention to the eyes. Charlie instantly forgot his pain and bit down as hard as he could onto the Direwolf's head. He felt his teeth sink into Delta's left eye. Delta began to howl loudly. He was frustrated by the wolf on his throat that he could not shake off as well as the wolf on his head that he could not buck off. Delta's left eye began to bleed and he bucked upwards like a bronco trying to rid himself of a cowboy.

All three of the K9 combatants were ferociously growling and rasping gravelly from deep in their throats. Their fighting noises filled the forest.

Justice watched with Trump and Reagan from a safe distance and realized they had no business in this fight. They could only watch in horror as the animals tore themselves apart.

Heston ran full speed up the trail to the sounds of the combat. Gene, Peggy Noah and Nancy were following closely.

Heston joined Ranger Hugh alongside Ben and Justice at the edge of the clearing. He saw Ben was obviously injured and bleeding from the eye socket. Heston removed his undershirt and gave it to Ranger Hugh to use on Ben's eye wound and hold his dangling eyeball.

The sight of a giant Direwolf with a large wolf on his back biting his head along with another large wolf biting his throat was astonishing. The Direwolf was spinning and jumping like a rodeo bull in frustration because he could not grab his assailants with his jaws to kill them.

Heston had his .44 magnum at the ready to shoot, but he wasn't sure what to shoot. If he shot at the Direwolf he could easily hit one of the wolves as quickly as they were spinning and jumping.

"Heston you must shoot" Justice said.

"Shoot at what? I could hit a wolf."

"All three of them."

"What? If I kill the wolves then…"

"Heston the wolf hanging on to the neck of the Direwolf is the wolf that attacked Ben."

"A wolf attacked Ben?"

"Yes. They are all bad. Shoot them all." Usually, Justice would not stop his enemies from killing each other. But this was different.

He knew the wolves would eventually identify him. He had a vested interest in all the wolves being killed as well as the Direwolf.

Heston leveled his large Colt revolver and fired twice at the bloody, spinning mass. He heard a yelp immediately. Charlie fell from on top the Direwolf and landed hard on the ground. He had been shot in the heart with a large Black Talon bullet. Charlie was dead before he hit the ground.

Justice thought 'Two wolves down, one to go.'

Delta felt immediate relief. He began to throw Beta side to side violently. The centrifugal force made Beta let go of Delta's neck, and he flew across the clearing, skidding to a stop. Beta was the only K9 that was not seriously injured.

He saw Delta bleeding from his left eye and obviously disoriented. He looked to see Charlie lying motionless across the clearing with a gunshot in his chest. It was an obvious heart shot. Beta knew his partner was dead. Then he looked to see his other partner Alpha laying in the same spot he was in when he attacked Delta's throat. That meant Alpha was either dead or rendered helpless. Now it was up to Beta to kill the giant Direwolf. In his estimation the odds were evened with the damage to Delta's eye.

Beta did what he had been trained to do. Attack.

He ran forward and jumped on the Direwolf's throat again. This time he changed his angle to better attack his thick muscle, windpipe and essential arteries. This was the angle that he was taught in training. This was a killing angle. The Direwolf would be in the throes of death after only moments. Beta was confident in his strength and conditioning. Until he heard three loud BOOMS!

Heston fired three times. All three of the Black Talon bullets hit Beta in the side. Heston had aimed to hit both the wolf and the Direwolf, but his missed the Direwolf. Beta fell to the ground in pain. He knew he was in trouble. He looked up at the Direwolf who stood over him dripping blood out of his eye. Then the Delta struck. The last thing Beta saw was the Delta open his jaws and grab him by the head. Beta felt Delta bite down on his head. Beta didn't feel the pain of his death. His death was too quick.

Heston fired at the very moment that Delta attacked Beta's head. Because of the quick movement of the Direwolf attack Heston missed with his 6th and final bullet in his Colt. Heston pulled the trigger again and the sound of Click! was heard by everyone including Delta.

Delta looked at the human and saw that he was grabbing a shotgun from one of his friends. He knew this was his time to escape and heal his wounds. Delta spun around and galloped into the forest. Delta heard a loud Boom from the shotgun but the slug flew harmlessly over his head. Sometimes a retreat is the best way to move forwards.

Heston, Gene, Peggy and Nancy ran to Ben. Noah stayed with Justice and inspected him for injury.

"His eye is out of its socket" Ranger Hugh said to the group.

Heston had seen a terrible eye wound like this before. He had seen medics hold the enucleated eye with a cloth close to the eye socket until he could get in the ambulance. Heston's problem was that they were at least four miles into the forest. An ambulance would not make it out here. They would have to get Ben to their vehicles and transport him to the hospital.

Gene looked at his cell phone. No bars.

"No cell phone signal Heston," Gene said.

"Let's make a litter and transport Ben out of here."

"I know how to do that," Noah said.

Everyone was surprised by Noah's statement. He didn't seem to be the likely one to know how to make a field litter.

"Ok Noah, what do you suggest?" Heston asked.

"Let me have your flannel shirt Heston." Noah said, "and let me have your uniform shirt." Noah said to Ranger Hugh.

"Next, we need those two long branches over there." Noah pointed to two long, relatively straight branches that had been blown off a tree by gunfire on the ground at the edge of the clearing.

Noah inverted the sleeves to the shirts so they were inside the body of the shirts, then he buttoned the shirts back up.

Noah took out his new Leatherman Multitool and opened the knife blade. He cut holes in the shoulders of the flannel shirts.

Heston, Gene, Peggy, Hugh and Nancy stared on with interest. As Noah inserted the first branch through the bottom of the shirt and extended it through the sleeve and the hole in the shoulder he'd just cut, they caught on.

"Great idea Noah!" Gene said.

Then they helped thread the pole through the other shirt and repeated the process with the other pole. They had a basic liter set up. Since Ben was not more than 160 pounds soaking wet it held him just fine.

With Ranger Hugh on the front of the litter and Heston on the back, they began to carry Ben out of the forest.

After about an hour Peggy checked her phone and noticed they had some cell phone service.

"Heston, we have cell service here."

"Ok, can you contact Captain Becky for me? Tell her we are hiking out and should be near the Smiley home in an hour or so. We will need an ambulance."

"Ok."

"And tell her the Direwolf is real and on the loose."

Bass and War

"OK, Bass I need you to head out now with War." Betty Porkter said.

"I haven't had enough time."

"That's all you get. You will have to make it work. I have faith in you."

"What about the new Navy Seal? He isn't here yet."

"I'll send him later if you need him."

"If I need him? You don't listen to me Betty." Bass looked at Betty. He knew she wasn't going to budge on this.

"We just picked up a call between The Texas Rangers and the tracking team. It appears Alpha, Beta and Charlie have been killed by Delta or the tracking team."

"Oh no! That's terrible!" Bass was shocked and saddened. He loved all three of the wolves.

"What's more terrible is Delta has escaped and is loose in the forest. He has killed two so far and our Navy Seal has been gravely injured."

"How was he injured?"

"Charlie attacked him. He pulled his gun to shoot Delta, and Charlie attacked. He has lost at least one eye."

"Yeah, I warned everyone that those wolves were not ready."

"Look Bass, 'I told you so's are not going to do us any good here."

"My warnings may have done that Seal some good if you would have listened."

"Bass, I need you to take War and go kill Delta." Betty was done being nice.

"This is crazy. I'm not the right guy." Bass considered resigning his job.

"You are the right guy, Bass."

"Yeah, well, Betty I don't like you."

Betty smiled, "I'm sorry you don't like me Bass, but get moving. Nobody else can do this. You are the only guy."

"The Texas Rangers can." Bass tried one last time to get out of it.

"Maybe yes, maybe no. They would probably lose a few Rangers in the process. War has been designed for this exact kind of situation. You can control War. War likes you. He may kill the Rangers if he goes with them. He won't kill you." Betty wasn't entirely sure of her last statement.

"I want a raise. And I'm not so sure I can control War."

"Effectively immediately, your pay is doubled. And yes, you can."

"Tripled. Triple my pay rate." Bass started at Betty, completely serious in his demand.

"OK, tripled."

"And it remains tripled even if I survive this crazy mission."

"Deal. Now go."

"Fine, I will do my best. But even my best may not be enough."

"You need to have the faith in yourself that I have in you." Betty said.

"Ok fine." Bass was tired of the argument. He got his pay tripled and he was good with that. Plus, he wasn't going to win the quarrel. He had to either quit and go home or have his pay tripled. He chose the money.

Bass went into the lab where War was kept.

"C'mon, buddy. We got our marching orders." Bass said to the huge beast.

War wagged his massive tail. He understood every word.

He took War down to the parking lot. Bass was given a company Ford Expedition, and he opened the rear hatch lift gate to let War jump in. He barely fit. The Direwolf completely filled the cargo area. Fur pressed up against the glass on all three sides and the rear of the vehicle lowered due to the heavy load.

As Bass sat in the driver's seat and started the engine, he heard a new voice.

"Hey Bass! Wait up!" A young man with long blond hair and a thick blond beard trotted up to his window and motioned for Bass to roll down the window.

"Hey, Bass. Sorry to surprise you like this but I have been asked to join you. My name is Barry McKockiner. Can I jump in real quick?"

"Sure." Bass pushed the unlock button, and the doors electronically unlocked.

Barry jumped into the passenger seat and reached to shake Bass' hand.

"Hi Bass," he said. "Thanks for letting me join you."

"I was told you may be joining me, but I really didn't believe it. I'm glad to have the company. I'm convinced I'm not the right guy for this job."

"Well, Bass, rest assured that I am the right guy."

266

"Why is that?"

"Ben is a teammate of mine. He and I have the same skillsets." Barry said.

"You do know he is injured? Almost killed?" Bass asked.

"Yes. I do know that. That's why I am here."

"Why do you think you are the right guy if the last right guy was almost killed?" Bass asked.

"We learn from our mistakes. We don't make the same mistakes twice." Barry said with confidence.

"Ok. I get that. So, you are a Navy Seal too?"

"Yes, Bass I am." Barry Smiled at him in an attempt to put Bass at ease. Barry knew that some people find Navy Seals intimidating.

Bass smiled and nodded as he put the big Ford into gear and headed to the Smiley home. He had noticed that Barry and Ben were the same size and of a smaller build. The biggest difference was the hair color. Neither man looked like a trained killer. But Barry had a huge pistol strapped around his waist.

"What kind of pistol is that?"

"It's a Desert Eagle." Barry said with an ease to his voice, "Have you ever shot one?"

"Ha! No, no, no. I've never shot a gun."

"Never?" `

"Nope. I told them I was the wrong guy for this. They wouldn't listen to me." Bass said.

"Don't worry about it. Your Direwolf and I will keep you safe. You control him and I will control the gun. Between us, we will kill the other Direwolf." Barry said confidently. "You will be home for dinner."

"That's a better plan than I had."

"What was your plan?"

"I didn't have one."

"OK, yeah, this is a better plan than yours." Barry laughed.

Barry's confidence and easy laugh put Bass at ease. Maybe they could do this.

After a 25-minute drive they arrived at the Smiley home in Driftwood.

They pulled into the driveway and noticed some Texas Rangers standing at the end with vehicles lined up on the side of the driveway. There was an ambulance with two EMTs waiting for the Heston's group to emerge from the forest.

Bass parked his vehicle at the end of the line of vehicles on the side of the driveway.

"They are going to freak out when they see War," Bass said.

"I haven't seen him yet outside of the vehicle anyway. So, I may too. I can tell he fills up the cargo space back there."

"Let me have a moment alone with him first, Barry. He can be a bit unpredictable around new people and guns."

"OK, sure."

They got out of the vehicle, and Barry proceeded up to the Texas Rangers and introduced himself as Bass went to the rear of the car to let War out. War jumped down and sat next to Bass. He knew what was coming. Bass was going to give him a speech about not attacking anyone. He was right.

"OK War, you need to understand we are going after Delta and Justice. I doubt we will find Justice. I think he is smart enough to be long gone by now. But we know Delta is out there killing people. Please War, don't kill or attack anyone other than Delta." Bass looked deep into War's eyes. "Please?"

War understood everything. He had no interest in killing anyone that didn't need killing. He remembered the success he had when he licked Bass' face earlier in front of the scientists. They immediately approved him for the mission. So, he did it again. He licked Bass' face.

Bass knew this meant War understood him.

"You understand everything don't you?"

War licked his face again. War's eyes were even with Bass' eyes when War was in the sitting position.

"You just played dumb with the scientists. You are way smarter than they gave you credit for. Why War? Why?"

War couldn't tell Bass anything. At best he could answer yes and no questions with a lick or wag of his tail. He could point at things with his nose. But answering complex questions was not in the cards for now.

War wagged his 48-inch tail.

"OK War, stay close to me and try not to scare the nice people we are going to meet."

War wagged his tail again.

"And don't eat anybody!"

War wagged his tail again and smiled.

Bass noticed the smile and smiled back at War, "We're going to get along just fine, War." Bass finally felt safe around a Direwolf.

Bass and War left the vehicle and walked towards the group of Texas Rangers and Barry at the end of the driveway.

As Bass and War approached the group the conversation between them slowed to a stop and they stared at War like they were looking at a giant green alien. One of the Texas Rangers dropped a cup of Starbucks coffee.

"Holy sweet Mother of Christ" one of the other star struck Rangers said.

The other two stood in silence as Bass and War joined them.

"Hello, I am Bass with Duralink and this is War, also from Duralink" Bass smiled nervously at the group.

One of the Rangers nervously moved his hand to his sidearm and unstrapped it from his holster.

War noticed and bared his teeth at the Ranger. When the Ranger's hand did not move from the gun, War began a deep growl and stared menacingly at him. His eyes left no doubt about his killer instinct.

The Ranger's khaki-colored pants showed a large wet spot growing around his zipper.

"Bass, buddy, he is on our team." Bass looked War in the eyes and stroked his ears.

"What was that about?" Captain Becky asked.

"Don't grab a gun while looking at War. He may take it as a threat." Bass said, with a weak smile.

The Ranger raised his hands over his head and said, "Sorry, War. I will never do it again."

All the other Rangers immediately moved their hands away from their guns.

"Hi, Bass I am Captain Becky Lawson with the Texas Rangers." Becky smiled and shook his hand. "The Ranger with the wet uniform pants is Ranger Holden Hisweiner, and over there is Ranger Chit Head." Everyone shook hands and exchanged their pleasantries.

"This gigantic wolf you have, he is going to help us find the other gigantic wolf, I assume?" Becky asked.

"Yes, Captain Lawson. War has been designed and programmed to… well, he is perfect for this assignment." Bass said. He couldn't explain much about War's programming and training because it was top secret.

Barry noticed Bass' uncomfortable nature, so he jumped in.

"We should tell you folks" then he paused for a second "actually *ask* you folks, to treat this mission we are all on like a top-secret project. I know it isn't fair to you. And I apologize for this, but War and I do not exist. We operate in the shadows by design. It is not typical that we operate inside of our country. Normally, we would be in the Middle East or some other area with plenty of bad guys. Honestly, we kill bad guys for a living. But due to a series of unfortunate events we are here." Barry smiled at them all. "Let me assure you we can handle this situation, and we will do so with the utmost professionalism and speed."

The team of Rangers looked at Barry and understood his message. However, they would want explanations later about how a Direwolf could escape Duralink and place the civilian population in danger.

"Bass we just explained to Barry that we are waiting for Heston and his team to emerge from that forest with Ben at any moment."

"I am going to run in there and help them get out," Barry said, and he turned to run.

At that moment, they emerged from the forest.

"There they are!" One of the Rangers said, and he pointed to the end of the Smiley yard.

Barry ran out to meet them. He looked at his teammate Ben Doverbich on the improvised stretcher as he held the bloody t-shirt over his eye.

"Holy Cow Buddy what happened to you?" Barry said, smiling at his friend.

"One of my wolves turned on me. Surprised me."

"Let's get you in the ambulance."

"Just pop my eye back in and I will go back out with you." Ben said in all seriousness. In his mind, he was ready for more action.

"No way brother. You are off this mission, and I have taken over. You can't have all the fun." Barry smiled at his long-time buddy.

"You are a dick."

"Don't tell anyone, brother."

"I'm gonna tell everyone."

"I bet you will."

"Take my Desert Eagle. You will need it more than I will."

Barry took the large handgun then handed it to Heston. Barry took over from Heston on the litter and they hurried to the ambulance.

"Can you give me a quick debrief? Captain Becky asked Ranger Holden.

"Yes. The three wolves from Duralink are dead. The other Direwolf is injured but still out there and dangerous."

"Is that it?"

"No, Captain Becky," Holden said. He took a deep breath. "Deputies Jesus and Waylon are dead. Killed by the Direwolf."

"How did that happen?"

"They were overwhelmed in the fight. These pistols are not enough. Basically useless." Ranger Holden paused for a moment "You were right about the Mossbergs being necessary."

"Where is yours?"

"It is still in my vehicle at Salt Lick." Ranger Holden sheepishly admitted.

Captain Becky shook her head and walked away from the young Ranger. He would answer for this later.

After Navy Seal Ben Doverbich was loaded into the ambulance Captain Becky called everyone over to her.

"OK here is the deal. We have an enormous Direwolf in the forest that is injured and extremely dangerous. In fact, he will kill anyone he comes in contact with." She looked in the eyes of those that assembled around her.

"We are going out there to kill it. This Navy Seal and his Direwolf named War will lead the way. They have experience with this type of operation. We will be in a support role."

"Wait a minute Becky," Heston said. "Why is the organization that put us in this position going to lead the way in getting us out of it? They already lost their first-string player." Heston was always brutally direct.

"I am not with Duralink. I am with the Navy. I am the most qualified person here." Barry said trying to get Heston on his team. "We will catch this Direwolf, and we will kill it."

"As long as your Direwolf plays along, right?"

"The Direwolf will 'Play along'." Barry McKockiner said. He noted to himself that he and Heston may not play nicely together.

"Look, Captain Becky, I will not cooperate with this, and I encourage you not to either. But you do what you want. I am taking my team back to enter the forest at Salt Lick. Based on what I have seen that's the best place to interdict him. He may even be drawn to the smell of Salt Lick if he is hungry." Heston said then looked at his team. He nodded for them to head to the vehicle. Heston was not going to wait for anyone's approval. He didn't like the way the Navy and a giant dog were taking over. In his eyes, they were a part of the problem. He wanted no part of it.

"Cell phone coverage is terrible out there Heston, take a radio." Captain Becky said. She knew Heston well enough not to argue with him. She didn't agree with him about the Navy Seal's involvement, but she could live with it.

"Captain Becky, keep a close eye on that giant dog. I don't trust it. Remember what happened to the other Navy Seal Duralink sent us." Heston said to her.

"War is a lot more manageable than Delta was." Bass Wooten jumped into the tense conversation. When everyone looked at him, he wished he'd kept his mouth shut.

"That's just great," Heston said "War is more manageable than the Direwolf that killed two deputies, two civilians and almost killed a Navy Seal. For your sake, I hope he is more manageable."

"For the record, Ben was attacked by another animal from Duralink. Not the Direwolf." Barry said.

"Well, isn't that great. It was a different trained animal from Duralink." Heston said with derision in his voice.

Captain Becky became a bit more nervous about the situation. She didn't want to see the result of a conflict between Heston and the Seal.

"Ranger Holden, go with Heston's team. You can retrieve your Mossberg when you get to Salt Lick. Carry it this time." She glared at the young Ranger. "Take my vehicle, I will be going with Barry."

"Yes Ma'am," was all Holden could say. He was grateful for the opportunity to prove himself again.

"Let's go," Heston said. He and his team headed for his truck while Holden got in Captain Becky's Ford Explorer. They left for The Salt Lick. It was now midafternoon, and they needed to make progress soon. Operating in the dark would be a problem against a Direwolf.

Heston realized he still carried the Desert Eagle from Ben Doverbich.

Delta is Injured

Delta sprinted into the forest. He navigated as best he could with one eye. His left eye was bleeding from the attack by Beta. The battle had been intense, and he may have lost had the human not shot the wolves attacking him. Delta was lucky.

Delta heard and smelled the large shady stream that ran nearby. He approached the cool water and smelled to see if anyone was nearby. He was alone. Delta eased into the deep stream and held his head underwater. He opened his eyes in the clear water to flush them of the blood and debris in them from the battle. The cool water felt great and refreshing. Delta raised his head and stayed in the stream for a few minutes to gather himself. The moving water flushed his fur of the caked blood. He closed his eyes and took a deep breath, realizing again how lucky he had been to survive the battle.

He was able to see much better now. The damage to his left eye was not as bad as he thought. The wound on his eyelid was worse than it was on his eyeball. The stream cleaned it out and he was able to see. Delta looked around the forest, he smelled something. Human scents were coming toward him. Could it be his adversaries? He did not think that was possible.

In a moment, a young man and a woman appeared out of the forest, laughing and talking. They carried fishing poles and a picnic basket. Delta remained still in the water as they approached. The water covered most of him, with only his visible above the water. The two young people approached the stream completely unaware of Delta's presence in the water. They talked and laughed about who would catch more fish. They took a spot on the bank of the stream only a few yards away from Delta, unaware of his presence.

Delta realized he was hungry. The battle had taken a lot from him, and he needed to replenish his lost calories. The two young humans were another stroke of luck for Delta. He was supremely lucky, he thought to himself. Between his natural skills and his good luck he could not be defeated. The world would soon belong to him.

After the young man finished getting his fishing rod ready to use, he looked at the stream. He looked directly at Delta.

"What the heck is that?" He asked his female friend.

Then the young woman looked at Delta.

"It's a gigantic dog!" She said, smiling. She was a dog lover at heart and was initially glad to see the Direwolf resting in the deep water of the stream.

Delta could see they posed no threat to him. Neither was armed.

Delta stood up from the stream showing the pair his full size. Their mouths dropped open in amazement. He turned to face them. They had no idea he was deciding which one to eat first.

"Hi Puppy," the female said in a friendly tone.

"That's no puppy." the young man said.

Delta decided on the man. The man would be first. He sprang forward splashing through the water and grabbed the man by the head. Delta whipped the man overhead, then downwards like he was cracking a whip. This was an effective movement Delta used for immobilizing and killing. The young man's back was broken, and he was rendered harmless. Delta began to feed upon him, as the woman started screaming in terror. Delta fed upon his arms while the young man was still alive but in shock and too dazed to

276

make a noise. He watched the giant Direwolf strip his arm of its meat before he passed out from the loss of blood.

The young woman very smartly did not stay to watch. She kept her wits about her and ran as fast as she could without making a noise. She ran up the small trail towards The Salt Lick Restaurant. As she neared the edge of the forest, she began to scream at the top of her lungs.

Heston Enters the Forest by Salt Lick

Heston and his team, including Ranger Holden, arrived at The Salt Lick Restaurant Parking lot by 3:45 pm.

They collected their weapons with Ranger Holden retrieving the Mossberg 12 gauge from his vehicle. He also carried a 9-millimeter Glock.

Heston carried a Colt .44 magnum, a Mossberg 12 gauge, and the Desert Eagle from Ben.

Gene and Peggy each carried 9-millimeter Glocks. Peggy also carried a Mossberg 12 gauge. Noah carried a .22 caliber Smith and Wesson that would be of no use. Nancy had a Glock 9-millimeter and a .38 revolver.

The entrance to the forest was behind a small stream behind The Salt Lick Barbeque restaurant in Driftwood.

Heston led the way towards the trailhead followed by Holden, Gene, Peggy, Noah and Nancy. The three dogs shot out in front of the team looking to pick up scents. The team of trackers was quiet and serious as they headed towards the forest. They knew danger was ahead and they had to be on top of their game today.

As they entered the forest they heard the screams of a woman. Then they spotted her. From further up the trail a young woman emerged from the forest running at top speed. She was running

277

their way with a terrified look on her face. There was no mistaking that she had been traumatized. When she saw them, the look of relief on her face was noticeable.

She ran up to Heston and caught her breath before she began her story.

"My boyfriend has been killed, I'm sure!"

"Slow down honey. How? How was he killed?" Heston asked, afraid he knew the answer.

"A giant dog! It must have been six feet tall. It was resting in the stream. Then it jumped out and grabbed him by the head!" She said tearfully. She expected amazement by them, but they appeared to anticipate the story.

"How far away was this?"

"I've only been running for ten minutes or so. Probably a mile that way" she said pointing down the trail.

"We will go find him," Heston said, glancing back at his team.

"I want to go too." The young woman said.

They looked at her and were stunned that she would say that.

"We can't take you, sweetie. You need to go to The Salt Lick and call someone to come get you." Heston said.

"That's bull crap, he was my boyfriend, and I want to watch that dog die." The young woman was angry and committed.

Heston thought for a moment. He had to respect the attitude. In his experience, women that were pissed off and committed were not to be quarreled with. He didn't have the time to argue with her. They needed to get going. He looked at his watch. 4:00 pm. Too late to waste time.

"OK suit yourself. Stay close to us." Was all Heston said.

"What's your name, sweetie? Peggy asked the young lady.

"Camille. Camille Tou" She said and held out her hand. Peggy smiled and shook her hand.

They entered the forest in single file following the hiking trail.

After a 20-minute hike, they got to the stream where the attack happened.

"This is the place," Camille said.

The entire team readied their guns. They looked in all directions but didn't see a giant Direwolf.

Then they spotted something unusual and out of place. Across the stream were the remains of a body. Camille began to sob.

"That's Stacy's head." She sobbed and pointed to the human head at the edge of the stream. "That was my boyfriend."

They approached carefully. The man had been eaten with most of his body gone. Only his head and spine remained attached. Meatless arms and legs were tossed nearby.

"What was his name?" Noah asked.

"Stacy. Stacy Recked. He was a great guy." Camille said sobbing.

"Must have been," Noah smiled at the young woman.

"Let's get going" Heston said. "I'm worried we'll run out of daylight."

They headed deeper into the forest.

Barry McKockiner and War

Barry and War ran far ahead of Captain Becky, Bass and Ranger Chit.

Barry knew enough to know he didn't want to fight in the dark. Not without night vision goggles. By his calculations they had about four hours left of daylight.

Captain Becky glanced at Ranger Chit and Bass Wooten. They were doing their best to keep up with the Navy Seal and the giant Direwolf but couldn't maintain their speed. In a matter of minutes Barry and War were out of sight.

"Well, it looks like our protection has left us in the Dust." Captain Becky said.

"I think Heston was right." Ranger Chit said, "That Seal has one job and that is to protect Duraink. He doesn't care about us."

"I think he's just excited to kill Delta. He will realize he left us and wait up." Bass tried to put them at ease. But inside he agreed with them. Delta presented a giant problem for Duralink that could terminate their programs if word got out about this debacle.

"Let's just stay sharp." Captain Becky said. She looked at Ranger Chit and realized that only she carried a Mossberg 12-gauge shotgun. He didn't have one of the large guns.

"What side arm are you carrying?" She asked Chit.

"Glock 9 mil."

"Bass, do you have a gun?"

"I have never even shot a gun."

"Ok this is now officially a Fuster Cluck." Captain Becky shook her head.

Captain Becky realized that Ranger Chit was too new to have been issued a Mossberg. He was a green rookie. So, his value on this mission was very limited. Bass was of no value whatsoever unless he had a bag full of hamburgers. Of which he didn't. So, he was dead weight.

So effectively, she was alone in the forest. "This is just great." She said out loud.

"Captain Becky, I tried to tell them I was the wrong guy for this, but they wouldn't listen."

"Yeah Bass, you can just be quiet from here on out." Becky said.

"I think I'm completely useless on this mission," Bass said.

"Don't be too tough on yourself, Bass. You can always be used as a bad example." Captain Becky was sick of Duralink employees. She didn't want to hear any more crap from one. The 'I tried to tell them' routine didn't fly with her.

They trudged on into the forest, listening to the forest sounds for signs they may be close to either the Navy Seal or to danger.

Bass remained quiet.

Delta found a ravine with soft leaves and shade. He knew his eye was rapidly getting better. Now that he had a full belly of protein he decided to rest for a few minutes. Then he would pick up the scent of Justice and track him down. He didn't want anyone to think he had neglected his mission to kill Justice. Killing Justice was the first step to his world dominance. Delta closed his eyes and drifted off into a comfortable sleep. His battered body would awake stronger and ready to take care of business.

Justice ran with the dogs. He was a dog at heart and loved his time with Trump and Reagan. While Justice was on another intellectual level from them, he was still a dog. They had a canine connection that he could never have with a human. His communication with Trump and Reagan was effective and efficient. They communicated with thoughts. They had a natural radio system between each other that allowed them to communicate much better than humans were possible of. Humans had to take ideas and reduce them to sounds or written words. Dogs didn't have that roadblock. They immediately knew what the other meant to say. No poorly chosen words. Efficient and effective.

They ran through the forest at top speed without worrying about leaving Heston behind. When they had their target, they would sing their song, and Heston would arrive shortly thereafter.

Justice was in the lead, closely followed by Trump then Reagan.

"I got it," Justice said without words.

"Yes, I smell it too."

"Me too!"

"This way!"

The three dogs raced between the trees and scrub brush excitedly following the scent that they picked up.

The smell grew so strong after a few minutes they knew they were moments away from seeing the Direwolf they were after.

"Don't sing yet," Justice said.

"Why? We have him. He is near." Trump said.

"Two reasons. Number one, we don't want to warn him we have him. Any surprise would be in our favor. Number two, we want to be right. We should see him before we make a noise."

"OK Justice, if you say so. But normally we would be singing now to tell Heston we are close."

282

The three dogs quietly approached a small stream. Across the stream was an upwards sloping hill. Justice suspected the target was on the other side of the hill.

The three dogs looked at each other and crossed the shoulder deep stream. On the other side they shook themselves off and headed towards the top of the hill they spotted. With the strong scent, they believed the target would be visible once they got to the top of the hill. Then they would sing.

Delta slept soundly until he awoke with the strong smell of Justice. It was curious to Delta how the scent hit him so suddenly. Normally scents grow stronger over time as distances are reduced. Now however, the strong smell appeared quickly.

Delta stood up. He looked in the direction of the smell. There was a ridge line that towered over his sleeping spot in the ravine. He knew Justice was approaching the ridge line.

Delta moved slowly and quietly towards the top of the sloped hill.

When he got to the top of the hill he saw them. Three dogs. Justice plus two others. As he saw them, they saw him. Delta ferociously growled and sprang forward to kill Justice. All three dogs began their loud cries and wailing. When they saw the size of Delta all three turned and ran. Justice ran in a different direction than the other two.

Delta didn't care about anything other than Justice. The other two disappeared into the forest, Justice was still visible off to Delta's right. Delta followed Justice.

-

Trump and Reagan were intimidated by a dog the size of Delta. They knew that despite their bravery, they would die if they attacked that giant. They did what they knew they should. They ran back to get Heston at the top of their speed.

They ran through the trees and almost collided into Heston who was running towards the sounds of them singing.

"What's up guys? You ran back to get me?" Heston spoke to his two dogs like they were people. He was not used to them running back for him. In fact, he couldn't remember it ever happening before.

As he stood over the dogs trying to understand what was happening, Gene, Peggy, Noah, Holden and Nancy ran up and joined him.

"What's going on, Heston?" Gene asked

"These dogs have never come back for me before."

"Where is Justice?" Noah asked nervously.

"He didn't run up with these two. He must still be out there."

"We have to go find him!" Noah yelled.

"Pipe down Noah," Heston said tensely.

"What do you want to do Heston?" Gene asked.

"We are going to kill this giant Duralink disaster."

Heston looked at his two dogs and said "Go!"

Trump and Reagan ran back into the forest leading Heston and his crew towards the giant Direwolf.

After 10 minutes they stopped at the stream they crossed earlier just before the encounter with Delta.

This time there was no new scent to follow. They found the scent that led up to the sighting of Delta, but after that the scent disappeared.

The dogs ran in large circles with their noses on the ground searching for scents of Justice or of Delta. Nothing could be found.

Barry and War heard the distant sounds of Heston's dogs singing that they had their target sighted. Then they listened as the singing stopped as abruptly as it started.

They rushed in the direction of the dog's sounds.

After 20 minutes they stopped and listened intently. Their speed through the forest left Becky, Bass and Chit were too far behind to catch them.

Then Barry heard the sounds of something large crashing through the forest.

War knew immediately it was the sounds of Delta.

Barry looked at War and said, "Stay here".

Barry's plan was to use himself as bait, to have Delta chase him into a trap. When he led Delta into the area in front of War, War could attack while Delta was occupied with Barry. The surprise nature of the attack would allow War to prevail quickly.

Barry quickly explained his plan to War, who understood every word.

With his understanding, War also knew this was not a solid plan. The odds were that Barry would be killed in the chase. But honestly, War didn't care about Barry. So be it. He would sit in this spot and wait for Barry to show up with Delta hot on his tail. Stupid is as stupid does.

Barry disappeared into the thick forest towards the sounds of Delta.

War sat silently, waiting for the action to arrive.

Justice Races through the Forest.

Justice reached the top of the hill and saw the giant Direwolf that was after him. Delta was ready for him. He had been waiting for him. Immediately Justice understood that crossing the stream washed away his scent blocker that was applied to him earlier, thanks to Peggy and Nancy.

Justice quickly analyzed that if he stayed with Trump and Reagan they would be killed. Justice told them to go left, and he would go right. Trump and Reagan complied and ran to find Heston while Justice tried to outrun the Direwolf in the other direction.

Justice was fast, but the Direwolf with his enormous legs was faster. He could hear the loud thumps of the Direwolf's running behind him. The only advantages Justice had were his smaller size and his intellect. He had to find a way to make his size work for him. He took a hard left off the trail and scooted under some scrub brush. He heard the thuds of a difficult turn made by the Direwolf behind him. Those sounds told Justice he also enjoyed an advantage of being nimbler than Delta.

By running through thick vegetation and darting around corners Justice was able to gain some distance from the Direwolf.

This evasion couldn't last forever though. Justice had to have a plan.

He approached a small clearing and spotted a cave entrance ahead and could tell that Delta would not fit in the opening. But going inside would only be wise if there was an exit from the cave; otherwise, he was trapping himself inside.

To the left of the cave was the stream that had snaked around through the forest and passed by the cave. Justice had an idea. He would enter the stream, then run into the cave. Next, he would double back to the stream.

He had to be fast. His distance from Delta had increased but not by much. He could hear Delta crashing through the thick scrub brush behind him. Justice calculated he had two minutes or less.

Justice sprinted into the stream and splashed out again. He left a solid trail to the entrance to the cave. That should be easy to follow, Justice thought to himself.

Then he went 20 feet into the dark cave, turned around and ran out again. Justice carefully followed his exact path to the stream he had created a few moments earlier. He could hear Delta crashing and straining through the thick forest growth towards him. Justice had to go faster. Delta was seconds away now.

Justice ran and jumped into the stream with a splash. He was grateful to discover that the center of the stream was deeper than Justice was tall.

Justice held his head underwater and swam with all his might following the current of the stream. When he opened his eyes underwater, he couldn't see well through the water of the stream.

Justice stayed underwater as long as he could. Soon his lungs felt like they were going to explode. He had to breath. He hoped when he raised his head above water that Delta would not see him. At the very last moment Justice raised his head and took a deep breath. When he did, he heard the sounds of loud growling and snarling. The sounds were behind him, from the area he had just left.

Justice stayed in the stream and allowed the current to take him far away. He realized he was safe.... for now.

———-

Delta followed Justice closely in the race through the forest. More than once Delta missed grabbing Justice by the tail by mere inches. Delta was faster than Justice and only missed catching

Justice due to erratic and unpredictable turns by the German Shepherd.

Delta again was moments away from killing the smaller beast when the animal turned sharply into an entanglement of jungle-like growth on the forest floor.

Delta fell behind his target as he crashed through tangled maze of growth. Delta had to jump through the vegetation instead of run through it. He was undeterred though. He knew the German Shepherd couldn't run forever and time was on Delta's side. Delta could smell the fear in Justice, and it was a satisfying smell.

Soon, a small clearing could be seen with a cave on the far side. Delta at first feared the cave would provide protection for the smaller beast. He followed the scent. The scent led to the stream off to the left. Had Justice crossed the stream? Or swam down the stream to escape? Delta allowed his nose to tell him the story.

He followed the scent to the stream, but then it led him to the cave. Delta surmised that the idiot Justice hadn't seen the cave until he was in the stream, then he made a tactically stupid decision to return to the cave.

Delta ran to the cave entrance and lowered his head to fit inside. He snarled and growled loudly to instill the fear into Justice that he would soon die. His loud, viscous roaring barks and snarls echoed deep into the cave. He was frustrated to discover that his shoulders wouldn't allow him to enter the cave, they were too broad. Delta's sense of smell told him Justice was deep in the cave. The scent trail was unmistakable. Justice was trapped and trapped deep in the cave. All Delta had to do was wait him out. Delta dislodged his head from the cave opening and sat outside.

Justice had to come out eventually, and Delta would be there when he did.

Barry heard the loud snarling that was a short distance away. He knew that the ferocious snarls and barks could only be made by a gigantic wolf.

He ran in the direction of the sounds with his Desert Eagle firmly in his right hand. Then the sounds stopped. If it was a fight, Barry thought, the fight was over.

Barry continued forward. When he turned a corner in the trail he found a stream. Across the stream he could see Delta sitting in front of a cave entrance. Delta's back was to Barry.

Barry stared at the giant wolf and realized it was almost as large as War. The sight was intimidating.

He decided not to follow his original plan. He decided to get closer and try shooting the beast with his Desert Eagle. End this hunt now. Barry had faith that the large 50 caliber gun would kill the beast. But he better not miss.

As he approached the stream he stopped just when his feet entered the water. This would give him a fairly easy 20-yard shot. Barry raised his weapon and took careful aim. Just as he had the giant beast sighted in, Delta turned his head and faced Barry. Barry felt his intimidation again as the beast stared at him. Barry squeezed off a shot with the large hand cannon. A roaring BOOM! echoed through the forest forcing birds to erupt from their trees in flight. The recoil of the gun, despite the designed off-gassing produced by the weapon, was enormous. With all of Barry's strength he tried to prevent the weapon from raising too high so he could squeeze off another shot. His footing in the stream was not good and his right foot slipped forward, forcing the gun even higher into the air as he tried to catch his balance. He shot again, this time into the trees.

When he lowered the weapon for another shot, he saw Delta running straight at him. He had clearly missed his important first two shots. After a few large strides Delta flew through the air across the stream, headed straight for Barry.

Barry squeezed off a third shot when Delta was in mid-air.

Barry's last thought was that he should have followed his original plan and baited Delta to follow him to War. He should have let War kill Delta.

The Desert Eagle's famous tendency to shoot high was Barry's downfall.

His final shot missed Delta.

Justice floated down the stream for less than five minutes when he heard three loud gunshots come from the area he had just left. He did not know what they meant or who fired them. From the sounds it was a very large caliber gun. Justice knew it was either Heston with his large caliber Colt or the Navy Seal with his large caliber Desert Eagle side arm.

The stream followed a long straight path allowing it to pick up speed. Justice felt more and more secure as the stream carried him further away from Delta. Any increasing distance from Delta was good.

Justice did his best to hold his head above water as he dog paddled with the stream current. Ahead, he could see a person approaching the stream from the forest. It was Heston!

Justice floated and dog paddled his way towards Heston as Heston stepped into the stream to cross it.

Heston looked up the stream and spotted Justice. Then out of the forest came Gene, Peggy. The rest of Heston's team would follow in moments.

"Look at this," Heston said with a smile.

Justice floated up to Heston.

"Help me out of here Heston" Justice said.

"I'll never get used to you talking, Justice. No matter how long I live." Heston said as he helped Justice out of the stream.

As Justice got his footing on the side of the stream, he shook the water off him. Noah came out of the forest and saw him.

"Justice! Thank goodness you are OK!" Noah crossed the stream and gave his dog a hug.

"I believe your Navy Seal friend is dead," Justice said.

"Why?"

"I heard his gun fire three loud shots then the forest went silent."

"We heard them too. Maybe he killed Delta."

"Maybe... I just don't think it would have been that easy."

"We need to investigate. They sounded like they came from up stream."

"Yes, they came from the area I just left. Delta was chasing me. I ran into a cave then doubled back out and jumped into the stream. He followed my scent into the cave and thought I was still in there."

"So, you saw Delta?"

"Yes, I did. He is slightly smaller than War."

"Ok Heston what's our plan?"

"Let's see if we can make our way to the cave Justice described. Hopefully Delta is still there."

"OK, by my watch we have about three hours of daylight."

"Yeah, that's about right."

"We can't waste time. I don't want to be out here after dark with this beast."

Delta ate until he was full. Barry had good meat on his arms that was now in Delta's belly. He checked the scent in the cave for Justice, and the scent had grown weaker. Apparently, Justice escaped while Delta attacked and ate the man in the stream that shot at him.

He knew he was now being hunted. It was time to be the hunter instead of the hunted. The humans that were after him would now be his prey. Delta decided to go back the way he had come.

He followed the trail back towards the Smiley residence.

After twenty minutes Delta heard people ahead. He was not hungry, but as usual, he could eat. Delta remained still behind a group of large oaks that gave him a view of the trail ahead. Delta surmised that there were two groups of hunters after him. Ahead, was one of the groups.

A female was in the lead with a large gun. Behind her was a Texas Ranger and the man from Duralink that Delta knew as Bass. Bass had been in the Language Lab and Delta only knew of him. They had not worked together before.

Delta decided to allow them to pass. He did not need to feed, nor did he want the female Texas Ranger to shoot the large gun at him. For one thing, it could kill him. For another thing the loud sound would summon the others that were hunting him. Delta decided to allow them to go deeper into the forest where he would not be.

Delta watched closely as the group passed within 20 yards from his obscured position in the trees. When they had passed and he could no longer see them, Delta crept around the trees and followed the trail that exited the forest, right into the Smiley backyard.

================================

Captain Becky led her team into the forest keeping her eyes and ears open for the Navy Seal and the gigantic wolf that had left earlier them hunting for Delta.

She did not like the feeling of being in the forest hunting for a big, human killing wolf. She was trained to hunt people, not enormous wolves.

They looked at each other when they heard three loud gunshots echoing in the distance.

"That was a large caliber handgun." Captain Becky said.

They hiked towards the sounds of gunshots that they heard.

After 15 minutes they saw a stream with a cave on the other side.

The smell of gunpowder was still in the air, so they knew they were in the right area.

As they approached the stream Becky focused her attention on the cave opening twenty yards across the stream.

She got to the edge of the stream and prepared to cross it when Bass noticed something in the water, downstream by a few yards.

"What is that, Captain Becky?"

"Where?"

"Look to your left."

Becky looked downstream and saw a mound of something hung up in a tree branch. It was covered by a t-shirt of some kind.

The longer she looked at it the less she liked what it could be.

"Ranger Chit, go down the stream and see what that is hung up on the tree branch."

"Yes, Captain."

Captain Becky turned her attention back to the cave.

She held her Mossberg even more tightly when she saw the scrub brush behind the cave move.

It could have been a deer or some other wildlife, however since they had been in the forest the wildlife had been noticeably absent.

Becky raised her Mossberg up to her shoulder and aimed at the moving brush.

"What is it, Captain Becky?"

"I don't know. But if a giant wolf comes out of there, it will get shot."

"Wait, it may be War."

"I don't care."

"Don't care?"

"Not really."

"Well remember, War can kill Delta for us. So, you may want to care a little bit."

Both Becky and Bass stared at the vegetation moving behind the cave when they heard Ranger Chit.

"Oh crap!"

"Oh crap, what?" Becky and Bass both said at once.

"Oh crap, our Navy Seal won't be helping us anymore."

"He never really did," Becky said.

"Ok, well, I hope you weren't counting on him."

"Why?"

"This is him."

Both Bass and Becky looked to their left and saw Chit standing knee deep in moving water. He held up the severed head of Ben Doverbich.

"This is him." Chit said.

"This day just gets better and better. Toss the head on shore. We can get someone to come back for him."

Chit tossed the head by swinging it by the hair onto the bank. Then it rolled down into some scrub brush near the water. Bass and Captain Becky looked at each other, then shrugged their shoulders.

"This is going to be difficult to explain," Bass said.

"Ehh, nobody liked him anyway." Becky said.

When they looked back at the cave, a giant Direwolf was staring at them in front of the opening.

Becky raised her Mossberg again.

"You should put that gun away Becky," Bass said.

"Why?" Becky said, preparing to shoot.

"That's War, and he is trained to attack anything he perceives as a threat. Pointing a gun at him is a great way to shorten your life."

Becky lowered her shotgun.

"Are you sure that's War?"

"Oh yeah. The coloring is different, and he is bigger than Delta. Plus, Delta would have killed you for pointing that gun at him. War has more discipline."

Bass crossed the stream and approached War. The giant wolf wagged his tail indicating he approved of Bass approaching him.

Bass held out his hand and rubbed War behind his large ears.

Becky and Chit walked up behind him.

"Why is War alive and Ben dead?" Becky asked.

"I dunno. Maybe they got split up." Bass said.

Just then War's tail wagged.

"Did you see that? He wagged his tail after you said that."

"OK War, did you get split up from Ben?" Bass asked the huge dog.

War wagged his tail again.

"So, he can communicate?" Becky asked with a surprised tone in her voice.

"I think so. Let's keep the questions to yes or no questions." Bass said.

Captain Becky stared at the gigantic wolf. Could he communicate? She had to admit it appeared he may be able to.

"OK, War if you want to answer a question as yes, wag your tail. If no, then just stay still. OK?" Bass said.

War wagged his tail.

"Holy Cow!" Chit said. "That freaking wolf understands!"

"Do you know where Heston and his group are?"

War sat still.

"Are they close?"

War wagged his tail.

"Ok let's try this" Becky said as she pulled out her sidearm.

"Wait! I told you guns may threaten War." Bass couldn't believe she pulled out her gun after what he had told her.

"War, I'd like to fire straight up in the air. Is that OK with you?" Becky asked the giant Direwolf.

War wagged his tail.

Becky fired three shots straight up in the air.

After ten seconds there was an answer. Three shots were fired in the distance.

"That's Heston," Becky said and fired once more indicating she understood his response.

"He will find us. We can give him a few minutes. Chit, take a look in that cave and see if anything is in there we should know about."

Ranger Chit did not like this idea at all. Entering the small dark cave ranked up there with biting the Direwolf on the nose. But he didn't think he had any room to argue.

Chit slowly walked to the cave entrance like he was being led to his execution.

"Oh, for crying out loud Chit! Get your butt in there!" Becky yelled at him. "Bravery must not be your strong suit!" She couldn't help but terrorize the young rookie.

Chit lowered his head and sped into the narrow cave, bumping his head on the top as he entered. He ducked down and walked as quickly as he could into the darkness.

The light from the entrance to the cave became very dim, providing no visibility into the rear of the cave. Chit remembered he had a small Mag light in his top pocket of his uniform shirt. He fumbled with his button then grabbed the small flashlight and twisted the top allowing his light to illuminate dimly.

"I knew I should have replaced these batteries last week," he said out loud.

"What did you say Chit?" Becky yelled at him.

"Nothing Captain Becky!" Chit yelled back. He realized he was more terrified of Captain Becky than he was of the dark cave.

When Chit was afraid, he had a habit of talking to himself.

"I'm not afraid of this cave." He said.

"Are you talking to yourself?" Becky yelled at him.

"No!" He didn't want to lie to her. But he had to.

Becky chuckled. She knew she had him scared of her.

Chit moved deeper into the poorly lit darkness.

"I am not afraid of the giant wolf that may be back here," Chit said out loud.

"Who the hell are you talking to Chit?" Becky yelled into the cave.

"Nobody!" Chit said then realized he had to go to the bathroom.

"Christ, not now!" Chit said to himself.

"Chit who are you talking to?"

"Nobody!" He said as he fumbled with the zipper on his wet pants.

Chit relieved himself on the side of the cave as he looked into the darkness with his flashlight.

As he was almost done a light came from 10 feet behind him and illuminated him. It was a light much bigger than his small light.

"For Christ's sake Chit! Did something scare the pee out of you?" Becky said laughing. She was pointing her much larger Mag Light at him.

Chit fumbled and dropped his smaller light on to the wet cave floor.

"Yucch Chit! Now your light is all wet."

Chit turned his back to Becky for a bit of privacy as he zipped up his business.

"There isn't anything in here," Chit said to Becky.

"Oh Really? I found a weirdo wagging his wiener around."

"I am not a weirdo. I just had to pee. And I wasn't wagging it around either." His feelings were a bit injured.

"Whatever you say. I'll see you outside. Weirdo." Becky said laughing. "And don't forget to zip."

"Yeah OK."

"And don't zip up that wiener you've been wagging around." Becky couldn't resist one more shot at the young Deputy.

"I haven't been…Oh, Christ." He knew he should just give up.

Moments later they all stood outside the cave.

"I wonder how far away Heston is?" Becky asked.

Becky pulled out her Glock to fire again when Trump and Reagan spotted them and splashed across the stream, followed closely by Justice.

"Oh, Hi fellas! Is Heston close by too? Becky said to the dogs. She spoke to them like they were people.

She was shocked when Justice answered.

"Heston is behind us by a few seconds." Justice looked at her.

"Ho-ooo- ly Cow" Becky said. "You can speak."

"I'm sorry Becky, I thought you knew. I didn't mean to surprise you." Justice said.

"Now I know why you are so special." Becky was blown away by the unbelievable sight of a dog speaking.

Chit and Bass just stared in silence.

Just then Heston was on the other side of the stream with Peggy, Gene, Holden, Noah and Camille.

When Camille took one look at War she screamed.

"That's the wolf!"

"No sweetie, this is a different wolf. He is helping us find the wolf that killed your boyfriend." Peggy said to the young woman.

The group crossed the river and approached Becky, Chit, Bass and War.

"Heston, this dog speaks!" Becky said excitedly.

"Yes, he does." Heston smiled at Becky. "He has been a top-secret project at Duralink for a couple of years now. That's why they are after him. Try to keep it a secret, OK?"

"Keep a talking dog a secret?" Becky said it like it would be impossible.

"Yeah, keep it a secret, please." Heston asked nicely.

Becky, Chit and Bass looked at each other.

"I want to work with that dog." Was all Bass said.

After a few moments, they regained their sense of what they were faced with.

"You see anything of Delta?"

"No, but Delta killed your favorite Navy Seal." Becky said.

"He did? When? How?" Heston asked.

"Barry ran ahead of us with War. Apparently, he and War split up, for unknown reasons, and Barry found Delta. Delta prevailed."

"Ok is anything in the cave? Did you look?"

"Well, here is what I can tell you about that. There was a guy in there wagging his little pink buddy around." Becky said with an evil smile.

"Oh my God." Chit groaned painfully. "This will never end."

"What?" Heston didn't understand.

"Oh, never mind. It's empty. Other than a large wet spot. Chit investigated it."

Chit breathed a sigh of relief. He had older sisters that Becky reminded him of.

"Ok, Captain Becky, do you have an idea about what to do next?" Heston asked trying to appear cooperative.

"Seems to me that Delta has evaded us successfully. I don't want to be in the forest with him at night. So, I would say let's get out of here while we still have some light."

"It will get dark fast now. It is 730 p.m. Dark in 30 minutes. We have an hour before we are out of the forest."

"Which way do you want to go? To Salt Lick or to the Smiley home?"

"It's 90 minutes to the Smiley residence." Becky said.

"It's about 60 minutes to Salt Lick. "Heston said.

"How many vehicles at Salt Lick?" Becky asked.

"Two. My truck and a Ranger SUV."

"Let's go to Salt Lick. If we need more room I can call in an extra vehicle." Becky said.

"Tell you what. Why don't you go to Salt Lick and I will cut through the forest to the Smiley home." Heston said.

"You just asked me what I wanted to do!" Becky was exasperated.

"I know, I was trying to be cooperative. But it just isn't in my DNA. You can take Camille and Bass out of here. They need to get to safety."

"I can take War and anyone else that wants to go with me through the forest. If we run into Delta I will let War kill him for us." Heston said.

"Heston, what if Delta kills War?" Becky asked.

"Then I will kill Delta."

"You have this all worked out in your simple, little male brain, don't you?" Becky glared at Heston.

"Pretty much." Heston smiled.

"OK, I will go to Salt Lick. When I get there I will call for back up to take Camille and Bass to their homes." Becky said.

"Wait," Bass said regretfully.

Everyone looked at Bass.

"If I let you take War without me, he is as likely to kill you as not. So, as much as I don't want to, and let's be very clear that I don't want to go, I need to go with Heston. Where War goes, I go."

"Look I don't need to be taken home. I want to go through the forest too." Camille said.

"For crying out loud," Becky said, exasperated again.

"OK, who wants to go back to Salt Lick? By show of hands." Heston asked the group.

Nobody raised their hands.

"OK let's get going. We are burning daylight."

"This is just great Heston. We are gonna hike through a dark forest with a giant Direwolf on the loose." Becky said exasperated.

"Hey, they all volunteered."

"Well, I'm going with you now to protect them. And you."

"No complaining." Heston said.

"Bite me, Heston." Becky said.

Heston smiled. Becky's stock price just went up in his estimation.

The sun was below the tree tops but not completely gone. Heston took the lead and the group followed in single file. The dogs including War and Justice were in the lead.

War and Justice Speak

After the group was on the trail for 15 minutes the dogs were substantially ahead of Heston.

War was in the lead of the four dogs. Suddenly he stopped and turned towards Justice who was immediately behind him.

"Look, I know you are Justice," War said.

"Justice who?" Justice decided to play dumb.

"Don't be stupid. I know you are not stupid."

"OK. Fine. You know I'm Justice. Do you want a doggie biscuit? I'm all out."

"No, I don't want a doggie biscuit."

"What then?"

"Two things. First, I just thought you should know I have no intention of harming you or capturing you. If I were you, I would have escaped from Duralink too."

"Ok that's good to know. Thanks."

"Second, Delta will smell you. He will not be as kind as I am."

"So, you are kind?"

"Not especially."

"So, what do you propose?"

"We use you as bait for Delta. When he comes for you I will kill him."

"Are you sure you can?"

"I am a superior fighter. I am smarter than he is. So, I believe it will be a short fight."

Trump and Reagan sat listening to the giant wolf speak to Justice speaking telepathically.

"OK, how do you want to do this?"

"I will take the lead, you stay close behind me. He will smell you coming and ambush us. But I will smell him and be warned of the ambush."

"Won't he know that?"

"Maybe. Maybe not. He is not as smart as either you or me. But it doesn't matter. Because his ambush is guaranteed."

"Ok let's go."

"Trump and Reagan, stay behind me." Justice said.

The four dogs raced through the forest in the dusk of the evening.

Delta was sore from the fighting. He traveled through the forest and felt his soreness more and more. When the stream approached, he gratefully lowered himself in and took a long soak. The cool water felt great, and he spent some time holding his head underwater to clean out his eyes from the blood and dirt.

He watched the sky grow dark and heard the cicadas begin their nightly songs.

He held his nose above water and submerged as much as he could while still breathing. After 30 minutes, darkness had moved in, and the stars were visible overhead.

It occurred to Delta he could sleep next to the stream then go back to Duralink tomorrow. Without the Navy Seal what could they expect him to do?

The longer he soaked in the water the better that idea sounded.

Then he heard them. Dogs.

Next, he smelled them. The scents were unmistakable.

It was War and Justice.

The intensity of the scents indicated they were quickly getting closer.

Delta realized his good fortune. His being submerged in the river would mask his scent. They wouldn't know he was there until it was too late.

Delta's night vision allowed him to see the trail easily as it meandered out of the trees.

Delta backed up a few feet away from the trail and positioned his feet so he could spring into action. He would kill War first, then kill Justice.

Only his nose, ears and eyes were above water. His nose and ears were wet and likely not to have a strong scent. His plan was perfect.

When the Direwolf and the German Shepherd were in mid-stream he would attack. This would be too easy. Delta patiently waited, soaking in the cool moving water of the stream.

In moments he heard them, then he saw them come running down the trail towards the stream.

Just before they got to the streams edge they abruptly stopped. Why? Could they smell him. No. That was not possible. Why then? Delta remained completely still and submerged in the cool water.

The group approached the water with War in the lead. Two other dogs ran up behind Justice. War moved cautiously into the stream. His instincts were trying to protect him. Ware looked side to side with each step, gradually sinking deeper into the stream. When War was in the middle of the stream, Delta struck. He used the strength of his massive legs and launched his huge body upwards out of the water. He flew over the water like a giant killer whale and then crashed downward onto War's back.

The massive Direwolf War was ready for him though. His sense of smell gave him a strong warning that Delta was extremely close. War heard the loud splashing sounds of Delta's burst out of the water, so before Delta landed War had partially turned to meet him.

The two giant creatures fought with a ferocity that Justice, Trump and Reagan had never seen. All they could do was watch from the edge of the stream as the two enormous Direwolves fought in the middle of the moving water. Their long-standing hatred for each other was now on full display. Loud snarls, yelps and howls were produced by the two warring carnivores that displayed their desire to destroy the other.

After moments War was in control. He was able to slip sideways and flip Delta off his back. Delta landed in the water allowing War to press his heavy weight on top of him. War mounted the top of Delta and held his head underwater with both of his giant paws. Delta thrashed underwater in vain attempts to get out from under War's weight. Delta used his rear paws to scratch at War, but War stepped back and forth avoiding them. The bulk of War's 300 pounds held Delta firmly underwater, helpless. After a long few moments, Delta knew the fight was over. War did too. The massive beast underwater stopped thrashing and bubbles from his face stopped rising to the surface. Soon, War relaxed and took his weight off Delta.

That was a mistake.

As soon as War's weight was removed from Delta's body, Delta magically sprang into a brutal assault. He burst out of the water and now ended up on War's back. Delta's massive jaws wrapped around War's neck and he bit downward with all his strength.

War twisted and flipped backward in an attempt to throw the beast off his back. Delta's grip was too tight. Delta held War's neck with his massive jaws, while his feet and legs held tightly around War's body. War knew if he wasn't successful in short order, he risked certain death.

After his last flip backward War was entirely underwater. The tables had turned. Delta would not release his grip on War's neck. The beast kept his nose and face underwater as long as he could as he bit down on War's neck. The water filled with a deep red color from the blood out of War's neck. His carotid artery had been penetrated. Now it was Delta that held War underwater. War's strong legs thrashed to gain some sort of footing to help him escape. He could not find any traction.

Finally, Delta had to breathe. He released his teeth out of War's neck but kept his body weight on top of War's body.

When Delta raised his head above water, he looked over at the three dogs that were spectators on the side of the stream. Delta took deep, triumphant breaths as he glared at the k-9 gallery watching. They had horrified looks on their faces. Clearly, they wanted War to win the fight. Now it looked as though that was not going to happen.

The realization must have hit all three of them at once because they immediately turned around and ran into the forest in terror.

Delta took his time now. He pressed down on War with his two enormous front paws. After a minute, he took his weight off War and slowly walked out of the stream and shook himself off. Water sprayed away in all directions from his vigorous shaking. Delta knew the fight was won; he was victorious again.

He decided to find the three dogs, kill Justice, and then go back to Duralink. The scientists would celebrate him for killing both War and Justice. He would be recognized as the greatest Direwolf and be rewarded with female Direwolves so that the repopulation of Direwolves could begin.

Delta looked back at the stream and watched War's lifeless body float to the surface, then move with the current downstream.

Justice turned and sprinted towards Heston, followed closely by Trump and Reagan. They raced through the darkness on the small game trail in the direction they had come from. In five minutes they almost collided with Heston and the rest of the group.

"Justice, what's going on? Where is War?" Heston asked.

"War is dead." Justice said.

"Dead? How?" Peggy asked, alarmed at the death of the huge dog.

"Delta killed him." Justice said.

Heston looked around at his team. They knew they were in trouble. Even more trouble than a few minutes ago.

"Where? I mean, where did it happen?" Noah asked.

"There is a stream five minutes away. He ambushed from the stream. It was quite brilliant. He hid underwater, so we could barely smell him. I couldn't smell him at all. Trump and Reagan picked up enough scent to give us a warning just before we got to the stream."

"Then why did War die?" Heston asked.

"We didn't know Delta was underwater at that point." Justice began, "He ambushed us, jumped on War's back and after a ten-minute fight that was… brutal barely describes it… Delta prevailed by drowning War underwater."

"OK, if Delta is five minutes that way, that means we are in trouble," Peggy stated the obvious.

"Any animal that can kill a beast like War will kill us in a matter of seconds," Noah said excitedly.

"Take a breath, Noah. We have guns. War did not." Heston looked at Noah grimly. "We will prevail." Heston said with all the confidence he could muster.

"Crap, I shoulda gone to Salt Lick," Camille said.

"Looks like I should have joined you." Bass moaned.

"I've made a huge mistake." Camille began to sob.

"Camille shut the hell up. You aren't helping." Peggy glared at the young woman. The time for mothering was over.

"Ok, Heston what do you want to do?" Nancy asked.

"Let's work on the belief that Delta is after Justice. That means we are going to be attacked. Let's get into a defensive position and wait for him." Heston's logic was sound.

"Or" Justice said, "I can go ahead and get him to follow me away from you."

"That won't work. He will just kill you, then come for us."

"I agree he may kill me, but I disagree that he will come for you." Justice said.

"I give you credit for bravery, Justice. But we stick together." Heston wasn't having it. He knew they were all safer if they stuck together. He wasn't prepared to sacrifice Justice. "Justice, we are a team. You are a part of this team. We will never sacrifice a member of our team."

Justice responded with silence. Silence because he was touched and proud that they would stand by him in a situation as dangerous as this. He didn't know what to say.

"I have an idea." Becky said, "I can hike out to Salt Lick and radio for help. If I double-time it, I can be there in an hour, maybe 90 minutes."

"That's a terrible idea, Becky. Number one, it splits us up. Number two, you can't do that in the dark. Not in 90 minutes."

"I think I can, Heston."

"In the dark? You think you can be to Salt Lick in 90 minutes in the dark? I doubt it."

"Well, I know I can be. I've lived in this forest since I was a kid." Ranger Holden said.

"Me too." Ranger Chit said.

Heston looked at Becky.

"I don't like the idea of splitting our forces." Heston said.

"Neither do I, but it may work if they can make it out and call for backup. Get us a dozen Texas Rangers with Mossbergs and Delta's days are numbered." Becky said.

"I get your point," Heston admitted.

"Plus, Heston," Gene said, "If Delta can kill War easily, we may not have a chance anyway. At least this idea gives us a chance. We will still have our guns, either way. If the guns are the difference makers, allowing these two to go get help won't change anything. We still have our guns."

"Do you think this is a good idea?" Heston looked at Gene.

"I think it is the best choice from a few bad choices." Gene said.

"Me too," Peggy said.

"Me too," Nancy said.

Heston nodded his understanding.

"OK, you two have been on my FUBAR list. But if you do this, you are forever off it." Becky said to the two young Rangers.

"Forever?" Holden smiled.

"Don't push it, Holden." Becky said.

"Ok, I'm ready."

"Me too."

"Then go. Holden, if you see the big mutt shoot it with your Mossberg."

"Yes, Captain."

"Remember, the end with the big hole is where it says boom." Becky looked at him and smiled. She was grateful he would take on this dangerous assignment.

"I'll try to remember that thanks Captain,"

"Here, take my Mag-Lite. It's bigger than yours."

"Thanks, Captain." Chit reached for her large steel flashlight.

"And it has fresh batteries."

Chit nodded his understanding.

Rangers Holden Hisweiner and Chit Head ran into the darkness towards The Salt Lick, following the bright beam from Becky's Mag-Lite.

"Let's find that clearing a ways back and wait. It is more defendable than this area is." Heston said.

The group hiked in the direction they had just come from looking for the small clearing so they may defend themselves. Heston, Gene and Peggy still had their Mag-Lites.

They hiked up the dark trail, pointing their Mag Lites at every noise in the forest.

After 10 minutes, they found the clearing. Heston positioned everyone in a circle with their backs to each other. This allowed them to get a 360-degree view of their surroundings.

Captain Becky and Heston carried Mossberg shotguns. Everyone else has sidearms. Gene and Peggy had taken charge of the two Desert Eagles that the Seals had left behind.

"Heston, any chance you'd swap your Mossberg for my Desert Eagle?" Peggy nicely asked. "I think this is too much gun for me to shoot. I'm afraid of the kick. But I know I can shoot a Mossberg." Peggy smiled, hoping he would make the trade.

"Sure Peggy" Heston handed Peggy his Mossberg and took her Desert Eagle. The weight of the large pistol told Heston she was probably right.

The group stood in nervous silence. Cicadas sang around them as they stood in a circle under the stars. Every noise in the forest caught their attention.

After 30 minutes, the tenseness seemed to be relieved, and they breathed a bit easier.

"My knees are killing me. I need to sit, Heston." Gene said.

"Me too." Nancy agreed

"I could sit," Camille said.

"OK fine, you all sit. I'll stand." Heston said.

"I'm standing too," Peggy said.

Heston remained standing with Peggy, who never liked to sit.

Peggy stood next to Gene as he sat on the forest floor and stretched out his legs. His knees were sore.

"I don't hear anything do you?" Peggy whispered.

"Nothing but cicadas."

"Justice, any scents?"

312

"Nothing but faint scents."

Then in the distance, in the direction of Salt Lick, came three loud Booms. They were from a shotgun.

"Uh-Oh," Becky said. "That sounds like Holden's Mossberg."

Then rapid fire from a smaller caliber weapon. Seven shots. Then silence.

"You want us to go check it out?" Justice asked.

"No, stay here with us. You are our early warning system."

"Heston, if Holden and Chit have been killed, no backup is coming."

Heston thought for a minute. If they split up, they were weaker in force.

If they stayed in place, they may be sitting ducks waiting for backup that would never come.

Heston knew any decision was better than no decision.

"Ok, let's head back to Salt Lick and find out what they were shooting at."

The group stood up, checked their weapons and hiked out in a single file line.

Heston and the three dogs took the lead. Gene took up the rear while Bass and Camille were in the middle since they were unarmed and defenseless. Peggy was in front of Gene, and Nancy was behind Heston.

Heston, Gene and Peggy held their Mag-Lites as well as their weapons. The trail was illuminated ahead by Heston's Mag-Lite. He wasn't sure it was a good idea to light up the trail, possibly warning Delta of their location, but figured that Delta would smell them sooner than he would see the lights coming up the trail. So, the lights wouldn't matter.

He was right. Delta's sense of smell was powerful.

They hiked through the dark forest with heightened senses, as ready as they could be for an ambush.

After 30 minutes, they knew they had to be close to the location of the gunfire they had heard earlier.

The lights from the Mag-Lites swept the trail and the areas off to the side of the trail.

Heston slowed the pace. Then he whistled for the dogs to come back to him.

"Justice, what scents are you picking up?" Heston asked. He understood the value the military saw in Justice every time he asked Justice a question about what he was smelling.

"We are getting close, Heston. I think that Delta may be on his way to Salt Lick. The scent is leading that way."

"We have to catch him before he gets to that restaurant. That would be a massacre."

"I agree."

"Ok, listen up" Heston said to his team. "We are going to have to pick up the Pace. Delta may be headed to the Salt Lick restaurant. He probably smells the barbecue and is hungry."

"Let's go."

The dogs ran ahead, followed by the team.

Delta's Trap

Justice noticed before they got out of the forest that the scent of Delta was getting intense.

Justice, Trump and Reagan slowed down and looked around. The scent was unmistakable and close by.

Delta hadn't gone to Salt Lick. He'd set an ambush! Justice was confident of his analysis. They were going to be ambushed.

Before Justice could run back to warn Heston, Delta sprang out of the forest from the side of the trail.

Justice narrowly missed being grabbed by Delta's open snapping jaws.

Trump and Reagan began their howling to call Heston.

Delta chased Justice in a large circle around the clearing with his massive snout just inches behind Justice.

As they howled, they bravely nipped at Delta's heels to get his attention away from Justice. But it didn't work.

Delta chased Justice around the small clearing frustrated that he couldn't catch the more nimble dog.

Delta was larger, but Justice was quicker. Justice was able to stay inches away from Delta's jaws.

Justice ran in a large circle, then when Delta thought he knew where Justice was going, Justice changed course and direction. Justice knew he didn't need to evade Delta forever, but just until Heston and the team arrived.

Justice changed directions for the 3rd time when Heston and Captain Becky arrived.

They both watched in horror as Justice ran out of luck. Delta cut off Justice's circle and trapped him, like a boxer traps an opponent in the corner. Delta sprang forward and grabbed Justice by his hips. He bit down fiercely and felt Justice's hips break.

Then three loud gun blasts broke through the night air and flashed brightly, briefly illuminating the forest.

Heston had fired his Desert Eagle twice while Nancy fired her Mossberg once. They both were worried about hitting Justice, so they didn't fire more shots.

Delta felt the searing pain enter his body. He knew he'd been shot.

All he could do was go into protective, defensive mode. He dropped Justice from his jaws and painfully ran down the trail in the direction of The Salt Lick, away from the gunfire.

Delta disappeared into the night.

Heston, Becky and Noah got to Justice first.

Justice lay still on the forest floor. His eyes were closed. Blood oozed out of his hips and abdomen.

"Justice, can you hear me!" Noah yelled.

Justice did not respond.

Becky felt for a pulse and breathing.

She was silent.

"What did you feel, Becky?" Peggy asked.

"He has a weak heartbeat. He isn't dead."

Heston inspected Justice's hips. He had experience with dogs being attacked before. Pigs in Texas often attacked the dogs tracking them.

"His hips are broken and his abdomen is bleeding. He probably has internal bleeding." Heston said.

"We have to get him to a doctor," Noah yelled.

"Noah, you have to understand this. Right now, Justice is not our primary concern. Delta just ran towards The Salt Lick restaurant. We have to kill him before he kills a bunch of people there." Heston explained to Noah.

Noah stared at Heston. He did not like it, but he understood what Heston was saying.

"OK, I will stay here with Justice." Noah said.

"Camille, I want you to stay here with Justice and Noah," Heston said, then he looked at Nancy. "Nancy, since you are armed and they are not, you should stay here too. Guard them. Bass, you aren't armed, so you stay here too."

"Nancy, here take my Colt .44 magnum. I have the Desert Eagle. If Delta comes back, shoot him with the Colt. Not your Glock. Got it?"

"I got it." Nancy said and nodded.

"OK, let's go." Heston said looking at the others.

Heston, Gene, Peggy and Captain Becky ran up the trail toward The Salt Lick Restaurant.

The Salt Lick

Delta had set the trap perfectly.

He used the same tactic Justice used on him earlier at the cave. Delta ran towards the edge of the forest, then doubled back and took up a hiding space behind some trees. He waited less than five minutes when the three dogs ran up the trail directly in front of him. Justice was in the lead. Justice was all he cared about, but he would happily kill the other two just for fun.

Delta sprang out upon Justice perfectly. The German Shepherd's luck was uncanny. Delta missed him by inches.

Delta chased Justice around the area over and over again. Just as Delta trapped him against some trees, he grabbed Justice by his hips. He bit down forcefully with his large, powerful jaws. He felt his teeth sink into Justice's hips and abdomen. He squeezed his jaws as tightly as he could.

Delta felt tremendous and powerful when he could tell Justice's hips had snapped in the power of his jaws.

Delta heard the unmistakable gunshots and felt a burning pain in his midsection. Instantly his feelings of incredible power and joy were demolished with searing pain.

He had been shot. Delta instinctively knew it was bad. Very bad. Possibly, life-ending bad.

He did what he knew he had to. For the sake of his life and for the future of the young Direwolves that he knew he would sire–he tossed Justice aside and ran.

He ran towards the end of the forest as fast as possible despite the pain.

He arrived at the end of the forest quickly. Ahead he could see lights. He saw the lights of a building and the lights from moving cars on the two-lane highway that divided him from the building.

Delta's pain was too intense to care about humans or automobiles. He had to escape the guns behind him.

Delta smelled the powerful scents of barbecued meats. He ran towards the smells. He knew his body would heal faster with protein consumption. He came to a two-lane highway. He saw car lights coming toward him in both directions. He sprinted across the two-lane blacktop road, jumping in front of the cars. Cars coming from both directions had to slam on their brakes to avoid the giant Direwolf. One of the cars was rear-ended by the car behind him, producing a loud crashing noise. Metal and broken glass sprayed across the blacktop highway.

Delta jumped over the guard rail on the opposite side of the road and ran through the dark towards the building with all the lights and smells.

His pain was intense. He could tell from the smell of the building that there was food inside. Meat. Delta's instincts told him he would need protein to start the healing process. He didn't want to die. He wanted to meet his future Direwolf puppies.

He ran as fast as he could. He approached the backside of the building, which was a stroke of luck for Delta. Sheriffs typically were stationed at the front side of the Salt Lick. The rear entrance was unguarded.

Delta slowly crept towards the rear entrance, and the smells became overwhelming as he approached. The beef, pork and chicken smelled beautiful. Delta wanted to feed.

Delta got to the back employee entrance of the restaurant just as a cook in a white apron came out the double delivery doors.

The cook was a smaller Latino man with a name tag that read 'Ernesto.' Ernesto looked at Delta, who stood taller than he did. Ernesto didn't know what to say or do. He froze in place, looking upwards into Delta's eyes.

Delta knew Ernesto didn't represent a threat. He wanted to feed on the food inside the building.

Delta used his giant nose and nudged Ernesto aside with a swift, strong push. Ernesto readily complied and moved aside.

As Delta entered the kitchen, he saw a mountain of beef and pork piled up on the cook's tables preparing to be chopped up. The three cooks in the kitchen did not notice Delta at first. They were busy chopping meat and filling customers' orders. Then one of the cooks named Julio looked up and saw Delta come through the doors and approach the table. Julio had never seen a six-foot tall dog before.

All he could do was stare for a moment. He looked at his partner cooks and said, "Look at that."

Both of the other cooks looked at Delta and quickly ran out the other side of the kitchen towards the customer seating area.

Delta got to the table with the meat and quickly began to feed. In four giant bites, he had consumed 12 pounds of beef. Next, he started on the pork. Julio hadn't moved an inch. He stared at Delta as he consumed the pile of pork.

Delta felt satisfied enough to turn around to leave. When he turned around, he saw Ernesto and a Sheriff's deputy standing in the doorway. The Sheriff grabbed his gun. Delta knew what that meant. He sprung towards the Sheriff and grabbed him by his head. The Deputy dropped his weapon as he waved his arms in wide circles to regain control of himself. Delta's tongue and teeth muffled his screams. With a quick bullwhip-like snap, the Deputy's feet left the ground and raised over his head, then slammed downwards again. A loud snap was heard throughout the kitchen as the Deputy's back was broken. The Deputy was quickly dead. Delta dropped the Deputy and looked at Ernesto who didn't move an inch. Delta was not hungry and didn't see Ernesto as a threat, so he walked by him, nudging him aside again so he could fit through the doors that he had passed through earlier. Ernesto stood in stunned silence, watching the giant wolf stroll away. He was in shock about what he had just witnessed.

Delta was able to see the road he had crossed earlier. Some vehicles were still on the highway stopped due to the wreck Delta had caused when he crossed. Then Delta picked up the scents of Trump and Reagan and the humans that followed them. He knew they were coming for him. Delta decided to turn around, run back through the restaurant, then loop around the building and go back into the forest and disappear.

Delta turned around and saw an empty kitchen. He proceeded around the prep tables and entered the customer seating area. There was a large fire pit with sausages hanging from an iron bar above. Servers stopped what they were doing at looked at Delta in awe. Delta reached his snout out, grabbed a rope of ten sausages, and ate them in seconds. When people saw Delta, they froze. Two women screamed and children began to cry. Delta glared at them all. He knew he had to leave. As much as he would like to stay and feast upon the vast amounts of beef and pork in front of him, he was full. He had to leave to escape the team he knew was after him. His injuries disallowed him from participating in battle.

If he were uninjured, he would have waited for them here, then enjoyed killing them all. However, his injuries were significant. He was in pain. He looked at the floor and could see he was leaving a trail of blood. He had to escape.

Delta walked out of the main entrance to the restaurant. All the people waiting outside looked horrified as he strolled toward them. None of them were threats. Delta did not worry about killing them. There was no need. Delta stepped towards the parking lot and spotted two more Sheriff's Deputies. They immediately pointed their weapons at Delta, mistakenly believing they could force him to stop. They hesitated to shoot because the civilian patrons of the restaurant were so close by. Delta's training took over and he charged one of the Deputies, immediately grabbing him by the head. The Deputy fired his weapon three times into the sky as Delta chewed on his head. The other Deputy moved to Delta's left to get a good shot at him. He worried about hitting his partner as well as the civilians. The deputy heard the muffled screams of his partner and fired his 9-millimeter sidearm into Delta's side.

Delta felt the sting of the small bullets and realized what was happening. He lifted the deputy in his mouth off the ground and swung him sideways back and forth violently. The screaming deputy in Delta's mouth knew death was close. He tried to use his hands to pry himself out of Delta's mouth. Delta swung the screaming Deputy into the other Deputy and knocked him off his feet. Delta spit out the bloody Deputy, who landed on his dazed partner. They were both lucky to be alive. Delta saw the forest 50 yards away that surrounded the restaurant. He tried to run, but he couldn't stand the pain. Delta walked as fast as he could. He turned left at the end of the restaurant and headed for the highway and the forest that lay beyond. Delta wanted to go to the forest area he was familiar with. There he could escape down known paths. It was just beyond the highway.

He approached the highway about 50 yards down from the accident he had caused earlier. He jumped over the guard rail and trotted painfully across the highway in front of stopped cars. The drivers watched him through their headlights with open mouths and gasps.

Once on the other side, he was 20 yards from the forest.

He could see the trailhead. There was no one around.

Delta entered the forest and was immediately put at ease. He was familiar with this area. Now he could escape.

Once he was a couple of minutes into the forest, he picked up the smell of Justice. Justice had to be dead, right? Delta had crushed his hips with his bite. If Justice were alive, lying ahead on the forest floor, Delta would put him down for good.

Heston, Becky, Peggy and Gene emerged from the forest and could see the accident on the highway ahead. It wasn't a major accident, but traffic was stopped.

People were milling around their damaged cars on the side of the road as the group approached.

Becky tried to use her radio to call for help, but her radio was dead. She pulled out her cell phone, called her supervisor, and appraised him of the situation. She told him they needed backup immediately. She asked him to send the backup to Driftwood's Salt Lick barbecue restaurant.

Heston wondered if Delta had something to do with the accident.

"What happened here?" Heston asked a man and woman standing next to their damaged car.

"A giant wolf ran in front of our car. We slammed on the brakes and got rear-ended." The man told Heston.

"A giant wolf, huh?" Heston knew the man was telling the truth.

322

"Yeah, I know it's hard to believe. The Deputy doesn't believe me." The man said.

"Where is the Deputy?"

"On the other side of the road talking to others who stopped."

"OK, Thanks."

As they approached the Sheriff's Deputy speaking with another motorist, Captain Becky knew she should take the lead.

"Heston, let me talk to him first." Becky said.

"Fine with me." Heston said.

"Hey Deputy, I'm Captain Lawson with the Texas Rangers." That usually got a Deputy's attention.

"Yes, ma'am?"

"Can you get on your radio and call for backup? We need all the support we can get."

"What's going on?"

"We have a giant rabid wolf out here, and we need to kill it."

"That's what these folks told me! They told me they saw a giant wolf. I didn't believe them."

"Well, you can believe them. Which way did it go?" Becky asked.

The Deputy shrugged his shoulders, but the man he spoke with spoke up.

"Over there towards The Salt Lick." The motorist said, pointing with his fingers.

"Call for backup." Becky ordered the deputy.

"Yes, ma'am"

Then the four marched over the guardrail toward the restaurant.

They approached the rear of the restaurant and immediately knew Delta was there. Or had been there. A dead deputy lay face down on the concrete just outside the double swinging loading doors. Blood from his head ran down the sloped concrete ramp towards the small asphalt parking area.

Heston gave the command for Trump and Reagan to circle the outside of the restaurant in different directions. Trump went left and Reagan went right. Heston, Gene and Peggy entered the kitchen. Captain Becky went right around the restaurant on the outside, following Reagan.

People were making loud panicky noises outside the kitchen in the restaurant area.

Gene, Peggy and Heston looked at each other.

"He's been here. That's for sure." Peggy said.

"Yeah, but is he still here?"

"We're gonna find out." All three had their guns out and ready to fire.

They walked around the prep tables and into the restaurant area. Nobody was sitting. Men, women and children stood against the walls. Everyone was talking in small groups about the giant wolf they had seen.

It was clear that Delta was not inside the restaurant. They went out the front door only to find more people talking about the unbelievable gigantic wolf that just walked through them. Then they saw the two Deputy's leaning up against the wall. Both were bleeding. One was worse than the other.

"What happened here?" Heston knelt next to the Deputy that seemed to be able to talk about the situation.

"A giant wolf just strolled through here. He was enormous. His head was as tall as mine. He attacked us and almost killed my partner. Unbelievable." The Deputy spoke like he was in shock.

324

"Did you call for backup?"

"I just radioed for help. They will be here soon."

Gene, Peggy and Heston looked at each other.

"That's him. It has to be Delta." Gene said.

"Who?" The Deputy asked softly.

"Let's just say you are lucky to be alive and tell the story."

"The wolf was bleeding. The blood on the sidewalk there is from the wolf." The Deputy said.

"Could you tell where it came from?"

"I shot him at least six times. It looked like he'd been shot in the stomach before I shot him. When he grabbed my partner, I shot him while it chewed on his head. It didn't seem to matter to him."

"The other wounds were larger? Larger than yours?"

"Yes. Looked like shotgun wounds."

"That would have been Ranger Holden and Ranger Chit." Gene said.

"Yep." Heston said.

Trump and Reagan ran up with their tails wagging. They were excited. Becky just was behind them.

"They have a scent to follow," Heston said.

"Let's go" Becky was ready to kill Delta.

Trump and Reagan went to the left around the restaurant, then took another left and headed to the highway.

"Oh no. Delta has doubled back to the forest."

"Crap. That means Justice, Bass, Camille, Nancy and Noah are in trouble."

The group ran towards the highway and the forest they had left just 30 minutes earlier.

Nancy stood guard with her Desert Eagle over Noah, Bass, Camille and Justice. Between them, they had one flashlight and one gun. Noah's .22 didn't count as a gun against a Direwolf.

The forest was cool and dark. Every noise they heard attracted the flashlight beam.

"We need to get Justice to the hospital soon," Noah said softly, stroking Justice's head.

"We can't do anything now but wait. Moving him could hurt him more than letting him rest."

"Here, take my Glock, Noah. That .22 won't do much to a Direwolf."

Noah held the much larger gun and recognized he better learn to shoot soon. He felt like a duck out of water. He figured he was safer with the larger gun.

Nancy listened carefully to the night sounds.

Just as she started to get a bit more relaxed, she heard a loud thudding up the trail. It was something large.

"Heads up, Noah," Nancy said.

"Where is the safety on this thing?" He thought it was a good question. He wanted to be ready.

"It doesn't have a safety. Just point and pull the trigger. Use two hands." Heston whispered.

"OK"

"Camille, hold this flashlight, point it up the trail." Heston said and passed his flashlight to her.

"I can do that."

Nancy and Noah held their guns up and pointed toward the flashlight beam.

Then Nancy heard something moving through the forest around them. Something large was cutting through the woods, trying to outmaneuver them.

"Flashlight to the right, Camille," Nancy commanded.

Camille pointed the flashlight into the dark forest on their right. Nothing moved

Five minutes passed. Nancy began to think it could have been a deer crashing through the forest to avoid them.

Camille did precisely as she was told. She kept the flashlight pointed to the right into the dark forest.

Nancy looked down the trail in the direction they had come from earlier. It was dark. Too dark.

Then Nancy saw two red eyes staring at her from the darkness down the trail.

"Camille flashlight! Move back to the trail!" Camille moved it the wrong way. She pointed up the trail in the wrong direction.

"No! The other way! Right, Right!" Nancy began to yell.

Camille quickly moved the light 180 degrees around. The flashlight illuminated the trail, and there stood Delta. Nancy saw his full height as he stood in the middle of the trail.

"Holy Christ," Nancy breathed quietly.

The flashlight was on Delta for another second before he rushed toward them.

Noah was so scared that he pulled the trigger as fast as he could. Pow pow pow pow pow! His bullets sprayed in every direction except Delta's. Many of the bullets went straight up into the surrounding trees.

As Delta was in mid-air, Nancy got off a shot with her big 50 caliber pistol. She missed high. The recoil of the Desert Eagle resulted in Nancy pointing the gun too high to shoot Delta with a second shot. Delta landed on Nancy and grabbed her by her left shoulder and arm. He bit down viciously, swung her side to side, then tossed her to the left into the forest scrub brush. Nancy flew high in the air tumbling with her feet spinning, then landed hard on the ground. Nancy lay with her feet over her head, tangled in the low forest growth.

Noah and Camille screamed and ran in both directions down the trail.

That left only Bass staring directly into Delta's eyes.

Bass stood between Justice and Delta. He was completely unarmed.

"Delta, you remember me, right?" Bass asked the Direwolf, hoping to exert some control over the beast.

Delta stared at Bass. He wanted to kill Justice, lying on the other side of Bass. Bass was in the way. Delta realized he was getting tired. He wondered if it was because of blood loss.

"Sit," Bass commanded the Direwolf.

"Delta didn't budge."

"Delta sit." Bass said bravely.

Delta thought about killing the small man.

Justice lay just beyond Bass. Delta could quickly kill him. Delta looked at Bass, then looked at Justice. Was Justice already dead?

Delta could not see signs of breathing, and the German Shepherd's eyes were closed. Maybe Justice was already dead.

Delta stepped towards Bass and used his giant snout to push Bass aside.

Bass tried to remain in place, but the giant Wolf was too strong. Bass skipped two paces to the side as the Direwolf pushed him aside with his enormous nose.

Delta put his nose on Justice's body and tried to determine if he was alive or not. He couldn't feel breathing or hear a heartbeat.

He decided to make sure that Justice was dead. Delta produced a low growl. The growl was instinctive. It always happened before he attacked something. He bared his huge teeth and prepared to finish the job on Justice.

Then he heard a female's voice.

"Bass, Catch!"

It was Camille. She had gone over to Nancy and retrieved her Desert Eagle. Camille knew the gun was too big for her to fire, so she did the only thing that made sense. She tossed it to Bass. She didn't know Bass had never fired a gun before.

Bass caught the gun. He knew how to hold it from watching Nancy and Heston.

Standing three feet away from Delta, he pointed the big pistol into Delta's face.

"I don't want to shoot you boy," Bass said honestly.

Then Delta's growl was directed at Bass.

Bass remembered that anyone that pointed a gun at either War or Delta was destined to be attacked and killed.

Delta quickly snapped with his giant jaws towards Bass, ready to grab Bass by the head.

Bass fired the giant gun directly into the open mouth of Delta. A gigantic BOOM! filled the forest. The fire from the end of the gun barrel lit the area briefly, almost like a bright flash from a camera.

Delta's head flew back away from Bass as Bass fell backward. The gun flew upwards and out of Bass' hands. Bass landed on his backside and the gun landed behind him.

Delta's huge body lay limp on top of Justice, with Delta's head unnaturally folded back and touching his spine.

Camille recognized that the weight of the Direwolf could kill Justice if he were still alive. She ran over to try to pull the Direwolf off Justice. But he was just too heavy.

"C'mon Bass, help me!" Camille yelled.

Bass stood up, his hands still stinging from firing the Desert Eagle and tried to roll Delta's body off Justice. Noah returned from the forest and rushed to help too.

They were not having the success they needed, and all of them lost faith that they would get the 300-pound wolf off Justice.

Then Heston, Becky, Peggy, Becky and Gene ran up and quickly realized what was happening.

Everyone grabbed a different side of Delta and lifted. Their combined strength allowed them to lift Delta off Justice.

Peggy looked at Delta's head which was splayed open from the snout backward. Brains were hanging out of the back of his head.

"That is yucky!" Peggy said with her nose curled up. "Who shot him?"

"Freaking great shot! Perfect! Who did it?" Heston asked.

"C'mon fess up. Who shot him?" Gene asked.

"Wish it had been me," Becky said.

"It was Bass," Noah said.

"Bass?" Nancy said in a daze. She had just regained consciousness. "I don't believe it."

"Neither do I," Becky said. The shot had been perfectly placed into the Direwolf's open mouth, with the huge bullet entering the brain and exiting through the skull. The hollow point bullet basically destroyed everything in its path.

"It was Bass. I gave him the gun." Camille said.

Everyone looked at Bass. The man who had never fired a gun before and loved dogs.

"Bass! Well, are you going to say anything?" Gene asked the small man staring back at them. "At least take a bow?"

"Let's get Justice to the animal hospital." Was all Bass could say.

"I agree with that," Noah said.

Heston checked the status of Justice while Gene and Peggy helped Nancy up. She had been bitten in the shoulder and neck. She had lost some blood but was otherwise OK. She was lucky that no major arteries were opened during the attack.

"Paramedics are on the way." Captain Becky said.

The group decided to wait for the paramedics to arrive rather than try to move Justice and possibly hurt him. They all sat on the ground around Justice and tried to relax before the paramedics arrived.

"Bass shot Delta," Becky said. "I woulda never guessed."

"His first time shooting a gun, he shoots a Desert Eagle, killing a Direwolf. Amazing." Peggy said, "We are proud of you, Bass."

"I woulda picked Heston for gender reassignment surgery before I picked Bass to shoot a Desert Eagle into the mouth of a Direwolf." Gene said with a smile.

"Me too." Heston smiled at Bass and patted him on the shoulder. "And to think that I thought Bass was dead weight on this hunt. I'm sorry Bass."

"I thought I was dead weight too, so don't be too tough on yourself."

"We have more stories to tell that nobody will believe." Gene looked at Peggy and smiled.

"Ah, the kids never believe any of your stories anyway."

"Yeah, but this one is true."

"Except for the parts you will make up."

In an hour, they delivered Justice to the Driftwood Animal Hospital where Dr. Frosty Moore was ready for him.

He took Justice directly into surgery.

Epilogue

Twenty-four hours later, Justice was back at home with Noah.

Noah had a bed set up for Justice in his favorite spot on the back porch, facing the forest.

The house was quiet and still as Noah attended to Justice like he was a family member. Noah was in the kitchen cooking for Justice when the doorbell rang. He walked through the living room and opened the front door. It was Gene, Peggy and Heston.

"How is our patient?" Peggy asked.

"Probably sleeping." Noah smiled.

"Can we see him?"

"Sure, he is in his favorite spot." Noah pointed to the porch.

The group moved out to the porch and looked at Justice lying in the bed Noah had made for him.

"Hey buddy, how are you feeling?" Gene asked.

Justice lifted his head off the pillow and looked at his visitors.

"Like a Mike Tyson opponent."

"Why am I not amazed you know who Mike Tyson is?" Heston chuckled.

"Everyone knows Mike Tyson," Justice said. "Duh."

"Reagan and Trump don't."

"OK smart ass, what is your point?" Justice was sore and a bit grumpy.

"Wow, Justice is better," Peggy said, smiling.

"I'd say so."

Just then, the doorbell rang.

"Who is that?"

"I dunno. We are all here." Noah said. "Maybe Nancy."

Noah went through the house again to open the front door. When he opened it, he immediately recognized Bass. Bass stood on the front porch with another man wearing sunglasses and a leather jacket.

"Hi, Bass. Come on in."

"Hey Noah, I'd like you to meet my friend Delon."

"Hello, Delon," Noah said. The two shook hands. "We are all out here on the porch with Justice. Come on back."

Noah led the way through the living room with Bass and his friend following him.

When they returned to the porch, the three other visitors looked up.

"Bass and his friend are here," Noah said." This is …."

"Delon Husk," Gene said wide-eyed. "He doesn't need an introduction."

Noah looked back at Delon and screamed, "Ahhh! Delon Husk! I didn't know you were that Delon! For all that is Holy, Bass! You're going to kill me!" Noah grabbed his chest.

Heston and Peggy were unimpressed. Both were pissed off that Duralink had allowed Direwolves into the community.

"Hi," Delon said as he looked around at the group.

"Hello," Gene said, holding out his hand to shake Delon's hand.

Delon gave Gene a firm handshake.

Heston and Peggy stared at Delon.

Delon looked at Peggy and Heston. He could feel their anger.

"Look," Delon said, "I feel like you may be angry."

"Ya think?" Peggy said. It wasn't a question. It was an accusation. She glared at him.

Heston just stared at him without smiling.

"I don't blame you. I'm not going to give you excuses. I'll say this: When I found out what happened, I fired over 20 people. I had the wrong management team in place and didn't find out until it was too late."

"OK, keep going," Peggy said. She wanted to like him.

Delon took a deep breath and paused as Heston watched.

"Look, it's like this," Delon said. "Justice is the most important work we have ever done. That includes everything at Tesla, SpaceX, The Boring Company, PayPal as well as Duralink."

"Justice is more than 'work,'" Noah said, sounding offended.

"Oh, I agree with you Noah," Delon said. "Justice is special to me. And I am grateful to you all for protecting him."

That's when it hit Noah that he may not own Justice. Delon Husk was Justice's legal owner. Was Noah going to lose his best friend?

"Are you going to take him from me?" Noah asked, sounding defeated. He didn't want to cry, but he knew he was close.

"Noah, I know you love Justice. Let me tell you what I have in mind." Delon started to explain.

"What?" Noah asked, holding back tears.

Delon noticed Noah getting emotional.

"First, understand this: if you do not approve of my idea, I will leave Justice with you. OK?" Delon looked directly at Noah, hoping he would feel better.

Noah felt like birds began to sing, and the sun was coming out. Maybe all was not lost!

"OK" was all Noah said. Inside he knew he would never approve of anything that resulted in him losing Justice, but it was nice of Delon to say that.

"Second, if you allow me to take Justice back, I promise he will never be in a cage again. He will have a full roam of the Duralink facility. I will ensure everyone at Duralink treats Justice as they treat me. He will be my representative walking through the hallways. Everyone will be instructed to open doors for Justice and ensure he gets all he can eat anytime he is hungry." Delon looked at the group, hoping to see some easing of the anger. "And he will eat human food, whatever he wants. As much as he wants. I will open an account with What-a-Burger if that is what he wants." Delon smiled at the group, hoping to break the ice. It didn't work.

"OK. Go on." Noah felt he would not agree to Justice leaving, but was smart enough to know Delon could take him if he wanted to. The courts would side with Delon for a million different reasons.

"Next, I promise no more surgeries on Justice. We have done everything to him that we need to. Now we have to reap the scientific rewards. Justice holds scientific treasures beyond belief." Delon removed his sunglasses.

"Would he ever work with the military?" Peggy asked.

"No. Not Justice. We may, no we will, enhance other dogs based upon what we learned from Justice. They will work with the military. But I promise Justice will lead a pampered life. He will be treasured. Treasured by me and everyone at Duralink."

"Where would he sleep?" Noah was concerned about Justice's comfort.

"He will go home with me every night. I have ten kids, I just had twins delivered a week ago." Delon smiled, again hoping to break the ice with the mention of twins. Only Peggy smiled back at him. "They will give him all the attention he can handle." Delon finally said.

"I don't want to lose him," Noah groaned.

"I understand that. And here is the last part. Maybe the best part. I will give you and Gene and Peggy and Heston 250 million dollars each for caring for Justice the way you all have." Delon looked at them all in the eyes. He wanted to convey that he was serious and grateful.

"That's a billion dollars," Gene said incredulously.

"Yes, it is. Bass here has told me how you cared for him, and I can see he is right."

"Bass is the one that killed Delta. He saved Justice's life." Noah said.

"Yes, I know." Delon smiled.

"Noah," Bass said, "Delon gave me 250 million dollars this morning. He transferred it right into my checking account."

"I don't believe it," Heston spoke up for the first time.

"I can show you," Bass said. He pulled out his phone and opened his bank app. In 30 seconds, he showed Heston, Gene and Peggy his account balance. It was $250,001,150.58

"I had 1150 bucks when he made the deposit."

"Sweet Baby Jesus," Gene said softly.

"Yeah, my bank manager has already called me three times, all puckered up to kiss my butt." Bass smiled.

"He'll do more than that for you I'll bet," Heston said.

"Hey, as much as we would appreciate the cash, it's still Noah's decision," Peggy said.

"Well, I know what my vote is," Gene said, smiling. Peggy elbowed him in the side with a 'Shhhh' sound.

"Noah," Justice spoke up, "You must take the money. I will still come to visit you. A billion dollars is too much for you folks to turn down. That is life-changing money. I will be fine." Justice knew he was taking care of Noah now, as well as Gene, Peggy and Heston. This was his best way to take care of them.

"Can I have visitation rights?" Noah asked.

"Sure, anytime," Delon smiled at Noah. He appreciated how Noah didn't jump at the money as most people would have.

Heston, Gene, Peggy and Noah all looked at each other.

The next day they each bought themselves a Tesla Model X Plaid. Peggy purchased a red one.

The End of the True story

<u>Thank you</u> for reading my story about Justice!
Check out my other books if you get a chance:
- Laconta- Killer Bigfoot in Texas.
- Thin Man and Mrs. Thin Man- Killer bugman from the center of the earth.
- The Mortician- Zombies invade Texas.
- Fesko- Vampires come to Texas from Ukraine.
- Kizma:Kidnapped- Crazy killer kidnaps women.
- Screams in the Forest.- Werewolves in Texas
- Dark Tales- Short stories. Great for kids.

Thanks again! - Gene

www.ingramcontent.com/pod-product-compliance
Lightning Source LLC
Chambersburg PA
CBHW061514020726
47502CB00006B/2066